Joanna McDona
falling in love with Scotland she moved north of the border in 1975. She joined the BBC straight from university and worked on *Today* as a producer and duty editor, going on to present *Good Morning Scotland* for six years under her maiden name. Joanna Hickson. She is now a full-time writer and lives in Edinburgh with her husband and family.

Joanna McDonald's children's novel REBELLION AT ORFORD CASTLE was broadcast on BBC1 on *Jackanory*. ISLAND GAMES is her first adult novel.

Island Games

Joanna McDonald

Fairest Isle, all isles excelling,
Seat of pleasures, and of loves;

John Dryden
King Arthur, V 'Song of Venus'

KNIGHT

First published in 1994
by HEADLINE BOOK PUBLISHING

First published in paperback in 1994
by HEADLINE BOOK PUBLISHING

This edition published 1999 by
Knight an imprint of Brockhampton Press

10 9 8 7 6 5 4 3 2 1

ISBN 184186 0247

Typeset by Letterpart Limited, Reigate, Surrey

Printed and bound in Great Britain by
Mackays of Chatham PLC, Chatham, Kent

Brockhampton Press
20 Bloomsbury Street
London
WC1B 3QA

For my mother who got me going
and my husband who kept me going.

ACKNOWLEDGEMENTS

Producing a first novel is not a one-person operation. I would like to thank Sophie McDonald, Carolyn Haldane and Robert Dudley for reading the original manuscript and making constructive criticisms, Robin and Sheena Buchanan-Smith for teaching me all there is to know about starting and running a luxury hotel, Derek Roy for advice on commodity dealing, Belinda Robertson for inside information on cashmere and the knitwear industry, Lisa Eveleigh for being a brilliant agent, Marion Donaldson for taking the risk and my husband Ian and daughter Katie for endless encouragement and for leaving me alone at crucial moments.

Chapter One

Salami sausages the size of bolsters hung in the dim shadows of the ceiling, garlanded with strings of dried red pimentos and bunches of garlic bulbs, their papery skins rustling in the breeze from the open door. Beneath them a score of different cheeses glistened under cold glass; creamy fat cylinders of *provolone*, slabs of *dolcelatte* veined like marble, squashy white mounds of *mozzarella* and *ricotta*, and strange ochre-coloured *cabrales* wrapped in an overcoat of brown maple leaves. Like blobs of colour on a giant artist's palette, tubs of green and black olives nestled alongside bowls of rosy *sugo*, emerald *pesto* and dark blue-grey *insalata di funghi*, interwoven with shiny pink strings of fresh country sausages and sun-dried tomatoes sparkling like rubies. Casa Gianelli sold six varieties of *ravioli* and twenty different shapes of pasta with names that flowed like virgin olive oil; *linguini, fusilli, tortellini, macaroni, tagliatelli lasagne*, plus the humble soft potato *gnocci*, vacuum-packed in three different flavours – natural, cheese and herb. Giant spiral jars of preserved vegetables offered a layered collage of spidery artichoke hearts, polka-dot stuffed olives and wreaths of pearly-white button mushrooms. Shelves climbed to the ceiling stacked with tins and bottles containing rare ingredients: pumpkin-seed oil, balsamic vinegar, white truffles and red peppercorns. Casa Gianelli was a culinary Aladdin's cave.

Nell McLean never failed to relish its fragrant aroma, a mélange of fresh-ground coffee, spicy marinades and ripe cheese and, today, the special earthy pungency of bright orange chanterelles, clustered like exotic butterflies in a wicker basket by the entrance. She inspected the rows of *prosciutto crudo*, suspended like giant fruit bats from a rack in the main aisle, and edged past the queue of people waiting to be served at the cold counter, smiling at them apologetically and waving to acknowledge a shout of welcome from the genial, balding proprietor of the shop, Signor Giuseppe Gianelli himself, who was theatrically grating Parmesan, performing like a busker before a fascinated audience.

Nell was a favoured customer in the Casa, welcome to browse at will and pay at leisure. She was the chief researcher for a television food-quiz programme called *Hot Gryll*. Its presenter, self-styled 'gourmet and food-wit' Gordon Gryll could wrest more puns per minute out of food and cooking than any other man alive. 'I prune my remarks to fit the compôte–ition!' he would quip with exaggerated delight, encouraging audience response with egregious exhortations like, 'Here on *Hot Gryll* the ingredients may sometimes be canned but your laughter is always fresh!' Behind the scenes Nell often found herself wincing inwardly while trying to convince some eminent chef that it was worth his reputation to take part in such a circus. However, the programme was hugely popular and even the most temperamental chef knew an appearance on it could boost his restaurant's fortunes enormously.

Nell was responsible for the visual element of the quiz, a form of Pelmanism with recipes. After several straightforward rounds of questions and answers, three competing chefs were shown a selection of ingredients for thirty seconds and then asked to list as many as they could recognise and remember. In the final round they were given kitchens and asked to concoct a dish from some or all of the items they had listed. The results, which were often spectacularly weird, were then judged by Gordon Gryll and a celebrity guest, usually a politician or an actor, on the grounds that people in these professions could be relied on to sound sincere under the most trying of gustatory experiences.

Speculatively fingering a tin of pâté de foie gras, Nell wondered how it would mix with spinach and macadamia nuts. She had worked on *Hot Gryll* long enough to be able to predict when the judges were likely to need liver salts after a recording. She herself had an iron stomach or, as her brother Tally described it, a concrete mixer – referring, she suspected, as much to its shape as to its digestive abilities.

When it came to appearance, Nell McLean knew she was no Nell Gwynne. An increasing interest in food and cooking throughout her twenties had left her a size which kind friends described as 'buxom' and dress manufacturers classed as Large. She was of medium height, had a good head of wavy light-brown hair, a fair complexion, bright blue eyes and a generous smile but by no stretch of her own imagination could she be described as pretty. Her face was too plump, her complexion too rosy and her body too round. Consequently she had little interest in clothes, preferring to shop for ingredients rather than fashions.

A large box of custard apples caught her eye in a display of fresh vegetables. Their pale-green, uneven skins reminded her wickedly of Gordon Gryll's complexion after the TV make-up had been removed. Custard apple, foie gras, nuts and spinach – such a mixture would surely test the chefs' competitive skills and the judges' taste buds . . . With a mischievous grin she selected three and dropped them into her service basket.

'Ciao, Joe,' she called as she passed through the checkout.

'Ciao darlin'!' Giuseppe Gianelli shouted back with his quaint, Cockney-Italian accent. His friends all called him 'Joe' on the grounds that the English version of Giuseppe was Joseph, and by the same rule, his shop was commonly known as *Joe's*. 'Give my best to Gordy!' For some reason which always amazed Nell, Gordon Gryll and Joe Gianelli were good friends. She, who hardly ever encountered the temperamental presenter away from the tensions of the studio hothouse, could not imagine anyone actually seeking his company voluntarily.

'Eye-Level's done it again!' exclaimed Caroline Cohen, the sloe-eyed, dark-haired pixie of a production assistant who shared Nell's office at Television Centre.

Nell dumped her bag of booty from *Joe's* on her already cluttered desk and shot an inquiring look across the room. Caroline was pounding away on the special large-print typewriter she used for scripts. A sheaf of dog-eared pink A4 sheets lay beside it, the typing on them covered in biroed hieroglyphics. 'Not another re-write?' Nell asked sympathetically. 'That must be the third this week!'

'Fourth, actually,' muttered Caroline without a

pause in her key-bashing. 'Please don't have any ingredients with complicated spellings, Nell, because the P as B always takes twice as long when you have.' After the programme was transmitted Caroline was responsible for preparing a detailed report known as a Programme as Broadcast sheet. It could take all day if there were too many complications.

'Only macadamia nuts. I'll leave one of the empty packets on your desk so you can check the spelling.' Nell began to unpack her carrier bag and add the fresh items to the large box full of dry ingredients she had ready to take to the studio for the recording.

'Why did you have to choose those?' cried Caroline. 'There are enough nuts involved in this programme as it is. And anyway I love them and they're lethally full of calories.'

Nell regarded the elfin-like figure perched on her typist's chair and cocked an incredulous eyebrow. 'You're not counting those again, are you Caro? You'd disappear if you got any thinner.'

'Well, a spreading waistline means a new wardrobe. And when you're paid as little as I am . . . damn!' Caroline stopped typing and pressed the reverse key. The electric typewriter stuttered like a machine gun firing as the carriage juddered backwards. 'Now I'll have to re-do that whole line. Please don't talk to me, Nell. Anyway it isn't for me, it's for David. He needs to lose weight and I've promised to help him.'

'David – David Guedalla? I thought you didn't fancy him.'

'I don't.' Caroline grinned impishly up at Nell. 'I thought if he got rid of his spare tyre he'd be irresistible to other girls and then he'd stop asking me out. I'm sure he only does it because his mother says he should.'

'David isn't a Mummy's boy,' protested Nell, self-consciously tucking her white blouse more neatly into the waistband of her floral skirt. There was less waistband than waist and the latter therefore spilled over the former. David Guedalla was an old friend of her brother's whom she had recently introduced to Caroline.

'Well, you know better than me what makes him tick,' said Caroline, frowning over the erase mechanism. 'Don't *you* fancy him at all, Nell? You've known him long enough. If you did the decent thing and kept him happy he wouldn't keep bothering me. Damn again! The rub-out ribbon's run out.'

Nell giggled. 'That sounds like one of Gordon's witticisms,' she remarked and fell to mimicry, at which she was quite skilled. ' "Rub in the flour and run up a few scones!" ' She could even screw up her face to look a bit like Gordon Gryll's jovial jowls.

But Caroline wasn't to be distracted. 'Don't change the subject, Nell,' she admonished, trying to give her friend a reproving look and search for a new ribbon at the same time. 'Why have you never had a fling with David? Or perhaps you have and you're now trying to palm him off on me.'

Nell looked indignant. 'Not at all! We go back too far to be romantic. I thought you might get on well together, that's all.'

'Why – just because we're both Jewish?'

'No – just because you're my friends. I like match-making, it gives me a thrill. That's why you're both coming to dinner tonight.'

'Well, dinner will be nice but you've met your match-making match I'm afraid,' said Caroline briskly. 'There are only calories between David Guedalla and me.' She glanced up at the clock which hung over the door, the red second hand ticking inexorably towards the midday programme recording time. 'I've got to have this finished in five minutes and you'd better concentrate on matching something with macadamia nuts.'

'Oh, don't worry! I've got the ideal mixture this week.' Nell picked up the box of ingredients and staggered towards the door.

'Ideal' proved to be not quite the right word. Required by the show's producer after the recording to drive home the celebrity judge – in this case an actress of a certain age and an uncertain constitution called Gloria Parker – Nell was too busy negotiating the traffic to notice that her passenger was becoming quieter and paler as the journey progressed. 'I shink I'm going to be shick,' slurred Gloria suddenly and promptly was – all over the dashboard of Nell's venerable hatchback.

Normally Nell would have been sympathetic, but somehow she couldn't bring herself to be pleasant to someone who had just consigned her to several weeks of nauseous motoring while deftly avoiding her own pale pink trousers. 'There is a window,' she muttered mutinously, wrenching the wheel round to navigate the quickest route to the kerb, and then instantly felt contrite. She supposed some of the blame lay with her choice of ingredients. Solicitously she helped her passenger into the relative cleanliness of the back seat.

'Shorry,' mumbled the discomforted actress. 'It musht have been those cushtard apples. Like shweet shcrambled eggsh!'

Nell got back behind the wheel and pulled out into the traffic. She said nothing but inwardly concluded that the copious amounts of wine the actress had drunk after the recording couldn't have helped. And then a wondrously appropriate thought occurred. 'Sick transit Gloria!' she almost cried aloud, regaining her sense of humour. 'God, I'm getting worse than Gordon Gryll!'

Tally McLean let himself into his first-floor flat. Through the open-plan hall and sitting room he could see the green panorama of Hyde Park, laid out beyond the three long sash windows. These had been completely replaced when the building was repaired and converted following the notorious siege which had violently ended its tenure by the Iranian Embassy ten years before. After the SAS had stormed it live on television, number 27 Princes Gate became one of the most infamous addresses in London, so that when Tally bought his flat there the price was artificially low. In time, however, it had become a very desirable residence. Tally was a speculator by nature and by profession, though normally he dealt in the futures' market, buying sugar or cocoa or coffee – any commodity in bulk which he could hope to sell on later at a profit.

'Gemma?' he called, dumping his slim black leather briefcase on the hall table and loosening his tie. He felt drained and elated at the same time, having sweated in his City office until the last minute to clinch a deal. The five-figure profit he'd made compensated enough to mellow his mood.

A tall, slim, tousled blonde in a blue silk kimono sauntered into view from a side door. She looked sulky and unreceptive. 'Hi,' she said dully.

'Well, you're a fountain of joy,' Tally remarked, veering off the move he had made in her direction. 'Don't tell me – *Vogue*'s put Naomi Campbell on the cover again.'

'Don't be so condescending,' retorted Gemma.

'*Vogue*'s got nothing to do with it. It's cellulite.'

'What's that – a new magazine?'

'Oh God, you wouldn't understand!' Gemma strode over to the television and switched it on. She moved with the predatory grace that was the hallmark of a catwalk model. Indeed, it had been on a catwalk that she had spent most of her day, and her feet were bruised and aching from being forced into shoes that were too narrow and too high.

'There's no time for that,' Tally reminded her. 'We're due at Nell's at eight.'

'I'm not coming.' Gemma flopped down into a deep brocade sofa. Tally had used an interior designer for his flat, and the sitting room was a tasteful symphony of yellow fabrics, cream walls and brown polished wood.

'Why the hell not?'

'I don't feel like it.' Gemma picked up the TV remote control and began to flick through the channels. Bursts of music and dialogue followed in quick succession until the grinning face of Gordon Gryll filled the screen, launching another half hour of culinary fun and games. 'Relax. Enjoy the show,' crooned Gordon. 'Let the sieve take the strain!'

Tally stood ominously still in the middle of the room, his back to the television, fair hair flopping over dark brows which glowcrcd above glittering blue eyes. He stared down at Gemma who stared past him at the screen. 'Are you ill?' he asked with a patience he did not feel.

'No.'

'Then you've no excuse. Hurry up and change.' Tally turned away and removed his tie completely.

'I don't need an excuse not to dine with your sister. She won't mind if I'm not there. She doesn't like me anyway.'

'Rubbish. And people don't snub a dinner party just because they think the hostess doesn't like them – that's fatuous.'

'I'm not fat . . . that thing you said,' retorted Gemma angrily. 'I'm not fat at all, whatever Mark Fothergill may say!'

Enlightenment spread over Tally's face, bringing amusement with it. 'Oh, I see,' he said, sitting down beside her. 'That's what all this is about. Mark bloody Fother-Bother has made some snide remark about your bum and you've taken umbrage.' He slid his hand under her thigh, pushing it up to cup her silk-clad buttock where it dented the cushion. 'Well, it's a fine bum – and I should know. Why take any notice of what that poncy designer says?' He leaned forward to nuzzle her ear, pressing his face into her long tumbled hair. 'A poof like him wouldn't know what a female buttock should look like. He's too busy buggering hairy male ones.'

For a moment Gemma brightened. 'Do you think so?' she asked, momentarily responding to his advance before putting up a petulant hand and pushing him away. 'No, he's right. I *am* putting on weight – and cellulite.' She stood up, leaving his curved hand lying empty on the sofa. 'I've got a photo session for swimwear tomorrow. I can't afford to eat tonight.'

'God al-bloody-mighty!' exploded Tally, losing patience and leaping up. 'You're as boring as hell, Gemma. How can anyone live with someone whose idea of dinner is a vitamin pill and a mug of herbal tea?' He strode towards the door which led to the bedrooms, opening it violently. 'And this whole place stinks of hair remover. If you've used my shaving brush to put it on again I'll put ground glass in your face cream.'

'It's not my fault,' Gemma shrieked, prowling after him with her arms wrapped defensively around herself. 'I'm a model! I have to be thin and I have to be smooth. We can't all make money by juggling sugar and cocoa and we can't all eat ourselves stupid without putting on a pound.'

He turned on her with a malevolent grin, unbuttoning his shirt. 'Some people are stupid without eating at all,' he sneered.

Nell was desperately wondering why she had arranged a dinner party for programme day. Clearing up Gloria's 'remains' in the car had left her precious little time to produce her planned menu, and so she had to plonk smoked salmon haphazardly on the plates instead of arranging it in 'flowers' with feathery dill foliage as she liked to do. Fortunately the veal in cream and fennel sauce, prepared last weekend, had defrosted without curdling and the new potatoes and baby leeks from Marks & Spencer needed no further attention other than boiling water at the right moment. Her dessert, however, which was to have been a freshly assembled *millefeuilles* of flaky pastry, raspberries and whipped cream, inevitably disintegrated under her too hasty ministrations into something resembling a thousand lumps rather than a thousand leaves.

'It looks like murder on the alps!' she groaned, struggling with soggy raspberries. It was nearing eight and she had yet to prepare herself for her guests. Abandoning the *millefeuilles*, she fled from the kitchen to the bedroom of her so-called garden flat, which was really a basement in any language other than estate-agentese. Its saving graces were her skill with patchwork, which decorated pelmets, cushions and chair-seats, and the rear exit which led straight into the beautifully maintained garden square behind the building – an arrangement which, on sunny June evenings like this one, meant she could entertain her guests outside for pre-dinner drinks.

'Thank goodness I only have one possible thing to wear,' she muttered aloud, ripping off her cotton blouse and skirt and throwing them unceremoniously into the bottom of a cupboard.

The item in question was a flamboyant flamingo print silk shirt she had acquired in *Monsoon*'s recent sale. It was loose and flowing, disguising and covering all her curves and bulges from the shoulders to the knee where a pair of tailored black trousers continued the deception of outline. Flat black pumps meant she would be able to rush about with plates and dishes unhampered by high heels.

Mummy would be horrified if she knew this was almost the only evening garb I possess, she thought, as she pulled a brush through her short, springy hair. She had no time to analyse her unaccountable twinge of guilt about this, however, for at that moment the front doorbell sounded. 'Oh God, no make-up!' she exclaimed, hurrying to answer it. Her long straight nose gleamed accusingly at her from the mirror in the hall. Its uncompromising shape was another of the faults which she felt counted against her.

The first arrival was Leo Turnbull, Nell's next-door neighbour. He was an artist who worked freelance in the BBC's set design department, painting scenery and props to make ends meet, but his real ambition was to paint murals. This evening Leo was in euphoric mood. 'I've got a commission! I've got a commission!' he cried as soon as she opened the door, grabbing her in a wild embrace and dancing with her down the narrow hall, bumping from wall to wall with careless disregard for sharp edges on door-jambs and picture-frames.

'Ouch – watch out. Hell, Leo, will you stop,' Nell shouted above his repeated cries of delight. When she managed to break free there were at least four new bruises which she needed to rub at once and couldn't. 'I'm delighted for you, of course,' she added ruefully, 'but take it easy!' His elation rubbed uncomfortably against her own uncharacteristic state of mild depression.

Leo looked only slightly crestfallen. 'Sorry,' he said, his long animated face looming over her apologetically. He was tall, dark and heartbreakingly handsome, wearing jeans and a faded blue shirt covered in paint splashes. Leo never believed in dressing up; Nell simply assumed that he owned nothing but spattered blue denim. He seldom had any money, but when he did earn a little extra he was the soul of generosity, purchasing gifts for his friends and presenting them with an eager smile like a puppy laying a bone at its master's feet. Now he laid his new commission before Nell in much the same fashion. 'I'm so excited. It only happened today – must tell you all about it.'

As he spoke the bell rang again. 'You can tell more than just me in a minute,' Nell assured him, edging past towards the door. 'Help yourself to wine. It's in the kitchen – you know.' Two people stood on the doorstep – Tally and Gemma.

'Hi Nell,' said Tally casually, bending to brush her cheek with his lips, and thrust a bottle into her hands. 'Hope you like it. It's a new import from Australia.' Tally prided himself on keeping close tabs on the wine trade.

Nell raised an eyebrow as her brother pushed straight into the hall ahead of Gemma. 'Thanks very much,' said Nell. 'Hello, Gemma.'

The two women exchanged vague kisses and Gemma swayed sulkily down the passage, entering the combined living and dining room in Tally's wake and then pointedly moving as far away from him as possible. Nell did not know that Tally had had to threaten Gemma with expulsion from his flat in order to get her to come at all, but she accurately detected that all was not sweetness and light in her brother's liaison. She shrugged. Tally's volatile love-life was a commonplace. She could hear Leo excitedly announcing his commission once more as she went to answer another peal of the bell.

'Greetings again, prog-mate!' said Caroline merrily, poking her head carefully round the front door before entering, and sniffing the air with exaggerated curiosity. 'Can't smell a familiar aftershave, can I? Don't tell me Eye-Level's here.'

Nell responded with indignation. 'Would I subject you to that at the end of such a day?' she expostulated. 'We've had enough punishment, I think. Hello, David,' she added warmly to the plump, dark, curly-haired man who stood behind Caroline wearing an immaculate three-piece city suit. This was the David Guedalla Nell had known since schooldays and whom she had tried to pair up with Caroline. Disappointingly she now knew that little should be assumed from the fact that they had arrived together.

As a rule, giving a dinner party was Nell's greatest pleasure in life. It delighted her to take infinite care in presenting dishes that were pleasing to the eye and delicious to the tongue. She spared no pains in exploring different recipes, experimenting with ingredients, trying sauces and accompaniments in the same way as many other women tried clothes and accessories. The enjoyment of friends at her table was more important to her than her appearance, and she derived great satisfaction from the appreciation she generally received. But on this occasion something seemed to go sour. Afterwards she wondered if the general disgruntlement had been a virus which she herself had incubated, for her mood was irritable from the first.

'I'm to paint Trevor Entwistle's swimming pool,' Leo announced as soon as the company was assembled around a white wrought-iron table laden with drinks and canapés under the plane trees in the garden-square. Although it was communal and other groups and individuals lay or sat enjoying the evening sunshine, they remained aloof, respecting the invisible barriers that existed between their territories.

'Trevver the Wevver?' exclaimed Caroline, intrigued. 'Is he building a new pool? They must be paying forecasters well these days.'

'Don't know about that,' confessed Leo. 'I think he's come into money or something because he's bought this fantastic house on the river at Bray and he's adding the pool on. He says he doesn't want it to look like a public toilet with tiles and everything, so he wants me to paint it, bottom, sides, ceiling and all.'

'What subject will you choose – bathing beauties?' Tally's cynical question was coloured by the row he'd had with Gemma. He was angry that she had tried to put her swimwear shoot over and above his sister's dinner party. He couldn't credit what he called 'poncing about in front of a camera' with the dignity of a profession for which it was worth making sacrifices.

'Do me a favour,' said Leo, somewhat offended. 'I've got to get Trevor's approval, of course, but I thought the weather would be an appropriate subject.'

'Dripping poached eggs, d'you mean?' asked David, amused. 'Like on the TV forecasts?'

Leo looked defensive. 'Not exactly, no. Cloudscapes though, and thunderheads and lightning and wind and snow and hail – and sunshine, of course. It might be every season at once.'

'Like a Turner,' suggested Caroline. 'Except it'll be a Turnbull.'

'People will travel miles to visit it,' cried Leo, carried away with the image of greatness thus thrust upon him. 'Like the Sistine Chapel.'

'Except it'll be the Entwistle Bath,' put in Tally prosaically. 'Doesn't have quite the same ring to it somehow.'

'Better than a tankerload of treacle,' scoffed Gemma, sending him a baleful glare. 'You can't plaster *that* all over a swimming pool.'

'Have a nibble,' said Nell, to cover the awkward silence that ensued. She had prepared small squares of filo pastry stuffed with cream cheese and spinach, tiny cubes of brie deep-fried in breadcrumbs, and baked circles of anchovies wound into pastry wheels. No one appeared to want them, though. Only David took one with an apologetic cough. Gemma just shook her head and sipped at her mineral water, studiously avoiding Tally's eye. Leo was too excited to eat, waving his arms and launching into further descriptions of his artistic intentions, and Tally was too busy glaring at Gemma to notice the proffered plate. Caroline simply smiled and murmured, 'I mustn't, honestly.'

Why do I bother? Nell asked herself, staring uncomprehendingly at Caroline. The girl was built like a fairy. Tiny hands and feet tipped limbs that looked as if they might snap in a high wind. She must be size eight, thought Nell. She needs a diet like the ocean needs water. But she said nothing, pouring wine into her own glass, suddenly not caring if she got drunk.

The meal progressed in similar vein. When the first course was over, Nell scraped slice after slice of uneaten smoked salmon into the cat's dish. Thatcher had disappeared as she always did when visitors came but she would have a glorious treat when she crept in during the night.

From the CD player in the corner the voice of Pavarotti lubricated the air like melted butter and the veal was just as rich and smooth, but Nell noticed that Gemma cut hers into tiny pieces and pushed them around the plate, occasionally forking a morsel of leek into her mouth with an expression that threatened to curdle the cream sauce. Caroline begged for 'Just the smallest portion!' and then played cat and mouse with it, consuming very little. Tally ate his fast and heedless, clearly not tasting a mouthful, and Leo waved his fork about in animated conversation, occasionally delivering its contents to his mouth, and occasionally to the tablecloth or the carpet. David, ever obliging, ate appreciatively and asked for seconds but Nell knew he only did so out of sympathy. He needed no extra nourishment. His spare tyre bulged over his waistband rather like her own, but at least he was aware how much effort Nell had gone to and hated to see it disregarded. He was a kind man, thought Nell, spooning sauce over his seconds of veal. Caroline frowned crossly at David as she passed the plate down the table.

Nell found herself eating furiously, as if to compensate for the general abstinence, even though she knew she would scold herself later for doing so. While part of her despised the metropolitan obsession with diet and weight, another part longed to share it, if only to reap the rewards of silhouette. It was uncomfortable to be round when the rest of the world was angular. At the same time she was annoyed that people should spurn her carefully prepared food. Why do people think they're asked to dinner? she thought mutinously. Just so that we can all sit around admiring their cut-glass jaw-lines and the salt-cellars behind their collarbones? I want to share food and witty conversation! They shouldn't come if they're not prepared to eat.

In view of the circumstances, she decided to dispense with the *millefeuilles* altogether. If people disdained a successful dish like the veal then she wouldn't give them the satisfaction of even glimpsing a failure. Instead she brought out cheese and fruit and a decanter of late-bottled vintage port which she noticed Tally consumed faster than anyone else.

Inevitably the party broke up prematurely, Gemma beginning the process at ten-thirty by pleading her early photo session and asking Nell if she would 'very sweetly forgive her'. Tally left with her, wearing such a murderous expression that Nell wondered whether Gemma would make it home alive. Caroline refused coffee, saying it kept her awake, and then claimed she had a headache, begging David to give her a lift home. Nell thought this request unreasonable, considering her remarks about him earlier in the day, but David seemed politely willing.

By eleven only Leo was left, still chattering on

about his commission and how much he was going to earn from it. Nell listened for several minutes, pouring fresh coffee and trying to analyse why the dinner had been such a fiasco. She liked Leo, especially since he had 'come out' on her sofa two years before and told her of his homosexuality. Now they usually compared notes on their various affairs and Nell was not jealous that beautiful, generous Leo attracted a queue of lovers when she did not, for none of them seemed to last long. She worried about his health in this age of AIDS but did not say so. His promiscuity was his own affair, and at least it provided plenty of scope for gossip. Tonight, though, this endless talk of his commission was proving unbearable.

'Why doesn't anyone eat any more?' she asked suddenly, when he came to a comma. 'I cook them dinner and pour them wine and all they can talk about is their diets and how much weight they've put on.'

Leo was nonplussed. How had the subject of diet suddenly arisen, when he had been musing at length over the relative merits of nimbus and cumulus? 'Do they?' he asked.

'You must have noticed,' she said impatiently. 'Even David looked as if the food was sawdust in his mouth, especially after Caroline had frowned at his second helping. Do you think it's wrong to enjoy food, Leo?'

'Of course not.'

'Rubens liked plump women,' she pointed out. 'You're an artist – do you?'

He shrugged. 'It's difficult to pass comment when you don't go for women much at all, in that way.'

She laughed ruefully. 'Silly me. I tell you, I'm not going to bother giving dinner parties any more. Food is obviously out of fashion. I'll have to find another hobby. The trouble is, I'm not very good at anything else.'

'It's all in the mind, you know,' said Leo thoughtfully, 'a matter of emphasis. All you have to do is make them think your meals are exquisitely delicious, and yet *won't* make them fat.'

Nell did not respond to this immediately but inside her head an idea began to buzz about like a firefly.

Chapter Two

It was 24 June – Midsummer Day, the Feast of St John, the day when the folk of 'Merrie Englande' used to light fires and leap through the flames to gain protective magic for the coming year. The weather continued exceptionally warm and sunny and London was full of tourists, thronging the parks, milling in the stores and packing the Thames' pleasure-boats. At discos and raves the peddlers of Ecstasy did a roaring trade. So many eager people, young and old, were seeking excitement and gratification, and perhaps a little Midsummer magic of their own.

In the City, those wine bars which had withstood the dive in business following the London Stock Exchange's Black Monday were lunchtime-full, although the recession meant that Australian sparkling wine had more or less replaced French champagne as the staple drink. David Guedalla had bought the genuine article, however, because he and Tally were celebrating.

'Happy Birthday, old man – and old really is the word,' grinned David, raising his *flûte*. 'How does it feel to see policemen getting younger?'

'You'll find out in a month's time yourself,' grumbled Tally, gulping half his glassful in one go. 'Twenty-nine. It's a watershed, I tell you. "A moist eye, a dry hand, a yellow cheek . . ." '

' ". . . a white beard, a decreasing leg, an increasing belly!" ' finished David. 'That last one only applies to me, however. *Henry IV, Part Two*, eh? We can't be that old if we still remember our school Shakespeare! What are you so miserable about, anyway? You're making a good whack, you're fit, trim and still under thirty. The world is your oyster.'

Tally grimaced. 'I've never liked oysters. Nasty, smelly wet things with sharp edges. Give me lobster any day. In fact, I think I'll sting my stepfather for one tonight.' He brightened perceptibly. 'It'll be some compensation for having to listen to him drone on about computers.'

'Birthday dinner?'

Tally nodded and gave a resigned shrug. 'Mother insisted, but Gemma's refused to come. Just as well, really, because they don't get on. I don't know that Gemma and I get on very well any more either. Familiarity and all that.'

'You've always been a bit of a "love 'em and leave 'em" man, haven't you? I don't know why you let them move in – you only have to move them out again. One day, some girl will do it to you. Is Nell going tonight?'

'Yes, of course. One of the few things we have in common is our birthday.'

David gave his friend a sideways glance. 'Oh, I don't know. There might be more than you think. How does she view being twenty-nine?'

Tally shook his head. 'I haven't asked her. She's happy enough, I reckon. There's nothing about her that losing a few stone and gaining a man wouldn't cure.'

'That's the trouble with you, Tally. You think sex is the answer to everything.' David's voice contained a note of mild exasperation.

'Well, isn't it? Mind you, a mega deal must run it a close second. If I could scoop the Big One I honestly think I'd give up this melting pot and start a chicken farm or something. They're right when they say broking is a young man's game. It gets you down after ten years.'

'Ah – so there *are* some compensations for us plodding actuaries.'

'Oh, you'll be wearing pin-stripes for ever, Guedalla. Rolling round town in your chauffeur-driven Bath chair when you're ninety!'

'Any sign of the Big One?'

'There might be, there just might be. I'm keeping my moist eye on the Gulf and the dollar.'

'Sounds like a good combination.'

'Oil and vinegar – with the emphasis on the oil!'

A twenty-ninth birthday is a milestone in any personal almanac. Nell's unaccustomed depression had deepened following her strained dinner party. Nothing seemed to go right. At the studio she had been unable to pacify a particularly famous and temperamental chef who had stormed out of the recording, infuriated by one of Gordon Gryll's facetious remarks. The whole programme had had to be scrapped and the other contestants re-scheduled to appear thc following week. The producer had raged, Gordon Gryll had sulked and Nell had gloomily eaten the avocado, crème fraiche and passion fruit from among her selection for the Pelmanism section. Afterwards she wished she could crawl home and curl up with a good book and a box of chocolates, but instead she had to face drinks with her father and dinner with her mother.

'You're both as dull as an Irish summer,' complained their stepmother that evening, glancing from one glum twin to the other as their father poured champagne. Ian McLean had married Sinead O'Brien when she was five months pregnant, two weeks after his divorce from his first wife, Donalda, the twins' mother. Tally and Nell had been collected from their separate boarding schools in a chauffeur-driven hire-car to attend the wedding. They had not been told about the baby and, at twelve, had been too steeped in childish self-obsession to notice the tell-tale bulge on the twenty-two-year-old, red-headed bride. The arrival of a half-sister four months later had not altered their attitude towards Sinead, whom they always considered more of a wacky older sister than a wicked stepmother.

'A drink'll set you right,' said their father cheerfully. He wasn't drinking champagne himself, preferring the whisky he manufactured, blended and marketed around the world. Ian McLean was a stocky, jaunty Scot who was nearing sixty and, as he liked to put it, plagiarising Muriel Spark, 'in his prime'. He raised his tumbler to their *flûtes*. 'Happy Birthday!'

'Happy Birthday!' echoed a firm, high, even more markedly Scottish voice at his elbow. His mother, Kirsty McLean, was on a visit from Glasgow. A doughty lady of eighty with strong, wavy white hair, she had piercing blue eyes and a short, plumply rounded body. A glance at Granny Kirsty told Nell exactly what she herself would look like in fifty years' time, should she live that long!

'Champagne – wicked!' said a flame-haired teenage siren in black jeans and a baggy pink sweatshirt printed with the word OINK! She poured out some more and gulped it down as if she feared it might evaporate.

'Careful, Niamh, you'll get hiccoughs,' warned

Sinead mildly. This seventeen-year-old was the child who had been the cause of her marriage, the awkward pregnancy which had torn her away from her much-cherished job as an air stewardess. Now Niamh was the cause of most of her heartache.

'Chance'd be a fine thing,' muttered the girl, hurling herself energetically onto the settee beside Tally and slopping champagne over his trousers. She brushed it off, grinning. 'Sorry, it doesn't stain, though. God, it must be great being twenty-nine. You can do whatever you like, not like me. I'm not even allowed to go to the Time Capsule because it's still term-time. Never mind that exams are over.' She glared at her mother as if she was some sort of hideous creepy-crawly.

'What on earth is the Time Capsule?' inquired Tally, ruefully feeling his damp leg.

'Ignorance, total ignorance!' Niamh declared incredulously. 'It's only the shittest-hot place in town, that's all.'

'Niamh,' protested Kirsty and Sinead in unison.

'I'd take you there for a birthday treat if I hadn't been grounded,' the girl grumbled sulkily. 'It's got great music and wild lighting, and it's only round the corner.' She swigged down the last of her champagne and looked at her father inquiringly, glass raised. Ian McLean pretended not to noticc.

'Sounds ace,' Tally grinned, 'but way ahead. I think I'll have to grow up before I go there.'

'Nah – if you're grown up they won't let you in,' scoffed Niamh. 'That's the great attraction.'

Nell smiled sympathetically at Sinead. The Time Capsule was a disco where drugs were known to circulate freely. It was haunted by the under-twenties and Niamh claimed that all her friends went there all the time. When Sinead had announced the ban, the only-just-seventeen-year-old had screamed that she would be mocked by her peers as a dribbling, knicker-wetting infant whose only knowledge of low joints was her mother's knee! Nell rather suspected that, despite the ban, Niamh still managed to hang out in the Time Capsule at least once a week.

Sinead returned the smile. 'Aren't you going to open your presents?' she asked, pushing several gaily wrapped parcels across the glass-topped coffee table. This branch of the McLean clan inhabited a terraced house in a street off the Fulham Road called Hollywood Gardens – a thoroughfare inappropriately but pleasantly lined with cherry trees. The house was on four floors, curtained and papered by Osborne & Little and hung with several of Anthony Green's vast asymmetric canvases depicting his family life. Sinead liked them because she said it was as chaotic as her own. The house had been immaculate when they first moved in five years before, during a flush period shortly after Ian had opened his entrepreneurial gold mine, a whisky distillery in India. But its rooms now showed signs of wear and tear, to which Sinead could not be bothered to attend.

'Happy Birthday, Tally and Nell.' An angelic-looking boy in dark grey, prep-school trousers and blazer had entered the room, his brown hair neatly combed, a hopeful smile on his lips. 'Can I have some champagne?'

'Of course you can't,' said Niamh.

'Of course you can,' said Sinead, reaching for the bottle.

'Thank you Ninian,' said Tally and Nell together, accepting the birthday cards he offered each of them.

'Creep!' muttered Niamh to her brother. She had remembered neither card nor present. She was in a perpetual state of feud with Ninian. He was everything she was not – conscientious, well-mannered, talented. A chorister at Westminster Cathedral, he had just arrived home from the choir school he attended daily. With gleeful sisterly anticipation, Niamh ached for the rapidly approaching day when his voice would break.

Having opened their cards, the twins attacked the presents. Kirsty had brought them each a bottle of single malt whisky, much to her son's disgust, for Ian dealt only in the blended variety. 'I hope you like it. It's Talisker – from the distillery on Skye,' Kirsty told them. 'Not to be confused with the Isle of Taliska where I grew up. Which, incidentally, is on the market, did you know?' From the needlework bag by her chair she produced a copy of the *Scottish Field*. The magazine was folded open at the *Property For Sale* section. Since no one else seemed particularly interested, Ninian took it from her and began to read.

Tally had opened his second parcel and stood up, holding a sea-green silk Armani shirt against his chest. 'Wow, see me in this!' he enthused, bending over to kiss Sinead. 'Thanks very much. Thanks, Dad.' He grinned across at his father whom he knew would have a fit when he learned what Sinead had paid for the shirt. Ian tended to think all clothes should cost under £20, with the possible exception of a McLean kilt, which might legitimately run into hundreds. He rarely questioned the cost of food and drink, however.

'Taliska looks a fab place, Gran,' said Ninian, lifting his head from the magazine. 'Did you really live there when you were young?'

Kirsty McLean nodded. 'Aye, I did that. Until I was eighteen and married your Granda'.'

' "Two hundred acres of natural grass and woodland, with white sand beaches and a private jetty," ' he quoted enthusiastically. 'It must have been great, like *Treasure Island*. Were there lots of different animals?' Ninian was mad about animals and kept several small rodents in his bedroom – another cause of friction with Niamh, who constantly accused him of planting them in hers.

'Hundreds,' Kirsty assured him. 'Badgers and deer and seals and otters. It is a paradise, ringed with silver.'

'Toady,' Niamh muttered to her brother. 'Smarmy greaseball.' Behind the magazine, out of his mother's line of sight, Ninian showed his sister a very un-chorister-like pair of fingers.

Sinead was looking dubiously at Nell who was opening her second parcel. It contained a pair of leggings in electric-blue Lycra, smothered in a design of gold chains, keys and padlocks. Nell held them up, to a chorus of whoops and cat-calls from the others. 'They look like Versace but I'm afraid they aren't,' Sinead said hurriedly. 'Have you seen the prices in his shop? I hope you like them. I wasn't sure what size, but with Lycra you can't go far wrong, can you?' She herself was wearing something similar in green and gold beneath a silky green over-shirt. She had good legs and the loose shirt disguised a slightly thickened waistline.

Nell stared at the leggings and tried to imagine her own sturdy limbs stretching the chains and padlocks.

'Oysters are *so* slimming, and *Bentley's* has such an *English* atmosphere!' Donalda had gushed on the telephone. Seated at the restaurant's white damask cloth, the twins' mother was immaculately coiffured, pencil-slim and resplendent in red silk Jean Muir and pearls. Her second husband, Hal Doxy, sat opposite, trim in a shark-grey worsted Savile Row suit to complement his abundant pewter-coloured hair.

The Doxys always ate at eight-thirty. 'The English hour for dinner,' Hal pontificated in his strange, mid-Atlantic drawl. Since marrying Donalda he had tried to round out his flat Yankee accent but had succeeded only in acquiring a hybrid twang which Tally described as 'a mouthful of mashed potato'. Hal loved all things English and Donalda had never dared admit to him that she had actually been born in Edinburgh. She excused this deception by telling herself that all Americans thought Scotland was part of England anyway!

'How's Gemma?' Hal asked. 'Sorry she couldn't make it.'

'Working,' lied Tally, recalling Gemma's categoric declaration that this time she definitely wouldn't bloat her stomach in order to eat dinner with his ghastly mother and stepfather. 'I'll make it up to you when you come home,' she had promised, whispering seductively in his ear, 'in my birthday suit, naturally . . .' A waiter placed a platter before Tally with a flourish and the sprawling legs of a cloven lobster inspired an image of Gemma's long, smooth lower limbs disappearing into the moist coral at their confluence. With relish he began to suck at the flesh.

Oysters were sliding down Donalda's throat like raw eggs. 'Isn't it intriguing?' she observed animatedly, clamping her long red nails around a wedge of lemon. 'You can actually see them flinch when you squeeze on the juice!'

Distaste made Nell gobble like a hungry puppy.

She had practically finished her *Coquilles St Jacques* before Hal had peeled his second langoustine. 'You shouldn't eat so fast, Nell,' admonished her mother, her glistening, pointed tongue delicately licking the pale mother-of-pearl interior of another oyster shell.

She's like a cat with the cream bowl, thought Nell, but knew Donalda would never dream of letting cream pass her lips. 'It comes of going to boarding school,' she said, unapologetically. 'If you ate fast you didn't taste the food.'

'But this food is delicious,' Donalda protested. 'And the dietitian at my health club says "fast makes fat, slow makes slim".'

'It's a good club,' commented Hal, wrestling with another crustacean, his napkin tucked carefully into his collar to protect his Pierre Cardin tie. He longed to be able to wear an old school tie but honesty forced him to make do with unidentifiable diagonal stripes. 'It's in Berkeley Square.'

'A nightingale slimmed in Berkeley Square,' crooned Tally softly, idly twirling his glass of Gewürztraminer. 'I used to go to a sandwich bar there. Fabulous banana croissants.'

'Croissants?' cried Donalda in amazement. 'And bananas? Only you could eat such things and not burst a zip, Tally. I don't believe your waist has expanded one inch since you were sixteen. It's positively disgusting.' There was no mistaking the pride in her voice.

Nell could almost hear her mother thinking, 'He takes after me!' Why does the whole world talk about nothing but dieting and getting fat? she thought despairingly, breaking another bread roll and smothering it defiantly with butter. Why don't they ask about the programme or Tally's deals? Why don't they tell us about their last holiday in

Bermuda? Anything but the sins of the stomach!

'It's the one thing wrong with the English,' Hal observed loudly. 'Their eating habits. All those business lunches. No wonder there are no elderly tycoons! They've all over-stoked their boilers and burnt themselves out.' His observation amused him and he choked on his prawn, spluttering and blowing his carefully stacked pile of shells all over the white tablecloth. They settled like pink confetti. Tally picked a fragment out of his wine with his finger, murmuring something about shell-shock. A waitress hurried up with a little silver brush and pan and began to sweep up the débris.

Once Hal was breathing normally again, Donalda proclaimed a shrill endorsement of her husband's last remark. 'You're so right, darling. Even when they take a weekend break they go to a country hotel just to eat and drink. It's not like that at Apple Corps. They *really* protect their employees' health. Did you know that Hal's introduced random breath tests? Anyone in the company can be asked to blow into a breathalyser at any time during working hours. Isn't that a good idea?' Hal was President of the British arm of an American computer giant.

'Wouldn't go down too well in Threadneedle Street,' remarked Tally. 'What happens if they fail? Do they lose their VDU licence?'

'They're given counselling,' explained Hal seriously. 'Drink can seriously affect reaction times. In computers that matters.' He turned to beckon the wine waiter. 'Obviously a sip or two in the evening's OK,' he added genially. 'Especially if it's a celebration.' He raised his long-stemmed glass to admire the pale liquid the waiter had poured.

'I'm glad I don't work at Apple Corps,' Tally whispered to Nell as he bent to retrieve his napkin from the floor. 'It would give me the pip!'

Nell giggled. At least Tally was on her side. He never talked about dieting or advocated abstention of any kind and he was enviably slim. Why hadn't she inherited Donalda's willowy physique as Tally had done, instead of taking after their father, who was short-boned and chunky? For 'chunky' in a man, read 'dumpy' in a woman, Nell sighed to herself.

'Will you give me a lift home afterwards?' she asked her brother suddenly. 'I didn't bring my car because it still smells awful and anyway, I want to talk to you about something.'

Tally glanced at her in surprise. These days they rarely exchanged much more than pleasantries and then only on social occasions. 'If there's a bobby with a breathalyser in Brook Green I'll blame you,' he said but she took that as a reply in the affirmative.

'We're not giving birthday presents this year,' declared Donalda as the waiter cleared their plates. 'At least, not pretty parcels. We've decided to give you vouchers instead – much more practical.' She extracted two envelopes from her gold lamé evening bag and stared pointedly at Nell's buttery knife and the remains of her second bread roll. 'Champneys for you, Nell. I know you won't mind. You're getting a bit *too* plump, darling!' She passed a thick, parchment envelope to Nell and a slim buff one to Tally. 'And British Airways for you, Tally. We didn't know where you'd like to go, but this way you can make up your own mind.'

'What a great idea,' said Tally with exaggerated enthusiasm, tearing open the brown sheath and extracting its contents. 'Thanks, Mother. Thanks, Hal.'

Mercifully the kiss of gratitude he delivered to his mother diverted attention from his sister. Nell stared in disbelief at the crisp, crackling cream envelope with its embossed red logo and felt tears of humiliation prick her eyelids. A voucher for a health farm! And this from her mother who seemed serenely unaware of the hurt she inflicted with it. Nell groped blindly for her shoulder-bag which she'd parked on the floor at her feet and stuffed the envelope unopened into it. The action gave her time to blink back the tears and force a smile to her lips. 'Thanks, Mummy,' she said, bending over to kiss the strong waft of *Poison* by her mother's left ear. 'Thanks a lot.'

'I really like to visit a health farm,' Hal told the world loudly. 'You come out feeling ten years younger.'

'And hopefully, ten pounds lighter,' trilled Donalda in her equally penetrating voice. 'Wouldn't that be marvellous, Nell? The poor girl finds it so hard to diet,' she informed the restaurant in general while appearing to address her husband confidentially. 'A little boost to get started is a fantastic help.'

Nell bit back the cry of indignation which rose to her lips. She felt sick. There was a huge knot in her stomach but she knew she wouldn't throw up. Once something went down her throat it stayed down. Emotional upheaval, illness, fright – all these things seemed to make her swallow rather than retch. 'Fantastic!' she agreed feebly.

Driving down Piccadilly after dinner Nell noticed, not for the first time, how Tally's long legs disappeared into the dark shadowy recess beneath the dashboard of his BMW. They seemed almost endless in the fine, dark-blue chinos he wore with his fashionably crumpled beige linen jacket. Even when he was folded behind the wheel of his car there was no sinful bulge where his pale-blue silk shirt tucked into the lizardskin belt at his waist. Through no apparent effort of his own, Tally carried hardly an ounce of spare flesh. His hands, skilfully manipulating the black leather-covered steering wheel, were the colour of milky coffee, the fingers long and tapering with neat oblong nails. As Nell wrung her own pale pink appendages with their rounded knuckles and ragged cuticles, she had to slide her seat forward in order to brace her considerably shorter legs against Tally's sharp acceleration. Through the car's tinted windows she could see pairs of elegant theatregoers returning to their hotels. Posses of laughing diners spilled out of the Pizza on the Park and the Hard Rock Café, jostling and calling to each other, lithe and supple in T-shirts and tight jeans. They seemed to be in another world, one from which Nell felt excluded by more than passing speed and tinted glass.

'What did you want to talk about?' Tally asked, shifting gear to rev out of the Piccadilly underpass. The twinkling fairy-lights of Harrods briefly beckoned on their left as they crossed the Knightsbridge junction and gunned up Kensington Gore. Nell suddenly had a vivid memory of once encountering the ample figure of a famous female pop star wandering disconsolately around Harrods food department. She'd been wearing a voluminous ethnic caftan and sipping constantly from a carton of freshly squeezed orange juice which she clutched tightly in a dimpled fist, like a baby clinging to its bottle. Surely it had been not long afterwards that the singer had died. Of what? At what age?

With an effort Nell returned to the present. 'Being twenty-nine,' she said in answer to Tally's question. 'Don't worry, it'll wait for the coffee. You will stay, won't you? I have some good brandy.'

Tally nodded absently and frowned. He was thinking of Gemma with her not-quite-flat stomach and hungry, slanting eyes and wondering if she really was waiting to give him his birthday present, her beautiful, not-quite-perfect body scented and smooth. An image of her naked form appeared in his mind, sprawled erotically on their king-size bed but curiously he felt no stirring of desire. Gemma's body was always available, although admittedly it was offered more eagerly to the camera these days than to him, but a confidence from his sister was a rare event, and one which at present seemed the greater attraction.

The streets of houses behind Olympia were empty and silent, but there were lights in most windows. In Brook Green people tended to live separate, secret lives behind net curtains. The houses had party walls but their owners seldom had parties. The only remains of Nell's dinner were some fading lilies bought for the occasion, now drooping over the hearth and exuding a strong, sweet fragrance. The dining table was pushed back against the wall and supported a sewing machine which sat in a sea of multicoloured fabrics, candy-flossed with loose threads, evidence of some developing new patchwork. Nell pointed to the table behind the calico-covered sofa. On it was a tray containing several bottles and glasses. 'You pour the Armagnac,' she said. 'I'll get coffee.'

When they were seated rather awkwardly at either end of the sofa, cradling well-charged brandy balloons and watching the steam rise from pretty porcelain mugs of black coffee, Nell asked: 'Where will you go with your airline voucher?'

Tally took a large sip of Armagnac, set down his glass and drew the buff envelope from his inside pocket, removing the thin British Airways booklet and flipping it open. 'I don't know really,' he said. 'It's for two hundred pounds. Not enough for two returns to Paris. Trust Mother! She never did like Gemma. Still, I suppose it's mutual.'

'What about two standbys to Glasgow?' Nell spoke in a rush, as if she must get the words out before she thought twice. 'There's enough for that.'

Tally stared at her in astonishment. 'Glasgow?' he repeated. 'Why on earth would I want to go there? The Glaswegians may think that "Glasgow's Alive", and bombard us with awful logos full of stars, but I'm afraid I'm not convinced.'

'Oh come on, Tally. What about the City of Culture – the Citizens' Theatre, the Tramway and all that? It's not "No Mean City" now, you know.'

'OK, I grant you all that.' Tally arched an inquiring eyebrow. 'But I'm no culture vulture. Give me one good reason why *I* should go to Glasgow? And don't say to return to my roots.'

'Granny Kirsty would say that,' Nell grinned wickedly, 'but I'll only whisper: *tattie scones*!'

Tally raised his hand in submission and laughed. With the habitual lines of cynicism suddenly smoothed from his face he looked years younger. 'OK – tattie scones is a very good reason. In fact, I could murder a pile of 'em now, fried with bacon. All those prawns and lettuce leaves don't seem to fill any cavities.'

'But you've just eaten Lobster Thermidor,' Nell objected. 'I hate to think what it cost.'

'Lobster, red in tail and claw,' agreed her brother with relish. 'No point in letting Big Hal off with cod and chips. You didn't stint yourself, I noticed,' he observed tartly. 'Especially on the bread rolls.'

Nell blushed. 'I only ate them to annoy Mummy.'

Her shining round face clouded. 'It was beastly of her to send me to Champneys. Fancy telling the whole world: "The poor girl finds it *so* hard to diet"!' Her mimicry of her mother's brittle tone was so accurate that Tally snorted with laughter once more. 'Don't snigger,' Nell told him crossly. 'It's all right for you. You're so bloody thin you could slip through a letterbox.' She took an enormous gulp of her brandy and shuddered at its fieriness. A silence fell. As children they had spent little time together, having been sent to different single-sex primary schools and, in their teens, to separate boarding schools. There was no automatic easiness between them as might seem natural with twins.

Tally cast surreptitious glances at his sister, wondering if he understood her any better than he understood Gemma. 'What did you mean in the car,' he said finally, 'about being twenty-nine?'

Nell reacted instantly, with a vehemence that surprised him. 'It's such a bloody age, don't you think? By the time you're twenty-nine you ought to have got somewhere – but supposing where you've got is not really where you want to be? And who you've become is not the kind of person you like?'

She expected Tally to explode with incredulous laughter and demand to know why she had brought him there at midnight to spout that kind of drivel, but to her surprise he did not. Instead he thought for several seconds, considering her outburst. When it came, his reply astonished her. 'I think what you're saying is that you don't like yourself – and I feel exactly the same.'

'You mean you don't like me either?'

'No, idiot. I mean I don't like *me* either.'

Nell gave a short disbelieving snort. 'That's ridiculous! You are just about everything I want to be –

thin, amusing, clever, sexy . . . altogether far more interesting than I am.' She had put down her glass and drawn her knees up, hugging them. Her face was pink with the abasement of self-revelation.

'Put it another way,' suggested Tally. 'You are warm, kind, cuddly and generous. You have real friends. Whereas I am a sarky, aggressive beanpole who seems totally incapable of a worthwhile relationship, especially with a woman. Christ, Nell, I can hardly even talk to you without wondering if I'm being macho enough! I don't seem to feel anything genuine any more. I just chase money around, siphon off as much as possible into my pocket, and spend it. What kind of achievement is that?'

With her head on one side, chin resting on her knees, Nell resembled a startled robin. 'In this yuppie age, most people would regard it as the pinnacle of achievement,' she replied. 'There must be advantages in being thin and rich, or why does everyone want to be like that?'

'Do they?' asked her brother. 'Anyway, I'm not rich. I just have gold cards and a good credit rating.'

'You have a BMW car, a Patek Philippe watch and a Mel Gibson profile,' said Nell. 'Seems a pretty good "tally" to me.'

'Ha ha, it must be pun-day,' Tally grumbled, looking unamused and taking another long pull at his brandy. His name annoyed him. It was short for Talleyrand, for God's sake! It had been his mother's choice. How much better off Nell was, he thought, being blessed with the Sunday name Ellen which had been Ian's choice – a classic, down-to-earth Scottish version of Helen. However, many people commented on the fact that the shortened version of his name suited him, whether Tally liked it or not. His long blond fringe of hair drooped untidily over his left eye, giving him a dishevelled, lost-boy look, exacerbated at present by a doleful expression. 'I may be good at sums but I'm a disaster at people,' he muttered bleakly. 'I don't think I could name one person who would mind if I disappeared tonight.'

'For heaven's sake, Tally!' Nell was surprised by her brother's sudden bout of self-pity. 'What about Gemma?'

He set his brandy glass down so hard that Nell winced, silently blessing the deceptive strength of Waterford crystal. 'I don't think Gemma and I are exactly Romeo and Juliet. Anyway, it isn't the Gemmas of this world that I want,' he declared sharply, 'though it's all I seem to get. What I *really* want is an angel with Bambi eyes and a healthy appetite, who'll fill the fridge with beer and butter and not Diet Coke and cottage cheese!'

Nell's brow furrowed. 'They always did say the way to a man's heart was through his stomach – but he never wants his woman to have one, surely?'

'I do,' said Tally fervently. 'I want a mate with the heart and stomach of a gourmet, and I want to be her favourite dish.' He had a sudden vision of slender Gemma, nude and beckoning and nibbling a carrot. 'And I don't want to have to impress her with trendy clothes and a stretchy bank account.'

Nell stared hard at her brother. How could onc know a person so little when one had actually shared a womb with him for nine months? He was more like her than she had ever suspected! 'Let's go and find out why,' she said suddenly.

'Why what?' he asked, puzzled.

'Why we're like this. It must have something to do with our background. Perhaps we're more Scottish than we think. Perhaps it's all Granny Kirsty's fault. Do you remember her mentioning that ad in the

Scottish Field?' Nell bent down to pick up her bag which lay beside the sofa and took out a folded piece of glossy newsprint. 'Here it is – I tore it out while no one was looking.' She handed it to Tally.

He opened the folds to reveal a colour photograph of a large grey castle set in green lawns, with a glint of blue water glimpsed through trees and flowering rhododendrons. Above the picture, in black lettering, was the name of a famous estate agency. ' "Island for sale, due to family bereavement," ' Tally read aloud. 'What are they saying – that owning it gives you a heart attack?'

'Of course not! Oh, I don't know,' exclaimed Nell, snatching the clipping from him. 'I just thought you might be interested, that's all.'

'What – in buying the island where Granny lived? In the depths of darkest Scotland! You must be joking.'

She stuffed the cutting back into her bag. She could feel Tally staring at her, eyes boring into her, but she refused to turn and look at him. 'Yes, I suppose I am,' she murmured, knowing it was a lie. She wasn't joking; she had never been more serious in her life. Twenty-nine was a number which terrified her, stirred her into wanting action of a radical nature. 'We don't have to buy it,' she went on tentatively. 'Just go and have a look, that's all. See where our roots are. I feel I've reached the age when I want to find out.'

She felt Tally's prolonged silence like a dull pain. Eventually he broke it, frowning darkly as if in the process of some great discovery. 'I used to think we had absolutely nothing in common except a birthday,' he said, 'but perhaps I was wrong. OK – let's fly to Scotland and find out.' He took his airline voucher out of his pocket once more and waved it at her, fanning her averted face. The draught made her turn and look at him, a broad smile breaking her previously solemn expression.

'Really?' she asked incredulously. 'Great! I'm sure the island can't be called Tally-ska for nothing!'

'What a wild idea,' cried Sinead when Nell told her their plan. 'It's a bit mad though, isn't it?'

Nell stared at her stepmother. Sinead could hardly accuse her of being wild. She herself had hardly had the key of the door before Ian had whisked her off a Far East flight and into his bed. *I'm Sinead, fly me!*

'What's the asking price?' The green eyes were curious.

'Offers over three hundred and fifty thousand,' replied Nell. 'Sounds rather cheap when you think of the average house in Hollywood Gardens.'

'We didn't pay that much for ours,' Sinead objected. 'Besides, Taliska's in the depths of nowhere – *and* it's probably got anthrax or something. What do you think of these?' She had been flicking through the *Next* catalogue and thrust the open page towards Nell. It showed photographs of models wearing leather gear, skirts and tight trousers with tank-tops and huge buckled belts.

Nell glanced at them idly. 'OK for a hoe-down,' she said. 'We're only going to look.'

Sinead wrote something on a form lying on the table beside her. 'I'll order this skirt, I think. It'll look good with my new Biggles jacket. Granny Kirsty says "One look and you'll fall".'

Nell giggled. 'Pregnant?'

'In love,' said Kirsty McLean, entering the conservatory where they were sitting. It had been built off the kitchen and occupied nearly half of the original square of ground at the back of the house.

'At first sight – you'll see. When do you go?' Kirsty placed her trug of thorny clippings on a window seat. Every time the old lady came to stay, Sinead complained that she over-pruned the riot of roses which trailed and clambered over every available wall and trellis in the small garden, but Kirsty firmly called it 'just a wee bit of deadheading'.

'At the weekend, which is the first possible opportunity. Tally says he can't take time off work and I can't really either while the programme's in mid-stream.'

'I like your programme,' said Kirsty. 'The last one had that young Scots chef on it – what's his name? Calum something.'

'Calum Strachan. He was a terror, Granny, all hot air and red hair. Even before the recording, when they were just getting voice level, he blew up because the floor manager asked him what the ingredients were of haggis. He seemed to think the poor man was being patronising, and bit his head off!'

'Perhaps he didna ken the ingredients,' observed Kirsty sagely. 'No' many folk do.' A lifelong member of the Scottish National Party, Kirsty's accent always seemed to deepen when she came to London. Nell guessed it was out of sheer cussedness.

'And if they did they'd never eat it again,' commented Sinead. 'Ugh! I can't think how anyone does, anyway.'

'That's because you're an Irish heathen,' retorted Kirsty. She enjoyed this verbal sparring with her daughter-in-law.

'Actually I rather liked him,' added Nell, remembering the sparky young man who'd succeeded in wiping the grin off Gordon Gryll's face several times during the course of the recording. Afterwards she'd underlined his name in her well-thumbed contacts book. Anyone who'd made life difficult for Eye-Level definitely merited another call.

'You wouldn't give up the programme, would you, Nell?' Sinead was incredulous. 'It's such a good job. All my friends are amazed when I tell them you work on *Hot Gryll*.'

Let them try it then, Nell thought. 'No, I shouldn't think so,' she said, winking at Granny Kirsty. 'We're just going to dig around our roots.'

Kirsty McLean stared back unblinkingly. Her shock of curly white hair framed her cherubic face like a nimbus and her eyes were blue and speculative. 'You don't know Taliska like I do,' she said.

Chapter Three

Scotland sits on the shoulders of England like the head of a tipsy dowager at a ball, whose tiara has slipped over one eye. The Mull of Kintyre is a stray lock of hair trailing down her shoulder and the hundreds of islands forming the Hebrides are the jewels in her tilted crown. Among them, Taliska is a tiny diamond chip right down on the dowager's temple, somewhere near her right ear.

Actually it looks more like a peridot, thought Nell, relishing her first view of the island from behind the perspex windshield of a helicopter. It was no more than half a mile across, an irregular rectangle lying midway down the edge of a long sea loch, like a gleaming gemstone bordering a swathe of dark watered silk. The centre of Taliska was mostly grass-covered, and the hot June sun had burnt the vegetation to a pale, yellowish-green and glinted off outcrops of siliceous rocks which broke through the surface where the ground rose gradually to a summit. At the north end, steep wooded slopes and rugged cliffs dropped to a narrow shingle shore, while in the south, smooth rocks and marram grass sloped gently down to a beach of shining white sand. Somewhere between the two, protected from the chill east winds by a belt of tall Scots pines but open to the balmier winds of the west and a stunning view across the loch, stood the castle – a tall, stark tower of grey granite, softened and extended by later additions built in a more elaborate architectural style. At the end of a driveway, which curved through massed ranks of dark-leaved rhododendrons, lay a bridge – a neat stone arch spanning a narrow strait of water. Such a narrow sound between island and mainland was called a 'kyle' in the old Scots' tongue and it was this kyle which made Taliska into an island with all the attendant myth and magic.

Myth was not mentioned, however, in the estate agent's brochure which Nell clutched nervously as the helicopter pilot tried to obey the wild gesticulations of a kilted man on the ground below, a man apparently torn between preserving decency by keeping his pleats under control in the treacherous downdraught of the rotor-blades and preserving safety by guiding the aircraft to the most suitable landing place on the stretch of shaggy green lawn in front of the castle.

'We'll hire a helicopter,' Tally had said when he learned that Taliska was a two-hour drive from Glasgow airport.

'Don't be daft,' Nell had protested. 'This is supposed to be a cheap trip, just to take a look.'

'It's also supposed to be a quick trip,' Tally reminded her. 'I've got to be back in London on Sunday. Come on, let's hire a helicopter. The return trip can't cost much more than hiring a car for two days.'

Nell didn't argue. If Tally wanted to dig into his pocket in order to fly high over Loch Lomond, Ben Lui and the Pass of Brander then she was happy to skim along, and it had indeed been a scenically thrilling trip with the hills rising bleak and grand above lochs of indigo, silver burns gouging purple scars down their steep, scree-scattered slopes. She had marvelled at agile sheep wandering nonchalantly along precipitous ridges, and lone rowan trees clinging tenaciously to crevices in dramatically sheer rockfaces. As an introduction to ancestral roots it had been spectacular.

'Andrew Ramsay-Miller,' yelled the kilted man, arm outstretched in greeting as Tally sprinted ahead of Nell under the still-turning rotor-blades. 'Representing the agents.' He was a genial-looking man of middle age, average height and ruddy complexion, with a full head of nut-brown hair and a trim, matching moustache. If his kilt had been partner to a cross-belted brass-buttoned tunic, instead of a baggy Harris tweed jacket, he might have been a major in a Highland regiment. The air of military precision was diffused, however, by an easy, almost shambling, gait and a loquacity which seemed unquenchable.

'I'm only here in an amateur capacity, I'm afraid,' he began, shaking both their hands and stowing their overnight bags in the back of the Range Rover which was parked in the drive. 'My brother is one of the agency's directors and he asked me to help.' His lips continued to move without pause but there was too much noise from the helicopter's take-off for the twins to hear his next words as he ushered them towards a pair of enormous iron-studded oak doors which stood open at the castle entrance. These led into a vaulted tunnel which ran under the great granite tower and into a stone-flagged courtyard where, in the relative quiet as the helicopter retreated, their guide continued his incessant monologue.

'You're staying at my pub tonight, if that's all right. I own the Lorn Castle, just down the coast. It's the old family home really but I run it as an hotel. Pays the bills, you know, and it keeps me out of mischief. I've often thought this place would make an ideal hotel, actually. Need a lot doing to it, of course. Terribly neglected, nothing's been touched for years. The old laird became rather reclusive as he got older. Wiring's in a frightful mess, there's no heating and as for the plumbing . . . Well, I can't pretend it's any good if it's absolutely on its last legs, can I? Still, I expect you know all that. This is the main entrance. It leads into the more recent part of the house, built about 1860. The family made some money out of the Glasgow tobacco trade, I believe. The rooms in this part are much larger than in the tower. That was built for defence rather than comfort, like most Highland castles, and it's not been altered much over the years. You reach it from the first floor. Now, what would you like to do? Shall I give you the guided tour or would you like to browse through the house and then I'll take you on a trip round the island? There's a cottage up the hill and of course the stables and farm buildings and the jetty and boathouse, you'll want to see those.'

As he paused for breath Tally leaped in with a firm acceptance of his offer to leave them to browse, encouraged by Nell's vigorous nods. 'That's all right,' responded the verbose Mr Ramsay-Miller amiably. 'I'll get my newspaper from the car and read it while you ramble about. I'll be here in the hall if you want me. It's all open.' Once more he jingled the bunch of giant iron keys which had orchestrated his long monologue, and wandered off towards the tunnel.

'Quick!' exclaimed Nell, grabbing Tally's arm and almost pushing him through a door. 'I don't care which way we go but let's get away before he comes back.'

'Ker-rist,' blasphemed Tally in awe. 'Talk about verbal diarrhoea. What was his name again?'

'Andrew Ramsay-Miller, I think he said.'

'More like Andrew Ramsay-Mouthful! Where are we?' Tally glanced round him, taking in the grimy cream paint on the walls of a passageway from which several doors led.

'Kitchen quarters, I think,' said Nell, consulting a floor-plan in her crumpled brochure. 'And those must be the back stairs at the end.'

'Good enough place to start,' murmured Tally. 'You map-read and I'll take notes.' He pulled a neat, morocco-bound notebook from a pocket in his leather flying jacket. When they had set off for Heathrow airport that morning, Nell had remarked to herself that Tally always seemed to have just the right clothes to fit the occasion. A leather jacket might have been thought too hot for June but it had been nippy in the helicopter and she had shivered in her lightweight jacket and trousers. Now she felt the chill of age and neglect lurking in the dim passageway. She also wondered why her brother should want to take notes when they were only sightseeing.

Taliska's original, fifteenth-century tower resembled a whole string of similar fortresses dotting the islands and promontories of Scotland's west coast. Built of grey granite, it stood square and solid with small, leaded casement windows, a slate roof with crow-stepped gables and several turrets, one of which contained a narrow circular staircase linking the three upper floors and the roof. This tower differed slightly from some other fortified houses in that it had been built over a tunnel gateway which had once led into a protected stone-walled corral where the clan cattle would have been driven in time of trouble, but which had been replaced in the nineteenth century by a baronial-style mansion befitting the incumbent laird's growing entrepreneurial wealth and his burgeoning family. It had been for the grandson of this early-Victorian businessman that Granny Kirsty's father had worked as estate factor. However, this once-numerous branch of the McLeod clan had petered out with the death a year ago of the last laird; his two daughters had married wealthy Englishmen and had no desire to maintain a crumbling castle and its surrounding acres of grazing fit only for deer, Highland cattle and black-faced moorland sheep.

The baronial mansion contained all the rooms required by a Victorian business magnate to house his family and entertain the friends and associates who would have travelled by steamer from Glasgow. There were six reception rooms, all panelled in stained oak and decorated with ornate plasterwork. They consisted of a book-lined library full of mouldering leather-covered volumes, a drawing room and a dining room, both hung with decaying red velvet curtains garlanded with rusty gold swags and tassels, a sunny morning room, an echoing billiard room and a smoke-blackened hall with an enormous fireplace from which a carved wooden staircase led to a galleried landing on the first floor. Here were situated the four principal bedrooms, all with dressing rooms and breathtaking views over loch and mountain. Each also contained a massive four-poster bed, majestically draped in cobwebbed brocade.

From the first-floor landing, a narrow arch and an uneven spiral stair led to the medieval tower, its principal chamber a dark, vaulted room with small square windows set deep into bare stone walls.

Above this were two rooms of a similar size and shape but without the vaulting. From each led a turret-garderobe or wardrobe-room with a small outer closet still fitted with the original medieval stone latrine seat. It was clear the tower had not been lived in for years because, in addition to the emptiness of the rooms and the primitive antiquity of the sanitation, the Edwardian electric wiring had not been extended there and the only available light filtered through the filthy windows.

'This is amazing!' Nell relished anything historic.

'This is grotesque,' grumbled Tally, scribbling frantically in his notebook. One whiff of the old latrines had sent him scurrying for the relative freshness of the draughty stairway.

The second floor of the Victorian wing contained more bedrooms, less elegant and imposing than those on the first floor but still mostly with spectacular views of loch and mountain. The top floor consisted of an extensive attic, some of which had been partitioned into servants' sleeping cubicles, the rest cluttered with the discarded domestic paraphernalia of several hundred years. Descending the back stairs, the twins explored further into the area behind the kitchen and discovered a servants' hall, a laundry, a stillroom and a large storeroom. On either side of the tunnel gateway were small musty rooms which might once have been guardhouses. Through a trapdoor in one of them a worn stone stair descended into a cold, damp cellar which ran under the length of the billiard room, completely lined with partitioned wine-bins. Two grilles high in the walls let in just enough light to see by, but the last laird had either consumed his entire stock of wine or else the cellar had been prudently cleared by his heirs, for it stood empty and forlorn.

'Now this *is* amazing!' Tally sniffed the grapey atmosphere appreciatively. 'There must be room for thousands of bottles in here.'

'It's all so decrepit,' Nell complained. 'It's hard to imagine what it must have been like when Granny Kirsty lived here.'

'Yes, it is a bit of an ancient monument, isn't it? Still, we might as well see the rest.' Tally pushed her gently back towards the stair. 'Don't be glum, Ellen McLean. I thought you liked old things.'

'I do, but I don't like to see them go mouldy.' Nell scuffed cautiously upwards, feeling her way in the dusty gloom. 'Besides, I'm starving, aren't you? It seems an age since our British Airways croissant.'

As they stepped into the relative brightness of the tunnel, Tally's teeth gleamed momentarily. 'What a Boy Scout I am,' he declared, thrusting his hands into his capacious jacket pocket. 'Always prepared.' He drew out two Mars bars and handed one to Nell. 'Eat that and cheer up. We've got to arm ourselves for another dose of Andrew Ramsay-Mouthful!'

Nell tore the paper off the Mars bar. 'Arm is the right word,' she giggled, cheered by the prospect of chocolate. 'Do you realise his initials are ARM?'

'So they are! Still, I suppose he's pretty arm-*less* really,' commented Tally, chewing contentedly. 'And it's very decent of him to turn out for us on a Saturday.' Perhaps it was the Scottish air but he was feeling unusually benevolent towards his fellow man.

Once re-started, their kilted guide kept up his verbal barrage all the way across an overgrown kitchen garden and orchard which stretched along the back of the house, dividing it from the stables and farm buildings. 'Of course, I remember Taliska when it was still quite a lively place,' he told them eagerly. 'Stalking and fishing parties, picnics, tennis, that sort of thing. You can see the old tennis court over there and at the end of the stable block the last laird had a squash court built. It caused quite a stir at the time because the locals didn't know squash from cricket, but the old boy had studied in Edinburgh in the thirties when squash was just beginning to become popular. The court's still there, of course, but I don't know what kind of condition it's in. Don't suppose it's been used for years, like the billiard room. Did you find that? It's off the tower on the other side – oh, you did? Good. Bit of a nightmare, eh? I don't know how they could see enough to play without electricity – must have used Tilley lamps or something. Of course, the electricity is a bit wonky now because of the wiring but at least the island's been connected to the main supply – which is more than can be said for the water. That comes from a reservoir up the hill which I'll show you later. Do you want to see the whole stable-block? There's a milking parlour and a dairy as well as staff accommodation and all the stalls and byres.'

The soft, endless stream of information and gossip accompanied the twins like a radio commentary as they explored the various outbuildings. Part of the stable-block had been turned into garages and tractor sheds but the old squash court was untouched, the walls cracked and flaking and the floor filthy but undamaged because the roof remained miraculously intact.

'I think they've been storing hay in here!' said Tally incredulously, dropping to his knees to examine the narrow, tightly laid boards. 'It's lucky the floor hasn't buckled or warped.'

'Play squash, do you?' asked Andrew Ramsay-Miller with interest. 'I used to play a fair game myself when I was at college but we don't have a court at Lorn, of course, and there are no others within a hundred miles of here as far as I know.'

'Where is the factor's house?' asked Tally, while he had their guide's attention. 'We haven't see that yet, have we?'

'No. It's up the hill. We can go there now if you've seen enough here.'

Granny Kirsty's old home was an eye-opener. It hardly qualified as a house; it was just a butt and ben – a kitchen and living room no bigger than a modern container wagon, constructed without foundations, with two additional rooms built into the roof-space and reached by a stair which was little more than a ladder. Perhaps it had been one of the original clan homes, dating from the time before the castle had been extended into a mansion, for its walls were two feet thick, constructed of rough stones gathered from the hillside, the cracks packed with heather and crudely plastered over on the inside. Even on that warm June day the interior was cold, and only small patches of sunlight falling through tiny square casement windows illuminated the gloomy rooms. The floors were stone-flagged downstairs and unevenly boarded upstairs, where the window dormers afforded the only places a grown man could stand upright. Nell wondered how Granny Kirsty's mother had managed to rear a family of six children in such cramped surroundings, and why Kirsty had nothing but fond memories of a home which had offered such poor accommodation.

Tally prowled angrily through the mean little cottage making no notes in his book but marking every deficiency and shortcoming with little grunts of disbelief. He clambered up the rickety steps which led to the upper floor, bending nearly double to inspect the attic rooms from end to end and peering through the cracked panes of the windows down the hill to the big house, standing grand and imposing in its gracious setting. He even shut himself for several minutes in the outside latrine, which smelled every bit as foul as the ancient conveniences he had disparaged in the tower.

When he eventually spoke it was to demand in disbelief: 'Is this really where the factor lived? I'd have thought the horses were better stabled!'

Andrew Ramsay-Miller nodded. 'Yes indeed,' he concurred. 'The old laird had a reputation as a tight-fisted employer. He was a mean old despot actually, if you want my opinion. Did nothing for the local people at all, except turn them off the island and tell them to find homes elsewhere. He valued his privacy, they say. The factor's family was the only one left, apart from house servants.'

On the walk down the hill Tally remained morose and silent, his earlier feelings of benevolence evaporated, his notebook closed in his pocket. Nell was suddenly grateful for their guide's continual patter because Tally kept up his Trappist-monk impersonation for a good half hour, appearing wrapped in his own thoughts and only vaguely glancing at the features pointed out to him. They took the Range Rover to inspect the bridge and Nell leaned on the stone parapet to peer into the dark, swirling waters of the kyle. The tide was at peak flow, lapping the granite arches just beneath her feet. 'It looks quite deep,' she remarked. 'Is is dangerous?'

'At certain stages of the tide I believe it may be,' Andrew Ramsay-Miller acknowledged with a frown. 'The maps call it the Kyle of Taliska but the locals call it the Kyleshee, meaning "fairy strait". Don't know about fairies, though. They're more likely to be water-sprites or Silkies. Now, who is this, I wonder?'

A stocky man in oil-stained blue overalls and ancient trainers was walking towards them down the narrow mainland road with a rolling, seaman's gait. He was carrying a dirty black holdall in one hand and a six-pack of McEwan's lager-cans in the other. His heavy-browed face bore an unfriendly scowl and several days' growth of dark stubble. In answer to Andrew Ramsay-Miller's hail he slowed reluctantly to a halt.

'There's nobody up at the house, you know,' Ramsay-Miller told him. 'Do you want something?'

'Who's asking?' demanded the man threateningly. He had untidy, almost black hair and was aged about thirty-five, strong and well muscled.

The man in the kilt was not deterred, however. 'I represent the agents,' he said mildly. 'My name is Ramsay-Miller. And you are?'

'Macpherson,' admitted the man grudgingly. 'I berth my fishing boat at the jetty. There's nobody to mind now. 'Tis handy for getting home. Closer than Oban.'

'Ah,' said Ramsay-Miller pleasantly. 'Your home's nearby then?'

The man jerked his head in the direction from which he had come, where the houses of a straggling village could be seen in the far distance, their roofs rising above roadside gorse. 'In Salach, on the main road.'

'And your boat, are you taking her out now? Without a crew?'

'No.' Macpherson shook his holdall and there was the clunk of heavy metal objects clashing together. 'I've my tools here. The engine's playing up.' He suddenly turned and stared at Tally. 'You buying the place?' he asked bluntly.

Tally shrugged noncommittally, returning the stare. 'I'm looking,' he said. 'What's the fishing like?'

'No' bad,' replied Macpherson, surprisingly readily. 'Prawns, lobsters, scallops. I've only an inshore boat.'

'You make a living though?' Tally seemed genuinely interested.

Macpherson gave a rough guffaw. 'Not what *you'd* call a living, no doubt. Are you from London?'

'Yes, as a matter of fact I am,' agreed Tally, grinning amiably. 'Have you been there?'

His inquiry was met with a scowl. 'No. What would I do in London?'

'Same as I'm doing in Taliska,' replied Tally. 'Have a look.'

'I'll no' bother. And you should do the same,' came the terse reply. With that Macpherson nodded at Nell and walked on over the bridge and through the open wrought-iron gates onto the island, swinging his heavy bag like a hammer-thrower at a Highland games.

'Hmm,' murmured Nell with relief. 'He seemed a bit edgy.'

'Och, they're a touchy lot, the west-coast fishermen,' Ramsay-Miller observed, watching the man disappear around the rhododendrons at a bend in the drive. 'Not without reason. They think every foreigner's a Eurocrat checking on fishing quotas. He'll loosen up when he's sunk the contents of that six-pack. I wonder if the agency knows he's berthing his boat at the jetty, though. Oh well, I suppose it can't do any harm. We'll go and take a look, shall we? It's quite a fine jetty, built for the steamers which used to call weekly, and the supply boats. All the coal for the house was brought in by puffer before the road was metalled.'

'What's a puffer?' asked Nell, climbing into the Range Rover.

'Little coastal tramp-steamer. Hardly any left now, of course. Collector's items only, owned by fanatics. There's one based at Oban takes tourists around the islands – a week's round trip with cordon-bleu cooking. Does quite well, I believe – though you have not to mind finding smuts in your syllabub!'

Their guide turned the car off the road and began to negotiate a rough pot-holed track which skirted a pale sandy beach lapped by opalescent green water.

'What a beautiful beach,' Nell enthused. 'Is the water cold?'

'Freezing,' Ramsay-Miller assured her. 'Swimming is advisable only in high summer, and even then a wet suit is recommended.'

'What a pity,' said Nell. 'It looks so inviting, rather like those pictures of the Caribbean only without palm trees.'

'If it was like the Caribbean, the west coast of Scotland would not be the glorious empty wilderness that it is,' her guide pointed out. 'For that we can thank the bracing climate and the great Highland midge.'

'Midges?' she queried but her question was lost in the distraction of a sudden violent lurch of the car and Tally's curses as his head hit the roof.

'Sorry.' Ramsay-Miller was wrestling with the wildly spinning steering wheel. 'Even four-wheel-drive sometimes isn't enough on these tracks.'

'Is this the only way to the jetty?' demanded Tally, rubbing his head furiously.

'No, there's a better track down from the stables

but I thought you'd like to see the beach. Are you all right?'

'I think my brains are addled but I can't have many anyway or I wouldn't be here,' grumbled Tally. His mood did not appear to have been improved by the bang on the head.

The Range Rover rounded a rocky outcrop and the island's jetty came into view, a pier of sturdy, creosoted tree-trunks supporting slats of seasoned grey wood, most of which were still intact. Only the odd gap appeared in the planking like missing teeth in a set of dentures. A snub-nosed, gaily painted wooden fishing boat with a distinctive short mast and net-boom was pulling away from the jetty, out into the choppy waters of the loch over which a fresh, afternoon breeze was blowing, whipping the surface into small, foam-flecked waves.

'I thought he said he was only going to work on the engine,' said Nell. 'I wonder why he lied? After all, why shouldn't he put to sea if he wants to?'

'They don't usually go alone,' remarked Ramsay-Miller in puzzled tones. 'Even a small inshore boat needs a crew of two to do any fishing. Still, perhaps he's not going to work. There's a pub just up the loch where a lot of fishermen go. He may be popping out for a few with the boys.'

'One way to beat the breathalyser,' remarked Tally. 'Can you be done for being drunk at the helm?'

'But he had that six-pack with him,' Nell pointed out. 'Why would he take a six-pack to the pub?'

'That's true,' Ramsay-Miller agreed. He swung the Range Rover into the lee of the jetty and stopped. There was a rough stone boat-shed tucked back into the rocks at the landward end. 'There used to be pleasure craft kept here – for fishing and outings, you know. Do you want to see inside? I think there's a key on this ring.'

It took him several minutes to locate the correct key, during which time Tally flung stones moodily into the loch, skimming them over the roughened surface while Nell simply stood and stared at the immense spread of land and water displayed before them. A mile away across the loch lay the low, fertile island of Lismore, appearing in the foreground like a humped strip of verdant green, while beyond it, across another ribbon of water, rose the steep barren mountains of Kingairloch on the Morvern peninsula. She knew the place-names because she had studied the map before she left home, but even the detailed colours and contour-lines of the Ordnance Survey could not have prepared her for the stunning spectacle they presented. The striking contrast of the low green fields of Lismore suspended between the dark, mysterious blue of the loch and the sweeping lavender shadows of the wild, rugged range of hills clinging to a gentian sky supplied a scene of such beauty that it caused in her a sudden eruption of emotion. Through tear-filled eyes she registered the dark round cannonball heads of a group of seals stretched out on a tide-washed skerry to her left and the low dipping flight of black and white oystercatchers foraging about the rocky shingle of the shoreline immediately to her right. She remembered Granny Kirsty's words in the conservatory in Hollywood Gardens – 'You don't know Taliska like I do,' – and she understood with a strange wonder that the surge of emotion welling in her must be an echo of something her grandmother had experienced as a child growing up in the sight of all this natural splendour.

After that the contents of the boat-shed were an

anti-climax – just a pair of twelve-foot clinker-built dinghies with mast-steps in the forward thwart and one modern fibreglass hull with a rusting outboard motor attached to the stern. They would take no prizes in West Highland Sailing Week.

With the freshening wind had come the cooler air of approaching evening. Time was running on and their guide said there was little else they could usefully see without donning boots to clamber over the island's rugged northern end and traverse the central grasslands. 'If you're still interested you could come back tomorrow and walk the island but you've seen all the buildings now. Shall we go to Lorn?'

Compared with Taliska, Lorn Castle was not really a castle at all. It was a crenellated lodge where Andrew Ramsay-Miller's ancestors had convened for the huge stalking and shooting parties so beloved of the Victorians, many of whom would travel up from London or their estates in the south for the autumn season. So it had the air of a home-counties hall, transplanted from Berkshire or Buckinghamshire and surrounded by the requisite parkland of deer-cropped grass and fenced groves of specimen trees, oaks, beeches and larches, stunted by the prevailing west wind and leaning visibly towards the hills as if seeking shelter in their comforting folds.

They approached along a narrow drive which plunged down a steep glen from the high main road running north from the port of Oban. Several cars were parked with their bonnets nosing the hotel's granite walls. 'Looks as if we may have picked up some guests off the road,' said Andrew Ramsay-Miller. 'The season is beginning to improve, thank God.'

There was no one behind the antique reception desk in the hall but their host didn't seem perturbed. 'The staff have a meal break at this time,' he explained. 'I'll take you up. I know which rooms you're in.' He strode up the wide, carpeted staircase which was lined with stag's horns and other trophies befitting a hunting lodge. Judging by the abundance of cobwebs adorning these, Lorn Castle had a shortage of reliable domestic staff, a situation underlined by the fact that the rooms to which Andrew Ramsay-Miller showed them were not prepared for new arrivals. The beds were still unmade, and dirty towels and linen lay piled in heaps. At this the hotelier looked peeved and plunged back down the stairs, muttering about fetching his wife. This left Tally and Nell standing disconsolately on the landing. They raised quizzical eyebrows at each other and shrugged, amused and exasperated at the same time.

'A hundred thousand welcomes,' said Tally dryly, quoting from the road sign they had seen on their way from Taliska. Andrew Ramsay-Miller had told them it was the traditional Gaelic greeting to strangers – *ceud mile failte*.

'Just one would do,' said Nell. 'And a hot bath!'

At that moment, a small, dark, energetic-looking woman bustled up the stairs, wearing a bright placatory smile and a PVC apron decorated with a large purple-sprouting thistle. 'Sorry about this,' she said, extending a slightly floury hand. 'I'm Fee Ramsay-Miller, Andrew's wife. He must have forgotten to tell me you were staying here tonight. Andrew does forget things sometimes – he has so much on his mind. Would you like to wait for these rooms to be done, or shall I show you two more? They'll be on the next floor, I'm afraid, and not quite so big but cheaper of course.'

She waited expectantly, trying not to look as if she was anxious to get back to her kitchen. 'Let's go upstairs,' said Nell, picking up both her bag and the impatient vibrations emanating from Mrs Ramsay-Miller. 'I'm sure the rooms up there are fine and they'll have a better view, won't they?'

Without confirming or denying this, Fee Ramsay-Miller turned immediately for the upper flight, narrower and steeper than the lower staircase. One of the proffered rooms turned out to be a small single, overlooking nothing more salubrious than a back yard, featuring overflowing dustbins. Nobly Tally accepted this room, leaving Nell to occupy a larger one containing a rather lumpy-looking double bed with a grubby white candlewick bedspread and a gratifyingly beautiful view looking west into the setting sun, now a huge, bright orange disc suspended over the ocean in a mauve haze. She also found a bathroom boasting a large, old-fashioned, only slightly copper-stained bath into which she ached to sink, but the off-the-road guests, upon whose arrival Andrew Ramsay-Miller had remarked with such delight, had obviously hurried to wash off the dust of that very road and used up the hotel's mcagrc supply of hot water in the process.

'This place is like Fawlty Towers,' Tally moaned, bursting in to compare notes. 'No rooms, no view and now no hot water! I wouldn't speculate on the future of Highland hospitality if this is an example of it. For God's sake let's go down and have a drink. They surely can't have run out of whisky.'

There was certainly no shortage of the Gaelic 'water of life' in the array of bottles crowding the sideboard in the barn-like hotel drawing room. The room itself was otherwise cheerless, devoid of people and furnished with dark, shiny leather armchairs scattered about a polished wood floor, upon which a few well-worn Persian-style rugs had been thrown to relieve the Spartan surface. The fire in the grate was laid but not lit.

'What, no table groaning with scones and shortbread?' demanded Tally, clutching his stomach in the apparent grip of acute hunger. 'Oh well, *uisge beag* will have to live up to its name and save our lives!'

One Gaelic road-sign seemed to have started a linguistic trend with Tally and he had recovered some of his normal light-hearted cynicism despite the frustrations of the hotel service. Spurning the assortment of single malt whiskies which offered a taste-excursion around the product of a dozen Highland distilleries, he opted for a blend and poured two hefty measures of Famous Grouse, topping them up from the contents of a water jug, though not without first inspecting the surface for signs of dust.

'At least there are good smells coming from the kitchen,' Nell remarked, sniffing the air. 'So we should get some dinner.' After a sip from her glass she was keen to seek Tally's opinion of Taliska but, as she opened her mouth to do so, Andrew Ramsay-Miller walked in beaming and rubbing his hands.

'Got yourselves a drink, I see. Good, good. Did you notice the form on the sideboard? Just fill in the details of what you've had and we'll put it on the bill. Ha ha! We'd love to have drinks on the house, of course, but I'm afraid in this present economic climate . . .'

'Feeling the recession a bit, are you?' inquired Tally, who hadn't noticed the clipboard with attached form, on which he had been expected to enter their drink consumption. He drew out his gold Parker and began to write, pausing before completing the action to inquire whether Mr Ramsay-Miller would like to join them?

Their host shook his head. 'No, I'll wait until a bit later, thanks. Yes, people don't seem to be spending as much as they used to. Although having said that, the bed and breakfast market is doing quite well, I'm told. Perhaps the tourists are trading down. We're certainly thinking of going down-market a bit next year. You know, not offering quite such high-class service and cutting prices, that sort of thing. It seems to be the trend.'

'So you don't think people have money to spend, then?' asked Tally, winking at Nell behind Andrew Ramsay-Miller's back.

'Well, if they do they're not coming to Scotland.'

'Perhaps they're not being offered the kind of thing they want to spend their money on,' Tally mused.

'Are you thinking of going into the hotel business?' asked Andrew Ramsay-Miller curiously. 'Is that why you're looking at Taliska?'

Tally made no immediate response so Nell intervened. 'Would you recommend it?' she asked, perching on the arm of one of the over-stuffed leather chairs. 'You've had some experience, after all.'

Smoothing his kilt underneath him, the hotelier lowered himself into another chair and leaned forward confidentially, elbows on his bare knees. Nell couldn't help thinking there was something faintly comic about the way his sporran kept his kilt decently anchored between his sturdy, tartan-wrapped thighs. 'Circumstances were much more favourable when we started this place ten years ago,' he said. 'If you *are* thinking of going into business I don't want to put you off but I personally wouldn't begin again now.'

He seemed more subdued than he had been earlier in the day, and Nell wondered if his wife had given him a piece of her mind over the matter of the rooms. She had the feeling that the real force behind this particular enterprise was not sitting here with them but slaving over a hot stove in the kitchen. 'Does your wife do all the cooking?' she asked, following her train of thought.

He looked almost guilty as he answered, 'Yes, she does. Paying off the chef was one of the economies we've already had to make. There just hasn't been the custom in the restaurant to justify keeping him on. The breathalyser has a lot to answer for.'

'Well, we look forward to sampling her fare,' said Nell warmly. 'It smells very good.'

Andrew Ramsay-Miller looked from one to the other of the twins. 'Do you work in this field at present?' he asked.

'No,' replied Tally. 'I work in the City and Nell works in television.'

'Television – really? Any programmes I might know?'

'Perhaps you do,' said Nell reluctantly. 'I'm a researcher on *Hot Gryll*. It's a sort of quiz with cooking . . .'

'Oh yes! We've often watched that. Even thought of trying to get our last chef onto it before he left, but he refused. I'm afraid he didn't like the compère, said he made fun of the competitors. I bet that's an interesting job, though. I can't imagine giving that up to run an hotel in Scotland.'

'At least I know how to handle temperamental chefs,' Nell pointed out. She felt dizzy. Strong whisky on an empty stomach was making her light-headed, and the conversation seemed to be taking a turn that she, for one, had not expected. Were they really discussing the possibility of opening an hotel at Taliska?

At that point, a spruce, freshly bathed middle-aged couple strolled into the room and began to inspect the bottles on the sideboard. Andrew Ramsay-Miller stood up. 'Well, dinner won't be long. I'll see you later.' He backed away, pausing to exchange pleasantries with the new arrivals and point out the clipboard.

As 'mine host' left the room Tally leaned forward to whisper to Nell, 'I promise never to go down-market, never to wear a kilt and never to bore our guests to death with chit-chat!'

She looked absolutely staggered. 'You're not seriously thinking of turning Taliska into an hotel?' she expostulated. 'Whatever gave you that idea?' She was on tenterhooks, astounded that his mind should have been running along the same lines as her own while all the time she had thought they were opposites in everything!

'It was you, the other night,' said Tally, taking another large sip of his drink, 'saying how, at twenty-nine, we should have done something worthwhile. I've been thinking about it ever since.'

'Really? You never said.'

'No. Well, I felt a bit of a fool really. I thought you'd think I was completely bonkers.'

She laughed delightedly. 'No, I don't. I was thinking exactly the same thing – ever since that awful dinner party when no one ate anything and Leo said something really interesting afterwards.'

'What did he say?'

A loud gong sounded just outside the room,

making them jump. They caught each other's eye and grinned. It was a moment of rare, unspoken understanding. 'I'll tell you over dinner,' said Nell, getting up and putting her empty glass on the cluttered sideboard. 'Right now, I'm starving!'

The dinner was as tempting as the rest of the hotel was offputting. A delicious cream of cauliflower soup was followed by a choice of roast veal or poached salmon, accompanied by fresh, lightly cooked vegetables and fragrant, subtle sauces, rounded off with a raspberry and hazelnut meringue cake. There was a party of locals among the diners and it was easy to see why they came.

'This soup is excellent,' said Nell, relishing the smooth Crème du Barry. 'Just enough cream to cauliflower. But very calorific, as Caroline would say. That's why Leo's remarks were so interesting. I complained to him that all anyone talked about these days was putting on weight and going on a diet and he said that if you opened a restaurant where people could enjoy delicious food that wouldn't make them fat, you'd earn a fortune. And I'm beginning to think he was right.'

Tally frowned. 'What would you do – list the calories on the menu beside the price, for God's sake?' he asked incredulously.

'No, of course not. It would have to be a bit more subtle than that.'

'I should hope so. And where does the sex come in?'

'What do you mean, sex?'

Tally snorted derisively. 'It's an equation, Nellie dear. Healthy meals mean healthy bodies, healthy bodies mean sex. Indirectly you're promoting light meals and heavy breathing. Honestly – I mean it!' He made this last assertion loudly to offset the burst of laughter with which Nell had greeted his remarks.

She shook her head, still gurgling with mirth, glancing round to see if the other diners were staring at her. 'I knew you wouldn't take me seriously,' she said eventually, with resignation. 'But since we're talking bed as well as board it all fits in, don't you see?'

'You mean a place for banting and bonking?'

'Well, not banting exactly. People hate to think they're being force-fed cottage cheese and radishes as you know. But just reducing the load a little. What do you think?'

Tally studied his sister's face for several seconds. She was right, he had never really taken her seriously. She was just his sister. Friendly, easygoing, popular, always a pleasant companion but never really a force to be reckoned with. And yet here she was proposing a mind-blowing change of life and making it sound a likely proposition. He must be getting senile. 'Well, it's certainly true that the rich and glamorous are always looking for ways to enjoy themselves without putting on weight,' he conceded. 'That's one of the problems with having money – you want the perfect image to go with it. So yes, I'm sure that if you could offer the lap of luxury without the middle-age spread you'd certainly be on to a winner. And if you could offer a setting for super-spicy sex as well, the sky's the limit!'

'Is Taliska the place, do you think?' Nell was tucking into her salmon now, noting at the back of her mind that if they did set up at Taliska they'd have Fee Ramsay-Miller's culinary skills to compete with.

'Yes, I do as a matter of fact. An island is always a bit of a magnet and we could promote it as a secret hideaway where the rich and famous could recover from jet-lag and a limp libido and lose a bit of flab at the same time. I honestly think it might work.'

'When did something like this first occur to you?' asked Nell, intrigued that his thoughts should have been following hers so closely, even if his seemed to concentrate more on the sex than the slimming. Part of her still suspected that her brother might be indulging in a bit of away-from-it-all fantasising – that he would change his mind as soon as he was back in the cold light of the London exchanges.

'It was when I saw the factor's house,' Tally said soberly. 'Can you imagine Granny Kirsty being reared in that miserable hovel, within sight and sound of that enormous castle? And yet she remembers Taliska as a magic and wonderful place . . . It must have a special Something therefore, and yet I don't understand quite what.'

'I do,' said Nell simply, thinking of her emotional experience down on the shore. 'Granny Kirsty didn't look at the castle, or even at the island really. She just looked out – at the loch and the sky and the mountains. It wasn't Taliska she loved as much as the things that Taliska had to offer.'

'Such as?' Tally probed.

'Space and air and beauty and scope for discovering yourself,' said Nell, surprising herself. The words came easily enough to her lips but it was as if they were someone else's thoughts.

'Very existential,' observed Tally dryly. 'But the fact remains that she and her family were exploited and degraded and I think it would be wonderful to balance the books. And if this hotel is an example of average Highland hospitality it shouldn't be too difficult to compete.' He gestured contemptuously at their surroundings. 'Apart from the food, it's a disaster.' He paused, fixing Nell with an earnest stare. 'I am serious you know, Nell. It would be simple justice if Granny Kirsty's descendants were to be the ones to rescue Taliska from the consequences of the laird's neglect.'

'Maybe it's not a case of us rescuing Taliska,' Nell observed thoughtfully, aware that her heart was thumping with nervous apprehension, 'but of Taliska rescuing us.'

Chapter Four

'You've got to be joking!' exclaimed David Guedalla a week later when Tally told him of his intention to buy Taliska. 'What are you going to do there – set up a sinecure?' During the 1980s several senior traders had established high-tech computer and fax links from remote rural locations where they attempted to combine city and country pursuits. They were viewed with derisive scorn by their urban peers, mostly young Turks like Tally who considered that pheasant shoots and commodity futures were mutually exclusive.

'Definitely not.' Tally tied the lace of his sports shoe decisively. He and David were about to embark on one of their regular games of squash at the London club to which they both belonged. Squash was Tally's one concession to fitness. 'I'm going to start an hotel for jaded city types like you to come and rediscover sex and a healthy diet.'

'An hotel? What in God's name do you know about running an hotel? Can you trade it? Can you stag it? Now I know you're joking!' David picked up his racquet and followed his friend out of the changing room. 'You can't even play squash in the Highlands,' he remarked, switching on the lights as they entered the bare white court. The neon strips spluttered into life, emitting a baleful glare.

'You can on Taliska,' said Tally smugly. 'There's a court there, so don't imagine you can avoid my winning ways in the future! Let's face it, you could do with a bit of refurbishment, Guedalla. Your upholstery is becoming distinctly overstuffed. I challenge you to be one of our first guests.' He swiped the small green ball at the wall to begin the warm-up.

'Our?' queried David, returning it.

'Mine and Nell's. I'm going into partnership with my sister.'

David mistimed his next shot and hit the metal strip below the red line on the front wall. There was a noise like a cannon shot. 'Sorry,' he said, retrieving the ball and restarting the rally. 'Did you say with *Nell*?' His expression was a comic mixture of dismay and disbelief.

'Yup.' Nothing further was said for a few moments as the ball slammed several times off racquet and wall, punctuating the silence with alternate twangs and splats. 'Well – what do you think?' Tally demanded eventually, catching the ball and staring inquiringly at his friend.

David shook his head as if to clear it. 'I don't know if you're serious, because I'm amazed that you're contemplating a partnership with Nell. You two have always been rather at arm's length, haven't you?' Then he shrugged and a slow smile spread over his amiable round face. 'Still, I've always thought Nell's a great girl,' he added, nodding sagely. 'I suppose it just takes a brother longer than most to realise it. It could be the best move you've ever made. And yes, I'll definitely be coming to stay.'

Tally tossed him the ball, returning the grin. 'See? You do know a good thing when you hear it. Now serve, you smarmy bastard!'

★ ★ ★

Gemma's initial reaction was similar. 'You're joking,' she laughed incredulously when Tally told her. 'You wouldn't last a month in the country.'

'I take it that means you won't be joining me?' he asked mildly. He had decided to tell her over dinner at one of her favourite restaurants, thinking that in public she could not throw the kind of tantrum she'd indulged in rather too often lately for someone of his emotional repression. She was not only eating that night but, until now, had also seemed rather pleased with herself. He knew he should have been more curious as to why. Perhaps she'd been offered a TV advertisement. She was desperate to break into acting.

'Come to Scotland? Would you like me to?' Gemma enjoyed a forkful of avocado mousse. They were dining at Langan's where she loved to be part of the cavalcade of stars and personalities who frequented its tables. She had chosen a dramatic black and grey Vivienne Westwood dress for the occasion, an outfit which had, as she'd hoped, attracted a few flashes from the paparazzi hovering round the entrance. Her long lissome figure and swinging blonde tresses usually showed up well even in the murky newsprint of the gossip columns.

'Of course I'd like you to,' Tally told her glibly, using a crust of bread to mop up the juices around the remains of his *escargots provençales*. 'You'd suit Taliska rather well. I can just see you standing on the stairs in cashmere and pearls.'

'Yes, but would it suit me?' she snapped, rising as usual to his bait.

'Why not? It's a bit grim right now but when we've done it up it will be the epitome of style and comfort. And it will have saunas and jacuzzis and a gym.

Cellulite will evaporate in Taliska's crystal air!' He had recently discovered what cellulite was but still did not completely comprehend the terrors it held for Gemma.

'Yes, but mould will probably form in its place,' she retorted.

Tally wrinkled his brow in amused surprise. Gemma had not produced much witty repartee lately. 'So I can't persuade you to come?' he asked, signalling a waiter to pour more wine. They were sharing a bottle of Bourgogne Algioté 1987 which he had chosen because he knew she liked it.

Gemma spread her hands expressively, threatening to spear another diner with her fork. 'Sorry!' she exclaimed and any protests which might have been forthcoming melted under her limpid apologetic gaze. Of Tally she asked, 'How could I, darling? I'd be history in ten minutes. No agent is going to bother ringing a model five hundred miles away in the sticks when he can summon twenty others straight off Sloane Street!'

'You underrate yourself,' Tally admonished her. 'Absence might make the lens grow fonder.'

Gemma shook her head. 'It's a lovely thought, but out of sight is out of *Vogue*, I'm afraid. Besides, I'm a city girl – and you're a city man. Why the hell do you want to leave London?'

'Time flies like a weaver's shuttle,' he replied enigmatically, quoting his old school motto, an epigram he had considered ridiculously whimsical as a callow youth but which he was now beginning to appreciate. 'And speaking of shuttles, there's one that flies to Scotland from Heathrow every two hours. You can come at any time. You just have to jump on.'

'You sound as if you're going tomorrow,' she

teased him. 'Surely there are one or two things to do first – like raise the money, for instance. How do you propose to do that?'

'I don't know why but I didn't expect you to ask that,' he told her with a pretence at offence. 'I thought you thought I was loaded.'

She frowned. 'I'm not a gold-digger you know, Tally.'

He squeezed her hand in guilty apology. 'I know you're not. You're a super-sexy super-model and I'm a fool to be leaving you. I'm sorry.' He raised his glass and stared at her over the rim. She really was looking stunning tonight. There was none of the sulky, dissatisfied droop to the mouth which had lately detracted from her fine regular features. 'I'm going to sell my flat,' he went on, 'and Nell's going to sell hers and we're going to get the rest from banks and grants. There are really good grants for bringing employment to these remote areas, you know – from the EC Regional Fund, Scottish Tourist Board, Highlands and Islands Enterprise and so on. I've been doing my homework.'

Gemma removed her hand from his, raising it defensively. 'Spare me, please. I don't want to hear about my rivals for your affections. When will you leave? I've got a new job starting next week and I'll be away for a while anyway. Should I move out before I go?'

'Oh, I think we might have a little more time than that,' he smiled. 'That's great news about the job. I thought you were in good form.' He leaned forward to whisper confidingly, 'Hey, don't look now but Jerry Hall has just walked in!'

Gemma had half-turned to verify this observation before she realised her mistake. 'You're having me on! You're an infuriating shit, Tally McLean. I'm bloody glad you're leaving!'

'I'm sorry, Thatcher,' Nell said contritely as she emptied a doggy-bag of *cervelles au beurre noir* into the cat's bowl. One of the chefs had prepared it for the programme and for once none of the studio crew had been eager to finish it off. 'I hope you like brains. Maybe it will make up for going to stay with Sinead. It's only for a few months, until everything gets a bit more organised. And you've got to promise me not to eat any of Ninian's pet mice. It's the cats' home for you if you do.'

Nell had sold her flat remarkably quickly and now had four weeks in which to pack up the last twenty-nine years and transport herself from one world into another. The *Hot Gryll* production team were already planning a farewell party. The whole pace of events was frightening in its velocity and the presence of the little cat, calmly and methodically chewing her banquet of brains, was both a sorrow and a solace. 'Oh God, Thatcher, have I done the right thing?' Nell asked, stroking the smooth, feline head. 'I suppose you'd tell me not to look back. What was the phrase? *The lady's not for turning!*'

'Talking to yourself?' said Leo, coming in from the garden. 'The door was open – I hope you don't mind.' Thatcher leaped down from her table-top feast and walked stiffly from the room. She tended to be standoffish with visitors, even frequent ones like Leo.

'You think I'm mad, don't you?' queried Nell. 'I hope you'll miss me when I've gone.'

'I'll come and visit you, if I can find the way – and the fare! It's a long journey to Broadmoor.' A teasing smile split Leo's fine-chiselled face as he sat down at the kitchen table and stuck his feet up on a second chair.

'It's called Taliska,' Nell reminded him patiently. 'And if you play your cards right it could be your next commission.'

'Wow! I'll have to brush up my technique with heather and thistles, then. Is there much of a face-lift needed?'

A hollow laugh greeted this inquiry. 'More like total reconstructive surgery,' Nell sighed. 'God knows where the money's coming from but I leave all that to Tally. He's the genius with figures.'

'His girlfriends always have good ones anyway,' agreed Leo.

'God, don't mention Tally's girlfriends. Gemma's flown off to film a commercial in Trinidad and won't be coming to Scotland. All those swimwear catalogues paid off, it seems. Meanwhile Tally has gone all caveman, thumbing through his little black book. It's as if he's determined to roger everything in skirts before he leaves London.'

Leo raised his fine, girlish eyebrows salaciously. 'The naughty ram. Has he sold his flat yet?'

'Not that I know of, but he only put it on the market a couple of weeks ago.' Nell handed Leo a bottle of white wine and a corkscrew. 'Here. I hate pulling corks. This is the Australian stuff Tally brought to that dreadful dinner party. We'd better see what it's like.'

'You and Tally are chalk and cheese, aren't you?' observed Leo when they were both furnished with full, chill glasses, beaded with condensation. 'Why are you doing it, Nell? Seriously.'

'Seriously?' She took a sip of wine and considered it appreciatively. 'That's not bad. Tally's quite good at vintages and things. That should prove useful anyway.'

'Surely you're going to get professionals in to run the place, though?'

'Some. I've been trying to get hold of a chef recently. A particular one I thought might be persuaded to join us, but he seems to be on his hols. I wonder where chefs go for a break? It must be awful for them if they don't like the food when they get there.'

'You're avoiding my question, Nell.' Leo wagged an admonitory finger at her. With his glossy dark hair tied back in a pony-tail he looked rather like a handsome, disapproving schoolmistress. 'Why are you doing this? You had a good career – "with prospects" as they say – and a nice cosy pad with resident cat. Why throw it all away on a risky business about which you know nothing? It's crazy! Did Tally talk you into it?'

'Oh no. We kind of convinced each other.' Nell ran her hand through her irrepressible brown curls and left them standing on end as if a mad crimper had been at work. In check cotton trousers and loose white T-shirt, she looked rather like one of the little rubber troll-dolls that were currently flooding the toyshops. 'You're very conservative for a bohemian artist, aren't you, Leo?' She laughed. 'Maybe I just want to get out of the rat race. You know the song. *Nellie the elephant packed her trunk and said goodbye to the circus*. . . Perhaps that's me!'

'Don't be silly,' admonished Leo with sudden concern. 'You're not an elephant and you're not a Nellie neither.'

'Faulty observation, good alliteration,' said Nell. 'Speaking of elephants,' she added suddenly as an idea dawned, 'would you fancy a week at a health farm? I haven't time to go now and I've still got Mummy's voucher. As soon as you've finished the Entwhistle Bath you could drop out at Champney's for a week. You might meet a whole lot of rich people who need *trompe l'oeils* in their back passages. Oops – sorry! That wasn't meant to sound as rude as it did.'

'The only person doing a *trompe l'oeil* is you,' grumbled Leo. 'I never heard so much eye-wash to avoid an issue.'

'You will go, won't you?' Nell jumped up and took an envelope down from among the miscellaneous items attached to a pinboard on the wall. 'Here's the voucher. Don't for God's sake lose any weight while you're there, though. You'll disappear if you do. Go and research a mural for the wall of our new gym. It's going to be in the old billiard-room, and Tally says he wants it looking like a bacchanalia in the Roman Baths. You know, naked bodies writhing in steam, so people will get worked up while they work out. What do you think?'

Leo took the envelope, shaking his head in confusion. 'I think I've just been snookered,' he said.

'We just couldn't believe you were serious.' Donalda sounded annoyed. They were sitting with pre-lunch drinks the following Sunday in the lounge of the Doxys' Marylebone penthouse. The flat had been chosen for its proximity to Hal's Baker Street office and Donalda's favourite shops in Bond Street and South Moulton Street. Ceiling-to-floor windows afforded a view over London's northern inner suburbs, serried ranks of brick and concrete marching to the horizon, relieved by patches of green where the trees and grass of Regent's Park and Primrose Hill intervened. The hum of traffic rose from below on updraughts of turgid fume-filled air. Nell could never understand why her fastidious mother lived so high up where the atmosphere, far from being rarefied by altitude, seemed second-hand and past its sell-by date.

'But now you've put your flat on the market as well, I suppose we must believe you really mean to do it,' remarked Hal, handing Tally a gin and tonic. He himself was drinking iced tea, one of the few remaining Yankee habits he still possessed – that and a penchant for sweatshirts with colourful logos. He was wearing one now that promoted his own firm; it showed an enormous half-bitten apple with technicolour pips that looked like micro-chips. *The byte of success* read the motto beneath.

'Oh yes, we mean it all right,' grinned Tally, raising his glass cheerfully and taking a serious gulp. 'Phew, I need this! Had a heavy night last night.'

'You are burning the candle at both ends,' admonished his mother, taking a sip of her mineral water. 'And who are all these strange females who answer your phone? Since Gemma left I never know who'll be there.'

'Oh, I expect they're agents showing the flat,' said Tally airily. 'I haven't time to do it. I leave it all to them.'

Nell choked slightly on her gin but said nothing. As she had remarked to Leo, her brother seemed hell-bent on sampling every succulent siren on the London circuit before he was confined forever to the wastelands of Scotland. This didn't seem to gel with his declaration that he was really looking for gingham and apple pie, but perhaps he was just sloughing off his old skin with a flourish. Tally heard her splutter and shot her a swift glance. He wondered whether his sister was really as virtuous as she appeared, or did she secretly sneak out to singles bars and pick up cruising men? Being sexually voracious himself he found it hard to believe that others were more restrained. His present rampage through the sylphs of Sloane Street was paralleled in his professional life where, with tension building in the Gulf yet again, he was conducting a final fling on the oil markets, hoping to land that elusive bonanza deal to supplement the daunting portfolio of grants and mortgages he was compiling to finance their island venture.

'I know estate agents are working all hours to combat the property slump but I don't imagine that includes showing flats at seven in the morning,' said Donalda sarcastically. 'I hope you're being careful, Tally.' Her words were tinged with a faint trace of admiration. Donalda came from the old school which condoned male promiscuity, considering it a sign of healthy virility, while at the same time condemning the women with whom such promiscuous behaviour was shared as being 'no better than they should be'.

'I thought you'd be glad to see the back of Gemma, Mother,' remarked Tally slyly. Gemma had been classed as undesirable in Donalda's book because she swore and worked as a model. 'You know you never liked her.'

'She was infinitely preferable to a Scottish island!' his mother exclaimed. 'This is all the fault of that old witch, Mother McLean.' With a sneer she made 'mother' rhyme with 'wither'.

'That's not fair,' protested Nell, leaping to Granny Kirsty's defence. 'She may have lived there but she herself had nothing to do with us buying Taliska. I think it's rather romantic anyway that we're going back to Granny's roots.'

'My dear Ellen, you can't make a living out of romantic notions,' put in Hal. 'Life is not just a bowl of cherries and you cannot expect anyone to bail you out when the going gets tough.' Hal pontificated readily, freely mixing English and American clichés.

'I'll remember that,' Nell promised, cringing as always under Hal's patronising tone. She tried to like her stepfather but he was everything she found irritating – earnest, opinionated and humourless – and it frightened her to think that her mother loved him. She wondered if such a lack of discrimination could be inherited. 'We're relying on you to drum up a few clients among your friends,' she went on. 'Some of those high-flying executives whom you say go in for super-octane weekend breaks. You could recommend Taliska as *the* low-fat high-luxury hideaway!'

'Is that how you intend to market it?' asked Hal with interest. 'Gee, that's not a bad idea. Doll, we might even go ourselves. I've never been to Scotland.'

Donalda shuddered visibly. Scotland was the place from which she had escaped as soon as possible and to which she wished never to return. She had spent all her second married life not so much denying her birthright as trying not to draw attention to it. She congratulated herself that Hal's failure to visit Scotland could be directly attributed to her Herculean efforts at avoiding both the place and the subject. 'I think I'd better see to lunch,' she said brightly, getting up. 'We're having poached sea trout but I wasn't going to bother with Hollandaise sauce. I hope nobody minds. It's so rich!' She strode briskly out of the room, deceptively sporty in her Sunday leisure suit and aerobics shoes. She looked as if she had just returned from an exercise class but in fact Donalda did not like to break sweat, so she went in for callanetics and yoga rather than 'going for the burn'. The merest hint of a hot flush had sent her rushing for hormone replacement therapy and Evening Primrose oil.

Hal winked at Tally, causing Nell intense surprise. 'Your mother doesn't believe I know she's Scotch,' he confided archly, making the common American mistake of confusing Scotch whisky with the Scottish nationality. 'But I've always known it. It had 'Edinborrow' on her birth certificate when I went for the marriage licence and even I know that's the capital of Scotland.' He chuckled, hugely enjoying his little joke and confounding Nell's long-held belief in his total lack of innate humour. 'Don't worry, we'll be up to see you at Taliska. I want to check out the tartans, see if there's a Doxy clan!'

'Are you having me on?' demanded Calum Strachan, supplying a variation on the usual 'You-must-be-joking' reaction. 'You – starting an hotel? In Scotland?'

'That's right,' agreed Nell patiently, her hand trembling on the telephone handset. It had cost her a lot in nervous energy to make this call. 'My brother and I. We are Scottish, you know.'

'Coulda fooled me,' grumbled the voice down the line, in an accent which offered no doubt as to its owner's place of origin. 'You sound like Delia Smith.'

Nell was angry. How dare this thistle-voiced chef criticise her accent? It wasn't as if she'd even enjoyed the public school which had imposed it on her. 'I'm flattered,' she said sarcastically. 'Are you interested in hearing more?'

'What do you want?'

'I have a proposition,' Nell continued primly,

regretting making the call at all. 'Perhaps we could meet?'

'Maybe,' came the indecisive reply. 'What kind of a proposition?' His tone suggested that it might be an improper one.

'We're looking for a chef who's interested in health as well as *haute cuisine*. I thought you might be a likely candidate.'

'Why me?'

Nell took a deep breath. This conversation was stretching her communication skills to the limit. 'Well, you're young, innovative and Scottish – and you took the mickey out of Gordon Gryll!'

'And why should taking the piss out of that pluke make me eligible to cook in your kitchen, even supposing I might want to?' Despite the belligerent words a genuine note of interest had crept into the chef's disembodied voice.

'I know you're ambitious. We're starting up in Scotland. You're Scottish. Our set-up might give you the opportunity to establish a personal reputation in your home territory. We're trying to do something a bit different – to provide exciting food that isn't fattening.'

'What, cucumber in aspic, you mean?' Scorn crackled down the line.

'No, not cucumber particularly – unless you insist, of course!' Nell was becoming increasingly impatient. The call had definitely been a mistake. 'Look, do you want to meet or not? When we talked at the studio I got the impression you'd like to get back to Scotland, that's all.' It was true. Calum Strachan was presently head chef at a well-known and exclusive hotel near Harrods. Professionally he had put its restaurant among the top star-ratings in the guides but personally he remained a fish out of water in

London. He had been born in Crieff, the Perthshire town which promoted itself as the gateway to the Highlands, and the asphalt jungles of south-east England were slowly stifling him.

'OK, let's meet,' he agreed tersely. 'Harrods Health Juice Bar, three-thirty.'

'How appropriate,' murmured Nell. 'Fine.'

The juice of the day was blackcurrant and raspberry. Nell sipped a glassful thoughtfully, one eye on the escalator which delivered customers almost to the door of the basement Health Bar. Behind the counter the noise of juice extractors whined incessantly. She recognised the slight, wiry figure of the chef as soon as he stepped onto the moving staircase. His mop of curly red hair was striking and he looked younger than she remembered, perhaps only in his mid-twenties. His face was set, almost belligerent, with its bushy russet eyebrows and short sharp nose, and he carried himself at full alert, as if he half-expected someone to accost him at any moment. He did not have the look of a happy young man.

'Ms McLean?' His voice was softer than it had sounded on the phone but even so Nell tensed at his words. She had always hated the use of the amorphous title Ms.

'Nell, please,' she said, offering her hand. She did not get up, gesturing him to join her at the table. 'Perhaps I could call you Calum? I'm not very used to using Mr and Mrs. Nobody does at the BBC.' She smiled placatingly.

He looked as if he might have something to say on the matter of the BBC and its informality, but instead he simply nodded acquiescence and sat down. He was wearing jeans and a sweatshirt and looked slightly incongruous among the dressed-up lady shoppers seated all around them, taking their mid-afternoon refreshment.

'Thanks for coming,' Nell went on rather nervously. She would have liked to make him smile, finding his scowl rather off-putting. She seemed to remember he was rather good-looking when he smiled. 'Will you have the juice of the day? It's quite tasty.'

'Aye, I will, thanks,' he agreed and gave the order to the waistcoated student-type who was wiping down the next table. A few moments of silence ensued while his gaze shifted from Nell to the busy juice counter and back to Nell again. 'What's this idea you have for a new cuisine, then?' he asked brusquely. 'Do you know anything about cooking?'

Somewhat taken aback that he should be the one to launch into the questions, Nell shrugged. 'I've picked up quite a lot over the years, but I've never been to cookery school or anything, if that's what you mean,' she said.

He looked unaccountably relieved. 'That's good,' he sighed, his face brightening. 'I thought you might be about to give me a lecture on low-fat cuisine! Actually, it's one of my special interests.'

'Is it?' asked Nell, amazed. 'I didn't know. I only approached you because I wanted to use a Scottish chef in a Scottish hotel. I thought a Scot would understand the available ingredients so much better.'

'There's no place better for ingredients!' he exclaimed, his pale-lashed, brownish-green eyes beginning to sparkle with enthusiasm. 'London thinks it's got everything, but no' as fresh and plentiful as Scotland.' His juice arrived and he grew noticeably more relaxed as he took several large gulps. 'But of course there aren't that many people to eat them. I wouldna want to find myself cooking for a handful a day. This place of yours sounds a bit remote,' he said dubiously.

'Well, it is an island,' Nell admitted. 'That's part of its attraction. But it is connected to the mainland by a bridge and it's not really far by helicopter from Glasgow.'

'Helicopter! What kind of customers are you expecting, then? Millionaires?' Calum looked nonplussed. 'You'll no' get *them* eating grated cucumber and a lettuce leaf.'

'I told you that cucumber wasn't particularly what I had in mind,' said Nell with irritation. 'Look, supposing I start at the beginning and describe the place to you and our ideas for developing it, and then you can tell me if you're at all interested in joining us. Perhaps an island on the west coast is rather too much of a culture shock for a product of the central belt to contemplate.'

It was his turn to look annoyed. 'Crieff isn't central belt,' he said. 'I'm a Highlander and proud of it.' Animation coloured his face and sharpened his features.

Nell thought he looked quite fascinating when he flared up, like a peacock spreading its tail. Life wouldn't be dull on Taliska if he came to work there, she decided. A wide smile softened the impact of her response to his indignant declaration. 'Well, the Highland line is a very wide line,' she amended. 'Anyway, it's a long way from London, which is the main thing.'

His shoulders relaxed from aggressive to acquiescent. 'Aye, you're right there. This city gives me the creeps. Tell me about this island, then.'

An hour later they were still head to head in the Health Juice Bar when Calum glanced at his watch. 'Jings! Is that the time? I'll need to go!' He stood up, all sign of belligerence gone. A slight smile gave her no inkling of the strength of his enthusiasm, but at least it told her she had made a friend. 'I'll think about all this,' he promised, leaning forward to shake her hand. 'And you keep me posted about progress with the development. Good luck!'

'Thanks,' said Nell, returning his smile and noting how it completely transformed his pale, taut face. 'I'll be in touch.' She watched his shock of red hair rise slowly up the escalator to the next floor, trying to work out what it was that had clicked between them. She wondered if perhaps they shared a mutual sense of misplacement in London. 'You're a fish out of water, Calum Strachan,' she said to herself. 'And I hope I've hooked you.'

★ ★ ★

'We hate to think you've found a thrill,
Greater than working on Hot Gryll*!*
But if this hotel is your will
We'll all be up to take our fill.

'It's hardly Wordsworth, is it?' commented Sinead dryly, closing the much-signed greetings card from which she'd been reading the central message. 'Still, I suppose it's the thought that counts. How was the party?'

Nell made a wry face. 'Pretty gross! They held it after the recording and Eye-Level was leaping about like a frog on hot coals. He's always hyper after a programme. The producer was desperate to get the whole thing over with so that he could get down to the editing channel and the rest of the team were already speculating about who would get my job.'

'And what did they give you? Something amazingly useless and unsuitable, I dare say.' When she had left her airline job Sinead had been given a *Times Atlas of the World* and a Gucci belt which, considering she had been grounded and was about to lose her waistline to her developing pregnancy, had seemed singularly inappropriate gifts.

'Actually they weren't bad,' Nell told her, self-consciously pulling at her T-shirt. Out of a sense of duty she was wearing the leggings Sinead had bought for her birthday but they made her feel like a hefty bondage freak and she had covered as much of them as possible with a baggy black top. 'A camping stove and a pair of green wellies! They probably thought they were a huge joke, but in fact they'll come in very useful, especially as I'll be more or less camping at Taliska for several months, until the builders finish.'

'Are you sure you'll be all right up there on your own?' asked Sinead solicitously. 'It sounds horribly isolated.'

'Well, I won't be on my own for long,' replied Nell. 'At least, I hope not. There should be surveyors and architects swarming all over the place within a week or so, and then the builders will start and we'll have to get the garden knocked into some kind of shape. I want to grow lots of vegetables and herbs for the kitchen.'

'Oh God, the energy of the girl!' exclaimed her stepmother with a touch of Irish melodrama. 'I tell you Nell, you'll be a shadow of your true self by the time you've finished with all that lot.'

'That would make a change but I doubt it somehow,' Nell observed wryly. 'Tally will be up there too, once he's finished wheedling money out of the bonny banks. He's in charge of marketing and he's got some great ideas – like putting pamphlets in health clubs and sports centres, even in football and rugby clubs. We might get Will Carling or Garry Lineker coming to Taliska!'

'You might even get Gordon Gryll, God help you,' cried Niamh, coming in with Thatcher in her arms. 'This cat is cool, Nell. And her name is really wild.'

Nell was gratified to see that Thatcher had taken so quickly to the rebellious teenager. It was rare that the little cat socialised with anyone except Nell, and leaving her was a wrench. 'The feeling is obviously mutual,' she told Niamh. 'Perhaps you share similar non-conformist attitudes. Just keep her away from Ninian's zoo! I don't want him charging her with grievous bodily harm to hamsters.'

'She can sleep in my room,' said Niamh accommodatingly. 'I'll even have her litter tray in there.'

'If she can ever find it amongst all the other litter,' sniffed her mother but she looked pleased that the girl was offering to help. Throughout the long summer holiday Niamh had been displaying all the classic symptoms of uncooperative adolescence. When she wasn't shut in her room giggling with one or two cronies or out in a brat-pack stalking unsuspecting male prey in the discos and cafés, she was barging selfishly about the house leaving a trail of apple cores and empty Diet Coke cans and complaining of terminal boredom. Her presence disrupted the whole household and distracted Sinead from her habitual disorderly regime.

'Where's Granny Kirsty?' Nell asked suddenly. 'I expected to see her today.'

'She's out shopping,' Sinead replied. 'She wants to

stock up on all the things she says she can't get in Glasgow.'

'Like Anello and Davide thigh-boots and Workers for Freedom dungarees,' giggled Niamh, tickling Thatcher's ears.

'Don't be so silly, Niamh,' admonished Sinead. 'She's probably stocking up on Harrods shopping bags to give all her friends for Christmas. Tell me what time you'll collect the old lady on Thursday, Nell?'

Nell and Kirsty McLean were flying to Glasgow together and Nell would then stay a few nights with her grandmother before travelling on to Oban. She wanted to investigate several firms of architects who had been recommended to her in Glasgow and also buy a more suitable vehicle for her needs. Her clapped-out hatchback so nauseously anointed by Gloria was about to be delivered to a second-hand car dealer whom Nell fervently hoped had no sense of smell. She intended to buy something more rugged and capacious for Taliska.

'About one o'clock,' said Nell. 'We'll catch the mid-afternoon shuttle.'

'I like flying,' said Granny Kirsty at 30,000 feet, tucking into her British Airways tea. 'I don't know why all my friends say it tires them out.'

Nell muttered vaguely in response. She was not really listening to her grandmother's pleasantries. For her this was a flight of great significance. It was extraordinary to think that she had probably left London for good. Almost her entire life since the age of three had been spent in or around the sprawling English capital, and now she would only visit as an outsider. Strangely, she could feel no sense of loss. Perhaps she had always been an outsider. So eager had she been to cut the ties that held her to London that she had almost thrown the keys of her flat at the estate agent. All her belongings and furniture had been consigned to a Pickfords container and would be delivered to Taliska in due course. For a week or so she would be peripatetic, belonging nowhere, carrying all she needed in a suitcase. She found the prospect both alarming and enticing, and used all the airline packs of jam, cream *and* butter on her scone in celebration.

'I may have hired a chef this week,' she remarked, licking her sticky fingers. 'He's a Scot. You might remember him. He was on *Hot Gryll* once and gave Gordon a run for his money! He's red-headed and fiery – quite a character. His name is Calum Strachan.'

'I do remember him,' agreed Granny Kirsty. 'A bright laddie with a sparkle in his eye.'

'There wasn't much evidence of that when I met him,' replied Nell dryly. 'More like an icicle! But he melted a bit later on. He said he'd consider my offer. I think he might come.'

'Taliska's like a magnet to the right people,' declared her grandmother.

'You must visit soon, Granny. Shall I come down and collect you in a month or so?'

'No, thank you,' came the decisive reply. 'I dinna want to see it all rundown and decrepit. Anyway, I'm too old for bad plumbing. I'll come when I can get a fine bedroom with an en suite bath.'

'I see! All right.' Nell watched her grandmother fondly as she popped a segment of buttered scone neatly into her mouth. For all her eighty years she was as perky as a little bird, like a sparrow bobbing about in a hedge or a robin pecking crumbs on a lawn. It was typical of her that she confidently expected to see out another winter in enough health and strength to postpone her return to Taliska until afterwards. 'You shall come to the grand opening and have the best room in the hotel.'

'I remembered a story the other day,' said Kirsty McLean, wiping her mouth carefully on the airline paper napkin. 'The laird always told stories at his children's parties. He used to hold them once a year and we'd all go – his own weans, the shepherd's brood, the cook's daughter and all of us from the factor's house. He'd tell stories about Taliska, about its past and its people – fairytales! I suspect he made most of them up, actually. This one I remember was about a two-headed monster that used to emerge from the kyle at high tide and terrorise the islanders. A kind of man-eating Push-me-pull-you, if you remember your Doctor Dolittle! It could have been the death of the place if it hadna been for two brave young islanders. You see, the monster had two heads so it had to be fought by two people who could think as one – twins, in other words. It was twins that killed the monster and saved the island. Isna that a good omen?' At the end of her story Granny Kirsty smiled with quiet self-satisfaction.

Nell stared at her grandmother speculatively. 'You made that up, Granny Kirsty,' she cried accusingly.

'Did I?' queried the old lady mildly, her blue eyes twinkling. 'Well, I'll tell you something else shall I, young Nell, whose real name is Ellen? Did you know that *ellen* is the Scots word for island – *eilan* in Gaelic? And *tallach* is the Gaelic word for a hall. *Tallach iasger* – *Taliska* – the hall of the fishermen. So the Isle of Taliska is *Eilan Tallach iasger* or *Ellen Taliska*. Now, I didn't make that up!'

Chapter Five

Nell stared across the desk at the grave, sandy-haired lawyer with the deep, speckled grey eyes. 'What are you telling me, Mr McInnes – that my brother has made a mistake?' she asked incredulously.

Alasdair McInnes fiddled with the mottled blue enamel fountain pen which his wife had given him for his fortieth birthday, nearly a year before. A corner of his mind registered unremitting grief, as it did whenever her image intruded, the rest of it he applied to scrutinising the young woman sitting opposite him. He thought her plumply pleasing to the eye, and had instinctively liked her as soon as she walked in the door, even before she had opened her mouth – and then, if anything, her speaking voice had inspired a faint shock of disappointment owing to its very Englishness. From her appearance – her relative lack of height, her curly brown hair, fresh, healthy complexion, firm jaw and candid blue eyes – he had immediately assumed that she was Scottish. Alasdair McInnes was *very* Scottish, from his comfortable, well-worn Harris tweed suit to the certificate on his wall declaring him to be a 'Writer to the Signet', that august Edinburgh institution which endorsed the proficiency and trustworthiness of the higher echelon of Scottish solicitors. Being an innately fair-minded man, he tried to banish this sense of disappointment which he knew to be a perfidious, chauvinistic reaction but, like many Highlanders, he couldn't help feeling more comfortable with his own kind.

'Not exactly a mistake, Miss McLean,' he said equivocally, not wishing to imply that someone had been careless. 'More of an *erratum ignorantis* – an error of judgment through ignorance.'

'Which amounts to the same thing,' Nell retorted impatiently. 'Explain again, if you wouldn't mind, Mr McInnes. I still don't quite grasp the difference between English and Scots law in this respect.'

Alasdair smiled understandingly. 'It's quite a subtle difference but an important one,' he said. 'In England, an agreement to buy is automatically subject to contract. The parties can withdraw or negotiatiate further, right up until the moment contracts are agreed and exchanged, whereas in Scotland a property transaction is normally conducted on the understanding that when an offer to purchase is made and accepted, then the contract is immediately binding – unless specific waivers have been agreed at the same time. Your brother made no stipulation about his offer being subject to planning permission when he agreed to buy Taliska.'

'So effectively we are committed to completing the sale whether or not we get planning permission to convert the castle into an hotel – that's what you're saying, isn't it?' Nell leaned forward inquiringly, unaware that by so doing she favoured Alasdair McInnes with a tempting glimpse of her undeniably eye-catching cleavage. August might have produced its customary deluge of rain but the temperature, even in the West Highlands, had remained seasonally high and Nell had left several of the top buttons of her loose cotton shirt open.

Alasdair experienced the kind of physical response he had almost forgotten existed, and blushed despite himself. The previous summer his wife of fifteen years had died in a car crash. The devastation of her loss meant that he had not thought amorously about the opposite sex since, and this sudden rush of blood to the face and to other more stirring places took him completely by surprise. His lapse of *sang froid* annoyed him. He felt disturbed and threatened by it and responded aggressively, shifting uncomfortably in his chair.

'In short, yes,' he snapped and then added more evenly, 'You are committed to paying for Taliska as agreed, whether or not the District Council Planning Committee grant a change of use.'

Nell was puzzled by his apparent rancour, but concluded that the cause must be something other than herself or her case – an indigestible lunch perhaps, or an ingrowing toenail. 'Oh well,' she sighed resignedly. 'We'll just have to hope that they have no objections. Do you think there could be any?' Her naivety was ingenuous, beguiling.

By now Alasdair McInnes had recovered his composure and was contrite, shaking off his frown and returning her smile. His strong, generous mouth was more apt for smiles than solemnity; as a lawyer, he sometimes found this a handicap, but as a man, it added greatly to his warmth of character. 'Let's hope not,' he said. 'This is quite an undertaking you're embarking on, Miss McLean. It would be a shame if you were tripped at the first hurdle.' He coughed slightly as if somewhat embarrassed about his next remark. 'Of course, a word or two in the right quarter might help. Do you or your brother know anyone who could put in a good word for your project?'

Nell studied his face. Did he genuinely mean that influence alone would smooth their path, or was he trying to tell her that a few fiscal sweeteners might do the trick? She felt terribly at sea, inexperienced in such matters. Then all at once she knew what she must do. 'How long have we got before the application is considered?' she asked, leaning forward earnestly once more.

With this second change of position she caught the involuntary flicker of his eyes towards her cleavage. Now it was her turn to blush and straighten up, but Alasdair was already consulting his desk-calendar, tracing the weeks with his pen-tip. 'The Planning Committee meets in the third week of every month, on a Wednesday,' he told her. 'You have two weeks.'

'I may have some family connections which might help,' she said, standing up and holding out her hand. 'I won't keep you any longer now. You've been very generous with your time. I'll come and see you again before the planning meeting, if that's all right – just to check whether you have wind of any specific problem.'

He rose in his turn, moving round the desk towards her. He did not mention, as he could have done, that his time was her money. He almost found himself regretting that this was the case. 'I'll look forward to that, Miss McLean. Please feel that you can rely on me for any help, legal or otherwise. We country lawyers tend to act as financial consultants, estate agents, even social workers on occasion!' His warm, wide smile seemed to envelop Nell as he shook her hand and ushered her to the door. Its generosity did not fit the collective image she had always had of dry, serious-minded solicitors. 'You'll be needing further legal help once you do get planning permission,' he added, 'for builders' contracts and so on. I strongly advise you not to sign anything without getting it checked.'

'I won't,' she assured him. 'McInnes and Murray will be Taliska's chief i-dotters and t-crossers!' She paused as he opened the door to see her out. 'Is there a Murray, by the way, or is it one of those official-sounding partnerships which disguise a one-man band?'

The smile faded and a shadow crossed his face. 'Murray was my wife's name,' he told her. 'She was also my partner but she died last year, so I'm afraid it is a one-man band now. I keep the name though, for continuity – and, perhaps, for remembrance.'

Nell was dismayed by the flippant way she had elicited such harrowing information. 'I am so sorry,' she told him simply. What more could she say?

Nell phoned her father that evening. 'I need you, Daddy,' she said. 'I need someone who can wheel and deal and chat people up. Tally is up to his eyes in some amazing transaction which he says will solve all our financial worries at once. That means it probably wears a D-cup and skirts up to the crutch! And I'm no good at handing out baksheesh without making it look like a bribe, which is what I suspect we may have to do here. Could you possibly come up for a few days?'

As she was speaking, Ian McLean scratched his balding head and pulled uncomfortably at his shirt collar. Not since primary school homework had his elder daughter actually asked for his help, apart from the odd financial sub as a student. He was absurdly proud that she felt she could turn to him, but an opportunity of obtaining used barrels from one of Spain's largest sherry manufacturers was in the balance and he knew he should be flying to Jerez the next day. Apart from the right quality of water and barley, the secret of good whisky was to age it in old sherry casks, but they weren't always available. Having taken huge risks in his own business career, he was entirely behind the twins' decision to break into the precarious hotel trade but why, he wondered, couldn't the request for help have come at a more convenient moment?

'Well of course I'll come,' he said, disguising his reluctance. 'Would next week be all right?'

Nell felt her heart sink. 'Y-yes, I suppose it would but we'll be sailing a bit close to the wind. Haven't you got any cousins in this area who might be in influential positions? Granny Kirsty had five brothers and sisters, didn't she? They must have families who live around here.'

'Afraid not, Nell. There was nothing for any of them to do up there, you see. They all drifted south or overseas. No, you'll have to make do with me. I'll fly up tomorrow. What time is the afternoon train from Glasgow to Oban?' The barrel deal would just have to wait. He hoped his Spanish contact would put up with a bit of British *mañana*.

'Two-thirty from Glasgow Queen Street. I'll meet you. I've bought a second-hand Daihatsu Fourtrack which looks a bit like a Jeep so you'll know me among all the Volvos and Vauxhalls. Thanks a million, Daddy! I'll really look forward to seeing you.'

The few days that Nell and Ian spent in Oban were probably the happiest time they had ever known together. Her departure to boarding school at eleven, his divorce, re-marriage and second family and her three student years away at Bristol University had all added up to a relationship based on little more than the fact of paternity. Nell knew almost nothing of Ian's foibles and fancies, other than his penchant for flirting with girls young enough to be his daughters – a habit which had always annoyed and disturbed her – and his ability to get on famously with just about everyone he met – a talent which had won him many friends but lost him a wife. Donalda had never been able to accept that Ian put his friends as high on his agenda as herself.

Ian was equally ignorant about Nell's true character. Becoming the father of twins had surprised and delighted him at first. He had thought that as they grew they would think and act alike, respond to his approaches in similar ways and look and behave much the same. The reality had disconcerted and deterred him. From birth they had developed along completely different lines. Tally woke at five a.m. and screamed; Nell woke at seven and gurgled. He spat his food out; she shovelled it in. Tally walked at ten months; Nell at eighteen. Through their childhood, what had been black for Tally had been white for Nell. He liked BMX bikes and skateboards; she liked kittens and ponies. He watched *Starsky and Hutch*; she watched *Blue Peter*. He ate pizza; she ate chocolate cake. He messed about with Airfix; she with Knitting Nancy. He was lanky and coltish; she was round and puppyish. The list of opposites was endless . . . It made family life a nightmare. By the time the twins were seven, Ian had more or less opted out of Nell's life, leaving her to her mother, not realising that it was he whom she resembled, he whom she looked up to and adored. He had given Tally the best of what little attention wasn't devoted to work and socialising, until he had turned his affections towards the spirited Sinead and subsequently her look-alike daughter, Niamh. These two had amused and delighted him in the early years of his second marriage until the arrival of Ninian, whose developing intellect had proceeded to impress and fascinate him. In the daily company of two sparky red-heads and a talented brain-box, he had found little time to monitor the progress of his firstborn twin opposites.

Having presented him with her dilemma, Nell watched with admiration as her father cut a swathe through the Oban power-brokers. A man who had scythed through the miles of red tape generated by the Indian Civil Service in order to achieve what everyone said was impossible – namely, the building of a distillery in an officially teetotal society – he found the relatively uncomplicated Scottish planning process easy going. Ian quickly established the identity of the individual members of the Argyll & Bute District Planning Committee and, having further ascertained through skilful inquiry and judicious probing just which of them were the most influential, he rapidly calculated that if he won over merely three people, the change of use from private residence to hotel would go through on the nod. It took him two days to isolate his targets and a further two days to nail them to Nell's mast, and somehow no one felt slighted or insulted in the process. As a demonstration of how to stage-manage a deal it was a *tour de force*.

And there was plenty of time left for Nell to show him Taliska, outline their plans and listen to his ideas and advice. They strolled through the house together, banging plaster to locate load-bearing walls, stirring up the dust of centuries and summoning up the ghosts of past glories. Ian discovered that his daughter shared his love of history and nostalgia, his sense of the ridiculous and his eye for detail. He admired her ability to grasp the enormity of the task ahead without becoming daunted by it, and he beamed proudly as she handled her first meeting with the architect she had selected following her own set of careful inquiries. Just as he charmed everyone else, her father charmed Nell with his teasing blue eyes and his smooth, witty conversation, his quick mind and his handsome, open face. He was a rogue but not a cheat, clever but not devious, a *bon viveur* but not a lush. For the first time, Nell forgot her despair at having inherited his square solidity and coveted his abundance of self-confidence and charm, not realising that she had also inherited a good proportion of these.

'Here's to your haven of lust and recuperation. To L and R!' declared Ian, raising his glass on their last night together. Although they had been staying at one of the many harbour-front hotels in Oban, they had driven out to Lorn Castle for their farewell dinner because Nell wanted to show Ian the local competition. As ever, Fee Ramsay-Miller's cooking was mouth-wateringly excellent and Nell found herself hoping that the Ramsay-Millers' intention to grade down their hotel would mean they would not be trying to attract the same clientèle as Taliska.

She saluted her father in return. She had not been surprised at his reaction to Tally's marketing idea of appealing to carnal as well as gastric appetites. Ian's shout of enthusiastic laughter had been typical and he had declared that a place which encouraged any kind of rejuvenation, whether sexual or corporeal, had his whole-hearted sexagenarian support! If Taliska did nothing else, Nell decided, it had achieved a welcome new accord between herself and her father.

When Ian left, Nell moved out to the island. With a sense of the inevitable she took over the old factor's house, unpacking enough of her belongings to furnish it and make it habitable. The *Hot Gryll* camping stove came into its own as there was nothing in the kitchen except a stone sink and an old range which she knew she would never master. It took her the best part of a day to make the outside latrine usable, employing a gallon of disinfectant and a litre of whitewash. As she scrubbed and painted she vowed that she would make Tally take his turn emptying the chemical toilet!

He arrived as if by telepathy on the day after the cottage was habitable, his BMW piled high with such essentials as his sound system, a television and the remains of his wine-cellar. He also wore a huge grin and the bleary-eyed remnants of a monumental hangover. 'I did it,' he cried by way of greeting. 'I am the shit-hottest trader on the commodity exchanges! I speculated on Iraq becoming the subject of an oil embargo and I made the biggest profit on one tanker deal *ever*. You should have been there, it was brilliant.'

Nell laughed uncertainly. Would she ever get such a financial whizz-kid to empty the Elsan? 'It sounds distinctly dodgy to me,' she said, staring dubiously at the contents of the car. Where would it all go in the tiny cottage? 'Will it buy a few beds or the odd jacuzzi, that's what I want to know.'

'It would buy a whole warehouse of jacuzzis, furnish a score of bedrooms, kit out a dozen kitchens, re-point the battlements and re-roof the squash court, to say nothing of building a swimming pool and hiring the Roux brothers for life!' He pointed a triumphant finger at Nell's astounded face and laughed again, even more loudly, wincing at the same time because it made his head pound painfully. 'That made you catch your breath, didn't it? Unfortunately, I only get a percentage of all that but still, it should be enough to pay the builder. And the rest of the readies, little sister, I have raised among the po-faced bankers and hard-hearted granters of this world. Tomorrow we will sit down with this nice lawyer you say you've found and work it all out properly. But first, aspirin and champagne! Aspirin to sort out my head and champagne to appease the kelpie, or whatever nasty creature lurks beneath the waters of the kyle.' He opened the boot and extracted a bottle of Bollinger from within a bundle of miscellaneous clothing. Tally tended to pack his car rather than a suitcase. 'Do we have any aspirin?' he asked plaintively. 'It's a hell of a long drive from London.'

'In the cottage,' she nodded. 'And we have glasses as well.'

As the cork popped and the wine fizzed, Nell decided that now might not be the right time to mention the Elsan, and Tally decided that he would not bother mentioning to Nell his days of nail-biting anxiety as his oil deal had hung in the balance, awaiting the whim of the world's leaders through the United Nations. As much as his success in pulling off the deal itself, his hangover had been earned celebrating not having to tell Nell that the whole Taliska project would have to be abandoned. She would never know how close they had been to failing before they'd even started.

For her part, Nell never told Tally about the question mark which had once hung over their vital planning permission. She had never doubted that Ian's skilful manipulation of local politicians would pay off and, sure enough, outline planning came through right on schedule. The grand Taliska enterprise began to take shape as the architects worked on the detailed conversion plans. The library was to become a lounge bar, the morning room a conference and television room, the dining room and drawing room were to be linked by folding doors so that they could be opened into each other for special functions, and part of the hall was to be turned into a reception area. Tally and Nell had their first argument over whether there should be double beds in all the bedrooms, Nell pointing out that not everyone would be coming to Taliska simply for bed and bonking. Some bonkers might bring their children, and some guests, particularly the more elderly and infirm, might come for the regenerative qualities of Taliska's peace and quiet.

'Some people prefer twins to doubles,' she maintained stubbornly.

Tally snorted in disbelief. 'Even if they're seventy, by the time they read our brochure their hormones will be hopping enough to make twin beds a positive hindrance,' he declared theatrically.

Nell wondered just who was going to write this wondrously sensual brochure but put the question temporarily to one side. Eventually they agreed on three twin rooms out of a total of ten and discovered that, however they juggled the walls and the plumbing, they could only wangle four rooms with giant beds *and* double jacuzzis. 'We're going to have double trouble,' predicted Tally gloomily. 'Demand will outstrip supply, you'll see.'

'Well, we can always tie the twin beds together if we get pushed. And speaking of stripping,' continued Nell, diplomatically changing the subject, 'the architect says it's possible to bleach the panelling down to a pale blond. I think that sounds brilliant for the dining room, don't you? Light and airy.'

'It sounds like a hairdressing salon,' protested Tally. 'Ash-blond panelling and Carmen-curled carpets. And while we're on the subject of carpets, on the phone the other day Hal suggested they should be McLean bloody tartan – can you believe that? I think he's going all Scotophile, now that Mother's Caledonian skeleton is out of the cupboard.'

'Oh God – he's probably taking secret lessons in Scottish country dancing!' exclaimed Nell. 'Mummy will *die*. Still, he's right about one thing: the carpets should have some pattern or they'll look like hell in a year. Perhaps a muted tartan might be an idea.'

'Well, I leave all that to you,' said Tally grandly. 'You're good at interiors. Your flat was well done. All that patchwork and calico, it lingered in the mind. Mine seemed not to exist when I wasn't there. It was a kind of Cheshire flat – it appeared when you opened the front door and disappeared completely as soon as you walked out. We don't want any of that interior-designed anonymity. Taliska should look as if it has always been here and always will be, like the Highlands, reassuringly timeless and enduringly beautiful.'

'You sound like a tourist brochure,' said Nell with inspiration. 'You may as well write ours. And I don't mind doing the interior design as long as it's not assumed that all the domestic arrangements are mine, too. And Tally – I don't want you to discuss costings and quantities without consulting me, as you have been doing. I hired the architects and I want as much say in what they do as anyone.'

'OK, OK. But while we're on the domestic front, we've forgotten one rather important matter,' Tally said. 'I'm not living in that draughty hovel up the hill for ever – in fact, not for much longer. Where are we going to put ourselves? We need our creature comforts as much as the guests.'

'Not sea views and spa baths,' protested Nell. 'We have to leave those to the PGs.'

Tally looked dubious. 'Well, I'm prepared to forego the view but I insist on a decent bed and a jacuzzi. I'm not thinking of taking a vow of celibacy while providing the ultimate romping-ground for others. I'll take the back rooms over the kitchen; two of them, and a bathroom with all the trimmings. How about you?'

Nell chewed her lip, considering. 'I thought about the tower. The first-floor room is a must for the guests with that wonderful vaulted ceiling, because we can furnish it like a medieval solar. You know, oak chests and tapestry wall-hangings.'

'Ugh,' interrupted Tally, shuddering. 'I'd imagine Polonius was lurking behind the arras all the time! Still, you're probably right. The Hals of this world would go ape in a place like that.'

'The top two rooms are different though,' Nell went on. 'The stair is very narrow and steep and the windows are too high in the wall to see the view unless you stand on tiptoe. But I could use them. I'd like it up there.'

'Nell's little eyrie,' grinned Tally, unconsciously jarring Nell's sensitivity about being patronised. 'You could tuck yourself up there all cosy with your patchwork and your paperbacks.'

'Oh yes.' She mimicked his condescending tone. 'The little lady knitting in her attic rocking chair while Big Brother is bonking his balls off in the first-floor bedroom! Come on, Tally, while we're at it let's get really stereotyped. Let's make sure the little lady is in charge of dirty loos and bedsheets while big macho-man deals with the really important things, like winebins and balance sheets!'

Tally looked hurt and puzzled. 'What are you talking about? How did we get on to this?'

'We got on to it because you presume that you will be doing the cerebral stuff while I do the dirty work. You do, don't you? How long have you been here now – two weeks? And when have you ever so much as vacuumed the cottage or cooked a meal, let alone emptied the Elsan!'

A breaking-point had to come. In the tiny factor's cottage they had been living in each other's pockets, two people who were accustomed to living their own lives, if not exactly alone in Tally's case then at least each according to their own style, styles which were basically incompatible. Nell was becoming exasperated by Tally's habit of living with perpetual noise (the television, his sound system, the radio) and perpetual mess (dirty clothes, wine glasses left unwashed until the lees dried in the stem, smelly newspaper wrappings from fish and chips). Tally was maddened by Nell's uncontrollable urge to tidy up, by her need for a daily routine and by her eating habits. Tally ate to live, Nell lived to eat. He liked instant nourishment when he felt like it, hence the fish and chips; she liked to prepare proper meals with fresh ingredients even when the only equipment was a camp stove and a toaster. Their way of living had never been alike and in that respect nothing had changed; and furthermore, despite numerous requests, Tally had only ever been near the Elsan to fill it up!

'Look, you don't need to get your knickers in a twist,' snapped Tally heatedly. 'I'll do my share when I get round to it. What's the point in keeping this place like *Good Housekeeping* if we're moving out in a few weeks anyway?'

'It's not just the cleaning up, it's your attitude in general. Either we're in this as equals or we're not in it at all. This isn't a game we're playing. Oh, I know you think it's all great fun – sex in the shower and romps in the rhododendrons – and it will be. But it needs to be organised properly, and to do that we have to work as a team. You must stop treating me like the little woman and letting me take care of all the domestic chores while you concentrate on what you consider the important issues. We each need to do both or it won't work, Tally. You've *got* to start pulling your weight domestically!'

Tally reacted in his normal way to what he called 'female tantrums'. He shouted and then he left. 'Christ, you women are all the same,' he yelled in sudden fury. 'If you're not whining about putting on weight you're whingeing about pulling it. Listen dear, I'm *not* humouring you. I don't care which bloody rooms you have or how you choose to live. You can waste time at that bloody stove and stuff yourself stupid if you like – *and* you can rush round washing up and sweeping up until you're blue in the face, as far as I'm concerned. All I can say is, I don't ask you to do any of it and I'm *not* emptying that FUCKING TOILET!' With that he strode noisily out of the door and slammed it.

With an unerring sense of direction he found his way to the pub. It was a head-clearing mile walk down the drive, over the bridge and on to the mainland village of Salach, which boasted the Ossian Hotel. This establishment was not really an hotel at all but a drinking shop for local fishermen and crofters. Tally was badly missing the almost exclusively male society of the City exchanges and their surrounding restaurants and wine-bars. He was beginning to realise just what an enormous change he had made in his life, and he needed to find a male companion whose conversation would prevent him from dwelling on the matter. It was not Tally's way to mull problems over or discuss them, but to distract himself from them and hope they would disappear. It was in this frame of mind that he once more encountered the fisherman, Mac Macpherson.

The pub was sparsely populated and the man who berthed his boat at Taliska was sitting alone on a stool brooding over a half-empty beer mug. Tally nodded at him pleasantly, approached the bar and asked for a pint of bitter. The request was greeted with a snort of derision, not from the barman, a fresh-faced young man who obligingly began to operate the tap, but from the man on the stool. 'Something wrong, Mac?' Tally asked evenly. Since buying Taliska he had only once spoken to 'Fishing Mac', as he had privately nicknamed him, and that was to tell him that, for the time being, he could continue to operate from the jetty.

' "A pe-int of bit-tar," ' sneered the fisherman, trying to emulate Tally's rounded vowels.

Tally's reaction was controlled but cold. He was already on edge and he was sick of being mimicked. Nell had given him enough of that rubbish! 'Any objection?' he said through his teeth.

'We don't drink bitter here, pal,' growled Mac. 'Bitter is an English drink.'

Tally accepted the pint from the barman, handed over the money and took a steadying gulp through the thin white head of froth. 'Tastes very like bitter to me, friend,' he observed, and took another gulp.

'Heavy,' said Mac. 'We call it "heavy".'

Tally placed his mug carefully down on the bar and pulled up a stool. His level of irritation was sinking with the beer. He was looking for something to take his mind off Nell and Taliska and an in-depth discussion on the mysterious discrepancies between English and Scottish alcoholic nomenclature might fill the bill admirably. 'That's very interesting,' he said seriously. 'I wonder why?'

Mac frowned, trying to decide if Tally was taking the mickey or was genuinely curious. 'I dunno,' he said cautiously. 'Could be because it's heavier than pale.'

'Heavier than pale,' repeated Tally reflectively. 'I take it that pale is what the English call light?'

'Mebbe,' came the noncommittal reply.

'It would be more logical then if the English were to call bitter heavy and the Scots were to call it dark!' Tally was pleased with his analysis and swigged half of his pint on the strength of it.

Mac leaned forward threateningly on his stool. 'You gullin' me?'

''Course I'm not,' replied Tally amiably. 'I'm being friendly. Let's have a Scotch on the strength of it.' He reached out and picked up Mac's glass which was almost empty. 'You look about ready for another drink.'

'Whisky,' muttered Mac wearily. 'We call it whisky.'

Tally thought about this briefly and then nodded. 'Right,' he acknowledged. 'There really is only one kind of whisky, isn't there, and that's Scotch whisky! Two doubles please, barman.'

Stoically Mac forbore to mention that in Scotland you either drank a whisky or a large whisky, there was no such thing as a 'double'. He didn't want to jeopardise the offer.

The net result of this encounter was a pair of grievous hangovers and the start of an unlikely friendship. Tally began to make regular forays to the

Ossian to meet Mac and to make the acquaintance of several other locals, confounding their initial hostility with his easy conversation and chameleon-like ability to blend with his surroundings. Since the laundry facilities at Taliska were at present nil and Nell was digging in her heels about being his washerwoman, his clothes became as grubby as those of the crofters and fishermen and, since shaving in cold water brought him out in a rash, his chin, like theirs, was habitually covered in a stubbly growth of beard.

Nell refused to display any concern at her brother's swift degeneration from City whizz-kid to local yokel. 'Since you look like a night-soil collector you can bloody well empty the Elsan,' was all she said. And, to her surprise, he finally did.

But, while Tally made friends at the pub, Nell became painfully lonely. The days passed busily enough as plumbers and joiners began swarming over the castle, filling the rooms with their jovial banter and perpetual hammering and sawing, to say nothing of the daily problems they turned up demanding to be solved. It was the evenings she found difficult, when the big house was dark and Tally had grabbed a lift to the pub from the last departing workman. In London she had been used to returning to an empty flat, but at least there had been Thatcher and the telephone and the continual underlying big-city hum of traffic and humanity and, when she felt like it, there had been friends to meet and people to see. On Taliska she discovered what it meant to be really alone, surrounded by empty wilderness. Every evening it met her, head-on like a brick wall, unyielding loneliness, stretching minute by minute, hour by hour through the waning light until at last Tally came scuffing up the track to the cottage, fumbling with the latch and swearing mildly as he undressed in the dark. She couldn't tell him of her loneliness for she felt it to be a symptom of her own inadequacy. He had found companionship at the pub but that was almost exclusively a masculine haunt, especially in the winter. Local wives and girlfriends did not go there with their men. They socialised at home or at church or at the weekly ceilidhs in the village hall. None of these meeting places was available to Nell, who was not a church-goer and had no introductions into local female society. Besides, her idea of a good night out was not centred on tea and cakes.

Being lonely didn't stop her eating, however. On the contrary, it was as if she thought she could fill the void in her life by filling her stomach. She ate huge, solitary evening meals of pasta and rice with rich, comforting cream sauces, concocted lovingly on her *Hot Gryll* camp cooker with its two companionable blue-flame jets which hissed conversationally in the empty cottage. And after these platefuls she munched on biscuits, absentmindedly devouring them straight from the packet as she buried her loneliness in the pages of one racy novel after another. If she couldn't yet live the high-life she might as well wallow in it at second-hand . . .

However, by November, when they were safely attached to the main water supply and the plumbers and electricians had finished pulling out old pipes and circuits and putting in new ones, and the joiners had completed their partitions for bathrooms and closets, the plasterers and decorators moved in and Nell saw the opportunity to relieve her personal Mafeking. She put through a call to Leo.

'How was the health farm?' she asked after the usual pleasantries.

'Steamy,' replied Leo with customary *double*

entendre. 'There were mixed saunas. I encountered parts of the female anatomy with which I never expected to become personally acquainted.'

'Kinky!' exclaimed Nell, delighted to hear his familiar nasal drawl with its slight hint of femininity. 'Don't tell me there was no temptation for a shocking-pink-blooded male like yourself.'

'Did I say that?' he asked in a reproachful tone. 'When have I ever passed up an opportunity? I'm still getting free friction rubs from a very muscle-bound masseur, as a matter of fact. How are things going at Broadmoor?'

'Well, there's plenty of friction here too but not as pleasant as yours. Tally's failed to find any female distraction, worse luck, so he bickers with me and drowns his sorrows in the pub. He's become quite one of the boys. Still, although he's getting plastered so are the walls and that's why I'm phoning. How about coming up on a recce? I'd like to discuss some murals.'

'Yes – you bet! I think I could produce quite a good Bacchanal now, after all my sauna research.'

'When can you come? The sooner the better. I could do with your company, to say nothing of your brushwork.'

'How can I resist? I'm tiring of friction rubs, anyway. I'll swap my scene-shifts and come next Friday.'

'I'll send you a plane ticket and you can test out our package deal for us. We've registered with a travel agent to do tickets and arrange transit and helicopters and everything.'

'A helicopter? I fancy that,' crooned Leo excitedly.

'Sorry, Leo. The landing pad isn't finished yet and the lawn's too boggy at present. You'll have to come to Oban by train. I'll meet you – look forward to it.'

Leo arrived like a puff of talcum, soothing Nell's emotional abrasions with his lightweight gossip and getting up Tally's aquiline nose.

'He's OK round a dinner table,' Tally grumbled, 'but he irritates like hell after prolonged exposure.'

'Well, I like him,' declared Nell. 'He makes me laugh and he's had some brilliant ideas for murals. He was browsing among the old library books and found one full of the most fantastic pictures of wildflowers. He wants to use them as the basis for a bedroom theme.'

'What's wrong with wallpaper?'

'God, Tally, you can be so crass at times! Wallpaper's fine but dull. You said yourself you wanted people to remember Taliska. What was your phrase – "reassuringly timeless and enduringly beautiful"?'

'Well, I reckon Leo's not very reassuringly talented and enduringly camp.'

'You wouldn't be just a tiny bit prejudiced, would you? Leo may be gay but he's not camp and he's actually very talented.'

'Well, I'll have to take your word for that.'

'Yes, I'm afraid you will.'

The weather had grown windy and misty and the leaves had lost their hold on the trees and, perversely, Leo asked questions which could only be answered in summer. 'What are the commonest wildflowers that grow on Taliska? Are there any which grow here more readily than elsewhere?'

Eventually Nell hit on the idea of putting him in touch with Granny Kirsty, and between them they came up with a list of ten attractive and unusual flowers after which to name the bedrooms and on which to base a mural for each and a complementary scheme for interior decoration.

Meanwhile the plumbers were battling to install the huge circular jacuzzi baths upon which Tally insisted for the four most luxurious suites. One of these had been fashioned out of two of the rooms on the second floor, but the bend in the upper staircase was too acute to allow the huge bath to be manhandled around it.

'What can we bloody do?' demanded Tally of the foreman builder as they were conferring over midmorning mugs of coffee. Tally's voice was dangerously tense and Nell predicted fireworks. She and Leo were sharing the coffee break, discussing the design of one of the murals. 'Come on, man,' Tally persisted. 'There must *be* a solution. In at the window, perhaps, or down through the cupola?'

The foreman frowned and ground his teeth in the way they had come to realise meant he was revving up to make objections. 'You don't want to touch that,' he muttered. 'They're notorious leakers those things so it's best to leave it well alone.'

Leo looked up from the clipboard on which he was incessantly doodling and drawing. 'Ding, dong, dell,' he said in a singsong voice.

Tally rounded on him belligerently. 'What the hell d'you mean, ding, dong, bloody dell?' he asked roughly. 'Another of your flower-fairy ideas?'

Leo shook his head. 'Ding, dong, dell,' he repeated, grinning hugely. 'Pulleys in the well!'

For a split second Tally looked as if he was going to succumb to his inbuilt aversion and plant a right-hook squarely on Leo's jaw. Then his murderous expression changed and he began to laugh. 'Pulleys in the well! Yes – a bloody good idea. We'll rig up some ropes and pulleys in the stairwell – that should do the trick. Thanks, Leo.' His intended right-hook was adjusted to a pat on the back and the foreman stopped grinding his teeth.

Leo shrugged nonchalantly. 'Scene-shifter's standby,' he said. 'All you need is the right block and tackle. I'll help if you like.'

'Any assistance gratefully received,' agreed Tally who, whatever his faults, did not harbour grudges. His attitude towards Leo changed from that moment.

A few days later the artist left, promising to return with his paints when the basic decoration was completed, and Nell began to scour pattern books and catalogues for fabrics with designs based on native Scottish flora and fauna. It took weeks of planning, which was followed by weeks of waiting while carpets and fabrics were woven to order before soft furnishings could be covered and curtains made.

In the long dark evenings Tally toiled over the brochure. The photographs could wait until decoration was complete but the prose was a major factor. It had to have the allure of a bestseller coupled with the conciseness of a sound-bite. 'Busy people won't read detail,' Tally declared, writing and re-writing on the lap-top personal computer he'd persuaded Hal to lend him until their office was ready and they could install a larger, more permanent system. 'If it takes more than two minutes, it's no good.' He read aloud the material he had assembled so far.

' "Kiss goodbye to care in Taliska's sparkling air. Frolic in our heathers and snuggle in our feathers. Bring us your jaded appetites, your tired relationships and your sagging spirits and we will restore them to prime condition! A few days in the champagne charm of a wild Scottish island, in the unbeatable comfort of our luxurious castle, sustained by the unparalleled lightness of our delicious low-fat cuisine, will put pep in your step and a glint in your eye.

Return romance to your life, by relaxing before blazing log fires or strolling through flower-strewn meadows. Tumble in blissful beds and soak in sensuous spa-baths. Watch the birds and listen to the bees. They know what makes life worth living! There is no dream too fantastic, no fantasy too dream-like for our magical island to bring to life." '

'Steady on, Tally,' warned Nell when she'd heard this latest effort. 'There is a Trades Description Act, you know!'

Towards Christmas the twins moved at last into the main house and then jetted south to spend the festive season between the Marylebone penthouse and Hollywood Gardens. Both agreed that they felt like clumsy strangers in London's sophisticated fairy-lit bustle. It seemed odd that people moved about in such close proximity without pausing to pass the time of day, and disturbing that the prevailing facial expression was disgruntlement, producing an unsettling lack of goodwill among all the tinsel and holly. With surprise and gratification, Nell found that she yearned for Taliska.

The major bonus of the trip was that she persuaded Donalda and Hal to take them to Christmas Eve dinner at Calum Strachan's Knightsbridge hotel-restaurant where she proceeded to sweet-talk the temperamental young chef into coming up to give Taliska the once-over in the New Year.

'I'm no' making any promises, mind,' he warned, staring at her fiercely with his pale-lashed hazel eyes. Nell suspected that his apparent antagonism was a front put up to disguise his desperate desire to be lured back over the border. She knew that they shared a common dissatisfaction, that London had provided the crock of gold but no rainbow to go with it.

'No strings attached,' she agreed equably. 'But since we're paying your fare you might give us some tips about how to equip the kitchen, whether or not it becomes yours.'

Before they flew north again Tally spent two pleasantly hazy days in the company of his father, who used his contacts in the wine and spirit trade to smooth his son's path to a superb selection of vintages for the Taliska cellar. And Nell dragged Sinead around Peter Jones and the General Trading Company browsing among the cutlery, china and glass. Later, when she had selected her designs she would order them direct from the manufacturers at wholesale prices.

Their final evening in London was spent in a small bistro with David and Caroline, who were as ever at arm's length but both agog to hear how the hotel was progressing. 'According to schedule,' Tally lied convincingly. 'There'll be a grand opening at Easter.'

Nell visualised Taliska's empty rooms, half-plastered walls, curtainless windows and cookerless kitchen quarters. 'You must both come,' she urged fervently. 'We should have cracked it by then.' Or cracked up in the attempt, she thought cynically.

Chapter Six

Uttering many a lewd and blasphemous oath, Tally wrestled with a set of giant fire-irons before the cavernous hall fireplace. He looks like a battle-stained knight errant, thought Ann Soutar admiringly, pausing on her way to the reception desk with a box of tariff sheets. Although they were kept as firmly in check as her greying-blonde hair under its wide black-velvet Alice band, Ann Soutar was given to romantic notions and it was true that, with the long, spear-tipped poker in one hand and an enormous pair of fire-tongs in the other, Tally's tall figure did display an air of medieval aggression, though his blue language, grubby jeans and rolled-up shirt-sleeves detracted somewhat from the image of a knight in shining armour.

Ann had joined the Taliska staff at the beginning of March as the hotel secretary-cum-receptionist and was so far proving to be a fairy godmother, able to conjure order out of the rather unbusinesslike chaos of paperwork presented to her, and to magic the complicated computer-printer system supplied by Hal mysteriously into life. Nell had breathed a sigh of relief and handed the secretarial side of things entirely over to her, freeing herself to concentrate on the furnishing and decoration. In the new office in one of the ground-floor tower rooms, Ann and

Tally quickly established the sort of relationship which might have been written into a television sitcom. He teased her unmercifully while she protested and demurred and harboured deeply secret and lustful longings.

Sensing this, Tally was fleetingly tempted to fulfil these repressed desires. After all, he mused lecherously one morning, confined to tedious office work and furtively studying his new secretary, she was only nudging forty, had a trim figure and, he suspected, a lively and passionate nature beneath her calm and ordered exterior. Tally's own demanding libido continued unsatisfied. However, perhaps fortunately for the efficient running of the office, his temptation towards Ann only flowered briefly and was soon obliterated by the arrival of Libby Cox.

'Jeeze, Mr McLean, you beaut!' Libby had purred to Tally on their first meeting, her antipodean slang plainly referring neither to the castle nor the view. She was Australian, a honey-blonde, honey-skinned 'Sheila' with a taut, athletic body and lascivious green eyes which candidly issued a gilt-edged invitation to any man she considered worth more than five seconds' perusal. Tally had rated at least fifteen. She had hitchhiked from London in answer to an advertisement for hotel staff which he had placed at his father's suggestion in the Australian High Commission, and she came wearing the shortest of shorts and the bulkiest of backpacks and trailing her friend and travelling companion, Ginny Thomson, a small, freckle-faced, auburn-haired girl who had shyly admitted during her telephone interview that she was seeking her family's Scottish roots.

'I'm glad you like the place,' responded Tally smoothly, thinking that in Libby's case the voice on the phone had not been misleading. In the flesh she was just as sexy as her telephone manner had suggested. 'We aim to please. Sling your packs in the Fourtrack and I'll take you down to your quarters. They're in the stables, but don't let that put you off. We've installed a few extra comforts we don't allow the animals.'

'I think a stable could be quite comfortable, given enough straw and the right company,' Libby had quipped with a sidelong glance, climbing into the back of the vehicle in such a way as to offer Tally the most advantageous view of her tight round buttocks emerging like large ripe peaches from the high-cut shorts. 'Don't you, Ginny?'

'Not really,' replied her more discreetly trousered friend, sliding into the front seat. 'I don't like horses much.'

Tally slammed the vehicle into first gear and revved off down the newly gravelled back drive which linked the hotel to the stable-block. Most of the living-in staff were to be housed there, the whole upper floor having been converted into bedrooms, bathrooms and a communal lounge/kitchen. 'Well, that's all right because there aren't any,' Tally laughed. 'The island isn't really suitable for riding, as most of it is too steep and rocky. The only animals in thc byrcs arc our two cows, Bridc and Marsali, but they only come in at night and the gardeners look after them.'

'Gardeners?' inquired Libby on a hopeful note. 'How many of them are there?'

'Two – Mick and Rob. They live at the stables as well. You'll meet them soon.'

'Are there many other staff?' asked Libby. 'I mean, the hotel isn't very large, is it?'

'When we open we'll have ten rooms to let, and

the dining room seats forty at full stretch. Some of the staff are local people who work part-time, mostly as cleaners and extra waitresses, when we need them. Then there's Calum, the chef, his assistant Craig, and Ann Soutar, the reception manager. There's a new wine-waiter-cum-barman arriving next week called Tony and then there's me and my sister Nell. Oh, and at the moment Leo's here – he's an artist who's painting some murals. I don't think he's quite your type, though,' he added, glancing sidelong at Libby who was leaning forward in the back seat, her arm resting blatantly along the back of his shoulders rather than the car seat. Her well-scented ear brushed his teasingly. 'You'll meet everyone at dinner. We have it at seven-thirty, though it'll have to be earlier when we open.'

'When will that be, Mr McLean?' Ginny asked, climbing out of the Fourtrack which had pulled up with a squeal of brakes in the stableyard. Like Nell, Tally had become fond of the battered four-wheel-drive vehicle she had bought as a hotel runabout. More often than not these days the BMW sat in the garage. In time it would be used to meet guests off the train in Oban or ferry them from the now-completed helicopter landing pad.

'Opening date is officially Good Friday, but we're having a kind of warm-up house-party for friends and relations the weekend before, just so we can iron out any problems before the paying guests arrive. In all, we have ten days to get the place shipshape.' He had eyed the two girls appraisingly, letting his gaze rest twice as long on Libby, who returned it with a frank and knowing smile. 'You look quite fit,' he remarked. 'I hope you're ready for some hard work.'

'I think you'll find us ready for anything, Mr

McLean,' Libby had replied emphatically and even Ginny, who was used to her friend's ways, blushed at the stress on 'anything'.

'Have you solved the problem with the fire?' Ann asked, rousing herself from her knightly reverie. 'It still seems a bit smoky in here.' She sniffed the distinctly acrid atmosphere then jumped as Tally turned on her, delivering a series of swashbuckling flourishes with the poker.

'She will not succumb to my will, Miss Soutar,' he complained in mock despair. 'I have poked her and bellowed her and fed her succulent fruitwood logs, but she will not lie down and burn for me. All she does is send out smoke signals like a demented Indian squaw.'

'Oh dear,' murmured Ann with a suppressed giggle. 'Perhaps you should try a blanket. My old auntie had a fire that smoked and she used to hang a blanket from the mantelpiece to make it draw.'

'It would have to be a damn big blanket for this fireplace.' Tally bent to poke angrily once more at the reluctant conflagration, knocking a log off-balance and dispatching a shower of sparks into the room. 'Bloody hell, look at that,' he declared, stamping on a glowing cinder which threatened to ignite the dustsheet he had prudently spread over the new carpet. 'If the sparks won't go up the chimney, what hope have we of the smoke rising in that direction? And I've got the fire inspector coming this afternoon.'

'Haven't you cured it yet?' Nell asked, echoing Ann's inquiry as she came in the main entrance, followed by two hefty-looking characters in overalls. 'These men need to empty their van but I don't want them bringing the new sofa and chairs in here if the cushions are going to end up stinking of smoke before anyone has even sat on them.'

'Stash them in the drawing room for now and shut the door,' suggested Tally, staring balefully at the sinister grey wreaths crawling under the mantelpiece and out into the room. 'We'll move them around later. This fire needs more than just a good poke. Perhaps we need new pots on the chimney.'

'The sweep said they were all right,' Nell reminded him, nodding at the two men to fetch their load.

'The sweep didn't know what was at stake,' retorted Tally. 'How can we expect our guests to fantasise about making love before blazing log fires when the first thing that greets them on arrival is a smoke-house?'

'And a kippered receptionist,' added Ann, who still did not wholly believe that Taliska was intended to be a haven for flagging libidos. The tone of Tally's brochure had made her blush but, truth be known, she was quite looking forward to observing the antics of the guests it attracted – outside the bedrooms, of course!

'You could ask the fire inspector if he has any ideas,' suggested Nell. 'He must know something about smoke. After all, there's no fire without it!'

The fire inspector, however, turned out to be rather unapproachable. He was a young, dark-suited Gestapo-type who marched noisily on steel-tipped soles and heels through every room, staircase and corridor clutching a clipboard holding an official form scattered with little boxes, in each of which he scribbled, one after the other. Accompanied by Tally and scarcely uttering a word, he tested the smoke alarms, which had only been re-connected just before his arrival owing to their propensity to squeal whenever the hall fire belched, checked every emergency light and every extinguisher, noted every hose and bucket, applied lighted matches to the curtains and upholstery and timed how long it took him to get from the top tower room down to the front drive. An exterior fire escape had been built at the far end of the Victorian wing, reached through specially adapted windows in the housemaids' pantries, and Tally was reasonably happy that he and Nell had complied with all the requirements specified by the regional fire authority, without whose licence an hotel could not open for business.

He was totally unprepared therefore for the inspector's response at the end of his route-march when he stopped so suddenly and with such military precision that for one mesmerising instant Tally thought the po-faced young man might actually shout 'Heil Hitler.' Instead he said grimly, 'I'm afraid it will not do, Mr McLean,' tucking his clipboard under his arm and fixing his escort with a stern glare.

Since they were standing in the hall Tally could only assume he was referring to the gently smoking fire in the grate. 'It only smokes a little,' he protested. 'I'm sure we'll solve the problem in a day or two. It's just that the fireplace hasn't been used for a long time.'

Himmler's Double shook his head. 'No, I don't mean the fireplace. I mean the question of access to and from the upper floors.'

'I don't understand,' said Tally, puzzled. 'There's a metal fire escape at the eastern end and a stone staircase at the western end. The regulations stipulate that for an hotel our size there must be two fire-proof staircases, isn't that so?'

'Precisely, Mr McLean. *Two* staircases,' agreed the official. 'Which means that *that* one will have to go.' He nodded his head emphatically in the direction of the ornate galleried staircase which was the central feature of Taliska's entrance hall. All traces of its original smoke-blackened state had been erased and the whole edifice was bathed in rainbow light from the newly washed stained-glass cupola in the roof. Its finely carved oak flights and banisters had been cleaned and polished to deep golden perfection, two noble lions supporting subtly coloured heraldic shields guarded its newel-posts and its shallow treads were carpeted in soft mushroom-coloured Wilton, especially woven and figured with dark purply-blue scabious – a wildflower which studded the island's grasslands from July to September. It was an architectural composition of grace and elegance, designed to transform any ascent or descent into a journey of sensuous delight.

There was a long silence during which Tally's astounded gaze shifted from the staircase to the fire inspector and then back to the staircase. He appeared to be counting each individual banister, so long did he stare at it, and then a fiercely quizzical look came over his face as he turned once more towards his visitor. 'Excuse me?' he inquired coldly. 'I see no staircase. If you are referring to this beautiful item of antique furniture then I must hasten to assure you that if, by any extraordinary chance, someone happened to set a foot upon it, it would only be in the same uneducated way that a Philistine might stand upon a priceless Chippendale chair in order to change a light bulb!'

There was another tense silence, during which the fresh, downy cheek of Himmler's Double turned deep red. He dropped his eyes uncertainly to the form on the clipboard with its mysterious boxes and entries. 'Well, yes,' he stuttered. 'I think I can see what you mean. An item of furniture . . . Very well, if you say so.' He made an indecipherable squiggle at the base of the form and removed it from its restraint. 'In that case everything seems to be in order. Your certificate, Mr McLean.'

Tally took the essential document and studied it carefully before turning and handing it to Ann who stood quietly behind her reception desk observing events. 'Our fire certificate, Ann. File it under F if you please and show Mr Himm . . . Hoskins out. I have urgent business in the attic. Goodbye, Mr Hoskins – and thank you.' Tally shook the young man's hand.

Ann placed the paper on the desk, put on a bright smile and approached the inspector whose face registered shocked astonishment as Tally turned and bounded blithely up his precious 'item of antique furniture', two steps at a time.

Tally's urgent business in the attic was, in fact, an afternoon rendezvous with Libby who, in her present pre-opening capacity as cleaner and chambermaid, had agreed to give his apartment the once-over. However, her plastic bucket of cleaning utensils stood untended in the small lobby between the bedroom and the sitting room when Tally arrived, almost tripping over it in his eagerness to make sure that the longer-than-expected fire-inspection did not mean Libby had been – and gone. He needn't have worried. The Australian girl was in his bedroom, twisting and turning before the long mirror on his wardrobe door while her hands tweaked irritably at the bodice and skirt of the deep blue silky dress she was wearing. Her working overall was lying where she had thrown it on the floor.

'Polishing your image?' inquired Tally languidly, leaning on the door-jamb and observing her writhings with an amused smile.

'Jeeze, it'll need some polishing in this dress,' exclaimed Libby, not in the least discomfited by his sudden arrival. 'I just thought I'd try it on while I was waiting. We're supposed to serve dinner in these, but they're enough to put anybody right off their grub. Look at the frumpy length of the skirt – and the bodice makes my top half look like a sack of spuds.'

'Which it certainly isn't.' Tally moved further into the room for a closer inspection, closing the door carefully behind him. 'Mm,' he pondered, his eyes sweeping Libby's lissome figure from her sandalled brown feet to her tumbled blonde hair. 'It would certainly look better off than on.'

Her green eyes met his in the mirror, wide open and innocent and entirely at odds with the wicked tilt of her smile. 'Are you suggesting we serve dinner in the nuddy?' she inquired archly in her flat, antipodean drawl.

'Only to me,' replied Tally baldly, returning her smile tilt for tilt.

'It isn't dinner-time, though,' she said, glancing pointedly at her watch. 'It's arvo tea-time.'

'Arvo tea? What the hell's that?' he demanded.

'What you drink in the arvo, of course! In the a-after no-oon!' she repeated, plumping out the vowels with English twee-ness.

'I'd like to try some of this arvo-tea,' he declared, sitting down pointedly on the bed. 'Is it sweet and wet and served from a billycan?'

She moved towards him, still smoothing down the

silky skirt of her dress. 'No, it's hot and steaming and served with honey.' Her blue silk breasts were level with his face and she knew he wanted to reach out and touch them but she turned to confront him with the zipper which ran the length of the back. 'Could you undo me, please?' she requested with a giggle in her voice.

'With pleasure,' Tally murmured, running the tab down the zip like lightning and pulling her on to his knee in almost the same movement. 'Which particular bit do you want undone first?'

Without waiting for any reply his hands were inside the dress and his mouth was on hers, his tongue probing through her parted teeth. He had been so many unaccustomed weeks without sex that his urgency was all too hard and obvious under her squirming buttocks, a fact which seemed to encourage rather than deter the enthusiastic Libby. Within seconds the dress was over her head and he realised with a shock of pleasure that she'd been wearing nothing underneath. A titillating thought occurred to spice his immediate oral exploration of her bouncy, honey-coloured breasts with their hard, burnt-sienna nipples. Did she scrub floors with no knickers on? God, he must watch her next time she was cleaning the stairs! Who knew what a view there might be between the banisters! Meanwhile she was struggling to release what seemed like a banister between his own legs from the restriction of his trousers, and very soon the king-size bed upon which he had insisted was being used for the specific purpose for which he had intended it, and Libby was urging him on with the kind of Australian expletives never heard in *Neighbours*!

★ ★ ★

The new kitchen at Taliska became Calum Strachan's kingdom. In it he was ruler, despot and, occasionally, a benign dictator. During his New Year visit, Nell and Tally had persuaded him that here was an opportunity not only to return to his beloved Scotland, but also to preserve his position at the top of his profession and to develop a whole new style of cuisine which might in time be as renowned as that of the Roux brothers or even the great Escoffier himself. While he worked out his notice in London, Calum had sent detailed plans of the fixtures and fittings he required at Taliska and, when he arrived at the beginning of March, the twins were granted one policy meeting which turned out to be more like an imperial audience. They were then banned entirely from the kitchen while Calum went about 'running in' the new equipment, and creating his menus. Only one other person was permitted into this culinary closed shop and that was a lad called Craig Armstrong, the gangling young son of the proprietor of the local craft-shop, a lady who just happened to be an old schoolfriend of Calum's mother. Craig was sixteen and had been begging to be allowed to leave school and start cooking, and his apprenticeship to Calum was by way of a test, to see if he really did want to make *haute cuisine* his career.

Calum did his best to make Craig's life a misery. The boy was kept peeling and chopping and pounding and pot-washing for ten hours a day, and when he was occasionally allowed near the stove, his culinary efforts were subjected to such minute inspection and scathing criticism that the average sixteen-year-old would have departed screaming after a week. Craig, on the other hand, just shrugged and set out to try again, telling his mother when he crawled exhausted to his home that Calum Strachan was the most fantastic person he had ever met.

As March wore on, new and imaginative dishes began to emerge from the kitchen's pristine, stainless-steel interior, and the staff were asked to comment on them at meal-times. Nell wasn't sure whether this was a good idea since she imagined Calum's tether to be extremely short when it came to criticism but, to her surprise, he listened attentively to what the others said, even when Mick the gardener, reared up a close in Glasgow, disgustedly pushed away a dish of stir-fried breast of duck with pine kernels and demanded 'a decent plate o' mince an' tatties'.

'He was right,' Calum remarked later, putting a red line through the rejected dish in his notebook. 'It was too greasy. Duck is fatty and pine kernels are oily, and I should never have put them together. Maybe I'll try turkey breast and toasted almonds instead.' He pronounced the 'l' in almonds in a soft Scottish way which Nell thought made them sound even tastier. She often shared a coffee break with Calum, enjoying his culinary obsessions and driving ambition.

'As long as it's not macadamia nuts,' she sniggered.

'What have you got against macadamia nuts?' inquired Calum with interest. When she told him about Gloria he laughed, his pale cheeks creasing with amusement.

'I think that's the first time I've seen you smile since you came here,' Nell told him. 'I've been worried that you weren't happy.'

Calum considered this, returning to his habitual gravity. 'Starting a new venture is no' a time for being happy,' he observed eventually. 'I havena exactly noticed you splitting your sides, either. Time for that when we're a success.'

'How do you feel about it, Calum? Will Taliska be a success, do you think?' she asked tentatively. Nell had to admit to herself that she found Calum rather attractive. Like his voice, the young chef's looks were pleasantly and distinctively Scottish. His deep red hair, white skin which would instantly freckle if it should ever be exposed to the sun, and intelligent hazel eyes set in a fringe of whitish lashes proved unexpectedly magnetic. He was of average height for his race, five foot seven or eight, and surprisingly lithe and trim for a man who spent almost his every waking hour preparing food.

Ruminatively he felt his chin where the stubble grew as red as his hair. 'Aye, I think it will,' he said at length. 'As long as that brother of yours has got his marketing right.'

There had been little sign of Tally during February. Once delivery of his wine cellar was complete he had disappeared with the BMW stacked high with promotional literature, and had returned just in time to find Ann moving in on the filing system. He brought with him a diary full of provisional bookings, mostly from financial contacts, but his theory was that everyone who possessed money had to be on sociable terms with their bankers and brokers and it was through these contacts that word would spread to the wealthy and jaded of Taliska's uniquely restorative character.

'It only takes one man to make a few nudge-nudge, wink-winks at a bankers' dinner for several of his colleagues to start thinking they're missing out on something and want to try it for themselves,' he predicted. 'You wait and see. I've already got the promise of an article in the *American Express* travel journal and we'll be in *Forbes* magazine next April.

Concorde will be booked up with randy traders flocking from Wall Street with their secretaries, no matter what the pound is doing to the dollar. British Airways should give us an award.'

'It's hotel guide awards we need,' Nell said. 'I hope Michelin and Egon Ronay hurry up and pay us a visit.' Their investment in Taliska was enormous and often at night, poring over the accounts in her tower room, she would crunch her way through a whole packet of chocolate biscuits in sheer panic at the size of the overdraft.

Tally was accustomed to million-pound accounting. On the commodity exchanges he had regularly handled eight-nought deals. He knew there was serious money always circulating in the world and, despite almost daily statistics reporting the soaring level of business failures, he remained confident that there was still a hard core of people who would happily part with considerable sums if they were convinced that what they were spending it on would add to their *cachet*, however grand that might already be. To him Taliska was like a mistress – beautiful and desirable, a possession to be cherished and adorned, which others would covet and which he would share with them for the right price. It was he who set the charges, putting such a spectacular tariff on the hotel's rooms and services that Nell protested that no one would ever come. 'You wait and see,' he said, smiling knowingly. 'People will pay a great deal for something they really want, and they will desire Taliska because she is irresistible. All we have to do is make sure they know about her.' It was significant that he consistently referred to the island in the feminine gender.

Alasdair McInnes had become a frequent visitor, kindly bringing contracts to sign and returning documents checked, rather than always expecting Tally or Nell to come to Oban. 'It gives me a pleasant break from the office,' he told them, 'and I enjoy watching the conversion develop.' Despite the fact that it had been she who had first contacted him, Nell noticed that although he always paused for a social chat with her, when it came to business, with the unspoken gravitation of male towards male, the lawyer tended to seek out Tally, as if unable to credit Nell with any real responsibility.

Nell felt increasingly that people saw Taliska as Tally's project. Yet it had been she who had initiated the whole idea in the first place, she who had chosen almost every item of furniture, crockery and glass, every fabric, carpet and colour scheme, even down to the bedlinen and towels. Her brother had appropriated it, like he acquired women, by sheer willpower, and these days Nell saw herself reduced to junior level, little more than a name on the notepaper. She knew it was a form of paranoia but could not dismiss it, and it grew stronger as the hotel staff began to arrive. They had all been recruited by Tally during his travels, with the result that, although the ownership arrangement had been explained to them, they all intuitively set out to please him rather than her. It was Tally whom they considered to be The Boss. Nell began to wonder if people thought her the wrong size and shape to be taken seriously. Perhaps fat was short for fatuous, she thought.

The exception was Calum. In so far as he considered himself contracted to anyone other than himself it was to Nell, and in mid-March he graciously allowed her into the kitchen. To begin with she watched, also doing her share of the chopping and peeling, much to Craig's relief, but gradually she began to move in on the ovens and hobs, making soup, preparing roasts, mixing batters. Calum used no pastry, made no cakes and included little cream in his recipes. All the milk which arrived daily from the two Jersey cows was separated and the cream was matured into a delicious Taliska cheese which was to be offered as a final course at dinner, mixed with fresh herbs from the garden and rolled in a traditional Scottish way in toasted oatmeal. Where milk was needed it was used skimmed. Calum himself jealously guarded the prerogative of creating and cooking the all-important sauces and stir-fries which were to become the hallmarks of his cuisine. His vegetables were cooked only enough to make them hot, soups were thickened with egg or left clear and thin, his sauces were reduced stocks or purées rather than buttery liaisons, and his fruity desserts were leavened with beaten egg-white rather than whipped cream. Every dish was feather-light and delicately flavoured, and guests were to be encouraged to have second helpings if they felt the five-course menus were not substantial enough. Nell and Calum agreed that they didn't want people leaving the dining room hungry, but nor did they want them liverish and lethargic. The ultimate intention was that their guests should leave Taliska refreshed, relaxed and restored, demanding more of everything so that they would come again.

'I think we might have a problem, Ms McLean.'

Nell noticed with irritation that Rob Fraser always used the ambiguous feminine form of address when he spoke to her, laying subtle stress on the *Ms* in a way she found rather disturbing. She couldn't persuade him to call her Nell and she couldn't help feeling there was some sinister motive for this. As a gardener-handyman Rob was an enigma. He was vastly over-qualified, having studied geology at Edinburgh University and worked subsequently for the National Geological Survey. But a year ago, for some reason which he had not divulged, he had resigned his post and taken to a wandering existence, fruit-picking, odd-jobbing and living off social security before applying for the Taliska job. However, his references from the Survey were good and Tally saw no objection to a graduate geologist digging the vegetable garden and milking the cows if that was what he chose to do.

For some reason Nell always found it difficult to meet Rob's eyes. They were yellowish-brown and slightly protuberant, and always seemed to be trying to add unspoken meaning to the mundane words which came out of his mouth. He was dark and good-looking in a wild, long-haired way and gave an overall impression of prowling intensity, occasionally illuminated by a dazzling grin revealing strong and even white teeth. He reminded Nell of what the young Sean Connery must have been like, before they dressed him in a dinner jacket and made him shaken and not stirred.

'What problem, Rob?' she asked reluctantly. He had cornered her in the storeroom where she was checking toiletry supplies and she was anxious to go straight to the kitchen afterwards because Calum had promised to show her how to clear consommé.

Rob leaned on the door-frame, blocking her exit. He was grinning and fiddling with the thin leather thong he habitually wore tied around his throat. 'Travellers,' he said. 'I saw them when I was putting up the new sign by the bridge. They're camping in McCandlish's field.'

'What sort of travellers?' Nell asked, resignedly

pausing in the midst of a loo-roll count, knowing she would have to start again.

'You know the sort – they call them New Age travellers. They drive old buses and vans and move all over the place. Mostly they live off the social.'

'As you used to?' Nell had voiced the question before she thought better of it.

Rob grinned slowly. 'Yes, Ms McLean, as I used to. That's how I know what they're like – and they're trouble.'

Nell sighed with exasperation. 'Oh God! Please explain what you mean. We have troubles enough with only a week to go. Why should they make more?'

'There's only a few of them at the moment but they'll be just an advance party, making the arrangements. There'll be more of them coming if they've found a good patch. Hundreds more.'

Nell finally grasped the significance of his words. 'Hundreds – right on our doorstep? Oh no! You're telling me that the guests will have to fight their way through a mob of gypsies to get here?' She slammed her stock-book down on a sack of oatmeal. 'Come on. You'd better show me.'

The Fourtrack was in the yard behind the storeroom. In her agitation Nell spun all four wheels and scattered the gravel as she accelerated. Rob gripped the dashboard with white knuckles. 'It's all right,' he muttered anxiously. 'They won't go away.'

The fresh new sign on the end of the bridge read ISLE OF TALISKA HOTEL: LUXURY AT ITS MOST REWARDING in elegant royal-blue lettering on a cream ground. Blue scabious-flowers, chosen as the hotel logo, decorated the scrolled border. Beyond the sign, in a field still straggly with long brown winter grasses and dead teasels, a motley collection of vehicles was parked in a rough circle. Smoke drizzled into the sky from a scattering of camp-fires, and several flea-bitten dogs nosed hopefully in holes for rabbits. The gate was open, sagging off its hinges, and Nell drove through it, the Fourtrack bouncing wildly over the dips and hillocks of the unkempt meadow. She halted within a few yards of a multicoloured double-decker bus covered in spray-painted graffiti.

A bedraggled man in a dark red shirt and dirty black jacket and trousers approached as Rob and Nell got out. 'What d'you want?' he demanded flatly.

'I was going to ask you the same question,' replied Nell. 'Do you have permission to camp here?'

'Yup,' said the man, crossing his arms belligerently over his chest. Two more individuals joined him from different corners of the camp, a large bullish bouncer-type in a filthy quilted waistcoat and a rather beautiful but grimy woman carrying a small child on her hip.

'What business is it of yours anyway, Fatty?' the woman asked Nell baldly. 'Waddle off and leave us alone! We don't like cows like you nosing around our camp.'

There was a loud snigger from the thug and a slow grin spread over the first man's face. 'If you don't like somfink darlin', go and bovver Farmer Giles. 'E says it's OK so it's OK – right?' He put his arm around the woman's shoulder, letting his hand drop possessively onto her grubby cheese-muslined breast, which he stroked absentmindedly while she smiled insolently at Nell. Several older children gathered around the group and a sprinkling of adults ceased what they were doing to stare in their direction.

Nell felt herself blushing furiously, acutely aware

that Rob was beside her and had heard the woman's taunts. Without further comment she turned on her heel and climbed back into the driving seat. Rob heaved himself silently in beside her and she drove back through the gateway, peering through tears of anger and humiliation.

The farmyard was two hundred yards further up the road. It was a tip of a place, hemmed in by rusting corrugated iron roofs and uneven breeze-block walls which looked as if they would tumble in the mildest zephyr. Dirty cattle milled about in an enclosure outside two ramshackle deep-litter sheds. Beneath their feet was a morass of rotting straw and trampled bovine excrement, and the stench was indescribable.

'Thank God our guests won't have to see this,' muttered Nell, who had controlled her tears of mortification with several shuddering breaths only to find that the air she inhaled made her gag. 'How can he treat his beasts like that? Where is the bloody man?'

The farmer's name was Duncan McCandlish. His run-down 300-acre farm marched along the opposite shore of the Kyleshee from Taliska. On it he reared beef cattle and a few pigs, and kept a huge red Shorthorn bull called Ruairidh. He was an eccentric, irascible bachelor who would do anything for an easy buck and had an irrational distrust of women.

The farmhouse was as derelict as the rest of the buildings. The bell did not work so Nell hammered loudly on the cracked door-frame, dislodging some of its flaking paintwork. It was several minutes before McCandlish responded but eventually he opened the door and stood silent, gloomily chewing a mouthful of his interrupted meal. He was short, thickset, middle-aged and balding and he wore filthy corduroy trousers slung on khaki braces and a fleecy cotton check shirt with a grubby kerchief tied as a sweat-band around his neck. His eyes were bleary and he stank of the whisky with which he had been washing down his meat pie.

'Have you given permission for those people to camp by the bridge?' asked Nell, firmly quashing her misgivings.

'Aye. I told 'em they could stay as long as they liked,' McCandlish said truculently, ignoring Nell and addressing Rob. Nell fumed at this snub but let Rob do the talking.

'Have they paid rent for the field, Mr McCandlish?' the handyman asked suspiciously.

''Course they have!' sneered the farmer. 'You don't think I'm letting them flatten some of my best grazing for nothing, do you? They paid rent fair and square, in advance.'

'How many months in advance?'

'Three, if it's any of your business,' replied McCandlish aggressively.

'They'll be here for three months?' exclaimed Nell, aghast. 'That's the best part of our season!'

'That's what they paid for,' said McCandlish, wiping his mouth on the edge of his kerchief. 'And that's what they'll get. So now you know. Good day!' He stepped back and shoved the door shut so hard that it almost took their noses off.

'Charming man,' snarled Nell, picking her way back to the Fourtrack over chicken-wire and dog dirt. Frenzied barking had orchestrated the entire encounter but, perhaps fortunately, the canine perpetrators were confined somewhere in the maze of decaying buildings.

'There must be something we can do,' she moaned as she drove back towards the bridge. Some of the older children from the camp were dancing like dervishes at the side of the road making V signs at them as they passed. 'I'd like to run the little brats down!' she stormed, clutching grimly at the steering wheel, fighting the temptation to swing it in their direction.

Rob laughed harshly. 'That would really put you up shit creek,' he commented. 'Dangerous driving, grievous bodily harm and the undying enmity of the entire New Age travelling fraternity all in one go. It's not worth it!'

'But they'll ruin everything,' she groaned, not noticing the unusual familiarity of his language. 'I'll have to see our lawyer.'

'Lawyers? Huh!' muttered Rob scathingly.

Nell steered the Fourtrack into its usual place in the back yard and angrily switched off the engine. She was reaching for the doorhandle when Rob suddenly said, 'It's not true, you know.'

'What isn't?' She paused in the action of opening the door.

'What that woman said. She called you a fat cow. It's not true.'

Nell did not respond. The woman's words were busy branding themselves on her brain. She did not wish to discuss them. It was the old story of instant judgments.

'You could be thinner, of course, but you would be if you had a man,' Rob went on conversationally. 'You should use a bit of what you have, to lose a bit of what you have. You might find it fun!'

Nell could not believe what she was hearing. She did not know whether to laugh or cry. In a not very subtle way, Rob was propositioning her! In one bound her paranoia leaped from the foothills to the high peaks. Did her roly-poly image make her a target for roly-poly? Tally was not only 'The Boss' it seemed but she, Nell, was just 'one of the girls', open to offers, a candidate for a bit of nooky in the storeroom!

'I bet I would,' she murmured, pushing the door fully open. 'But right now, Rob, "fun" is rather low on my agenda. It comes somewhere below Paracetamol and a hot bath. If you see my brother, tell him about the travellers, would you? And tell him I'm ringing the lawyer.' She jumped down from the car and slammed the door, stalking away with what she hoped was an expressively affronted back.

'I'm afraid there's very little we can do,' Alasdair said gloomily, staring across the Kyleshee at the travellers' camp-site. There were at least thirty vehicles there now, with more arriving by the minute. 'They have permission and they've paid rent. They're entitled to stay.'

'What about health regulations?' Nell asked with a shudder. 'Surely the authorities must be able to enforce certain standards? The kyle will be a sewer soon.'

'The council has sent out inspectors,' Alasdair explained. 'They've ensured that latrine pits have been dug and a fresh water source is available.'

'But they don't use them,' growled Tally. 'We've already found piles of crap under the bridge.'

'It's disgusting!' snarled Nell. 'And they don't keep to their side of the kyle. We've found plenty of evidence that they've been on the island. Mick discovered rabbit snares in the east meadow. If the cows get those round their feet they'll be badly injured.'

In fact, Mick's report from the meadow at breakfast that morning had had the whole staff in hysterics. Rob's fellow outdoor worker was a stocky, talkative Irish-Glaswegian called Mick Lenahan, who had learned his agricultural and horticultural skills on the farm at a rural List D school for young offenders to which he'd been sent at the age of sixteen after a Glasgow Children's Panel had declared him to be 'an habitual petty criminal'. Emerging from the school at nineteen he had been found an agricultural job and had never returned to the city, thus avoiding the strain its influences exerted on his negligible respect for the law. Consequently his record had remained clean and he came to Taliska with a glowing recommendation from his former employer, an Ayrshire dairy-farmer. Mick's experience with stock was invaluable when it came to the Taliska cows.

Returning to breakfast after milking them and turning them out as usual, he described the snares he had found and then he also baldly announced that he had seen Marsali 'bulling' Bride. 'She's needin' done,' he added with a sheepish grin and the hint of a blush on his stubbly cheek. Further probing by Tally had elicited the information that Marsali was showing all the signs of a cow ready for insemination and that if she was left unattended, her milk supply would start to dry up. Amid raucous laughter from the rest of the staff, Tally had stared blankly at Mick and finally asked what he would suggest.

'Well, if ye havena a bull handy, you'll need to call the AI man,' said Mick simply. 'The local Farmers' Union'll ken the number.'

An arrangement was duly made with the artificial insemination agency, who agreed to call as soon as possible with some suitable Jersey-bull semen. And all this, thought Tally wryly, before he had even cracked his breakfast egg!

'The police will be keeping a close eye on the camp,' Alasdair continued sympathetically. 'You must report all incidents of illegal action to them.' He noticed Nell's somewhat puffy eyes and cracked lips and decided that the strain of the feverish preparations for the opening must be telling.

'Have you been to see McCandlish?' Tally asked. 'Isn't he concerned that they'll overrun his farm, injure his stock? Apart from anything else they have scores of wild-looking dogs which must surely get into fights with his aggressive curs.' Tally had already run foul of McCandlish's cattle dogs. Returning half-cut from the Ossian one night he'd had to leg it for the bridge and had only just managed to slam the wrought-iron gate in their snarling teeth. The gate worked on an electronic control and was monitored from the house by a remote TV-camera high in one of the Scots pines. If the worst came to the worst, they could keep it closed against the travellers but there were disadvantages. They'd have to keep a permanent vigil on the monitor in order to operate the gate for guests, and a closed gate did not exactly encourage the casual, bona fide visitors which no new hotel could afford to deter.

'I did see McCandlish and I must say he seemed almost gleefully unconcerned,' Alasdair replied. He found himself wishing he could smooth the lines of anxiety from Nell's tense face, but knew his words would have the opposite effect. 'He said that as long as they were here the travellers could have the run of the place. They'd paid for it, he said.'

'The man's a rogue!' exclaimed Tally. 'I wonder how much he fleeced them for it.'

'At least *he's* got compensation,' muttered Nell darkly. 'And what's the betting he's already had an

EC set-aside grant for that field? He's laughing all the way to the bank, whereas we shall end up having to explain to some po-faced investment banker why people are not exactly eager to flock through a mass of broken-down vehicles and unwashed bodies to use our luxurious facilities.' She turned an anguished face to the lawyer. 'Oh Alasdair, can't you do anything?' Through all the meetings and signing of contracts and agreements over the past six months they, at least, had come to first-name terms.

'I really don't see that I can, Nell. I'm very sorry.' Alasdair kept his educated Scots brogue carefully precise while regretting the nature of his answer.

'God! What the hell's the use of a lawyer who can't use the law?' she flared angrily.

'Steady on, Nell,' murmured Tally. 'It's not Alasdair's fault. At least most of the Easter guests are coming in by helicopter so they won't have to run the travellers' gauntlet . . . Christ, just look, will you? Here come some more. There are hundreds of them!'

'I'm afraid you've got wolves at the gate,' observed Alasdair with powerless sympathy.

'More like snakes in the bloody grass,' retorted Nell, stomping away up the drive, unable to stand the sight of yet another procession of rattle-trap vehicles bearing down on their painstakingly created paradise island.

Chapter Seven

The pre-opening house-party at Taliska had to be held behind locked gates. So many travellers had gathered by the Friday that a spectacular selection of clapped-out vehicles, having failed to find room in McCandlish's field, now occupied every available yard of grass verge leading up to the bridge. Only the thin strip of metalled road was accessible to through-traffic and, since the travellers had by now become all too familiar with the black BMW, each time it passed they greeted it with a particularly rich medley of taunts and catcalls. Alasdair McInnes had taken out a court injunction which was supposed to guarantee hotel staff and guests unchallenged access, but a flimsy bit of paper meant little to the travellers and, as Alasdair pointed out to a despairing Nell, they didn't actually do any physical harm to anyone; they simply made entering or leaving the island a laborious and nerve-wracking experience. Also a smelly one, since there was no longer anything fairy-like about the Kyleshee. Fast though the current ran with the ebb and flow of the tide, it could not cope with the wave of raw sewage from the travellers' camp.

'Well, me old mate,' drawled David Guedalla, having fought through to be greeted by Tally at the great, studded castle door. 'I see your creditors have finally caught up with you.'

'Yeah,' Tally responded, slipping back instantly into City-comrade mode. '*Mea* bloody *culpa*! What a cock-up. It's like Alcatraz, isn't it? Still, at least this prison is a damn sight more comfortable. Come and see your cell. If Caroline has finally succumbed to your masculine charms you'll be able to have a ball.'

'I've given up that particular chase,' said David cheerfully, following his friend up the main stair. 'I have other schemes afoot,' he added, too softly for Tally's ear.

'You don't get a sea view until you bloody well pay for it,' Tally told him as he opened the door to David's room on the second floor. 'It's the back drab for you, I'm afraid.'

'Phew!' whistled David in awe as he entered. 'Some back drab.'

He had been allocated the only letting room which did not look out over the loch. It was situated above Tally's flat which was over the kitchen but, in order to compensate for the lack of external spectacle, Nell had furnished and finished the room with extra care. One of the original four-poster beds had been carried up from the floor below and fully restored, the carved oak uprights picked out in gold leaf and hung with deep royal-blue damask curtains topped by a gold-braided tester. There were bright blue and gold print armchairs either side of a beautiful inlaid rosewood table, on which stood a huge vase of spring flowers, and the window curtains were in the same royal-blue damask, the swagged pelmet fringed and piped with gold to soften and frame the stark landscape of rocks and grass and bare, stunted trees beyond the glass. The walls were sponge-painted pale green with a Leo frieze of hand-painted blue scabious trailing sinuously around the room at head height. It was elegant and restful, and unquestionably earned David's admiring whistle.

'I detect the Nell touch here, do I not?' he inquired.

'Yes, the girl's gone mad on wildflowers,' said Tally, briefly reaching up to touch the frieze. 'She's called all the rooms after flowers that bloom on the island and this is her favourite – *Scabious*. She calls it Taliska's emblem. Leo's been here for weeks painting a frieze in each room. He's been so hard at it he hasn't got round to my mural in the gym yet. He probably won't care, but after all these petals and sepals, if I were him I couldn't wait to paint a bit of tit and bum for a change.'

'You're still a Philistine, Tally,' remarked David, opening the bathroom door. Inside was all gilt-edged mirrors and white tiles with the same blue-flowered frieze on the walls, gold taps and fitting gleaming on bath and basins. He fingered the shower door made of thick smoked glass engraved with the hotel emblem. 'There's also a pretty plant called thrift that grows about these parts, I believe, but I bet there's not a room called after that.'

'I should think not!' Tally was horrified. '*Spend*-thrift would be more like it.'

David laughed. 'Well, if you've got it, flaunt it. How is Nell, by the way? Are you two still speaking to each other?'

Tally made a wry face. 'Just about. She's fine. She's in her element these days helping the chef in the kitchen. I think it must be true love. You can't keep her out of the place.'

'Oh, really?' David raised a quizzical eyebrow and chewed his lower lip pensively for a few seconds. Something had given him pause for thought. But after a time he asked, 'So, no regrets, Tally?'

'No, not really. Not now that Libby Cox has

breezed in from Oz, anyway. She's raised the temperature a bit, I'm glad to say. You'll meet her at dinner. She's one of the waitresses – the one with the satisfied smile!' Tally made a lewd gesture and chuckled, heading for the door. 'I'll let you unpack. Drinks in the bar at seven-thirty. I hope you'll go away with a satisfied smile too, when you leave here.'

'I'll be working on it,' David called to his friend's departing back.

The first floor of the hotel had been allocated to the twins' family, many and various, and Nell was nervously wondering how successfully the parental pairs would co-habit. Apart from the odd unscheduled and stilted encounter, Donalda and Ian had not been under the same roof for more than fifteen years. The twins had toyed with the idea of postponing the Doxys' invitation to the official opening at Easter, but then decided that they would be justifiably hurt if they were not included in the family party. So they had taken a gamble, putting Ian and Sinead in *Wild Iris* – the largest and most luxurious bronze and gold suite at one end of the castle – and Hal and Donalda in the ancient vaulted tower chamber at the other, hoping it would appeal to Hal's passion for 'his-tory'.

'We'll put Ninian and Granny Kirsty in the two rooms in between,' said Nell scribbling on the allocation sheet. 'They should be able to keep the peace.'

'And we'd better leave plenty of space between them in the dining room as well,' added Tally. 'I don't want any of my Victorian decanters flying around in the middle of dinner.'

'Let's hope they're so impressed they don't dare step out of line the whole weekend,' breathed Nell, mentally crossing as many fingers as she could. Just the thought of her mother could still make her feel like a naughty little girl.

'Well, they bloody well ought to be,' Tally said. 'At least Father can't grumble about the wine list, since he helped me select it.'

Fortunately, the early April weather was calm, bright and sunny – which made for spectacular aerial views. Granny Kirsty had met Ian, Sinead, Niamh and Ninian at Glasgow airport and joined them for a chartered helicopter flight to Taliska, which also meant they could avoid the rabble at the gates. Construction of the helicopter landing pad was now complete beyond the garden perimeter fence on a grassy coastal strip of the type of terrain called *machair* in Gaelic. A quarter of a mile of newly gravelled track led from it to the house.

Tally loaded Ian, Sinead, Kirsty and the luggage into the BMW and Nell smiled a welcome from the driver's seat of the Fourtrack as her half-brother and sister climbed in excitedly, both talking at once.

'Aren't helicopters just *the coolest*. I wish we had one in London,' enthused Niamh.

'I spotted thirty-three deer running in the hills,' cried Ninian in his newly broken tenor. He'd left the choir now and taken up wildlife while he waited for his new voice to stabilise. 'And I think I saw a golden eagle. Could it have been a golden eagle, Nell?'

'Yes, it very well could, Ninian. And it's very nice to see you, too,' replied Nell dryly, secretly delighted that the two sophisticated London teenagers were sufficiently thrilled by their first sight of Taliska and the Highlands to forget any form of greeting.

'Jeeze, this is *some place*,' breathed Niamh, still speaking in italics. 'Is it a real castle? Does it have a drawbridge and everything?'

At the main door of the hotel Nell braked to a halt behind the BMW. 'No drawbridge, I'm afraid, but it still has the old loos in the tower – except that we've cleaned them up a bit and made them flush, of course.'

'Yuk!' Niamh pulled a face. 'Who wants a medieval loo?'

'Some people love the idea – but your room's got an ordinary low-down suite so you're OK.' Nell opened the door. 'I'll show you where you're sleeping when I've made Granny Kirsty comfortable. Have a look around in the meanwhile.'

She almost ran forward to where her father, stepmother and grandmother were disembarking and fussing around the luggage. 'Granny Kirsty! Welcome back to Taliska,' she cried, her arms held wide. For Nell, Kirsty McLean's was the most important arrival of the whole weekend. She was thirsting for her grandmother's approval.

Kirsty returned her hug warmly. 'It's good to see you, wee Nell,' the old lady said. 'Very, very good!'

Nobody but Kirsty ever called her wee, and Nell loved her for it. 'I'm dying to show you everything, Granny. Are you very tired after your journey?'

'Of course I am not,' retorted Kirsty. 'It was only a short hop. But my, they're noisy, those machines.' She raised her voice above the roar of the helicopter taking off.

'How's my girl?' boomed Ian McLean, giving Nell a hearty kiss over Granny Kirsty's head. 'You look fine, considering.'

'Considering what?' laughed Nell, kissing her father back. 'The overdraft?'

Tally was heaving bags out of the boot. 'Did you see the travellers on the other side of the bridge?' he fretted. 'They're an infernal nuisance. We don't seem to be able to get them shifted.'

'It's ridiculous,' said Sinead. 'Really bad luck. But never mind – we're not going to let it spoil our stay. We don't have to go anywhere near them, do we? My God, Tally, this place is magical.' She stood, red hair lifting in the breeze, staring out across the loch which glistened silver-blue in the sunlight, rippled and frilled by dark eddies of current and flurries of wind. In the foreground, the pale green *machair* stirred and undulated in grassy waves, and divers and gulls swooped and called among the grey rocks and heaped black seaweed on the shore. The loch seemed to stretch to infinity, only a faint, smudged line of mauve indicating where sea gave way to sky. To the north-west, the mountains of Morvern loomed in sharp outline like the coarse teeth of a saw, while to the south the coastline reflected the afternoon sun, shining cliffs plunging from gleaming grasslands down to a series of sparkling white-sand beaches disappearing into a distant spring haze. As Sinead said, it was a sight truly magical.

'But still a bit bracing,' remarked Nell pragmatically, tucking her arm in her grandmother's. 'You can see it even better from your rooms. Come on in!'

'I like all that stuff in your brochure, Tally, about low-fat cuisine,' said Sinead as they clattered through the echoing tunnel entrance. Tubs of bay trees and winter-jasmine had now been placed in the sheltered courtyard at the main door, softening the harsh grey granite walls into a verdant welcome. 'Will it tackle my middle-aged spread, do you think?' Sinead patted her tummy under the donkey-brown leather trouser suit she had chosen to wear for her journey from London. She had complained as she fastened the wide, studded belt of the jacket that it was tighter than it had been.

'Well, you might have to stay more than two days to see a real difference, wicked stepmother, but at least the problem won't get any worse while you're here – that our Calum can promise,' Tally told her.

'Thank goodness. Oh, will you just look at that!' Sinead stopped short in the hall doorway to appreciate her first impression of the hotel's interior. 'Isn't this beautiful? It looks like everyone's dream of home.'

Sunlight streamed into the hall through the stained-glass over the stairs and lit the warm, mellow panelling and the wide sweep of scabious-figured carpet. Under the arch of the staircase, sofas and chairs covered in old-fashioned floral chintz offered a cosy nook to sit in and a large, carved oak sideboard supported a copper kettle singing on a spirit lamp and a silver teaset laid out in readiness. Calum's only concession to traditional Scottish tea-breads were featherlight fruit scones made with skimmed milk and minimal fat, and these were offered with fromage frais and honey instead of butter and jam. A week of early spring sunshine had stirred the thousands of bulbs that lay hidden under the mossy lawns surrounding the castle, and daffodils now bloomed in generous clumps under every tree, so armfuls of these had been brought into the house and their starry yellow trumpets brightened dark corners, massed in vases together with branches of budding cherry blossom. A blazing log fire in the grate promised every romantic notion suggested in Tally's promotional literature, and the smoke problem had been solved by a refinement of Ann's auntie's blanket-cure. A large heatproof perspex sheet had been secured beneath the mantel and almost invisibly reduced the fireplace opening by a third so that now the smoke rose obediently up the chimney.

'We'll have tea in a few minutes, after you've seen your rooms. Is it as you remember it, Granny?' asked Nell anxiously as she accompanied her grandmother up Tally's famous 'item of antique furniture'.

Kirsty McLean shook her head vigorously. 'Not at all,' she said emphatically. 'When the laird told us stories at his annual children's party, it was always smoky in the hall. It used to make us cough!'

Nell caught Tally's eye as he ascended behind them, leading Ian and Sinead. The twins grinned fleetingly at each other, sharing a secret triumph. They were one up on the old laird anyway!

'Heavens, what an amazing room,' exclaimed Donalda when she and Hal were shown to their tower chamber. 'However old is it?'

'Wow! This is historic all right,' crowed Hal, thrilled. 'Look at that ceiling – it's just like a church.'

'And the bed – and that hanging! Wherever did you get that fabulous hanging, Nell?' Donalda was transfixed by the woven woodland scene of deer, badgers, squirrels, pheasants, ferns and fungi, all framed in a border of heather and bluebells, which covered the wall opposite the imposing four-poster bed. The bed itself was hung with a complementary tapestry-style fabric, the stylised floral pattern of which echoed the theme on the wall. Nell had found it difficult to buy suitably ancient furniture to complete the medieval atmosphere, but had luckily found an old oak kist in the stables which had been restored and polished and now stood between the window embrasures supporting a pair of magnificent sixteenth-century pewter candlesticks acquired in a local house-sale which she had attended. There was no central light but illumination came from the old ironwork sconces, still fixed into the walls but now electrified and freed of their burden of ancient cobwebs. The whole room gave the impression of existing way back in time. Only the dust of ages had been removed and the comforts of modern living subtly introduced. There were fat cushions on the stone window-seats and a very unmedieval upholstered sofa which, because it was covered in a simple heathery tweed, blended discreetly into the background. At the foot of the bed an oak coffer with a carved lid bore the ubiquitous vase of daffodils and blossom. The bathroom had been installed in the old garderobe and still boasted the original separate latrine, now plumbed and padded but retaining the five-hundred-year-old dressed stone box-seat built into the thickness of the tower wall.

'The hanging is a bit of serendipity. Tally found it in a tapestry workshop in Edinburgh on one of his trips,' Nell told her mother. 'It was commissioned by an earl who couldn't afford to pay for it.'

'Can you afford to pay for it?' asked Donalda seriously. 'Darling, you seem to have spent a fortune on this place. Are you sure it's worth it? I mean, it's so far from anywhere and now all those awful people at the gate! Are we safe, do you think?' On Tally's insistence, Donalda and Hal had helicoptered into Taliska precisely because of the travellers but they had nevertheless received a bird's-eye view of the teeming camp-site with its press of battered vehicles and tattered humanity.

'Mummy, of course we're safe,' Nell reassured her hastily. 'They're quite harmless – drugged up to the eyeballs most of the time, though God knows where they get hold of the stuff around here. They may be many and smelly but they're not going to invade or anything.'

'You never know,' observed Donalda sagely. 'This is Scotland and the Scots in my experience have a great capacity for violence – and they harbour grudges.'

Nell stared in amazement at her mother, hardly able to believe what she was hearing. 'How can you say that, Mummy, when you're a Scot yourself?'

Donalda shook her head firmly and bestowed an old-fashioned look on her daughter. 'Not any more, darling, not any more. I ceased being a Scot the day I divorced your father.'

'But you were born in Scotland,' Nell protested indignantly.

'Unfortunately yes, but as soon as I realised my mistake I left,' said her mother with a rare flash of humour. 'And why you had to come back, I will *never* understand.'

Nell realised that if her mother pursued this theme the whole weekend would be in jeopardy. Donalda was capable of arguing herself into a mood of implacability which could sour an atmosphere in five minutes.

'Well, anyway, the travellers aren't Scottish as far as I know. I don't think they can remember where they came from, actually. I just wish they'd go away.'

Donalda was about to launch into further plaintive strictures against her self-denied heritage when Hal emerged from inspecting the bathroom, a wide grin on his smooth, moon face.

'Doll, you should just see the john in there. I can't believe the Scots were so civilised back in the Dark Ages. I think this place – everything in Scotland – is just fantastic!'

If Donalda had intended further deprecations against the Scots, they died on her lips.

'Mummy is brewing a tantrum, I know she is,' wailed Nell to Caroline, who was busy unpacking. 'Having her here at the same time as Daddy was a big mistake.'

'Why? Surely they don't still argue. They've been divorced for years now, haven't they?' Caroline hung a startling red sheath dress in the cupboard. Her room on the second floor was named after the Burnet Rose, a wild flower rarely seen in the south of Britain but which flourished on the coastal sand dunes of the Hebridean islands. Rather than painting a frieze, Leo had copied the way the roses grew on the shore and distributed several flowering clumps on walls and ceiling, and the colour scheme of the furnishings echoed that of the plant, the cream and pale pink of the blooms, the dark green of the leaves and the deep aubergine of the Burnet's hips. On close inspection, Caroline had exclaimed with delight over a tiny hedgehog Leo had painted, peering out from beneath one of the briar-clumps.

'They don't argue because they never meet. We shouldn't have forced them together. It'll all end in tears.' Nell was wandering dejectedly around, twitching compulsively at the cushions and bedspreads. *Burnet Rose* was one of the twin-bedded rooms.

'Oh, I shouldn't worry. Anyway, even if there is a row it will be jolly entertaining for the rest of us. There's nothing like observing other people's wars.'

'You sound as if you're in the midst of one yourself,' remarked Nell. 'Who's the enemy?'

Caroline shrugged. 'It's David. He's not an enemy though, just a pest.'

'I'd have thought you two would have got this thing sorted out by now,' declared Nell. 'I don't know why you can't either give in or tell him to eff off. It's criminal, the way you string the poor man along. I suspect you secretly rather enjoy it.' She had not intended to blast off at her friend quite so vehemently, but her mother had stirred up her emotions and she had to let off steam.

Caroline gave a hollow laugh. 'Ha – listen to her,' she said. 'I suspect it's not *me* David fancies at all, but *you*! Whenever he sees me he talks about you. He's probably fancied you ever since you played Monopoly together on days out from school.'

Nell had a flashback memory of the chubby teen-age schoolchum Tally had frequently brought home on half-term visits. David's parents always seemed to be abroad on business during these breaks and it was true that as adolescents she and he had shared many a tussle over Park Lane, but she was incredulous about Caroline's theory. 'That is rubbish,' she scoffed. 'We're just good friends – and I need my friends. Please don't go spreading stories like that or he'll probably never speak to me again.'

Caroline tossed her dark head, rather miffed that Nell seemed perfectly happy to dish out advice but unwilling to accept any herself. 'Don't say I didn't warn you,' she muttered, stowing frothy underwear in a drawer.

Nell was instantly contrite. 'God, I'm sorry, I didn't mean to go off the deep end. Mummy's got me going this evening. Hell – is that the time? I'd better get back to the kitchen. Calum will be doing his nut.'

'Ah, now what about this little affair you've been cooking up in the kitchen, Nell McLean?' Caroline rounded on her. 'Rumour has it that you and your calorie-counting chef are spooning around together. Tell me about him.'

'There's nothing to tell,' Nell confided. 'I can't figure Calum out. Either he's shy or gay or doesn't believe in sleeping with the boss. I thought at one time we were getting on quite well but now . . . He's quite communicative in the kitchen but as soon as he's away from it he sprints for his little cottage up the hill and shuts himself away.' Calum had taken over the factor's old house in preference to a room in the stables or the attic, saying he preferred to live apart.

Caroline gave Nell a sympathetic smile. 'Bad luck. You might have had your cake and eaten it there. Still, anything could happen yet, given time. Speaking of which, when's dinner?'

'Eight-thirty – wouldn't dare have it at any other time, with Hal and Mummy here. I'll have to go now. Drinks in the bar at half-seven. See you then.' And Nell whirled out of the door leaving Caroline pensively holding a sponge bag, pausing on her way to the bathroom.

'Oh, what a tangled web we weave,' she mused cryptically.

The old library had hardly needed altering for use as the hotel bar. The panelling had been left dark and reassuring, preserving the clubby atmosphere of a Victorian gentleman's retreat. The musty, leathery smell of the books, dusted and restored, lent a quality of easy intellect to counteract the prevailing whiff of alcohol. Deep brown leather armchairs clustered around polished oak tables and there was a high, padded hearth-surround on which guests could perch and chat over the fire. In order to blend discreetly into the rest of the panelling, the actual bar had been constructed from the original shutters. Biscuit-coloured velvet curtains with deep chocolate-brown fringes replaced them at the long French windows which overlooked a terracotta-tiled terrace with a carved stone balustrade and steps leading down to the garden. In summer it was intended that guests could enjoy drinks outside.

A rather subdued company gathered there on that first evening. A formal dinner was to take place on the Saturday night so it was the twins' intention to make this meal a casual one, albeit with various groups of friends and family seated at separate tables so as to give the dining-room staff some serving practice. People had been told not to dress up and Donalda had scoured London for just the sort of outfit she considered suitable for such a 'neither-here-nor-there' occasion. It was a pale blue knitted silk suit with a neat, gilt-buttoned jacket and a straight skirt cut just above the knee. A strikingly long rope of real pearls given to her by Hal for their tenth wedding anniversary and matching pearl and gold earrings completed her 'casual' look. Nell felt like searching the hotel for a stowaway coiffeur because somehow Donalda had managed to shed the after-effects of the helicopter's fierce down draught and emerge with her ash-blonde crowning glory smoothly groomed and gleaming. As usual, in her mother's presence Nell felt like a messy scullery-maid. She had enjoyed the absence of such feelings of sartorial inferiority of late and she rather resented their return.

'Champagne all round!' announced Tally, flourishing a frosted green bottle with a label bearing the distinctive blue hotel logo. 'I've had a hundred cases of Bollinger specially shipped and labelled so I hope you like it.' There were simultaneous explosions as he and Tony the barman both released corks at once and a dozen glasses were quickly filled. 'There's whisky of course, Dad, if you'd rather.'

Ian shook his head and accepted a glass of champagne. 'Having spent all that time doing the city cellars with you I'd better taste the result,' he said, raising the glass and smiling genially around the rather sedate gathering. 'This is quite an occasion, isn't it? Are we going to have a toast?'

Donalda made a small noise, audible only to those nearest her, including Hal who placed a warning hand on her arm. Throughout their marriage, Ian's hearty bonhomie had been a source of continuous chagrin to Donalda.

'We certainly are, and I'm going to make it,' said Tally firmly, displaying some of his father's social élan. He gestured fondly in the direction of his grandmother who sat in one of the leather chairs, tiny and beaming in a lace-collared white blouse with a Celtic figured silver brooch at the neck. 'To the lady who inspired the whole venture and who has finally come home again to Taliska. To Granny Kirsty!'

Behind the old lady's back Donalda hardly raised her glass but there was a tear in Kirsty McLean's eye as she acknowledged the salutations of the others. 'No, no,' she protested in her soft, west-coast lilt. 'It is the twins we should toast – Nell and Tally who're fulfilling the legend and rescuing Taliska from oblivion.'

Nell had told Tally Kirsty's dubious two-heads-are-better-than-one tale and now he summed it up for the others. 'Granny tells us some twins of old killed a marauding two-headed dragon,' he explained. 'So in her book that makes us Saints George and Georgina! I suspect it's more myth than truth but we could certainly do with dispatching the marauding beast that is presently at our gates. Sadly, we have yet to come up with the method. With all respect to our lawyer, Alasdair McInnes, injunctions seem about as much use as a flying haggis.' He smiled genially at Alasdair who was among the house-party guests and stood diffidently in a corner in one of his familiar flecked-tweed suits.

'How about claymores at dawn?' called David from the fireplace, where he was perched beside Niamh on the padded surround. 'I'd even offer to hold your jacket, Tally, if you were gentleman enough to wear one.'

Sticking firmly to the casual ruling, Tally had dispensed with that particular item of apparel but had at least shaved and put on a new deep blue lambswool pullover with an abstract intarsia design down one side. Nell thought it made him look rather cuddly, as she had no doubt she also looked in the plain black sweater-dress she had decided to wear herself. She had rushed away from the kitchen at the last minute and knew her face was flushed, her hair untidy and her tights wrinkled at the ankle. She dropped her gaze in confusion as David caught her eye and winked. With Caroline's surprise statement still fresh in her mind, she took a steadying gulp of champagne. Like the whole weekend, she seemed to be poised on a knife-edge.

'Jacket? That's a dirty word on Taliska,' declared Tally blithely, seemingly unaffected by nerves of any kind. 'Which reminds me . . . I've invited one of my fishermen friends to dinner tomorrow night, and I've asked him to take you all on a boat trip on Sunday if the weather's OK. He operates from our jetty.'

This was the first Nell had heard of 'Fishing Mac's' inclusion in the celebration dinner. Tally's cavalier issuing of such an invitation without consultation incensed her and added to her growing inferiority complex. Then David sidled up and gave her a peck on the cheek. 'I haven't been able to do that since I arrived,' he said cheerfully. 'I hope you haven't been avoiding me.'

A general hum of conversation had broken out around the room but Nell nevertheless had the uncanny feeling that everyone was staring at her. She felt about aged ten and size twenty. 'Of course not,' she said hurriedly. 'It's great to see you here. I'm afraid I've been rather busy with Calum in the kitchen.'

'Ah, the mysterious Calum. When do we get to meet this paragon of yours?' David asked. 'You poached him from the Classic Hotel, I gather. Quite a coup – a classic culinary kidnap!'

Nell's tension eased slightly. She laughed and lapsed into broad Cockney. 'Not guilty, m'lud! 'E came of 'is own accord – just jumped into me sack, 'onest!'

David assumed the attitude of a Dirty Old Magistrate, twiddling imaginary moustaches and leering at her. 'But what wicked wiles did you use to lure him, my dear? Tell me that, eh?'

She bridled, fluttering her eyelashes. 'Wot are you implyin', sir?' she asked, instantly the Wronged Heroine. As youngsters she, Tally and David had played out many such conversational melodramas together. 'You impugn my reputashun! I'll tell the vicar.'

'I *am* the vicar.' David spluttered into laughter, unable to keep the act going. 'A good kosher vicar!'

Nell giggled gratefully. Temporarily at least his schoolboy ragging had dispelled her fit of paranoia. Glancing round she caught sight of Alasdair still standing rather awkwardly aloof. She tucked her arm in David's and assumed her normal voice, 'Well, Vicar, come and meet the lawyer.' She led him across the bar. 'Alasdair, you haven't met my old friend David Guedalla. David, Alasdair McInnes. I'm sure you two must have something in common, even if it's only me! I'm afraid I'll have to leave you to discover it though, or there won't be any dinner.'

For that evening at least, Nell's misgivings were unfounded. As a subtle introduction to his new style of cooking Calum had produced a meal which gave promise of spectacular things to come. There was a light pheasant consommé served with finely sliced crêpes, a terrine of chicken breast stuffed with truffles and served with crab-apple purée, caramelised spring vegetables and wild rice, and a speciality Scottish dessert called *cranachan* made with toasted oatmeal soaked in whisky and whipped not into cream as was usual but into fromage frais, sweetened with honey and topped off with preserved brambles. Portions of home-made Taliska cheese completed the repast, served with rosy apple quarters. Light Alsatian wines accompanied the various courses in sufficient quantity to leaven the atmosphere considerably.

Tally had arranged the seating and, partly to give Libby and Ginny a taste of waiting on tables of varying sizes and partly to diffuse any potential family embarrassment, he had put Hal and Donalda on their own as far away as possible from Ian and Sinead, who had a table of five with Granny Kirsty, Niamh and Ninian. Alasdair McInnes sat with Ann Soutar and Andrew and Fee Ramsay-Miller, who'd taken an evening off to inspect the opposition, and he placed David, Caroline and Leo with Nell and himself.

'Has Libby altered her dress?' Nell asked Tally in a whisper during the meal. She was only too aware that her brother and the Australian girl had become what Leo called 'an item'. An early sisterly complaint that the affair would lead to complications had been refuted by Tally, who declared angrily that he was quite capable of 'having it off without cocking it up!' At least Libby's arrival on the scene had relieved the build-up of tension which had developed between Nell and Tally, and furthermore 'Women's Lib' as he called her, referring to her liberal sexual attitude rather than any political stand on female emancipation, soon revealed an additional and fortuitous weapon in her armoury. She was a qualified masseuse, a talent which she was prepared to put at the disposal of the guests, as long as she could pocket the proceeds. There was no question of anyone taking undue advantage of Libby!

'Altered her dress – how should I know? She looks pretty good to me.' Tally cast an appreciative glance at the waitress as she passed the table with a pile of dirty plates skilfully balanced on wrist and hand. The silky blue dress clung provocatively in a way Nell had not foreseen when she ordered the uniform, and it ended a good six inches above Libby's knees, leaving a long expanse of honey-gold leg below. 'She looks as if she's jumped off the dessert trolley,' added Tally, grinning.

'She looks like a tart,' commented Nell.

'Exactly,' responded her brother. 'And a very tasty one, too.'

'I heard that, Tally,' said Caroline, who was happily eating most of Calum's carefully prepared food, confident that it wouldn't compromise her bulgeless figure in its clinging cream jersey and black ski-pants. 'Have you been tasting the tart then?'

'Just a nibble or two,' Tally admitted with a roguish grin. 'Incidentally, how's our favourite TV poisonality, the gabbling gourmet?'

'Eye-Level, you mean? The red-hot Gryll?' Caroline made a face. 'As gross as ever. He won a *Time Out* award the other day for the worst-phrased man on television!'

'I can't think of anyone who deserves it more,' said David. 'You're well out of that, Nell.'

Nell shrugged. 'Yes, but what have I got myself into? Hello – what's up with Mummy?' She had been keeping one anxious eye on Donalda and now observed her mother waving vigorously at Ginny who responded, held a brief exchange and then sped off towards the kitchen.

'Don't get so agitated, Nell,' remonstrated Tally. 'She probably only wants some gripe water or something. Ginny will sort it out.'

'Well, at least the rest of the family look as if they're enjoying themselves,' remarked Leo, laid-back in his usual blue denim.

There were frequent gusts of laughter from Ian McLean's table where Sinead was supplying a flow of Irish witticisms and Niamh and Ninian were trying to see who could kick the other under the rather wide table at which they were seated on opposite sides. The two younger McLeans had spent a good hour before dinner in the gym, frolicking in the communal jacuzzi, broiling in the sauna and trying out all the Nautilus equipment with pop music blaring loudly on the audio system. The gym was the only place where there was any background music available, both Tally and Nell being in total harmony about not wanting it in the other public rooms. They'd installed television and video facilities in the conference room for anyone who simply couldn't do without them, but there were none in the bedrooms. As all their advertising stressed, the aim of a visit to Taliska was to get away from the noise and distraction of the outside world and find other games to play!

'I think Granny Kirsty is quite happy to be back, don't you?' Nell asked the table in general. 'Tomorrow I'm going to take her on a tour round her old childhood haunts.'

'I wonder how she feels, coming back after so long?' pondered Caroline. 'It must be strange to think that tonight she's going to sleep on the island where she was born, for the first time in sixty years.'

'Perhaps the earth will move,' quipped Tally, who found such temporal musings faintly disturbing.

'I just hope she finds the bed comfortable,' remarked Nell prosaically.

Calum emerged from the kitchen after dinner and sat rather quietly on the sidelines until Nell introduced him to her grandmother over the bar-list of single malt whiskies. Tally had laid in a good selection of the more than fifty different malts distilled in Scotland, and the two aficionados were soon locked in animated discussion about which ones they had tasted and which ones they preferred. Calum revealed to Kirsty something he had not vouchsafed to anyone else, that it was his intention to introduce a series of dishes flavoured with various malts.

'It'll be interesting to see if the guests appreciate their different characters,' he confided. 'I think the peatier ones go with game and venison, and the smoother ones with shellfish and light meats.'

'Imagine a Scots version of Lobster Thermidor,' Kirsty enthused, 'using a malt whisky instead of brandy.'

'Exactly,' agreed Calum, smiling secretly. 'I have just such a dish on the menu tomorrow, and if you can name the malt I've used in it I'll call it after you, Mrs McLean!'

Tally took Alasdair to meet his mother and step-father over coffee and liqueurs in the drawing room, while Ian and Sinead and the Ramsay-Millers formed a more rowdy foursome in the bar. Niamh and Ninian started a wild game of Picasso with Leo, who was brilliant at drawing but hopeless at guessing, and Nell offered to take David and Caroline up to the roof of the tower. 'The view is fantastic in the moonlight,' she assured them. 'Well worth the climb.'

The narrow, spiral stone stair bypassed the two rooms which formed Nell's quarters and terminated in a small corbelled turret which led onto a narrow battlemented walkway skirting the steep rake of the roof, its distinctive crow-stepped gables sharply defined against a navy sky. On a flagpole the blue and white saltire of St Andrew drooped in the still air. Low among scattered stars, a huge spring moon hung heavy and luminous, sending long, ink-black shadows from the leafless trees across the bleached expanse of lawn which surrounded the house. Beyond the jagged line of fence-posts the empty *machair* stretched towards hillocks of silver marram grass, shimmering mermaid's tresses trailing down to the phosphorescent sheen of the loch. An owl called from the Scots-pine wood, lending the scene an unearthly quality.

'It's like *Brigadoon*,' whispered Caroline, her dark eyes gleaming. 'It looks as if it might disappear in a thunderclap and a swirl of mist.'

'Heavens, Caro, I didn't know you were so poetic,' murmured David, whose hand had dropped gently but unmistakably onto Nell's shoulder, his thumb casually ruffling the fine hairs on the back of her neck. She froze into immobility, waiting to detect her body's reaction to this tiniest of caresses, and to her amazement it was as magic as the moonlight. Small shivers began radiating from the focus of that featherlight touch. She turned her head and smiled, moving almost imperceptibly closer into the circle of David's arm.

'It's funny,' she said softly, wondering at the suddenness with which the signals had changed between them, 'how lightning can strike out of an empty sky.'

'Perhaps because the sky wasn't empty at all. A thunderbolt might have been waiting behind the moon,' responded David, moving his hand to run his fingers upwards through her hair, sending urgent, surging messages downward through her throat to her fluttering belly. How did he know that this was one of the most erogenous of her zones?

Caroline turned her head and her teeth glinted. 'I suppose the fact that you two are talking such utter nonsense must mean that three has suddenly become a crowd. Well, I've seen enough of moon and June. I'm off!' She slipped past them like a night elf, disappearing through the lighted rectangle of the open turret door. 'Byee! Have fun.'

'Shall we?' asked David, bending to brush his lips across Nell's temple.

Another erogenous zone instantly established itself. 'It seems a shame to waste the moonlight,' she murmured, turning to meet his lips and finding that their bodies only had to move inches to be touching at every curve and contour, of which they had plenty between them. Nevertheless, Nell reflected, enjoying symptoms of arousal she had not felt for some time, his arms seemed quite strong enough to hold her up!

Lying sleepless in bed alone later that night, Nell considered her feelings for David. She didn't love him, of that much she was certain, but he was a familiar friend and most of the barriers were already down between them. Memories of the kisses she had shared with him on the roof were still sending thrilling messages to secret places inside her body, and she suspected that inevitably they might lead to something more. And, just as she was contemplating whether or not she would like 'something more', she heard a slight noise on the spiral stair beyond her door. David, she thought with instinctive certainty. Oh God, but he can't – we can't. Not here in the room above my mother's! For however hard Donalda denied her Scottish heritage, Nell knew that her mother retained all the straight-laced attitudes of her Calvinist upbringing, attitudes which she, Nell, could not bring herself to offend. She lay quiet and still, hoping a hostile silence would repel all boarders. It's ironic, she thought, her brain racing as her body lay rigid, I suppose David and I could have been lovers a score of times in the past, only we just hadn't woken up to the idea. And now that the spirit and the flesh seem willing, the circumstances are decidedly weak. We really can't, not now, not here . . . *Please go away, David!* She willed her thoughts into sound waves and beamed them towards the door and after several tense minutes the silence was once again disturbed by the slow, reluctant shuffle of footsteps retreating down the spiral stair.

'This is the view that made me decide I wanted to buy Taliska,' said Nell to her grandmother the next day.

They were sitting in the cab of the Fourtrack looking out over the loch. Mac's fishing boat was riding gently on the calm water by the jetty and the low green mound of Lismore appeared deceptively close in the grey, limpid light. The bright sunshine of the previous day had softened and diffused; clouds had rolled in, high and livid, giving the sky a washed-out pallor.

'It was my favourite place when I was a child,' Kirsty told her. 'I used to sit and watch the puffers unload at the jetty. There were sometimes two or three a day in the summer.'

'It must have been quite different then. Is it strange to come back?' Nell asked.

'Very strange and rather disturbing. I think you've done a wonderful job, dear, don't get me wrong. Everything is looking magnificent but it's all for visitors now, isn't it? There's no one here who really belongs.'

'What about you? If we don't belong where we're born, where do we belong?' asked Nell, still astounded by her mother's incomprehensible denial of her Scottish birth.

'Where our loyalties lie, where our instincts tell us we belong, not somewhere that's written on our birth certificate. I don't belong here any more.' Kirsty sounded wistful but certain.

'But that makes us all like those people camping over the bridge,' protested Nell. 'They can probably hardly remember where they've come from – and they certainly don't know where they're going next. Surely you and I belong here far more than they belong anywhere?'

'Well, perhaps you have the right of ownership, dear, but the land itself will eventually absorb everyone and everything that's on it.' Kirsty McLean sat quite still, her age-blotched, wrinkled hands quietly folded in her lap.

'Dust to dust, you mean?' inquired Nell, thinking scattily how much of that particular stuff they'd removed from the castle rooms over the past few months.

'Yes and no,' said her grandmother. After a pause she added, 'I don't want to be buried here, Nell. I was happy here as a child but it's over now. Memories matter but you can make those anywhere.'

Nell was conscious of a terrible sense of disappointment. She had been so acutely aware of her family ties to Taliska but now it seemed that this had been merely the misplaced fervour of youth. Kirsty felt no such ties.

'You make us all sound as rootless as the travellers,' she said sadly.

Kirsty shrugged. 'Why have you chosen the scabious for your emblem?' she asked.

Nell was surprised. 'I suppose because I liked the colour, and the shape made a good design. It was you who told me they appeared all over the island in the summer.'

'Oh yes, they do,' Kirsty agreed. 'But the name they use for that particular specimen is "Devilsbit Scabious". Do you know why? Because it has very shallow roots. It's said that the Devil bit off its roots in a fit of pique.' Her grandmother took one of Nell's hands gently in hers and patted it. 'I hope your roots here are not shallow, wee Nell. You have a very generous nature and you seem to be giving your all to this island. I just hope it's going to give you something in return.'

Chapter Eight

Having several hundred New Age travellers camped on the doorstep did not encourage merry excursions to Oban for souvenir shopping, or pleasant afternoon drives to view the West Highland scenery. Lacking the inclination to contend with groups of grubby, garrulous children shouting 'Rich fat pigs!' or their equally grubby and drug-sluggish parents smiling their curiously superior smiles, the house-party guests were thrown upon their own resources for entertainment. Niamh, Ninian and Caroline put on jeans and wellies and set out to walk round the island. Leo returned to his paintbrushes, and Tally and David renewed their squash challenge. Nell took Granny Kirsty on her trip down Memory Lane and the separate parental couples spent the morning trying to avoid each other in the gym, plunge-pool and sauna. The staff had work to do and only Fee and Andrew Ramsay-Miller and Alasdair McInnes braved the strangers at the gates in order to drive to their own places of work. Alasdair promised to return but the Ramsay-Millers would be unable to attend Saturday night's celebration because there was dinner to prepare at their own hotel.

'Good luck to you,' said Andrew before he left, for once fairly dumbstruck by the luxurious standard of the Taliska accommodation. 'The place looks marvellous,' he added generously. 'I don't think we'll be competing for the same clientèle at all, but if you're ever full you know where to send people. And we'll do the same – if they can afford your prices!'

The explorers took a picnic lunch with them and Donalda and Hal said they would not eat at midday if they were going to do justice to the feast in the evening, so it was only Leo, David, and the older McLeans who joined the twins in the dining room for Calum's lunchtime broth and home-made bread. Nell was conscious of a feeling of relief that Caroline had gone with the picnickers. She was not certain how to handle the triangular situation between herself, Caroline and David now that it had begun to take a new tack. She was unsure how Caroline would react in the cold light of day, for it was one thing to constantly spurn an importunate suitor, and quite another to contemplate his sudden defection!

'Your mother doesn't change, does she?' Ian remarked to Tally, knocking back his second large whisky. 'Figure still comes before family.'

'She does look good on it, though,' retorted Tally, leaping to Donalda's defence. 'There's not an ounce of fat on Mother.'

'Not many ounces of fun either,' murmured Sinead, who had restricted her alcohol consumption to white wine with soda, which nevertheless seemed to go to her head just as fast as the undiluted grape. 'Life's too short to be a living denial, if you ask me. Don't you agree, Nell?'

Nell wished her opinion had not been solicited on the matter. She was a size-sixteen living proof of someone who did not operate according to Donalda's rules of consumption.

'If there's one thing Nell has never been able to

deny anyone, it's a kindness,' David said warmly, coming to her rescue. 'And Tally, too, for that matter. We'd none of us be here if it weren't for their generosity.'

Tally raised an inquiring eyebrow at his friend. Why such fervent praise for Nell's good nature, he asked himself, unless an ulterior motive lurked beneath? He was under no illusion that his inclusion in David's eulogy was anything more than a smoke screen. Something was afoot between his twin sister and his friend. Come to think of it, the signs had been there before they left London. 'You're only saying that because I let you win at squash, Guedalla,' he commented. 'But it's true – my generosity knows no bounds.' During their morning squash challenge Tally had been surprised to find himself totally out of condition and had puffed his way to a three-two defeat.

'That may be so in your case,' agreed David, smiling, 'but in Nell's there's no squash about it.'

'There's plenty of blush, though,' muttered a flustered Nell, slicing up a crusty home-baked loaf. 'Spare mine, please.'

'Anyway, you're not just here for fun you know,' Tally declared, accepting a hunk of bread from the tip of the knife. 'You're supposed to sing for your supper by sending us all your friends and acquaintances who will happily pay for the privilege of finding a new lease of life at Taliska.'

'We're trying out some live music tonight,' Nell informed them, hastily changing the subject. 'Our apprentice chef's sister is a music student in Glasgow but she's home for the Easter break. She's going to play the clarsach.'

'The clarsach? That's rather like the Irish harp, isn't it?' asked Sinead.

'Yes, I think they're quite similar. Tonight's sort of like a trial run for the official opening.'

'I wanted to hire Luciano Pavarotti but then I thought he might find the local talent too tempting,' added Tally, flashing an appreciative smile at Libby who was ladling broth in a gingham dress that checked out every curve on her body in much the same way as the blue uniform had done the night before. Libby had been busy with her needle and thread again.

'Speaking of locals, when are the Macphersons coming?' Nell asked her brother in a narked tone. 'And incidentally, you might have mentioned that you were asking them.'

'I did mention it – last night!' was Tally's unrepentant riposte. 'They'll be here around half-seven.'

'What's Mrs Mac like?'

'I've no idea – I've never met her. You'll like him though, Dad. He's a real salt of the earth type,' said Tally.

'Sea-salt would be more accurate,' said Nell. 'He's a fisherman and a drinking crony of Tally's, Granny,' she confided to Kirsty. 'They practically keep the local pub going between them.'

'Do you no' drink in your own bar, Tally?' asked Kirsty.

'Well, I will now it's open, I suppose. But it's a bit restricting.'

'A dog doesn't pee on its own doorstep,' David put in. 'Sorry, Mrs McLean, but you know what I mean. What are we all doing this afternoon?' He stared pointedly at Nell. 'No one's going to town, I imagine, not with the unwashed hordes still at the gate.'

'Well, I don't know about Granny Kirsty but I'm going to have a snooze,' announced Sinead. 'This island air is too much for me.'

'Aye, I think I'll do the same,' agreed Kirsty. 'All that nostalgia this morning has quite worn me out.'

'Nonsense, Granny, nothing seems to tire you.' Nell smiled fondly at her. 'You'll go on for ever.'

'Not without a bit of a rest I won't,' said Granny Kirsty firmly. 'You can get one of those nice Australian girls to bring me a cup of tea in bed at five o'clock.'

Tally hid a smile and winked at Libby. 'Tea in bed at five, that sounds like a good idea,' he murmured. 'What about me showing you the cellar after lunch, Dad?' he added more loudly. 'Or are you intending to punch out the Zs too?'

'I might give in a bit later but the cellar's a must after all that work I put in in London. I want to see which wines you finally ordered,' replied his father, tackling his soup with gusto. 'Lord, I haven't had broth like this since my Glasgow days.'

'That just leaves you and me, Nell,' said David very casually. 'We've done the roof, what are you going to show me next?'

'The kitchen door, I'm afraid,' replied Nell apologetically, realising guiltily that David would probably be hoping for something a little more romantic. 'I've got to help Calum and he won't allow strangers in his holy of holies.'

'Couldn't you smuggle me in as a hygiene inspector?' David persisted.

She shook her head contritely. 'Not even as a sack of potatoes. It's more than my life's worth.'

'Oh well,' he sighed. 'I'll just have to drown my sorrows in the cellar.'

'Not on my château-bottled you won't, buddy,' declared Tally. 'You can look but you can't taste.'

David smiled ruefully at this and caught Nell's

eye. 'Story of my life,' he lamented.

There was a light tapping on the heavy oak door of the upper tower room. Nell was lying prostrate on her bed and glanced round at the clock on the table beside it – six-thirty. 'Damn!' she muttered, thinking that whoever it was she did not want to forego the half hour she had planned with her feet up before she had to change for dinner. She was still not used to spending long periods of time standing on the hard tiled floor in the kitchen and her legs and feet ached appallingly. 'Who is it?' she called out.

'It's only me, darling.' Her mother's voice was swiftly followed round the door by Donalda's face, beautifully made-up and smiling. 'May I come in for a minute?'

Nell swung her feet to the floor, forcing herself to smile back. 'Of course, Mummy,' she said, marvelling at how easily her lips could say the exact opposite of what she was thinking.

For that night's dinner, Donalda had chosen to wear a stunning black velvet jump suit with a white satin collar. I can see why she didn't want to eat lunch, thought Nell, regarding the skin-tight outfit. She looks incredible, though. You'd never think she was fifty-four. And where she had ever managed to tuck twin babies into that tiny frame, God alone knows. Perhaps only Tally was really there and I was a changeling, carried into the labour ward in a bed-pan when Mummy wasn't looking . . .

'I just wanted a quick chat, darling, before we go down to dinner. You can dress while we talk, I don't mind.' Donalda pulled up one of Nell's patchwork chairs and sat down.

You may not mind but I do, thought Nell, who was still in the loose white cotton trousers and

T-shirt which she wore for cooking. Under her mother's scrutiny she felt as lumpy and ill at ease as she did in one of those communal dress-shop changing rooms where girls with wonderful figures writhed half-naked and moaned about not being able to squeeze into a size ten, whilst she scrabbled about trying to conceal both her spare tyre and the size of the ample garments she was trying on. 'It's OK, I don't have to change for a few minutes,' she said aloud, still sitting awkwardly on the side of her bed. 'What did you want to talk about?'

Donalda leaned forward with an expression of deep concern, resting her elbows on her velvet-clad knees, held decorously together even in trousers. She looked like a dark angel with her pale halo of hair fluffed around her immaculately painted face. 'We haven't had a moment alone together since I arrived and I just want to know if you're happy, darling. This is such an enormous change in your life and I want to know whether you feel you've done the right thing.'

Nell sighed and closed her eyes momentarily. 'To be honest, Mummy, I haven't had a minute to think even about what I'm going to wear tonight, never mind whether I'm happy or not. There'll be time for all that when the hotel is open and running smoothly – if it ever is!'

'But darling, I'm worried about you. You've isolated yourself from everything up here and you've taken on so much. Surely you were better off working with those interesting television people and having lots of friends around you in London?'

'Honestly, Mummy, I'm fine,' Nell assured her. 'I'm tired, I admit, but once we're open I'll be able to relax a bit more. It's been the most hectic six months of my life but it's been worth it, don't you think? Of course, you didn't see the place before we bought it or you'd realise just how much there has been to do.'

'Well, you don't *look* fine,' Donalda told her bluntly. 'You have bags under your eyes, your skin is sallow and I believe you have actually put on weight, although how you've managed to do that when you've had so much to do, I simply don't know. You look as if you've given up on yourself, Nell.'

'God, Mummy, thanks a lot,' her daughter snapped back. 'You make me feel like a million dollars.' In her present low spirits Nell's tether was too short to let her mother's remarks pass, as she usually tried to do. 'Look, I've a hundred things on my mind other than the brightness of my eyes, the glow of my skin or the trimness of my figure. How long will it take you to realise that I am just not the Cindy Crawford type? I know all that is very important to you, but it's not remotely important to me!'

Donalda coughed nervously, raising her almost transparent hand with its pearly-painted fingernails to her mouth. She looked pained. 'What *is* very important to me is your happiness, Nell. This kind of thing is all right for Tally, he's used to handling large business concerns, but you're different. You're a gentle soul who likes cooking. You should be married and having babies, not trying to be high-powered and assertive. It doesn't suit you.'

'Well, it's a bit late to think about that now, Mummy, even if you're right – which you're not.' Nell heaved herself reluctantly to her feet, feeling every pedal bone graunch painfully as she did so. 'It's sweet of you to worry about me, it really is, but I'm a big girl now, and not just in the sense you mean. I have to get on and finish what I started.

Anyway, I don't remember you ever recommending nappy-changing as an occupation before . . . Look, I'm sorry if I'm not exactly the daughter you would have liked but at least I'm not on drugs or living in a cardboard box on the Thames Embankment.'

'I really don't want to change you, darling,' said Donalda, whose black-mascaraed eyelashes were glistening with tears. 'I just want you to be happy and I don't think you ever will be, lost up here, however beautiful it may be.'

Nell swallowed a protest on Taliska's behalf and bent down to put her hands placatingly on her mother's shoulders. 'I'm going to change my clothes now, Mummy, and I'm sorry but I'd rather do it without an audience, if you don't mind. I'll see you downstairs in half an hour.' She kissed her mother firmly on the cheek and went slowly into the bathroom which, as in the vaulted chamber below, had been installed in the ancient garderobe.

Donalda looked surprised and hurt. She stood up and walked across to examine her reflection in the pier-glass which stood in a corner of the room, dabbing carefully at her eyes with a tissue taken from a box by Nell's bed. Thoughtfully she fingered the matching navy-blue silk blouse and trousers which Nell had obviously hung out to wear that evening, despite her claim not to have had time to think about her apparel. With an angry little shrug Donalda left the room.

Craig Armstrong's elder sister Tina was a pretty dark-haired girl who looked enchanting in white broderie Anglaise sashed with black velvet, seated at her harp at the foot of the main stairs. Her clarsach stood shoulder-high, a carved and polished wood frame shaped like a curved triangle, carrying a single row of strings which released a lyrical, plaintive, rippling sound under her flying fingers. The music conjured up images of windswept hills and fast-flowing rivers, racing clouds and the soaring voice of the lark which haunts the Scottish moors in spring and summer. It flooded the stairwell and the corridors, greeting family and friends as they emerged from their rooms for dinner, making their descent a melodic advance into gracious living. The hotel's public rooms were lit entirely by candles, and the smell of hot beeswax hung fragrant and heady in the air, mingling with the scent of the cherry blossom in the flower arrangements, now brought into full bloom by the warmth of blazing fires. Flickering flamelight gleamed off the panelling and weirdly animated the gilt-framed landscapes and still-lifes hung upon it, so that their delicate brushwork of trees and grasses seemed to sway, and the corpses of hares and pheasants to develop a macabre posthumous twitch. The men wore dinner suits or kilts with silver-buttoned black jackets, their white shirts ruffled and frilled. The women were in multicoloured silk and taffeta, velvet and lace, skirts long and short, trousers flowing or slim, jewels sparkling at ear and throat. Really, thought Tally, gazing round the assembled company, they all look rich enough to have paid our prices. Pity they haven't!

His pecuniary speculation was interrupted by the sudden arrival of the Macphersons. In fact, for Tally all rational thought was smothered by his first view of Fishing Mac's wife. It was like fireworks exploding in his head, closing his throat and setting his heart pounding like thunder. Flora Macpherson had the kind of beauty which comes from within; it shone through her gentle, deep-blue eyes and flitted over her soft, curving lips. With her pale gold hair and fair, luminous complexion she was a complete contrast to her swarthy husband with his heavy brows and sensual red mouth. She wore a rather old-fashioned embroidered blue blouse which revealed smooth, extremely white shoulders and the swell of plentiful snowy breasts, and was tucked into a full, mid-calf royal-blue taffeta skirt and wide black patent leather belt. She looked shy and charming while her husband stood glowering at her shoulder, his strong neck bulging uncomfortably over a collar and tie that were too tight, apparently trying both to push her into the room and to dare anyone to accost her.

Nell, seeing that Tally appeared suddenly to have acquired the pop-eyes and speechless gape of a bullfrog, stepped forward to greet the newcomers. 'Come in,' she said, offering her hand. 'Welcome to Taliska. You must be Mrs Macpherson.'

The cause of Tally's incapacity smiled and nodded, briefly returning Nell's handshake. 'Flora,' she said, in a rich Scots voice. 'My name is Flora. It's so kind of you to invite us.'

'Not at all,' said Nell hospitably. 'We're so glad you could come. It's our first chance to show off what we've been doing here. Did you have any trouble getting through the gate?'

'Oh no. Mac knows the travellers. We just drove on through.' Nell expressed surprise but did not pursue the matter.

By this time Tally's eyes had returned to their sockets and he moved into action with a warm, enraptured smile. 'Welcome, Flora. What a lovely name . . . So good to meet you at last, after knowing your husband this long. How're you doing, Mac?' He put his hands on both their elbows and urged them towards the bar. 'Come and have a drink. We'll be eating soon.'

Aware that his local guests might be ill at ease among his more sophisticated London visitors, Tally remained solicitously attentive towards the Macphersons. In the dining room he shared a separate table with them, a fact which Nell could see badly annoyed their mother who had barely been able to bring herself to acknowledge them when Tally introduced her. 'I don't understand what they say,' Nell heard Donalda whisper afterwards to Hal. 'Their accent is so *overpowering*.'

'She's quite a looker though, isn't she, Doll?' Hal replied. 'I wonder where Mac found her.'

Tally had been thinking exactly the same thing. Flora Macpherson would have attracted attention in any company, if only because of the deep-blue wonder of her eyes. They had certainly captivated Tally, whose conversation became quite gentle and sincere under their benign influence. It seemed to him foolish to risk offending the sweet Flora with any of the flippant cynicism which normally characterised his social intercourse.

'Have you two been married long?' he asked, as they waited for Calum's first culinary surprise. There was a handwritten menu on each table which stipulated that they were to expect something called *Taliska Tumult* followed by *Crème de Kyleshee* and *Lobster?* – the latter to be named after Granny Kirsty had tasted and attempted to identify its alcoholic ingredient.

'Ten years now,' Mac vouchsafed, since Flora seemed somewhat tongue-tied under Tally's scrutiny.

'You must have been a child bride,' Tally told her disbelievingly, rendering her even more flustered. He relished the giggle which she attempted to smother with her hand like an artless schoolgirl. The effort widened her enormous lapis lazuli eyes into profound pools in which he thought it would be bliss to drown.

'No, no,' she protested.

'Shame on you, Mac, you snatched her from the cradle,' Tally remonstrated.

'I did not,' Mac retorted indignantly. 'She was eighteen. Working with her father on the croft.'

'Where was that?' inquired Tally, suddenly finding crofts of riveting interest, although until now he had thought they were something to do with a dog show.

'On Lismore,' said Mac. 'Port Ramsay. I used to put in there on fishing trips. 'Tis a good sheltering harbour.'

'Well, it certainly sheltered a beauty.' Tally was not teasing. To him, Flora was a Madonna. One did not tease a Madonna. Nor, somehow, did one ask her if she had children. He had never heard Mac talk about any children.

At this point Libby presented them with the *Taliska Tumult* – a melt-in-the-mouth roulade, stuffed with minced mushroom and chicken livers and surrounded by a sea of purêed sorrel and lovage, both of which were already to be found among the new spring herbage sprouting wild on the island. Calum had sent Craig out foraging for them at dawn like a sorcerer's apprentice.

'Flora's mother died when she was fifteen,' said Mac, touching his wife's hand briefly. 'It was lonely for her living on Lismore with just her father. Then he couldna stand it either, after she left. He's in Oban now, living with his sister.'

'Mac sees to the croft,' said Flora, smiling at him. 'He goes quite often to Lismore but I've never been back. I dinna care to.'

Gazing at Flora, Tally scarcely noticed the pungent whiff of *Diorissimo* as Libby's arm brushed his shoulder, banging his plate of *Taliska Tumult* down just a fraction too tumultuously.

Despite her lack of lunch, Donalda discovered she had no appetite for dinner, not even for the *Lobster?* She fiddled with the rosy claws and nibbled at the malty flesh but her stomach revolted. Calum's food might be lightness itself but even that was too heavy for her present state of nervous tension. Her guts had been knotted nauseously ever since her conversation with Nell. She knew she had mishandled it and yet she could not fathom out how or why. She seemed to have no point of contact with her daughter and now her son, invariably her ally and support, had also apparently abandoned her in preference for a couple who sounded like half-strangled hyenas and who were disgustingly and unforgivably Scottish! What was more, he was looking at the woman as if she was made of Dresden china and might break at the slightest touch.

To add to Donalda's discomfort and dismay, her ex-husband and his wife appeared to be on the most amicable terms with the twins, so much so that she had even heard the Irishwoman suggest that her daughter with the outlandish name (which sounded a bit like 'naïve' except she was patently anything but!) might come up to Taliska in her summer holidays and work for them. The whole Taliska venture, which had always seemed to Donalda a foolish aberration, appeared now to have developed into an all-absorbing family affair from which she was almost totally excluded. The less she ate the more she seethed and the less likely it became that she would be able to contain her fury. Even the few sips she took of Tally's carefully selected French wines did nothing to mellow her mood.

Not wishing to attack either of her children directly she selected the most obvious alternative target. Declining a sweet course she pleaded a headache and excused herself, stopping at Ian's table on her way out of the dining room. She fixed her former husband with accusing grey eyes and said in her most penetrating voice: 'If you can't control your daughter yourself don't you think it's a little unfair to expect Tally and Nell to cope with her? They have enough on their plate without worrying about the behaviour of a seventeen-year-old baggage.'

Her words were audible to everyone in the dining room and acted on Sinead like the proverbial red rag. 'Just who do you think you're calling a baggage?' she snarled, waving her cheese knife like a weapon.

'It's all right, darling, I'll sort this out,' said Ian swiftly, shaking his head warningly at his wife.

'It's your daughter you have to sort out,' retorted Donalda icily. 'But not by palming the little hoyden off on my children, if you don't mind.'

'How dare you call me names, you old witch!' shrilled Niamh, standing up so abruptly that she knocked her glass over, splashing red wine onto the white tablecloth like a fresh bloodstain. 'At least I don't go about pretending to be something I haven't been for years.'

'Sit down, Niamh,' said Ian menacingly. 'You're making things worse.'

'There's nothing much worse than a spiteful middle-aged female,' Sinead continued, disregarding her husband's thunderous look of discouragement. 'The bloody woman's been spoiling for a fight the whole weekend but I don't damn well see why it should be my daughter who bears the brunt!'

'If you have insufferable children what can you expect?' returned Donalda.

It was Sinead's turn to stand up. 'Listen, you bleached bag of bones, I don't have to take this from you. Ian spent a fortune buying the little legal document that says we don't have to put up with your poison!' She advanced fiercely on Donalda and her shocking-pink talons might have inflicted serious damage if Hal had not hastily stepped between them.

'Aw, come on you two,' he said, his transatlantic drawl becoming more pronounced in his agitation. 'There's no need for this.'

'No, there is not!' boomed Ian, now also on his feet. 'I don't know what's got you so worked up, Donalda, but whatever it is can we drop it – or shall we go outside and sort it out between the two of us just like we used to do in the old days? Only I should warn you that I make one exception to my rule about not hitting women – and that's my ex-wife!'

'It's always been the same with you,' yelled Donalda. 'You've always been more concerned about upsetting everyone else than me. It doesn't matter to you that you've turned my children against me and lured them back to this benighted country when I thought I'd managed to wipe Scotland out of them for ever. It doesn't matter that you've encouraged them to sink every penny they have in this idiotic scheme just because your mother used to live here. It doesn't matter that Nell is a bag of nerves and that Tally's career is ruined and that a horde of your so-delightful countrymen are doing unspeakable things at the very gates of this fool's paradise. All you're worried about is how *I might be upsetting other people!*'

'Doll!' shouted Hal suddenly in a stentorian voice. 'This is embarrassing. Please be quiet.' He grabbed his wife's elbow and pulled her towards the door and, her face a mask of misery, Donalda allowed herself to be steered out of the dining room.

Sinead sat down again and began to mop angrily at the spilled red wine with her napkin. 'The bloody woman's menopausal,' she muttered. 'It's the only excuse. Sit down, Niamh.'

Ian wiped his brow with his handkerchief and turned to Tally who was sitting at the next table. 'I am sorry that happened, old chap,' he said, trying to smile. 'Don't know how these things blow up.'

David looked with concern at Nell's white face and reached out to squeeze her hand under the table. 'Well, you said you wanted Taliska to be a place where people let off steam,' he said bracingly. 'And that was some blast!'

She returned his smile a little wanly. 'Poor Mummy. She thinks everyone is against her.'

Caroline, who had returned to her usual habit of fiddling and nibbling and eating very little, looked up from her scrap-filled plate and said quietly, 'Well, it's not very nice feeling like a spare part.'

Tally stood up, excusing himself. 'I'd better go to my mother,' he told the Macphersons. 'Please enjoy the rest of your meal. I'll be back in a minute.' He made for the door.

'Tally ho!' called David softly after him and his friend raised a hand in rueful acknowledgement.

Tally had ushered Donalda and Hal into the small conference room, so when the meal was over the others spread themselves between the drawing room, the hall and the bar. Leaving her mother and stepfather to her brother, Nell brought coffee to the Macphersons and sat down to keep them company. Flora interested her, even though she had initially been irritated by Tally's invitation to them.

'Yours is the newish house next door to the craft shop in the village, isn't it?' she asked the fisherman's wife. 'How long have you lived there?'

'Five or six years now,' Flora said shyly. 'Mac bought it after he'd paid off the boat.'

'And do you have children?' Nell inquired, having none of Tally's neo-religious compunction.

A shadow seemed to pass over Flora's face and Nell suddenly wished she hadn't asked. 'No, we havena been lucky there,' the woman said. 'And you and your brother – you're no' wed?'

'No. I guess we haven't been lucky *there*,' Nell responded, smiling. 'But don't give up on us yet.'

'Most folk in these parts marry very young,' Flora observed, blushing. 'I didna mean to imply that you're washed up.'

'Like a greasy pot, do you mean?'

Flora laughed, a low, musical sound that was both infectious and sexy. 'No – like driftwood, I think.'

Nell considered this and nodded. 'Yes, driftwood is nicer. I'd rather be flotsam than a dirty dish. Someone might come along some day and pick me up and take me home.'

'Where is your home?' Flora asked.

'Well, I thought it was here,' replied Nell.

'No, I mean where are you from?' Flora blushed again. Conversation with strangers was such a minefield.

'Like you're from Lismore, you mean? Well, I don't really think I'm from anywhere much. I was born in Glasgow but we moved to London very soon afterwards. I was rather hoping to come from Taliska eventually.'

Mac shook his head at this, entering into the conversation for the first time. Up to this moment he'd been looking as if he'd rather be several miles away on a heaving deck. 'Ye canna do that!'

'Do what?' Nell asked, surprised by his sudden interjection.

'Just move in here and think you belong. It doesna work like that. Folk'll never accept it.' Mac was red with the effort and embarrassment of his contribution.

Nell swallowed several times, pondering his words. Mac's was a reaction she might have anticipated but somehow she had not. 'Well, perhaps you're right. In that case we'll just have to be the twins from nowhere.'

'May I join you?'

Nell was grateful that Alasdair appeared and sat down beside her, nodding amiably at the Macs. 'Was that delicious lobster caught by you, Mr Macpherson?' he asked. 'Tally tells me you're going to supply all the hotel shellfish.'

'Aye, if I can,' Mac agreed.

'It works out well all round really,' Nell pointed out. 'Mac doesn't have to pay Oban harbour fees and we don't have to pay a wholesaler.' She smiled rather pointedly at Mac. 'We may not belong but we're quite useful, aren't we?'

Alasdair took a sip from the coffee cup he had brought with him. 'I saw you talking to the travellers down at the camp this morning when I was passing through,' he told Mac. 'You're not having any trouble with them, then?'

A wary look crossed Mac's face. 'Trouble? Why should I have trouble?'

Alasdair shrugged. 'Only because there are so many of them and only one of you. You must have to pass through the camp every day.'

'Aye, but I'm no' bothered,' said Mac. 'They dinna bother me and I dinna bother them.'

'You might even be able to do the odd deal with them, I suppose,' observed Alasdair mildly. Too mildly, Nell thought. What was the wily lawyer getting at?

'How do you mean, deal?' Mac's forefinger eased his collar from his neck.

'Well, I saw you taking money off one of the women. I presume you've been selling your surplus fish. Seems a good idea, and at least those children will be getting some fresh food.'

'Oh aye,' Mac admitted, the flush on his face receding. 'I sell them what I canna sell here or in Oban. The odd squabs and squid that get into the lobster pots – you know.'

'Well, I'm glad someone's making a bit out of the travellers, apart from Farmer McCandlish,' Nell said. 'He's not our favourite person, as you can imagine.'

'Duncan's a strange one,' nodded Mac, an amused look in his dark eyes. 'But he's no' stupid, I can tell you that! He knows exactly what he's doing with them travellers.' A satisfied chuckle rumbled in his throat but he did not elaborate and Nell decided it was time she found out how Tally was getting on calming Donalda down.

She stood up. 'Well, in case I don't see you before you go I'll say good night. I have some things to do in the kitchen. I'm sure Tally will see you before you leave.' She shook hands with Mac and Flora. With easy good manners Alasdair stood up when she did and she smiled warmly at him. 'I might see you before bedtime,' she said prophetically, 'but if I don't, good night.'

'She wants to go home tomorrow,' Tally announced when Nell tracked him down to the office. Donalda had retired to her room and Hal was drowning his sorrows in the bar. 'I said I'd drive them to Glasgow airport.'

'Oh shit', sighed Nell dejectedly. 'Though I can't say I'm sorry. We should never have asked them all together.'

'No, it was a bit of a mistake,' agreed Tally. 'Mind you, it didn't help, you being so pally with Dad and Sinead. Agreeing to have Niamh in the summer was too much for Mother to take.'

Nell saw red. She was damned if she was taking the blame for this fiasco over Donalda. 'Well, I don't think she was delirious either about you sitting with the Macphersons at dinner in preference to her and Hal. You know how she dotes on you. You should never have asked the Macs anyway. He looked thoroughly uncomfortable the entire time.'

'He's my friend, for Christ's sake. I'd have gone bloody nuts over the past few months if it hadn't been for Mac.' Tally was sitting in front of the glowing computer screen and began to tap feverishly on the keyboard.

'What are you doing?' she asked, irritated. In the past few weeks Tally and Ann Soutar had moved all the hotel business onto the computer, effectively excluding Nell from the books until such a time as she also managed to learn the intricacies of the machine. It irked her to be put at such a disadvantage. 'There are still guests out there to entertain, you know – including your beloved Macphersons.'

Tally made an impatient noise. 'You're right, I

must say good night to Flora. I'm just seeing what we would have made if we'd charged them all at the going rate.'

'Counting the cost of entertaining your family?' Nell was incredulous. 'That's charming! You'd better include Fishing Mac, then, as he's busy consuming a bottle of Oban malt, single-handed!'

Tally grinned. 'He'll be pissed as a fart,' he observed indulgently. 'I'd better give them a lift home. Can't have him running over happy campers on the way back, can we? Besides, she's worth protecting.'

There was something in her brother's voice that rang warning bells in Nell's head. 'Don't mess about with that one, Tally,' she said suddenly. 'You'd be getting into something you can't handle if you do.'

Lit by the luminous computer screen, Tally's face was no longer the usual pleasant mask. 'Mind your own bloody business, damn you,' he snarled. 'When you've done a few years pokey yourself you can start shelling out the advice. Meanwhile, I wish you'd stop sticking your nose in my affairs and go and fuck David. He seems to have lusted after you secretly for months, though God knows why. As far as I'm concerned you're a fat bloody nuisance and I wish I'd never included you in the Taliska deal!'

This sudden and, to her, unprovoked attack took Nell off-guard and it was several seconds before she recovered enough to retaliate, but when she caught her breath, retaliate she did, with gloves off. 'That's rich,' she sneered, her heart leaping with violent indignation. 'The one-time City whizz-kid thinks it's *his* deal! Thinks he's the big boss man with all the power and all the glory! Well, I tell you, Tally the Wally-Dug, if you think you'd have got one room of this hotel open without me working my bloody guts out while you and Mac got pickled as herrings in the Ossian, you can think again. And now, for God's sake, you've taken a shine to his wife! Well, you can drool over the sugary Flora as much as you like, but don't expect me to mend your head when Mac whams you with an axe, or sew up the cuts when Libby starts making *Fatal Attraction* look like *Noddy in Toytown*. I may be a "fat bloody nuisance", as you so gallantly put it, but you're a nasty big prick who uses women and abuses friendships and I'm ashamed to have to call you my brother!'

The office door slammed loudly behind her retreating figure and Tally stared at the screen before him. Making an angry noise, he pressed *Enter* and a total appeared at the end of his column of figures. 'Five thousand three hundred and forty quid,' he breathed incredulously. 'That's a helluva lot to pay for a fucked-up weekend!'

Donalda might have felt a certain satisfaction, could she have heard Nell holding forth to David later that night. Everyone else had gone up to bed and Tally had driven off with the Macphersons, having shoved his drunken fishing friend into the back of the BMW, smirking at his slurred ramblings about 'bailing in' and 'bailing out' or some similar sea-going rigmarole. For his own part, Tally found sitting beside the gentle Flora a much-needed restorative and was more than happy that the journey took twice as long as usual owing to the necessity of navigating at a snail's pace around various bodies and objects lying on the edge of the roadway beyond the gate.

'It's not that I want to be patted on the back all the time,' grumbled Nell to David, harking back to her quarrel with her brother. 'God knows, Tally and I have never got on that well anyway. It's just that everyone is so negative! Mummy says I'll never be happy in Scotland. Mac says I'll never belong at Taliska, and Tally says he wishes I wasn't here. Even Granny Kirsty wonders if I've done the right thing! And all that before we've even officially opened. It's not what you'd call a good start, is it?'

'It could be better,' David agreed. 'But look, there's still me. Could you put me down on the plus side, do you think?'

Nell stared at him thoughtfully. Caroline's pensiveness during dinner led Nell to suspect that the other girl was beginning to have second thoughts about losing David and, in a perverse way, this endeared him more to her. He was so attractively safe – dark and solid like the skerries out on the loch. There was something about him she found irresistibly dependable at this time of uncertainty in her life. Caroline could look out for herself – she'd had more than her chance. Nell felt rather like one of the wide-eyed seals which swam onto the skerries to bask in the sun and escape the swirl of the tide. David's arms would provide a good place to escape to for a few hours when she felt in dire danger of being swamped. She held out her hand gratefully, taking his plump, blunt fingers in hers, noticing the fuzz of soft black hairs that adorned them. 'There wouldn't be a plus side at all without you,' she said emphatically, squeezing them gently. 'Just at the moment you are it.'

'Oh, I don't know,' he said modestly, entwining her fingers in his and bending to kiss their pink tips. 'I think we could include *Lobster Kirsty*. It was delicious!' Shortly after tasting the lobster dish, Granny Kirsty had correctly identified the malt used as Laphroaig and Calum had sent her a menu with the *?* altered to *Kirsty*.

'Yes, it was,' she agreed. 'So we'd better stick Calum on the plus list too. And Granny Kirsty, of course. And Ginny who's a honey and Leo who paints like a demon, and Tina Armstrong who played like an angel, and all the people who've actually booked to pay real money to stay here next weekend. Perhaps there are more pluses than I thought.'

'And what about the law-man? I get the impression that he's rather on your side,' suggested David.

'Alasdair?' She looked dubious. 'I'm not sure about him. He's a bit cautious, sees everything from all sides at once. I suppose a lawyer's bound to do that but at this moment I require unquestioned bias in my favour.'

They were sitting on the sofa in the hall. The fire had died to a few glowing cinders and the creaking and shuffling sounds of the settling household were gradually diminishing around them. 'Is everyone in bed, do you think?' whispered David, taking the opportunity of nibbling her ear at the same time.

'I think so,' she whispered back, hoping the butterfly clip of her pierced earring did not work loose. There were so many unexpected obstacles to seduction. 'Alasdair went out for a breath of air but I think I heard him come back.'

'Good. We don't need to wait up any longer, then.' David stood up and pulled her after him, his eyes asking meaningful and erotic questions.

Postponing her answer to this mute appeal, Nell felt with her free hand in the pocket of her silk trousers. There was a jingling sound and a large bunch of keys appeared from which she carefully selected one, disentangling her other hand from

David's in order to do so. 'The bar key,' she confided with a sly smile. 'There's some more of that Taliska champagne in the fridge and, frankly, I haven't had nearly enough of it yet. How about you?'

He shook his head, grinning, and took the keys from her, prowling towards the bar door with the exaggerated steps of a sneakthief. 'Do you know the combination, kid?' he asked in a stage-whispered James Cagney drawl.

'Naw, but some jelly should do it,' she replied in the same style.

'Don't be a stoopid moll,' he admonished, fiddling the key into the lock. 'We cain't use jelly to get into the fridge because da jelly's inside it already, wid de ice cream. Ah,' he announced triumphantly, opening the door. 'Voyla!'

Several minutes later they crept giggling down the passage to David's room with the champagne in an ice-bucket. At the door of *Scabious* they stopped for another key ceremony, David fumbling with the lock, chirruping with excitement because Nell, in her turn, was fumbling with the fastening of his trousers and giggling like a lascivious leprechaun. Reaction to the night's events had left her flirtatious and uninhibited, and all before she had even tasted the champagne! Having finally got the door open, David made an exclamation of triumph and turned to kiss her, just as his trousers fell down. She was gurgling with victorious glee when the next door along the corridor also opened, from the inside.

'Oh, sorry!' It was Alasdair McInnes in his dressing gown, his face a flaming study in astonishment. 'I thought I heard something.'

With exaggerated dignity David stepped out of his trousers and kicked them through the bedroom door with a flourish. 'It seems you can't trust Moss Bros,' he told Alasdair solemnly and stepped after them, pulling Nell behind him. Both bedroom doors closed simultaneously and David and Nell burst into hysterical mirth, stumbling in the dark towards the bed.

'Don't spill it,' hissed Nell, stifling a shriek as the ice-cold bucket came into contact with her bare midriff. Somehow the buttons on her silk shirt seemed to have come undone and David was trying to kiss her breasts without putting down the champagne. 'Here.' She grabbed the bucket, leaving his hands free to follow where his mouth had been. They were also ice-cold. 'Ahh!' she yelled in shock. 'It's like mating with an iceberg. Ouch!' This as she hit her head on the gilt-edged bedpost, recklessly depositing the ice-bucket so that its freezing contents spilled all over the bed. It was a tribute to their total absorption in their subsequent activities that neither of them noticed. And by the time they came to drink it they did not care that what champagne remained in the bottle was rather warm.

Chapter Nine

Nell was never sure whether it was bedding with David or sailing with Mac which started her throwing up. Perhaps it was both, combined with her escalating inferiority complex. Whatever the cause, it was at this time that she discovered not only that she *could* throw up but that she actually enjoyed the glorious, empty, weightless feeling the process induced. Having spent a lifetime so far when even gastric flu resulted in nothing more than aches and pains and continuous nausea without vomiting, the physical relief of sudden voiding produced an unexpected exhilaration.

She embarked on the Sunday loch excursion feeling lousy anyway, a state she put down to overconsumption of post-coital champagne and lack of sleep. She had stumbled out of David's room before dawn still wearing her crumpled blue silk trouser suit and wondering if her face and body looked as well-used as they felt. Cooking breakfast for twenty had induced the first rush of bitter fluid to her mouth, the smell of eggs and bacon for once stimulating acute antipathy rather than ravenous appetite. Then, shortly after ten o'clock, she had kissed her mother goodbye with as much warmth as her fluttering stomach and crashing headache would allow and tried to harden her heart against the querulous misery in Donalda's thin, pale face as it peered from the window of the retreating car. Tally seemed maddeningly unaffected by the emotional turbulence of the night before but Nell was in no mood to bury the hatchet with her brother, especially as his conciliatory offer to drive Hal and Donalda to Glasgow airport left her with all the responsibility of organising Mac's boat trip – an outing which he, Tally, had instigated without her knowledge and which she considered misguided. Spitefully she rather hoped he would run foul of the New Age travellers and have to spend fraught minutes negotiating his way through the gates. That would teach him not to be so smug!

As she was packing the picnic hampers, Mac shuffled into the kitchen looking like the inside of a cucumber sandwich and she began to wonder whether there would actually be a boat trip. Oban might be his home port but, if the after-effects of his previous night's consumption were anything to go by, it certainly didn't seem to be his home malt. Fortunately, several cups of strong coffee and two bacon baps seemed to put new heart into him and he climbed nimbly enough into the cab of the Fourtrack when Nell offered to drive him down to the jetty along with the day's supply of food and drink.

'Is your wife not coming with us, Mac?' she asked, enviously imagining he had left Flora cosily curled up in bed, sleeping off her late night.

'No, she goes to see her dad in Oban Sundays. And she gets sea-sick,' added Mac succinctly.

'On a day like this?' Nell said disbelievingly, as they halted at the jetty. The tide was flowing in calm spring sunlight and the loch glimmered like a silver salver, hardly a ripple denting its mirrored surface.

'You'd be amazed,' he muttered.

Despite his wife's unseaworthiness, Mac's boat was named after her. The *Flora* was a small but immensely sturdy timber-built fishing smack with a wheelhouse perched amidships like an up-ended matchbox in front of a short, stubby mast which supported the net boom at a forty-five-degree angle. Like most inshore boats she had little protection to offer from the weather, the wheelhouse being just large enough for the skipper and his crew, and the area below decks suitable only for stowing the catch. So the dozen people who embarked that Sunday would be exposed to whatever conditions the day provided. The forecast, however, was good.

Granny Kirsty had opted to stay on dry land with Leo, who said he was no sailor and wanted to get on with his mural in the gym. Calum and Craig were having the morning off but had promised to cook the landlubbers a late roast-beef lunch with all the trimmings. Of the rest of the staff, Rob came along to act as deckhand since Mac's regular crew always had Sunday off, and Libby and Ginny were simply not to be denied their first chance of seeing more of Scotland than the Taliska bedrooms and dining room.

'Are you OK?' David asked Nell with concern as he hastened to help her unload hampers, cold-boxes and rugs from the back of the Fourtrack. He and the rest of the visitors had walked down to the jetty from the hotel ready for the agreed eleven o'clock start. 'You look a bit pale.'

Nell straightened up and smiled ruefully at the pleasant, round face framed in its mop of dark curls which she had left snoring gently on the pillow at five-thirty that morning. Wearing jeans and a sweat-shirt, David looked relaxed and slightly pleased with himself – as any man would who had spent the kind of night he had, thought Nell self-consciously. Of course, he'd also had an extra four hours' sleep. 'I'm fine,' she lied. 'Although I could do with a brisk sea breeze to blow away a few cobwebs.'

'I don't think you'll be lucky there,' remarked David, squinting across the loch. Even this early in April, the rising sun had warmed the air enough to cause him to discard his waxed cotton jacket. 'Looks as calm as a millpond out there. Really fantastic.'

Niamh and Ninian were arguing over who would occupy the central fork of the bow. The boy was armed with his binoculars and a bird-book and had asked Mac whether they might see any puffins on their trip. 'Maybe,' muttered Mac, whom Nell had several times caught sipping surreptitiously from a battered thermos-flask which she suspected did not contain tea. 'It's a wee bit early in the year for them to be coming ashore for nesting. Still, keep your eyes peeled. Plenty of sea birds where we're going!'

At least he looks a bit more human now, Nell thought, wondering whether she might ask for a nip from the flask herself.

'Where are we going?' demanded Niamh. 'I hope we won't just be tooling about like a rowboat on the Serpentine. Can we go right out to sea?'

'No, that we canna,' said Mac firmly, eyeing his substantial human cargo. 'With this many aboard I'm no' going out of sight of land.'

'Well, where *are* we going, then?' Ninian repeated his sister's question. 'Somewhere near some cliffs, so I can see some nest-sites? Please!'

Nell interposed at this point. 'Where do you suggest we go, Mac?'

'Well, it's a nice run round the tip of Lismore and we can put in at Port Ramsay for a couple of hours.

Give you time to eat your piece and stretch your legs.'

Nell nodded, relieved to have the decision made. 'Great,' she said. 'That sounds perfect.' She was just grateful that Calum was not there to hear his sumptuous picnic described as a 'piece'.

The outward journey was uneventful. The steady beat of the diesel engine powered the *Flora* effortlessly over the glassy surface of the loch and within an hour everyone on board seemed to have grown used to the strong smell of shellfish which inevitably permeated the planks of what was, after all, a regular working boat. Everyone that is, except Nell, who began to doubt if she would ever be able to look a lobster in the eye again. Ninian was in his element, identifying the sea-birds which cruised above them, bobbed on the *Flora*'s wake and preened on the rocks of the small islands and steep peninsulas which they passed en route.

'Common gulls,' he pronounced dismissively, turning his binoculars skywards. 'But those zappy flyers must be fulmars, I think – look how they play chicken with the water! They could be kittiwakes, though.'

'Any puffins then, show-off?' demanded Niamh, secretly interested but unwilling to admit it.

'Not that I can see. They wouldn't be flying about anyway. They fish from the surface. Those big black things on the rocks must be cormorants and the ones bobbing on the water are guillemots or razorbills, I can't tell which. They're not puffins, though.'

'Don't they have beaut names?' remarked Ginny, who was following the commentary, clinging to a cleat on the leeward bow. 'Razorbill and guillemot. Somehow you can just imagine what they look like from their names.'

'They're all auks,' put in Alasdair over his shoulder. After doing his bit helping to stow the picnic things, he'd been leaning against the wheelhouse pointing out landmarks to Caroline who seemed to be keeping as far away from David and Nell as possible. 'Which is not quite such a "beaut" name perhaps.' He emphasised the Australian slang word with amusement.

'What are?' asked Niamh, puzzled.

'Razorbills and guillemots.'

'Puffins too?'

'Yes, puffins are auks too.' Alasdair looked gratified at her interest. Nell simply wondered where it was leading.

'But we haven't seen a puffin yet, have we?' There was a glint of mischief in Niamh's eye. 'Have we, little brother?' she persisted, digging Ninian in the ribs.

Ninian gave her an irritated look and admitted that so far he hadn't managed to sight one of the endearing clown-birds with their distinctive red, blue and yellow beaks. 'But I bet I will, before the day is out,' he declared defiantly.

'Oh yes, I bet you will, because we'll all help you. We'll track one down,' shouted Niamh exultantly. 'And what does that make us?'

David and Nell said it in unison, having followed her train of thought. 'Raiders of the Lost Auk!'

Niamh was furious. 'Damn you,' she cried. 'That was my line!'

Although it was one of the largest communities on Lismore, Port Ramsay was little more than a single terrace of twelve stone-built cottages running along one wall of a rather silted-up harbour. Some were in good repair, with doors and windows painted bright colours – ochre, red and green – but on others the paintwork was of an ancient nondescript grey and peeling badly, the difference being, Alasdair explained, between the spick and span holiday cottages of the city-dwellers and the less well-endowed homes of the crofters, who eked out a living off land and sea. The ruined walls of several abandoned crofts could be seen scattering the enclosing slopes of the bay. Mac skilfully docked the *Flora* against the seaward side of the harbour wall, unwilling to take her inside where burgeoning reeds and rushes were beginning to clog up the channels. There was no sign of life in the village although one or two small boats were pulled up on the muddy shingle beach and an ancient Land Rover was tucked into a lean-to at the far end of the terrace.

'It's too early in the year for the city slickers to be coming, and the islanders'll be away to the kirk,' Mac explained. 'They've a right grand one about two miles up the brae. Used to be a cathedral, they say.'

'That's right,' Alasdair agreed. They were all gathered in the stern, preparing to disembark and offload the picnic. 'Lismore was the home of the bishops of Argyll in the thirteenth century.'

'A cathedral!' exclaimed Caroline, shielding her eyes against the southern sun. 'From what I can see you wouldn't think there'd be enough people to fill a chapel.'

Alasdair laughed. 'Obviously the population's shrunk a bit since then. There are only about a hundred and twenty living here now, but there were once nearly two thousand people on Lismore. There are plenty of ruins – a large monastery on the southern shore and three castles. It's an island worth exploring.'

'Pity we haven't got much time,' remarked Nell,

who had personally spotted a primrose-strewn, sun-dappled glade on the wooded peninsula beyond the village. She fully intended to spread a rug out there and doze. Exploring could wait for another day.

'Well, I'm going to make a start,' said Ninian enthusiastically. 'Who's coming with me?'

After the picnic hampers and rugs had been ferried up to the clearing, Nell gratefully watched a chattering group straggle off up the stony, unmade road which led from the shore, armed with drinks and apples to keep them going until a late lunch. Even Ian and Sinead had decided that a bit of a walk would do them good and Alasdair promised them spectacular views from the central ridge of the island. Mac wandered off on some unspecified errand of his own but David lingered, saying he would help Nell prepare the picnic, at which Caroline had given a derisive snort, declaring: 'You wouldn't know a bap from a bannock!' and turned huffily on her heel, hurrying to catch up with the others.

Normally she might have rushed to pacify her girlfriend but Nell was feeling too wiped-out to be concerned for Caroline's feelings. 'I'm poleaxed,' she declared, flopping down in the sun, eyes closed and head spinning. Technicolour whorls and dancing black dots performed acrobatics behind her eyelids.

'I suppose I should be flattered,' remarked David, seating himself more sedately beside her.

Blindly, Nell waved an admonishing arm. 'Beast! You're a wild ravening beast, David Guedalla.'

He bent over her as if to savage her throat, growling like a tiger. 'And you love it, my beauty, you love it.'

She pushed him away violently and sat up, blinking. 'Idiot – get off! You've had far more sleep than me.' David stared at her, suddenly alarmed. She had gone sheet-white and her mouth was working as if she was in pain.

Nell thought she was going to pass out. Her skin felt clammy, despite the hot sun, and the whirling in her head increased to spin-dry speed. Her mouth filled with saliva and she threw herself off the rug and into some long grass where she proceeded to retch and vomit for several long minutes.

David had never been faced with such undisguised physical weakness before. Like most good Jewish boys he had relied on his mother to handle the effects of all his own bodily functions or dysfunctions, and had no experience himself of mopping or patting or dispensing tender loving care. He was completely at a loss. He just stood up and hovered helplessly, eyes averted, waiting for the crisis to subside.

When her diaphragm had stopped heaving and the blood began to disperse from her belly to the parts of her body it did not seem to have been reaching for several minutes, Nell sat back on her heels and took several deep breaths. Immediately she began to cough. Anyone who has ever crouched, retching, over bowl, basin or toilet knows that what comes out of the mouth also goes up the nose, and the action of straightening up sends it back down the nasal passages in a choking and foul-tasting stream. But Nell did not know this. 'There's some kitchen paper,' she spluttered furiously at David who seemed transfixed into immobility. 'In that basket – please!'

Rousing himself into action he found the desired roll of soft tissue and handed it to her without comment. When she had spent several minutes blowing her nose and wiping her eyes and mouth she crawled back to the rug and sank down prostrate once more, exhausted. 'Can I do anything?' he asked at last, wrinkling his nose. The stench of vomit was beginning to taint the fresh smell of earth and primroses. She shook her head, eyes tight shut, her hand still clamped firmly over her mouth as if to forestall a repeat performance.

'Water,' muttered David, hastily hunting in the boxes and baskets. 'There must be some water here somewhere.' With a small cry of triumph he found a bottle of Highland Spring, poured some into a cup and some over a paper napkin. 'Here,' he said to the prone figure on the rug. 'My best rugside manner.'

More than an hour later the explorers returned to find the clearing laid out for a feast, gay checked cloths spread over tartan rugs and food displayed in tempting array. Since they had not really noticed the first location they did not realise that the picnic had been strategically moved from the site of Nell's distress to a less polluted position, with all traces of her sickness buried under grass and stones. Nell was now feeling wonderful, as if shedding a physical discomfort had also rid her of all mental despondency. She felt a stone lighter, filled with new energy, like someone who has drunk half a bottle of champagne rather than a glass or two of fizzy mineral water.

David still felt somewhat inhibited, embarrassed at having witnessed her indisposition and guilty that he might partly be the cause of it. 'You look a different person,' he remarked shortly before the others returned.

'That's because I'm no longer a virgin!' exclaimed Nell quixotically, shaking out a tablecloth. 'Oh no, not last night, don't worry,' she added, giggling at his expression of shocked disbelief. 'I'm a bit long in the tooth for defloration. Although perhaps, in a way, you are responsible. You see, I've never vomited before in my life – and now I have. It's almost like being released from jail.'

'Is that how you felt when you did lose your virginity?' he asked with what she considered typical male prurience.

She shook her head. 'No, that wasn't nearly as exciting as this. So, see what you've done for me? You should be proud of yourself.' She flung her arms wide and began to dance about wildly, as if one act of regurgitation had changed her from an elephant into an elf. Half of him wanted to embrace her, to share this mood of elation but the other half could not erase the memory of her retching from his mind. He felt disinclined to kiss the mouth from which such foulness had so recently flowed. He was quite grateful when the others returned.

'You should have come with us,' Sinead told them as she sank gratefully down on a rug. 'Alasdair was right, the views from the top are just dazzling.'

'We could see six Munros!' cried Ninian. 'Do you know what they are?' he asked David solemnly. 'They're mountains over three thousand feet high and you can see six of them at once from up there, including Ben Nevis. That's the highest mountain in Britain.'

'We were lucky to see that,' added Alasdair, accepting the silvered metal tumbler of white wine Nell offered him. 'Thank you. Ben Nevis is usually hiding under a cap of cloud but it looks magnificent today. Sinead is right, you should have come.' He smiled at her and raised his drink.

Nell smiled back. 'There'll be another day for me, I'm sure,' she said happily. 'Old Ben won't dare to hide from me for ever.' As she said it she felt certain it was true. Despite the slings and arrows of the past twenty-four hours she was suddenly positive that she belonged here in this part of the world. After all, she had poured her own special libation upon the ground!

'No,' responded Alasdair, instinctively recognising her new sense of purpose. He himself looked like a natural extension of the landscape in his well-worn walking boots, checked shirt and rather battered cords. 'I'm sure he won't.'

Glasgow airport was thronged with people. It was the first weekend of the school holidays and a dozen charter flights were scheduled to fly families off to Easter breaks in Spanish sun-spots. Also the terminal building was in the process of being altered and extended and there were complicated detours between check-in and embarkation. Donalda and Hal were puzzled and perplexed by the disorder, following so closely on their emotional weekend and also on a rather unpleasant experience they'd had as they left the island. Despite it being only ten a.m. – an hour of the day rarely encountered by New Age travellers – many of those parked in McCandlish's field had been up and about, irritable and fractious due to some unrevealed cause. There had been much shouting and yelling as the BMW appeared through the gates and a particularly obnoxious little thug, whom Tally recognised as one of the pre-teen pack-leaders, threw something brown and viscous at the car which hit the tinted window right by Donalda's head. She ducked involuntarily but not before she had recognised the identity of the missile. 'Ugh!' she cried with revulsion. 'Tally, that was—!' She couldn't bring herself to complete the sentence.

'Crap – yes, I know.' Tally said it for her. 'Bloody little morons. I hope they drown in the stuff one day, preferably their own!' Furiously he had slammed his foot on the accelerator and fortunately the aforementioned morons had proved agile enough to get out of the way. But the sticky brown substance had clung tenaciously to the window glass, sullying Donalda's view of Loch Lomond as they drove along its length.

'I shall be glad to get back to London,' she complained when the check-in clerk had asked her twice if she wanted smoking or non-smoking and she had failed to comprehend the girl's refined Glasgow accent. 'At least the people I don't understand there are foreigners.'

Tally did not, as Nell might have done, remind his mother that she had lived in Glasgow herself for several years at the start of her first marriage and that she ought to speak the local lingo quite fluently. He knew that Donalda had long ago erased what she considered such a pollutant from her memory.

'Well, next time you come we'll have cleared the travellers away somehow, I promise you,' said Tally grimly. 'And we might have some real celebrities for you to meet.'

'That'd be great, Tally,' enthused Hal, trying to make up for Donalda's ominous silence at the very mention of a return visit. 'Who have you got coming for the opening?'

'Oh, they're mostly money men. The chairman of the Scottish Tourist Board is going to cut the ribbon for us and there are some bankers and their wives, the local MEP, the chairman of the local Enterprise Board. A pretty dry lot really but at least most of them are paying.'

'Well, all the best, my boy. I hope it goes with a bang.'

Tally disliked being called 'my boy' by his stepfather but he was so relieved to be saying goodbye he scarcely noticed. Donalda kissed him briefly on the cheek and said firmly, 'See you in London, darling,' before tucking her arm in Hal's and carefully setting her high-heels onto the escalator which conveyed them to the shuttle departure lounge.

It would not take a mindreader to detect that she had not had a good time, thought Tally. He took some paper towels from the gents, returned to the car park and gingerly cleaned the mess from the passenger window of the BMW.

Driving back up Loch Lomondside he suddenly realised almost for the first time that it was a glorious day. The loch sparkled like a basketful of diamonds, occasionally dulled by the passing shadow of a fat, fluffy cloud in a sky of purest azure. To his right Ben Lomond rose above thickly forested foothills as the loch narrowed, leading him northwards between the peaks of Ben Lui and Ben More surrounded by their lesser satellites. After climbing through the villages of Crianlarich and Tyndrum the road split, running north towards Rannoch Moor and the mysteries of Glen Coe, and west towards Oban and the Isles. Shortly after taking the left turn, Tally swung the car right-handed at the crest of a hill and all at once a huge and awe-inspiring vista opened out before him. He had driven this road a dozen times in the past few months but never previously witnessed the phenomenon produced by this particular combination of cloud and sun. He felt impelled to stop the car at a strategically provided viewpoint.

A tumbled mass of hills and glens stretched far and wide under a surging skyscape of heaped and foaming clouds which slowly gathered and parted, allowing brilliant, slanted rays of sunshine to illuminate patches of heather or sections of pine forest below. Pools of golden light flickered over the landscape as if the gods of legend were staging a laser show in a vast celestial discotheque. Tally thought it resembled a Renaissance artist's impression of the Day of Judgment, when the Hand of God reaches through clouds of heavenly radiance to dispense justice to all men. He sat for a long time simply staring through the windscreen while the clouds continued their slow, ethereal waltz, now opening new windows for fresh beams, now closing a curtain against the sun's rays.

'Great balls of fire,' murmured Tally to himself, moved beyond the previous scope of his imagination. 'Whatever the kids may say, I bet this kicks taking Ecstasy into touch.'

It was mid-afternoon when he drove through the village of Salach. He was hungry and tired but he dreaded the prospect of running the gauntlet of the travellers. He had caught sight of several small groups hanging about the petrol station and the general store, both of which were firmly closed and shuttered because the local Presbyterian community held staunchly to the Christian sabbath. The people from the camp were easily identifiable by their unisex long hair, usually tied back in a ponytail by the men and left straggly and unkempt by the women. It was strange, thought Tally, in view of their lifestyle that, rather than jeans or shorts, the women invariably wore ankle-length skirts and dressed their daughters in droopy, oversized frocks. Grubby femininity rather than rampant feminism seemed to rule among these rootless wanderers.

He considered turning in at the Ossian, but he was not in the mood for darts or pool and, after viewing the Hand of God in the hills, he did not feel inclined to sit in a dim, sour-smelling bar. The neat, modern house next to the craft shop drew him like a magnet. 'Well, why not?' he argued with himself. 'A pleasant cup of tea with Flora is just what I need.'

She opened the door warily in answer to his ring and looked surprised but not displeased. Smiling shyly she led him into a cosy living-kitchen at the back of the house which boasted a wide window with a view over gorse-scattered grassland leading down to the loch. A shining enamel range gave off comforting warmth and supported a singing kettle.

'I hope you don't mind my dropping in,' Tally said, accepting the offer of a comfortable Scots pine armchair at one end of the central table.

'I dinna mind at all. I was just a wee bit worried you might be the travellers. They ring the bell sometimes, trying to sell us things. Mac says they're all right but . . . Anyway, you'll have a cup of tea?' Flora was busy with teapot and caddy. 'I was going to have one myself. I'm only just back from Oban.'

'Of course.' Tally remembered being told of her regular Sunday visits. 'How is your father?' She did not seem to notice his awkward formality. To her it was natural good manners.

'No' bad. A wee bit more cheerful. He went awful morbid after he left Lismore.'

'It's hard to adjust to a new way of life,' Tally remarked, noting with glee the arrival on the table of generous platefuls of shortbread and jam sponge.

'It's no' that,' Flora said through a cloud of steam as she filled the teapot. 'He didna like me marrying Mac. He still doesna speak to him really.' She brought the pot to the table and sat down. Her face was flushed pink with steam and self-consciousness but she seemed confident in her own home. There was no sign of the shy reticence she had displayed the night before.

Tally thought that she looked even more alluring in the harsh light of her own kitchen than she had in the Taliska candlelight. She was wearing a short-sleeved, hand-knitted jumper in a soft shade of hyacinth blue which almost exactly matched her eyes. It had slightly puffed sleeves and a scalloped neckline and Tally thought it made her look like a schoolgirl. He wanted to take her on his knee and feed her sweets.

'I'll just let it draw a wee bit,' she said, pulling a knitted tea-cosy over the pot. 'Have some short-bread meanwhile.' She pushed the plate across the table.

Tally took a piece with alacrity. He had not eaten since breakfast and felt famished. 'Did you make this?' he asked through a mouthful of crumbs. 'It's delicious!'

Her blush deepened slightly but she smiled gratefully. 'Mac says I dinna make it as good as his mother,' she said.

Tally frowned. 'He doesn't appreciate you.'

She shrugged. 'He didna look too good when he left this morning. I hope he's all right.'

'He can take his drink, can Mac,' grinned Tally. 'He'll be OK.'

She poured the tea and offered him cake, taking a slice herself. He watched her eat it, appreciating her appetite, enjoying the way she licked the icing sugar off her fingers. She was a world away from Gemma, even from Libby – a throw-back to a bygone era when women were soft and sympathetic and went in and out in the right places and didn't smoke and swear. He had never met anyone like her.

'It's no' just the drink, though, is it?' she said

suddenly, dragging Tally sharply back from his reverie.

'What do you mean?' he asked, puzzled and off-guard.

'We can all take our drink here in the Highlands. It's our way of life.' She said it as if it were a commonplace. 'But lately sometimes there's something about Mac I dinna fathom. Something different. You see a lot of him, have you no' noticed?'

Tally pursed his lips, shook his head. 'No, I can't say I have.'

She leaned forward confidingly, as if about to whisper a secret in a crowded room. 'I can trust you, can't I?' she asked. 'You wouldna say anything to anyone else?'

He looked nonplussed. 'Say what? About whom?' The tea party was turning out quite unexpectedly.

'About Mac. I dinna want people talking but I want to ask someone's advice. Will you help me?'

'Of course I will, if I can,' he assured her. 'But there's nothing wrong with Mac that I can see.'

'I think he's taking drugs,' she said in a rush. 'I don't know what, but he's on something.'

Tally's eyebrows disappeared upwards, beneath the fair forelock of his hair. 'What? No!' he stuttered, astounded. 'Do drugs circulate around here?'

She shook her head. 'No' so far as I know. Mostly people just drink. Mebbe around the harbour though, among the fishermen. I've heard rumours.'

'Mac hardly goes to the harbour these days,' Tally pointed out. 'He sells most of his catch to us and he keeps the boat at the jetty. Anyway, I'm sure you're wrong. Tell me why you suspect him?'

She looked troubled at that. 'It doesna sound nice, put like that. A woman shouldna suspect her man.'

'All right, why are you worried about him then?'

She hesitated. Eventually she said, 'You know how he's grumpy sometimes, 'specially if he's had a few the night before?'

'He can be a bit gloomy, yes,' agreed Tally, unwilling to commit himself to more serious criticism.

'Well, lately he isna grumpy, he's wafty! Away with the fairies some days. I canna get a proper sentence out of him.'

'Perhaps he's had the odd smoke with the travellers. They're on something pretty strong by the look of them.'

But she shook her head. 'No. It started before they arrived,' she said firmly, 'around the beginning of March. At first I thought it must be something you were giving him because it wasna long after you and he started meeting at the Ossian.'

Tally was amused at that. He had smoked the odd joint and popped the odd pill in his time but preferred the traditional alcoholic stimulants. 'What made you change your mind?' he asked gently.

She looked at him shrewdly. 'After I met you I decided you wouldna be on drugs,' she said simply.

'Too much of a drunkard, you mean?' he asked lightly.

'No. I just knew, that's all.'

'Well, I'm glad you feel you can trust me,' he said, 'but I don't know what I can do to help.'

'Just watch him and let me know what you think. Then I'll decide what to do.'

She was no witless female, this crofter's daughter, thought Tally with renewed respect. When she decided what to do, woe betide Mac!

As so often happened, the wind had freshened in the late afternoon and angry little waves were nipping at the *Flora*'s planks as the picnickers carried the baskets back to Port Ramsay harbour. They were all replete with Calum's rillettes of wild salmon and cold Drambuie soufflés, and as they had consumed a fair quantity of Muscadet and Beaujolais between them, conversation had become uninhibited. Having cast surreptitious looks at them all afternoon, Caroline grabbed the other end of a hamper with Nell and asked outright if she and David were 'hitting it off'.

'Well, the odd spark has flown,' admitted Nell guardedly, wondering what was coming next. She could not discern the other girl's expression for it was dusk and they both had their heads down picking their way over the ruts and stones of the rough track. 'Why? You didn't want him yourself anyway, did you?'

'Oh no, you're welcome!' Caroline's words were casual but her tone made Nell frown in the gloaming. It would be bloody typical, she thought, if Caroline were to sulk about losing David, having kept him at arm's length for so long. Nell was not certain enough of her own feelings for David to want them compromised by any jealousy on the part of her friend. Ahead she heard Rob and Libby giggling over the burden they carried between them. Those two had teased each other merrily and joked together most of the day. There might be trouble brewing there, too, if Tally got wind of it!

When picnic and passengers were safely embarked, Mac eased the *Flora* out into the open waters of the loch. There was a very different sea running compared to the millpond of the morning. Within minutes the swell hit them and the boat was dipping and rolling with the jerky, uncoordinated action of a middle-aged swinger at a disco.

Mac seemed perfectly calm, standing at the helm

inside the wheelhouse and gazing out at the fiery path burned across the frisky water by the setting sun. The sky ahead was a pale shade of lavender, deepening behind them to violet, magenta and orange, among clouds massing into a spectacular sunset. The swell was breaking into a luminous greenish-white spume over the rocky outcrops off the northern tip of Lismore. There were few birds about now, only a skein of geese flighting east and the occasional late herring gull winging back to its roost in the dark cliffs of the mainland peninsula. Ninian had sorrowfully decided he was not going to find a puffin.

When the *Flora* rounded the outermost skerry and turned for home, the waves began to hit them amidships. The motion of the boat changed. She started to twirl and surge as well as rock and roll, and for the second time that day Nell felt her stomach churn and tasted the rush of bitter fluids to her mouth. She leaned swiftly over the side. Mac had switched on the big searchlight to probe the darkening waters ahead but she was sitting in its shadow, not immediately noticeable to the others, except David who had sat cosily close and who now clung tightly to her arm to prevent her from falling overboard. Mercifully the sound of her retching was swamped by the pounding of the diesel-engine. For a few moments after her personal storm subsided she continued to clutch the gunwale of the pitching boat and let the intermittent spray from the bow-wave soak her face, washing away any grim residue. Then she straightened, panting slightly, hair dripping, face pale in the gathering dusk.

'I'm OK, really,' she told an anxious David. 'Fine, in fact.'

'Well, at least you followed the sailor's code,' said

a voice above their heads. Nell looked up to see Alasdair, who had obviously witnessed at least the closing stages of her tiger-shoot, offering her a clean white handkerchief like a flag of truce: 'You know what they say. Always puke over the leeward rail!' He gave her a sympathetic, lopsided grin. It was the second time Alasdair had found her in a compromising situation and remained apparently unmoved. He was not, it seemed, such a dry stick as his legal calling might suggest. Gratefully accepting the handkerchief from him, Nell began softly to laugh into its folds.

Chapter Ten

Artemis Clover leafed impatiently through the pile of glossy magazines on her desk. She was not a glossy magazine person, would far rather have been reading the *Financial Times* despite her deceptively glamorous forty-something image, but Clover Cosmetics had recently placed a series of advertisements in the fashion journals and she wanted to check that what had been paid for had been properly provided. Strictly speaking, this was her personal assistant's job but Artemis was a perfectionist, which was partly why the company which she and her husband had started ten years before was such a runaway success today. Its flotation on the Stock Exchange two weeks before had been so over-subscribed that the share premium had turned them both into millionaires overnight.

As she picked up *Cosmopolitan* and began to fan its pages, a small colour-printed leaflet fluttered out onto the polished surface of the desk, catching her eye. A stunning aerial photograph of what was unmistakably a Scottish castle, set against a sparkling blue loch and a backdrop of purple-misted mountains, imposed itself under a caption which Artemis found instantly riveting. *Taliska revives jaded lives!* It was one of the special promotional leaflets Tally had placed to coincide with the hotel's opening, and if there was one thing Artemis had felt ever since the flotation it was jaded. As well as being a perfectionist in business she also sought perfection in all other aspects of her life, and at present things were falling well short.

She and Richard had thrown all their efforts into launching Clover Cosmetics onto the stock market and had almost totally ignored everything else in the process. As a result their personal relationship, once healthy and vibrant, had now gone absent without leave. Sometimes she wondered how they managed to discuss profit margins in the office when they could hardly pass the time of day at home. While the Clovers' laboratories and factories were hives of industry, their bed and board were deserts of apathy.

In the early days it had been so different. Soon after their marriage Richard, a cosmetic chemist who had worked for ten years with a famous pharmaceutical company, suddenly went 'green' and began to take an interest in the ozone layer and the effect of toxic emissions, and to devise formulae for cosmetics and toiletries which were ecologically friendly. At the same time Artemis, an international buyer who had worked for a City of London company which imported bulk commodities from developing countries, began to realise that there might be sound business reasons for basing beauty products on natural ingredients readily available in the Third World, instead of on expensive chemically manufactured materials. Clover Cosmetics had been born on a tide of happy connubial energy. There had been all the heady excitement of starting the business and as much as they had enjoyed devising their business plan they had both also enjoyed the sensual thrills of experimenting with Richard's new formulae, rubbing the mandarin-oil body lotions and coconut-milk foot balms eagerly into each other's flesh and wallowing together in pine-kernel bath essences and jojoba shower gels. But, as business boomed, play-times plummeted and Artemis could hardly remember the last time they had even approached an erogenous zone with an essential oil. These days she got more thrill out of the 'Footsie' report than Richard's love-making.

'Right' she said to herself as she perused Tally's Taliska teaser. 'Let's see if this new business can spice up some old business!' She thrust her stockinged feet into her high-heels and rose from her desk. She had a habit of kicking her shoes off when she worked, which often caused amusement in mixed meetings and even some painful encounters under boardroom tables! At least, she still attracted the odd game of 'footsie', she thought, even if the rest of her body was drooping a bit from lack of attention.

'Sarah,' she said decisively to her sleek, raven-haired assistant whom she'd hired partly to offset her own tousled, burning-bush look, though she'd never admitted as much to anyone: 'Have a word with Ossie and see when Richard's got a few free days that coincide with mine and then book us into this place.' She put the Taliska leaflet firmly down in front of the surprised girl. Ossie was to Richard what Sarah was to Artemis. 'Yes, I know it's an eon since we've taken time off together but now that the flotation is over I think it's time we did. In fact, the sooner the better. Book a double room with all the trimmings – and I *mean* a double. Don't let them fob you off with twin beds. If we're going away together to restore our jaded appetites, as this blurb says, we'd better get the props right!'

Sarah's face registered several levels of surprise. She had worked for Artemis for eighteen months and in that time had come to the conclusion that whatever passion had brought her bosses together in the first place, it had been completely supplanted by profit and loss accounting. They never seemed to show the least affection for each other and, as far as she could tell, only accompanied each other to business functions, never on recreational activities. Richard Clover had become a sailing fanatic and regularly entered his Swan-built yacht in international races, taking a selection of his company staff with him as companions and crew. For her part, Artemis tended to spend her time off at their country house in Gloucestershire where she kept a thoroughbred hunter and rode to hounds with royalty. As she studied the leaflet and lifted the phone, Sarah wondered whether Taliska could possibly work enough magic to bring the supercharged Clovers back to their marital grass-roots . . .

Alasdair McInnes left Oban Sheriff Court frowning deeply. He had scant regard for Sheriff Farquharson, whose courtroom he had just quitted. His Honour was nearing seventy, lived in remote seclusion in a comfortable residence overlooking Loch Awe and, when it came to grasping the realities of the present day, had a mind about as sharp as a well-buttered scone. He had never been within hailing distance of a travellers' camp and had no conception of the effect such a seething cauldron of visiting humanity could have upon a small rural community or, for that matter, upon a new business venture which advertised itself as a haven of peace, free from the stresses and strains of modern life! A phenomenon of the said modern life had driven, truck, van and ramshackle bus, into the middle of the Taliska idyll and His Honour Sheriff Farquharson could only state with legal exactitude that until proper charges were brought and prosecutions and defences prepared and presented, he could not rule on the matter. As a pompous postscript he'd added that Mr McInnes should not presume to approach him again for an injunction unless he wanted to be considered in serious breach of court etiquette.

'The trouble is it was old Sheriff Farquharson,' Alasdair explained on the phone to Tally after the hearing. 'He wouldn't know a New Age traveller from a Stone Age caveman. I think he imagines them to be a bunch of merry, peg-pedalling gypsies living in picturesque painted caravans.'

He grimaced privately at Tally's immediate consignment of the Sheriff to self-inflicted intercourse and made a mental note to explain to his client at a less inflammatory moment the curious Scottish law against 'murmuring' a judge – a law which Tally had just irretrievably broken.

When he had put the phone down Alasdair sat at his desk for several minutes ruminating on the situation at Taliska. It was one which he found progressively more puzzling. After months of apparently working harmoniously together, just as they were on the point of pulling the rabbit out of the hat and actually opening their beautiful pleasure palace to the world, the McLean twins appeared to be at loggerheads. In Alasdair's opinion it was more than just a petty disagreement catalysed by the travellers; it appeared to be a fundamental split in direction. Tally, it seemed, preferred the company of the taciturn fisherman Macpherson and his pretty island wife, while Nell had apparently embarked on some ill-judged relationship with David, the pleasant but, to Alasdair's mind, rather shallow city-type who had joined the house-party. Far from being shocked at finding them almost *in flagrante delicto* outside his room, Alasdair had been both amused and irritated by the incident, considering Nell to be worth far more than a furtive fumble in a doorway, however much she seemed to be enjoying it! David Guedalla had now returned to London with the others and, although he couldn't have explained why, Alasdair felt a curious sense of relief.

As was his habitual solitary pleasure, he reached for the battered volume of poetry he always kept to hand. If anyone had asked him, he would have said that the poetry of Norman MacCaig was the main thing which had held him together after his wife's death. Somehow the poet, who had suffered similar loss himself, in his poem called 'Memorial' caught the essence of grief for Alasdair and encapsulated it in words of elegance and simplicity which were a continual solace:

Everywhere she dies. Everywhere I go she dies.
No sunrise, no city square, no lurking beautiful mountain
but has her death in it.
The silence of her dying sounds through
the carousel of language, it's a web
on which laughter stitches itself. How can my hand
clasp another's when between them
is that thick death, that intolerable distance?

His wife's death seemed like an eternal barrier between himself and the rest of humanity, an inescapable pain that stabbed fiercely and repeatedly in the midst of the most mundane activities. But the initial agony was easing. Almost imperceptibly the period between each sudden sense of anguish was lengthening. *That thick death* was becoming infinitesimally thinner by the day, *that intolerable distance* a tiny bit shorter and more bearable. It was just that he had, as yet, hardly registered time's insidious effect.

No one was more concerned than Alasdair that the Taliska opening should go with a swing and the whole project be a success. He put the hotel and its twin proprietors high on his list of priority clients, where they lodged incongruously alongside two child-abuse cases and several fishermen's compensation claims. He tried to be a good lawyer for all clients but, inevitably, some got just that little bit more personal attention than others. Which was why he was so disappointed that he had failed to persuade Sheriff Farquharson of the seriousness of the McLeans' dilemma.

Tally slammed down the phone still 'murmuring' the Sheriff loudly, in language as blue as the waters of the loch beyond the office window. He stared angrily out at the sparkling, sun-drenched scene. What in hell's name was the use of all this perfect weather if Taliska's wealthy and fastidious guests were going to have their pleasure spoilt before they even set foot in the bloody hotel?

'Half of the joy of staying on an island is going on and off it,' he moaned to Ann who was only too sympathetic having, like the rest of the staff, been more or less marooned on Taliska since the travellers arrived. 'And now the bloody delivery boys have started refusing to drive through the gate since word got out about that theft from the butcher's van.' Half a side of beef had mysteriously disappeared the day before whilst the butcher was waiting for the gates to open, his attention distracted by children yelling and tapping on his window and making rude signs and faces at him. 'And that's another charge we can't bring because there were no witnesses other than those bloody brats who couldn't tell truth from a bag of humbugs!' exclaimed Tally.

'I wondered why there were such mouthwatering smells coming from the camp-fires last night,' commented Ann. 'It was a lovely evening and I went down to the beach for a walk. The smell of barbecued beef even overcame the whiff of sewage from the Kyleshee.' As she spoke she scratched surreptitiously at some insect bites on her legs. It had been so finc an evening that she had made the mistake of going out bare-legged and had fallen victim to a man-eating fly-hatch.

'Well, I've had enough!' Tally reached for the phone once more. 'If the law insists on being an ass I'm going to call in the reptiles. It may ruin our image but the tabloids will leap on this story I'm certain – especially since they're short of any juicy political scandal at present. We may lose a few camera-shy guests but at least the whole country will learn about Taliska.'

Tally made his call on Tuesday. By Wednesday the Ossian was overflowing with reporters, and journalists were swarming over the travellers' camp and the hotel. Nell became furious as photographers and television crews shoved furniture about and stubbed out cigarettes in all the rooms which she and her team of cleaners had made perfect for the first paying guests due at the weekend. But Tally was unrepentant. 'It'll be mega publicity,' he assured her. 'We'll never have another chance like this and some good has got to come out of that filthy rabble.'

The headlines were predictable. They ranged from the pithy ISLAND SHOWDOWN (the *Express*), HEARTBREAK HOTEL (the *Sun*), to the whimsical RICH MAN *In his Castle*, POOR MAN *At his Gate* (the *Mirror*) over pictures of Tally and one of the travellers' leaders, to the precise THE SIEGE OF TALISKA, *The Haves v. the Have-Nots* (the *Independent*). But being a capitalist press, most sympathised with Tally and Nell, showing photographic spreads contrasting the inside of one of the travellers' vans with a Taliska bedroom, and a pile of empties littering the travellers' camp with the neat array of bottles on the shelves of the Taliska bar. Wednesday evening's television news showed aerial shots of the sprawling mass of vehicles and humanity on the mainland and the wild, almost empty island with its beautifully restored buildings and its neat gravel drive leading to the firmly closed gates on the bridge, with a commentary pursuing the siege theme and introducing clips of interviews with the police and the local public health authority, justifying their lack of intervention. Tally and Nell were filmed walking out of the tunnel-arch and interviewed against the ancient iron-studded wooden doors, under the hotel banner with its scabious emblem. On the whole the coverage was in Taliska's favour, although most versions of the story did point out that the travellers had paid rent for their camp-site and were not, in principle, breaking the law.

Tally was jubilant about the results of his gamble in calling in the press. There had been a risk that the twins would be crucified, accused of being the rich flaunting their wealth before the unfortunate homeless, but that had not happened. 'We must keep taking the tabloids,' he enthused as he perused their coverage in minute detail. 'For once they got it right.'

His euphoria waned somewhat, however, when the phone began to ring very shortly after the main television news had ended. First the Tourist Board publicity officer rang to ask whether it was safe for his chairman to come to the island in view of the present state of siege, then, one by one, other guests or their representatives rang, either to query whether or not the opening was going ahead or simply to make an outright cancellation of their arrangements. By Thursday afternoon the grand Easter opening was looking rather dog-eared and Tally was feeling more than a little dejected.

Onc glimpse of the television coverage had sent Nell straight to her bathroom to stick her fingers down her throat. Watching herself on the screen had inspired instant nausea and she was fast becoming skilled at converting the mood to the action. Now that she had discovered the ecstasy of emptiness she found herself throwing up frequently, usually after dinner, her largest meal of the day. In effect, although she still found solace in eating she was also beginning to revel in vomiting. She began to consume huge amounts of food, purely and simply in order to have the secret and sordid pleasure of bringing it all back up again. This latest episode, however, came about not because she had overeaten but because she had over-reacted to the sight of herself on film. Shown standing next to Tally, she thought she looked like a duck beside a heron and filmed walking alongside him she appeared to waddle while he stalked. It was a contrast she had long been aware of, but she had never before been so starkly confronted with it and the spectacle reinforced her self-loathing.

It was Mick who brought the good news from the gate. Having escorted the cows to their pasture after milking as usual, he came stomping into breakfast where all the staff were busy speculating whether there would be an opening or not, wiped his perspiring brow with his handkerchief and said with dramatic simplicity: 'They're leaving.'

'Who's leaving?' Tally said tersely. He and Nell made a point of eating breakfast with the staff because it was a good time for airing grievances and solving problems, of which today there had already been plenty but, to his knowledge, no one had actually handed in their notice.

'The mob on the mainland. The travellers.' Mick poured some milk into a glass and downed it swiftly. 'Jings, it's hot out there! It feels more like August than April.'

Tally slammed down his knife, with which he had been buttering toast, and demanded: '*Leaving?* Getting into their bloody rattletraps and driving away? Are you sure?'

''Course I'm sure,' declared Mick, somewhat miffed that his word might not be believed. 'There's a bliddy great queue of vans and trucks waiting to get onto the road. They're all moving out.'

'I don't believe it,' cried Tally. He pushed back his chair with a triumphant 'Yessss!' and strode to the kitchen door. Nell was inside cooking breakfast which she often did to give Calum a morning off. 'Nell – drop all that and come with me. Mick says the travellers are leaving!'

Nell took the frying pan off the heat with a cry of surprise and flung it into the sink, contents and all. Still in her white apron she raced to the Fourtrack, leaping into the passenger seat as Tally started the engine. Burning the tarmac like Nigel Mansell, in less than a minute they had skidded to a halt at the end of the drive and were staring through the gate with incredulity.

The narrow road that led from the bridge to the village was clogged with vehicles, all heading towards the main road that would take them north to Fort William or south to Oban, but in whichever direction, gloriously away from McCandlish's field, away from the Kyleshee and away from Taliska! So determined were the travellers to leave as soon as possible that there was a log-jam of vehicles in the gateway and a violent argument was developing between the driver of a former Post Office van, now painted camouflage green, and a woman at the wheel of an old ambulance, now painted a patchy, funereal black. They were shouting at each other in the kind of language which had no roots in comradely affection, while behind them a cacophony of horns chorused in protest at the delay.

'They may need a real ambulance at this rate,' commented Nell with genuine concern. She was worried about the numerous dogs and children to be seen wandering haphazardly among the slow-moving vehicles, at considerable risk to their own safety.

'Stand not upon the order of your going, but go at once!' yelled Tally euphorically, now literally dancing about behind the gate. It had always impressed Nell, who was not of a Shakespearean bent, how Tally could summon relevant images and quotations from the bard, apparently at will. He was more erudite than his habitual flippancy suggested. 'Great balls of fire, Nell. They're really going!' He grabbed his sister in a bear-hug and planted two ecstatic kisses on her pale cheeks. 'Aren't you pleased?'

'Well, of course I am,' cried Nell, taken aback. She had not anticipated how much relief of tension this exodus would inspire in her brother. He had obviously been wound up like a watchspring beneath his relatively calm exterior.

Tally simmered down and turned to count the vehicles still waiting to go through the gate. The chorus of horns had ceased since the woman in the ambulance had won the battle for the gate by dint of her vehicle's superior size. 'About a hundred to go,' he said at length. 'How long do you think they'll take? Should we ring the Tourist Board and tell them we're on schedule for the opening?'

'Yes, I think we should,' replied Nell eagerly. 'As long as nothing stops them they should all be gone by this afternoon and then perhaps we can get the local refuse department to send a team to clear the place up a bit. That's the least they could do for us.' Piles of rubbish and discarded objects littered the field and the verges where the vehicles had been parked, and blackened patches disfigured the ground where their camp-fires had been.

'I wonder why they've suddenly packed up?' Tally queried, frowning. 'According to McCandlish they paid three months' rent in advance for that field, so why are they leaving after less than three weeks?'

Nell had spotted an opportunist photographer snapping away amongst the queue of vehicles. The press had not abandoned the story. 'Perhaps they didn't like the company,' she said, indicating the pressman and taking note of several more individuals with notebooks and cameras dodging along the road among the column of vehicles. 'Frightened they might be recognised in the papers and get done for social security fraud.'

'Possibly,' muttered Tally, pointing the electronic key at the gate mechanism. 'I'm going out there to investigate.'

★ ★ ★

The reason for the exodus was all over the lunchtime television news. A helicopter had taken aerial shots soon after breakfast and a reporter was shown standing on the road speaking to camera with the motley cavalcade of departing vehicles behind him and an unmistakable smirk on his face. 'The New Age traveller is retreating under a fierce attack,' he told his viewers. 'The unseasonably warm weather has brought the midges out of their larval stage earlier than usual this year and just three nights of their vicious attentions persuaded three hundred confirmed outdoor enthusiasts that there must be more comfortable places in which to make their camp. And so the Siege of Taliska is over, thanks not to the long arm of the law or the action of the authorities but to the extremely effective bite of *Chironomus Culicoides*, the mighty Highland Midge.'

'God bless the midge!' yelled Tally, recklessly exploding a champagne cork in the staff dining room, so that the precious fizzy liquid frothed over his hand, the table and the floor before some of it found its way into a glass. 'Long may it breed and prosper, the small gilded fly.'

'I detect another quote from Shakespeare,' groaned Nell, who was nevertheless unable to conceal her own delight in the outcome of the affair.

'Who else?' demanded Tally haughtily. '*King Lear*, no less! The wren goes to't, and the small gilded fly does lecher in my sight. Let copulation thrive . . .'

'Sounds like Taliska,' Nell remarked. 'Or how you reckon Taliska should be!'

'And so it will be now, thanks to that small grey-coated gnat.' Tally's glee was Mercutio-like.

'Don't forget that the same midge will still be here when the travellers leave,' warned Nell, tempering his elation. 'And our guests won't like it any more than they did.'

'Our guests don't sleep outside or anywhere near the shore,' retorted Tally. 'And we haven't detected any midges near the house at all. But you're right – we must lay in a supply of midge-repellent to issue to adventurous guests. I'll get some at the cash and carry.'

At midday the last of the travellers' vehicles had turned onto the main road, heading, as the driver told Alasdair while scratching irritably at his badly bitten neck, 'As far as possible from man-eating-midge country. That farmer was a bloody crook!'

Alasdair had encountered the traffic jam as he tried to drive to Taliska. He had to wait for a dozen vehicles to turn out of the single-track road before he could turn in, so he got out of his car to speak to the driver of the last of them. The traveller's final comment prompted Alasdair to pay Duncan McCandlish a visit on the way. Like any prudent country lawyer he always carried a pair of Wellington boots in the back of his Range Rover and these came in very handy, as he was forced to seek the farmer out in the fields. He found him leading his massive Shorthorn bull, Ruairidh, by the ring in his nose from a far pasture to one closer to the house.

'I had to put him far frae the campers,' muttered McCandlish when Alasdair warily approached man and beast, maintaining a safe distance from the bull, even though the lumbering creature seemed docile enough, patiently hanging his head, keeping the strain off the ring in his sensitive nostrils. 'They might hae scunnered him.'

'Or he them,' suggested Alasdair, thinking that

the travellers might very well have been put off by the great red and white bull with his sharp, stubby horns. 'Where have you been keeping him?'

'Away up the kyle,' the farmer told him, grinning. 'Out of mischief, I hope.'

'So do I,' agreed Alasdair, skipping backwards to avoid being caught between the half-ton bull and a shed wall. 'He's a great deal too large to be roaming free.'

'Funny you should say that,' remarked McCandlish, frowning. 'He's a swimmer, you know. I found him soaking wet once whiles he was in that field by the kyle. Lucky he didna swim away!'

'You'll be glad to see the travellers away, though.'

McCandlish scratched his head and winked at the lawyer. 'I knew they'd be off soon as the midges woke up. Mind you, the wee sookers were guy early. Still, I didna gie their money back. Nae question of that!' He chuckled with wicked glee.

'No refund, eh?'

'Not a penny. I'll be needing all of it to mend the fences and put the gate back.'

'But they were like that before the travellers arrived,' protested Alasdair.

'Well, of course,' nodded McCandlish solemnly. 'I wouldna let a rabble like that ruin my best field now, would I?'

So, after an initial hiccough caused by the late arrival of the Tourist Board chairman who had gone fishing as soon as he sniffed a cancelled weekend appointment and had to be hauled, protesting, off the river by his public relations officer, the opening ceremony went off without a hitch. The chairman and his wife were helicoptered in to be met by a gratifying battery of press photographers, most of whom had been ordered by their editors to stay on to cover the happy ending to the siege, along with their pen-pushing reporter sidekicks who were busy looking for spin-off stories to pad out Easter Sunday coverage. The twin angle took the fancy of several, who wanted details of Tally and Nell's different careers and sniffed about for any love-interest, without much success. THE LONG AND THE SHORT OF IT screeched one headline over a picture of Tally and Nell, which immediately had her stomach churning again. LOW FAT HI LIFE trumpeted another over a picture of Libby wearing very little and lounging in the big communal jacuzzi, together with some copy giving samples of Calum's meals. Only the *Scotsman* used a rather more staid picture of the Tourist Board chairman cutting a ribbon at the castle entrance to illustrate a think-piece questioning the grant made by Highlands and Islands Enterprise to a venture which provided only part-time employment to local people and recruited its permanent staff from outside Scotland.

This last angle infuriated Tally who rang up to complain to the paper in question that both he and his sister were Scottish, to say nothing of the chef, his apprentice, the receptionist, the garden staff and the barman, leaving only the two head waitresses who qualified as coming from 'outside Scotland'. He demanded a correction but failed to get one. However, this did not trouble him for long, since on the whole no new enterprise which was dependent on the public for its future survival could have wished for more free publicity than Taliska had received. Out of the jaws of defeat there was no doubt that a victory had been snatched. Even the MEP for the Highlands, who was a Socialist and therefore not automatically in favour of such ventures, had gone away declaring that he would spread the word about Taliska in Brussels, Luxembourg and Strasbourg where he was sure the low-fat, high-luxury image would act as a magnet to Eurocrats.

There was a picture story about the midge war in the Weekend section of the *Financial Times* which Artemis Clover managed to draw to her husband's attention just before he left to join his crew for the Easter channel-race at Cowes. The Clovers had actually spent Good Friday and Easter Saturday together at High Combe, their five-bedroomed Gloucestershire 'cottage', although Richard had been on the phone most of the time arranging his crew, and Artemis was absorbed in preparing and watching her horse race in the Berkeley Hunt's Easter Point to Point. She'd let the son of their caretaker ride him because she herself felt neither fit enough nor light enough to do so. Perhaps after Taliska she might be, she thought, and then had been surprised to see the article in the paper.

'Well, I hope they've got rid of all the travellers,' snorted Richard immediately. 'We don't want to be surrounded by weirdos as well as water.'

'And I hope they've got rid of the midges,' fretted Artemis. 'I won't stay if I'm going to end up with bite-speckled legs.'

'I doubt we'll stay long anyway,' grumbled Richard, spreading butter thickly on his breakfast toast. 'It was a damn silly idea of yours. As if we have a whole week to spare.'

Artemis watched him eat the toast, thinking that his incipient paunch and juddering jowl were more than enough warning of the health risk he ran now that he was nearing fifty. Besides, they spoiled his distinguished English-gentleman good looks.

'What's seven days compared with the rest of your life?' she demanded crossly. 'You promised!'

'Yes, I know. I promised to come, but I didn't promise to enjoy myself.'

'Coming will be a new experience,' retorted his wife acidly, picking up the canvas fishing bag she used for her point-to-point picnics and heading for the door. 'And I don't mean to Scotland!'

They were booked in for the last week of April, by which time the hotel had more or less settled into a routine. Tally had persuaded Flora to join the staff, working as housekeeper, thus easing the load on Nell who found she was having to take on more and more in the kitchen as her skills improved. And it was undeniable that since Flora knew most of them personally, she was better at organising the local women who acted as chambermaids. This arrangement also held the advantage for Tally of bringing Flora into his daily orbit, especially since Mac was away every weekday from dawn until dusk. Tally delighted in Flora's company, perching on the sink in the housekeeper's pantry while she was washing up early-morning tea trays or sorting sheets and towels, hearing about her childhood on Lismore and trying to describe to her the dubious delights of his own boarding-school upbringing. The rest of the staff gossiped about the growing friendship and Libby defiantly flitted between a slightly bemused Rob and the ever-ready barman, Tony Demarco, flaunting them under Tally's nose but leaving him unmoved. 'Women's Lib' was last month's story as far as he was concerned and, fortunately for him, she did not seem to be the clinging sort.

However, although Libby was no longer to be seen slipping out of Tally's flat at dawn, Flora never slipped in there either. His careful pursuit met with giggles and blushes on her part but no amorous submission and, uncharacteristically, he seemed content to have it that way. Beneath Tally's casual nonchalance was growing an emotion which he had never experienced before and which he found as thrilling and awe-inspiring as his first sight of 'Hand of God' country. Slowly and insidiously, succumbing to a gentle grace and a subtle sorcery, Tally was falling in love.

Mac, meanwhile, remained as much his friend as ever. The fisherman had bought himself a new car, claiming to have made 'a fair killing' in his dealings with the travellers, on top of his lucrative contract with the hotel. He no longer displayed the vague 'away with the fairies' symptoms which had worried Flora earlier in the year, and both she and Tally agreed that it must have been something to do with the travellers and forgot about it in the distraction of their own kindling relationship.

It was Ann who welcomed the Clovers to Taliska, full of excitement because, as an avid reader of glossy magazines and a regular user of Clover Cosmetics, she was eager to meet the company's high-profile proprietors. 'They invented natural beauty,' she enthused to Nell before their arrival.

'I thought nature did that,' protested Nell. 'But they certainly seem to have made nature pay. Tally says their share flotation broke records on the Stock Exchange.'

'We don't use their products in the hotel, though. Do you think they'll be offended?' asked Ann earnestly.

'I hope not. Perhaps they'll see an opportunity and offer us a good deal!'

Richard and Artemis had argued throughout their journey north and it was clear from their frosty attitude over the reception formalities that Taliska had a lot of work to do if they were to consider it worth the trip. However, by the time they had inspected their accommodation, wallowed in the jacuzzi and eaten one of Calum's delectably digestible meals they were mellowing slightly. After Libby took their breakfast up to their room the next morning she reported that Artemis had been sitting up in bed holding forth loudly on the telephone while Richard was prowling about fully dressed. But she also added significantly, 'The bed was a complete tip. It looked as if they'd been prize-fighting in it.'

'Fifteen rounds and a submission?' smirked Mick over his porridge, always an avid consumer of anecdote about the guests.

'Well, there were no black eyes but there were certainly black looks,' recounted Libby. 'Whatever joy they found last night seems to have fizzled out in the light of dawn. I think we should start a book on how long they'll stay.'

'Well, she's booked a massage with you later this morning, so don't wish her gone before that,' commented Ann. 'And he's asked if there's anyone who'll give him a game of squash.'

'I'll do it,' said Tally. 'I hope he's not too bloody good, though. I haven't played for a while.'

'He doesn't look very fit,' Ginny remarked. 'In fact, last night in the dining room I thought he looked rather pasty. Shaping up well for a heart attack, I'd say.'

'That's why they're here, dear girl,' Tally told her. 'He couldn't be much wealthier but he should leave here a bit healthier. If they stay the course, that is.' He looked pessimistic on the latter count. 'Taliska's got a bit of wand-waving to do there, I fear.'

By the morning of the fourth day Artemis was

gloomily considering giving up on their stay, their marriage and their business – for that was the awful sum total of what was at stake. She felt tempted to blame Taliska for not working the miracles of which it claimed to be capable, but realised that that would be unfair. After a bad start things had progressed reasonably well. In their tempting emperor-sized bed she and Richard had enjoyed a romp which had been quite like old times and, until she'd telephoned the office the next morning, everything had been almost cosy between them. She'd tried to leave work behind but had woken in the night remembering an instruction she'd forgotten to give Sarah. She'd regretted the call almost instantly, however, because as soon as the outside world intruded, the fragile mood of intimacy generated by their love-making evaporated. Richard had begun to growl and prowl like the proverbial caged tiger and she could once more feel the familiar tingle of tension crawling up her spine. The bed-time romp had been part of an illusion. There was no improvement in the prevailing climate of indifference between them. On the massage table even Libby's expert fingers had not prevented the spread of depression from Artemis's spine to the rest of her bones.

And when the massage was over she discovered that Richard had borrowed the hotel BMW and gone off on his own, without saying where or for how long, leaving Artemis furious and worried at the same time. With growing despondency she cycled thirty miles on the exercise bike in the gym and skipped lunch entirely, even though she'd been finding the Taliska meals a regular source of enjoyment. They were also having their effect. She noticed that her belts had eased a little and her silhouette was decidedly sleeker and felt that this, at least, should have been some source of satisfaction. But somehow it was not. After cutting short a stilted conversation in the hall with another lady-guest who threatened to pour out her life-story, Artemis decided waiting in the hotel for Richard was too frustrating and donned jeans and wellies for an invigorating scramble over the island's interior. Standing on the summit with the wind playing in her great mass of auburn hair she experienced a long-forgotten sense of freedom. Perhaps freedom was what she needed. Freedom from constant work, constant stress and constant Richard!

For his part, Richard was never happy for long without some sort of contact with fellow scientists. Having investigated the details of Taliska's water-supply and analysed the chemical reason for its incredible softness, he'd sought further environmental stimulation and, during a walk by the shore, noticed the heaps of black seaweed piled up among the rocks. On further inquiry he'd learned that it was in such plentiful supply on this particular stretch of coast that a company called Maritima had established a factory a few miles up the loch to manufacture products from it and, without telling Artemis, he'd rung the company's head office and arranged a personal guided tour.

Artemis saw the BMW sweep back down the drive as she was returning from her walk, refreshed but determined, intent on a showdown. They were booked in for a week but she'd decided there was no shame in crying a halt after five days. They'd tried and they'd failed. She was thrown off-balance, however, on entering their suite to find Richard's broad, handsome face wreathed in the kind of smile she had not seen for years. She could hear the jacuzzi filling behind the closed bathroom door.

'I've got a surprise for you,' her husband said before she could demand to know where he'd been. 'Look!' With the air of a magician he held up a white plastic tub containing a dark, glutinous substance which seemed to gleam with phosphorescence.

Her intended 'Where the hell have you been?' seemed to become entangled with a reactive 'Ugh, what the hell's that?' so that she was not sure which question she actually uttered, but it didn't really matter because Richard was oblivious to anything but his new plaything.

'It's called Algina and I'm certain it's going to revolutionise our product lines. Come on – we're going to try it!'

Postponing her showdown, Artemis moved forward to sniff gingerly at the contents of the pot. Contrary to its rather sinister, ectoplasmic appearance it had a fresh, salty smell reminiscent of the seashore or the breeze which had ruffled her hair during her walk. 'It smells like Taliska,' she said, curious despite herself.

'That's not surprising, since it's made of seaweed.' Richard carried the pot through to the bathroom, placed it on the vanity unit and turned off the taps. 'Come on, get your clothes off.' He was already pulling off the blazer and lightweight wool trousers he'd worn for his factory visit and hurling them through the bathroom door. They missed the chair at which he was aiming and landed on the floor.

Artemis took a deep breath and moved to pick them up, automatically placing them neatly on the bed. Her perfectionism meant she was also fanatically tidy. 'Exactly what have you got in mind?' she asked, her aggression subsiding. Richard's sunny eagerness had taken the edge off her confrontational mood. All at once she recognised the unpredictable, eccentric experimenter she had married, even down to the uncombed hair and the wild gleam in his eye. And, judging by the speed with which he was discarding his clothes, he was also about to become the great, skin-worshipping lover he had once been as well.

'What do you think I've got in mind?' he cried gaily. 'It's party-time! I'm going to rub you all over with Algina and then you can rub me all over with Algina and then we'll see whether it does what it's supposed to.'

Artemis raised an eyebrow and then, almost without realising she was doing it, began pulling her sweater over her head. 'What's it supposed to do?' Her question was muffled by lavender-coloured lambswool.

'It's supposed to sensitise the skin, stimulate the circulation and drive one into a mad sexual frenzy!' declared the now-naked Richard, standing just inside the bathroom door with the pot of black gunge in his hand, a naughty-boy expression on his face and a determinedly beckoning finger.

Another, more intimate part of his anatomy also began signalling wildly as Artemis stepped out of her jeans and removed her bra and panties. 'It doesn't look as if you need driving,' she said, swaying gracefully towards him. 'And I'm not sure that I do, either.' She reached out a searching hand but he stopped her with a peremptory gesture.

'No,' he said with mock severity. 'Science first, sex later.'

Her brows arched and her eyes wandered meaningfully down to the erect organ between his legs. 'If nature will wait upon science,' she observed slyly.

By way of answer he dug his hand into the black gunge and reached out to stroke it down her body from her throat to the plentiful red bush at the base of her belly. The dark, glistening gel made a wavy black line in startling contrast to her peachy skin, sliding down between her breasts in a slow, larval rivulet. 'Have I told you, Mrs Clover, just what a fantastic figure of a female you are?' he asked, standing back to admire his handiwork, his own bodywork growing larger and harder by the minute.

'Not for a long time,' she admonished him, silently thanking Calum's low-fat diet for streamlining the very line that Richard had traced. 'And don't think you're going to get away without gunge treatment, Richard Clover. Flattery won't keep you free of the dreaded slimy sensitiser!' She made a dive at the pot, and plunged her fist into the dark, glutinous contents. Surprisingly it was not unpleasant to handle, slipping between the fingers almost without clinging, rather like jelly. But it smoothed over the skin of his stomach with satisfyingly inky opacity and before long they were both slapping it on like wrestlers in a Hamburg dive-bar.

'Well, does it work?' asked Richard breathlessly, kneading the stuff voluptuously into her breasts while she spread a swift layer over his shoulders and neck. 'Are we zooped up into ze frenzy?'

In order to check this, Artemis slid her slimy palms down his body to its most urgently 'zooped-up' part and then knelt to follow with her lips. 'Mmm,' she mumbled with her mouth full. 'Tastes like lobster!' Her hair was soon also streaked with black gel because his gunge-covered hands encouraged her chosen activity by burying themselves in the tangled mass of her auburn curls. If they hadn't been indulging in such an obviously adult pastime they might have been a couple of over-grown urchins playing on a muddy riverbank and badly in need of a wash. And as if to reinforce that notion Artemis stood up and began to gently push Richard backwards while still continuing her organ recital with nimble fingers, finally tipping him, gasping with ecstasy, into the full bath. 'No more mud pies. Time for grown-up games,' she exclaimed, leaping after him so that water slopped everywhere, mingling with the black slime already streaking the white-tiled floor. It was a snug fit but a satisfactory one!

The Clovers came down for dinner looking like a different couple. They were chattering and laughing, full of plans and ideas for the final two days of their holiday, mostly based around obtaining more Maritima products upon which to conduct their enjoyable experiments. In the servery Libby took a fiver off Rob. 'Told you Taliska would do it,' she gloated.

When the Clovers checked out at the end of their week Ann was astounded to find they'd added a thousand pounds to the total of their bill, enclosing a note which said succinctly: *The small gratuity is to make up for the appalling state of our bathroom. Taliska is a treasure. We'll be back! Richard and Artemis Clover.*

In the normal way Nell would have noticed and been worried about the growing relationship between her brother and Flora, but during the first weeks of the season she was too taken up with her own personal problems. The events of the opening weekends had left their mark on her, both physically and mentally. She had been tired and stressed when the ability to throw up first manifested itself and yet, when the pace eased and the strain lessened, she found herself seeking the solace of the finger down the throat more rather than less, sometimes retiring to the bathroom three times a day to, in her own words, 'do a Gloria'. She dubbed the toilet 'the big white telephone' and the calls she made on it were ugly and addictive.

Inevitably she got thinner. In six weeks she went from a solid, spare-tyred citizen to a slightly flabby Miss Average. Her clothes drooped, her mouth drooped and her spirits drooped but she was decidedly no longer fat. David noticed it at once when he returned to Taliska one weekend late in May.

'What have you been doing to yourself?' he asked, not five minutes after she had collected him off the Glasgow train.

'What do you mean?' retorted Nell, peering through the windscreen into the rain ahead. The weather had deteriorated during May so that now it was unseasonably cold and, according to Calum, '*dreich*'. 'Strangely enough,' Nell remarked as an aside in the kitchen one day, 'the *dreicher* the weather the jollier the guests! After a walk in the rain they seem to discard all inhibitions along with their wellies and macs. It's amazing how many room-service orders we have for cocoa in bed at five in the afternoon.'

Calum had grumbled, 'Cocoa is not on my health menu.'

'Oh, I think they work it off,' Nell assured him. 'They're not ordering it to help them sleep.'

She knew what David was going to say before he uttered the words. 'You've lost weight, Nell. Are you all right? You look a bit peaky.'

A sharp stab of anger stung her into a biting retort. 'It's funny how when you're overweight people always tell you how well you look. They don't say you look marvellous, or great, or sensational, they say you look well. So I suppose it's inevitable that when you lose weight they say you *don't* look well. And of course you'd rather they didn't say anything at all.'

David was puzzled and offended. 'I'm sorry,' he said. 'I only mentioned it out of concern.'

There was an uneasy silence for several minutes as the car sped along the gorse-lined coast road, the bright yellow flowers dripping mournfully under the steady drizzle. Nell drove fast, angrily cursing herself for being a bad-tempered bitch. She knew that her reaction to David's well-meant remarks had been over the top but her emotions fluctuated as much as her food intake these days. She had spent the last weeks asking herself whether she had made a mistake jumping into bed with David with such hasty abandon after her row with Tally.

'Look,' she said, turning briefly to flash him a weak, apologetic smile, 'I know I've lost weight but it's intentional. I don't look great because I've just rushed straight from the kitchen to meet the train. I wanted to get my share of the dessert trolley finished so that we could sit down to dinner together this evening. I'm sorry if I was foul.' Coward, she berated herself inwardly. You're going to pretend everything is all right because you're too much of a weed to tell him he might as well get on the next train back. Mentally she tried to recall the boost to her self-esteem which David's love-making had inspired the last time he'd been up.

He looked relieved at the softening of her tone. 'It's OK. I shouldn't have passed comment like that. No one likes to be told they're not looking their best. I'm a crass idiot.'

She laughed. 'But a well-meaning one. Tell me the news. Have you seen Caroline at all?'

He looked slightly shifty at that. 'Yes, I have, as a matter of fact. We had dinner together last week.

She says Gordon Gryll's been asked to do a Christmas special this year. Can you imagine – turkey-stuffing races and mince-pie contests.'

'Jolly holly and other old chestnuts,' cried Nell, delighted. 'Oh yes, Eye-Level will be in his element!' She was faintly surprised to hear that David and Caroline had dined together, thinking that he, at least, would have steered clear of trouble from that direction.

'How are things now that you have real guests, paying real money?' inquired David conversationally.

'Not bad at all, considering. We've nearly a full house this weekend because of the Bank Holiday. You're lucky to get a room.'

'I rather thought you might let me share yours,' he said, a hint of petulance in his voice.

'If you play your cards right I might,' she told him, only half-teasing. 'But not officially, if you don't mind. A girl's got her reputation to consider.' She knew that was an excuse. She'd fling her reputation to the wolves for the right man!

He laughed ruefully. 'Oh, I see. Pity they didn't teach us corridor creeping at school.'

'Didn't they?' she asked, raising an eyebrow. 'That's not what Tally told me.'

'Oh well,' he said, blushing. 'I never had a penchant for grubby little boys.'

'I think it was the sixth-form girls Tally was after.' At that moment she drove past Mac and Flora's house and waved at the fisherman who was backing his shiny new car into the drive. 'He's changed tack a bit now, however,' she added.

David followed the direction of her wave and frowned. 'Still enthralled by the fisherman's wife, then?' he asked.

'Yes, but this time the glory is not in winning, nor even in having taken part, not so far anyway.'

'Heavens! Tally's technique must be slipping.'

Under the influence of Taliska's seductive atmosphere it was almost inevitable that Nell would shelve her uncertainty over David. And when he saw her enter the bar before dinner he decided that, far from not looking well, Nell looked really quite splendid. He was deceived by the carefully made-up face and the freshly washed and styled hair. With the loss of a stone in weight her habitual loose-fitting clothes seemed to emphasise rather than disguise her figure, which was now curvaceous rather than plump, and her dark pink flowing shirt and straight black slit skirt were stylish and eye-catching, even if she did not yet dare to flaunt her narrowing waist and disappearing tummy. Although she found no time to use the Nautilus equipment in the gym, the fact that she rarely sat down all day meant that she was walking herself into a decent figure, as well as literally throwing the weight off. David's compliments over the candlelit table were genuine and gratifying to Nell's easily bruised ego. They and the bottle of Pouilly Fuissé he ordered successfully melted her misgivings so that by the time she had held brief, proprietorial after-dinner conversation with several of the guests and settled down beside him with a large brandy, she was happily flirting with mischievous blue eyes, offering exactly the kind of wordless promises he hoped to receive.

Nevertheless, Nell insisted on retiring to her own room first, telling him suggestively that she had 'things to do'. As she held her habitual nightly conversation with the big white telephone she felt a twinge of guilt. Calum's menu had been particularly light and delicious that evening and she knew that he, as much as anyone, would have been horrified if he could see the way she disposed of it like so much unwanted garbage. For the first time she experienced a faint feeling of disgust at her own behaviour but it was only momentary. The effect her 'conversations' were having on her shape was too desirable to allow any thought of ceasing them.

David's soft knock came almost too soon, while she was still cleaning her teeth. Swiftly she sprayed air freshener around the bathroom.

'I'm glad you've left me the pleasure of undressing you,' he declared on entering, putting two well-charged brandy balloons down before advancing towards her with the air of an old satyr, all groping fingers and lecherous grin. 'I want to investigate this disappearing Nell personally, limb by limb.'

She giggled self-consciously, letting him unfasten the zipper of her skirt. 'I hope you find more than just arms and legs,' she murmured. 'There should be something in between.'

'And there is,' he crowed triumphantly, dropping on his knees to the floor, along with her skirt and a pair of rather loose black panties. 'A beautiful, juicy, wonderful cunt!' He lapsed into a silence dictated by the fact that his mouth and tongue suddenly had other things to do than form words, and their investigative activity made Nell grab his shoulders for support.

'I can't stand up if you do that,' she said faintly, pulling his head away and stepping unsteadily over her skirt and underwear. She moved towards the bed, still wearing her loose pink shirt and high-heeled black shoes and looking alluringly like a pantomime principal boy. 'Can't you continue your investigations lying down?'

David readily agreed that he could and within

seconds the principal boy had become a naked lady and David was using tongue and hands in such a way as to warm the coldest feet and dissipate the gravest doubts. His clothes joined hers on the floor and the bed became a rapturous tangle of sheets and limbs.

'I don't really like that particular four-letter word,' declared Nell later, when things had calmed down a bit and she was lying back against David's shoulder sipping her brandy.

'We seem to have made reference to one or two of those over the past half-hour,' he remarked drowsily. 'Which particular four-letter word did you have in mind?'

'Cunt,' she said bluntly. 'I don't like the word. It's not descriptive enough. In fact, it's rather insulting.'

He leaned forward to scrutinise the curly, thatched entrance to that portion of her anatomy. 'All right,' he said at length. 'Let's try some others. How about slit?'

She screwed up her face and shook her head. 'Nope. It's descriptive, I grant you, and accurate. But nasty. Too surgical.'

He tried again. 'I suppose if you don't like slit you won't like twat either?'

'Absolutely not – no resonance whatever! And don't suggest hole or I'll pinch your prick.'

'I prefer cock, while we're on the subject,' he told her primly. 'More masculine.'

'Trust a man to go all macho about it,' she teased, idly stroking the item in question. 'The great thing about whatever-you-want-to-call-it is the way it stirs in response. Mind you, so does my whatever-I-want-to-call-it, only you can't see it.'

'I can if I get close enough,' he said, bending over to stare so intently that Nell could feel definite stirring sensations beginning all over again.

'Nothing doing until you find a word for it,' she told him firmly.

He looked up, smiling cunningly. 'How about quim?' he asked, repeating the word in a low, sexy tone which had Nell giggling irrepressibly again. '*Qu-u-u-wim.*'

'That's it!' she cried, sitting up, snatching his brandy balloon and placing both his and hers hurriedly on the bedside table. 'It has resonance *and* alliteration. Quivering quim, quiescent quim, queenly quim – oh yes, I like that!'

'Querulous quim, quaking quim,' David added excitedly to the list, at the same time arranging her limbs so that the object under discussion was displayed to its best advantage. 'Quarrelsome quim questing to be quelled,' he crooned and began to attend to some serious quelling.

Nell wriggled with pleasure, wondering vaguely in how many other rooms in the hotel similar games were being played and similar dilemmas resolved in a similarly sensational fashion.

Chapter Eleven

As May ended, the wind and rain petered out and Taliska began to bask in warm June sunshine. This was the time of year when the island burst into full flower. The first scabious began to dance among the long grasses on the summit and beneath their dark blue pom-pom caps clustered trailing purple vetch and clumps of wild thyme, the latter giving off an instant and fragrant aroma when crushed underfoot. On the coastal strip, carpets of pink thrift released their honey scent to the swooping sea-birds and pads of creamy sea campion littered the rocks and ledges. Ranks of wild yellow iris marched along the banks of the freshwater burns and gathered in regiments around the springs; golden buttercups and bright-eyed daisies and pansies strewed the *machair*. The air was alive with the sound of bees and the thin crescendo of larks climbing high above their nests, singing their hearts out to the spirit of summer.

Although it was probably the most magical season of the year the hotel was relatively quiet, perhaps because society holds so many rival attractions during the month of June. Ascot, Henley, Wimbledon, Glyndebourne . . . these magnets drew people south, little knowing what pleasures they were missing in the wild, secret places of the north.

However, in sun-dried southern Spain, Ian

McLean's sherry cask deal finally came good and a certain member of one of the sherry-triangle's most prominent families found himself unexpectedly in funds. And because the twins' father had sung the praises of Taliska so enthusiastically during the negotiations, Gabriel Garvey-Byass decided to invest at least part of his profits in taking his wife, Isabella, for a restorative break in the Scottish Highlands. In line with the custom among the very British-oriented sherry families of the Jerez region, the three teenage Garvey-Byass children were all at boarding school in England, so before collecting them for the school holidays their parents could consider a week together in Taliska's champagne air. Isabella Garvey-Byass secretly hoped that the healthy regime boasted by the hotel might begin to repair some of the damage inflicted on her husband's constitution by a constant professional barrage of *fino, amontillado* and *oloroso*! Gabriel was still under forty but sometimes looked fifty with his dark-shadowed panda eyes and heavy, jaundiced complexion. He'd been a heart-throb at twenty-two when she'd married him, but now he was fast becoming a liver-throb . . .

'I would like to go to Scotland,' she told him in her deep, faintly accented voice, speaking English as they so often did together, since he had been educated at the famous Roman Catholic public school of Ampleforth and she at a convent in Surrey. 'I have not been since I went to the Skye ball with a school-friend.'

'Very well, we will go,' said Gabriel, replacing in the ice-bucket the half-bottle of Tio Pepe from which he'd been pouring. 'As long as they serve the *fino* on ice.'

She waggled a long, lacquer-tipped finger at him.

'We will not drink *fino*, Gabriel. We will not drink *anything*.'

He looked horrified. 'What? Not even a medicinal Carlos Treseros?' naming his favourite Spanish brandy.

'Definitely not. Not even white tea. And if I can give up the *gin y tonicas* you can give up Carlos Treseros.' She gazed at him fondly with her pale blue-green eyes. Isabella came from Irish stock and had striking wavy blonde hair to contrast with her sun-tanned Spanish skin. Unlike her husband she had not gone to seed but only sprouted a few extra centimetres amidships. 'Why don't we go at the end of June, just before the children break up?'

Tally decided to use the first of the good weather to spruce up the Taliska boats. The two wooden skiffs and the buoyant fibreglass dinghy were dragged out of the boat-shed, scrubbed, sanded, varnished and painted until they were all shipshape and seaworthy. A new outboard motor was acquired for the dinghy and loch excursions and rowboat hire were added to the hotel's list of recreational facilities. Mac warned Tally that guests should be told to keep close inshore because of the strong prevailing currents, and it was agreed that although rowboats would be issued unescorted, allowing guests to paddle round the island's coves and inlets, the dinghy with its outboard motor, which could travel further afield, would always be skippered. Rob and Mick agreed to deputise if Tally was unable to perform this function. The dinghy was equipped with oars and emergency flares and Mac gave all three men rudimentary instruction in seagoing safety and the direction of local currents and tidal rips.

To Nell's intense irritation, in order to look the

part Tally bought himself a peaked white sailor's cap and was instantly referred to by the staff as 'Cap'n Tally', while she secretly christened him Captain Hogwash.

Soon after the boats were launched, an unusual trio of guests arrived at Taliska. Robert Burke was an eminent London surgeon whose grip on the scalpel was beginning to waver. His physician colleagues had as yet been unable to diagnose the cause of his shakes and, while they were analysing their latest tests, Mr Burke had decided to take two weeks' holiday in the luxury and peace which the brochure assured him Taliska offered, in the hope that they might work a miracle cure. With him came his thin, taciturn wife Jean and their fat, brindle Boston terrier Lancet.

Tally watched Ann handle their registration and then offered to take them and their luggage up to *Lovage*, the central first-floor room with the best view in the hotel, an emperor-size bed and the circular double jacuzzi bath which had now been cleansed of its anointing with slimy black Algina. Since its former gunge-wielding occupants had left, Tally had wanted to change the name *Lovage* to *Clover* but had not persuaded Nell. 'Well, I don't think the Burkes will put bed and bath through their paces much,' Tally confided to Ann when he returned to reception. 'The way they climbed the stairs I shouldn't think it will be long before they're candidates for the body-snatchers.'

'Tally, that's terrible,' admonished Ann, who was nevertheless unable to stifle a squawk of mirth when she glanced once more at their surname in the register. 'Do you know, I'm sure she wears a wig,' she added in a whisper. 'That dark red colour doesn't seem natural, and somehow her hair doesn't sit quite right on her head.'

Fortunately there were no guests within earshot, for Tally let out an undignified whoop of delight. 'It's Burke and Hair!' he cried ecstatically. 'They *are* the body-snatchers!'

The names stuck. It was as Burke and Hair they were subsequently known throughout the hotel, though not of course to their faces.

However frail they may have looked at first sight, the pair were soon to be seen daily tramping the island with Lancet snuffling along in their wake. Hair had a *Field Guide To British Wild Flowers* and seemed determined to identify as many as possible, while Burke took photographs of them with a venerable but serviceable Pentax. Watching him cut his food at meal-times with a rather shaky knife, Ginny wondered just how steady his hand might be with the camera, but assured the rest of the staff over their own dinner that the couple were 'Really sweet, and enjoying every minute of their holiday.'

Indeed, Tally was forced to eat his words when Flora, using her skeleton key to enter *Lovage* one morning in order to make the beds at a time when she thought the trio would be out wildflower-hunting, found that instead the Burkes were actively sowing wild oats under the duvet while Lancet stood faithful guard over the red wig, which was carefully perched on a stand on the bedside table. Either Burke's shakes did not extend to all parts of his body or Taliska had triumphed again! Flora retreated in confusion, while Lancet's angry barking at the interruption probably also vividly expressed Burke and Hair's feelings on the matter. However, nothing was said and Hair's sensual rejuvenation subsequently stretched to allowing herself one of Libby's stimulating massages, during which she confided that the death of her son in a rugby accident several years before had been the cause of her acute hair loss. When this story was told at the tea table, the whole staff began to warm to the body-snatchers.

It was well into their second week that Burke approached Tally about getting across to Lismore where his wife had heard that the wildflowers grew even more prolifically than on Taliska. Was there a way of spending a day on the larger island, he wondered, without wasting time going both ways on the ferry? After due discussion, Tally agreed that if the weather continued sunny and calm then he would gladly take them to Oban in the morning to catch the ferry for Achnacroish on Lismore. They could take a packed lunch and spend the day searching for wildflowers and walking half the length of the island to the northern point, where he would collect them with the outboard-dinghy in the late afternoon and bring them back to Taliska in time to ease their aching muscles with a bath before dinner. It was partly the same route Mac had taken with the house-party, but Tally knew the fisherman would be unable to help this time because he would be out working until dusk, which at this season and latitude did not fall until well after ten. Tally had already spent several cosy evenings in Flora's kitchen drinking tea and talking, until Mac came unsuspiciously home just in time to accompany him across the road for last orders at the Ossian.

Burke, Hair and Lancet were duly delivered to the Lismore ferry the next morning and in mid-afternoon Tally set off across a calm loch with the outboard purring steadily behind. It was hot enough for him to strip down to his shorts; a clear blue sky was reflected in water of similar clarity and hue and the air was still and warm, the sun beating down to gild his already tanned skin. He encountered no other vessels on his outward trip. There was never much commercial traffic on this part of the loch, the main navigation lane being the other side of Lismore, and there was too little wind for pleasure sailing.

The long green island's only road ran the length of its spine and ended abruptly at the edge of a shingle beach on the northern shore where Tally raised the outboard and hauled the dinghy out of the water. It was only just after four and he didn't expect to see Burke and Hair for a while yet so he strolled up to a solitary red telephone box which stood stark and lonely, just off the road on a rocky, treeless peninsula. It was such an incongruous sight in that bleak, uninhabited spot that he couldn't resist making use of it. He decided to pass the time by ringing Flora, who would have just got home after her day's work at the hotel.

When he told her where he was she laughed delightedly. 'Oh aye, I know that phone box,' she said. 'You could use it to ring the ferryman in Port Appin and tell him to come and collect you. I never wanted to go, though. I dinna like boats.'

'And you born and bred on an island!' he exclaimed. 'What have you got against them?'

'I dinna really know,' she said reluctantly. 'The sea's a fickle creature and boats are chancy. No islander trusts them completely.'

'You get seasick, that's what it is,' he teased. 'Mac told me.'

'Aye, there's that, too,' she agreed. 'But I think that's because I'm feart. What're you doing on Lismore?'

'Looking for another lovely lady like you, since you're not available, it seems.'

She laughed again. 'Oh, there are plenty more like me.'

'Do you *want* me to find one?' he demanded, offended.

She relented. 'No' really. Then you wouldna come to my kitchen and eat all my shortbread.'

'Oh well, I'll just come back then.' He sounded mollified. 'I'd better wait for the others, though.'

'Others? What others?'

'Burke and Hair. They're hunting marsh orchids and nipplewort.'

'Nipple-what?' she spluttered, giggling.

'You heard me, you wee besom.' He was beginning to pick up Scots words from her. 'What are you doing right now? Have you got your clothes on?'

'Of course I have! Well, nearly.'

'Aha! I can hear you blushing. You haven't got your blouse on, have you? You're frolicking around in your bra giving the boys in the Ossian a thrill.' From the phone box Tally could see a motley threesome coming into view – Burke, Hair and Lancet, toiling down the road towards the shore looking hot and thirsty.

Flora was giggling wildly now. 'No, no,' she protested. 'I took my skirt off as it was so hot and I was just about to put my shorts on when the phone rang. I'm quite decent, really.'

'Pity,' said Tally. 'Look, I'll have to go. Can I come down for tea and sympathy later? But only if you promise to leave your shorts on. I bet you've got fantastic legs.'

'Oh aye, fantastic,' she repeated dryly. 'I'm making no promises. And no shortbread! You've eaten it all.'

'See you later then,' said Tally.

'You take care,' she ordered, seriously this time.

'Remember what I said about boats and the sea.'

'Yes, they're fickle – just like women. Byee!' He put down the phone, grinning happily. These days life was never complete without a teasing blether with Flora.

Burke and Hair were tired but enthusiastic about their day. Lancet collapsed panting in the bottom of the boat, walked off his feet. Tally shoved off and started the outboard and, when its roar had declined to a steady purr, Hair confided that she had found a globe flower which she said was quite rare, and showed Tally a picture of it in her book. He wanted to tell her that her wig had slipped slightly in all the excitement, but discretion forbade it. The flower looked rather like a large buttercup to him and hardly worth making a fuss about.

'I thought it was orchids and things that were rare,' he said when he had steered successfully around the rocks at the entrance to the bay and they were heading into mid-channel. 'Not buttercups.'

'Oh, some orchids *are* rare,' Hair assured him in her small, refined voice. 'We found some marsh orchids today – at least, I think they were marsh orchids. There are so many different types and they all look quite similar.'

'You've caught the sun a bit, Jean,' her husband remarked solicitously, reaching out to touch her glowing forehead and surreptitiously straightening her wig at the same time. 'I told you you should have worn a hat.'

'Hats are too hot,' complained his wife but she looked pleased with his solicitude.

They must be, thought Tally sympathetically, especially when you've already got one on, so to speak.

At this point the outboard motor suddenly began

to make the most alarming screeching noise. It rose rapidly to ear-splitting level before Tally found the presence of mind to cut the engine and then it whined slowly down in a relentlessly depressing diminuendo, ending in a dull clunk.

Gingerly Tally felt the engine housing. It was burning hot. 'Damn!' he exclaimed.

'What's happened?' asked Hair in agitation. 'Is the engine all right? Have we broken down?'

Manfully resisting the temptation to tell her to keep her hair on, Tally bent to slip his hand down into the water to feel the propeller. It was stuck fast. 'Yes, Mrs Burke,' he said. 'I'm rather afraid we have.'

'What can we do?' asked her husband anxiously. 'Can you fix it?'

Tally shook his head. 'I don't think so. We must have fouled a rope or a discarded fishing-line. The whole thing has seized up.' He glanced around to get his bearings. They were in mid-channel, a very empty channel with no other boats in sight. Taliska appeared deceptively close to the south-east but, after his coaching from Mac, Tally knew there was no time to be lost. He began to manoeuvre the oars from under the thwarts. 'I'm very sorry, we'll have to row. If we take turns we ought to be able to make a landfall on Taliska but we'll have to really put our backs into it.'

'Right,' said Mr Burke calmly. 'I'll take one oar. Let's get a move on. We don't want to miss dinner!'

They did miss dinner. At eight-thirty Nell was in the kitchen plating starters when Ginny came in to report that everyone was in the dining room except the Burkes.

'And they're usually so punctual. They like to eat

at eight so I think there might be something wrong. Should I go up to their room?'

'No, you carry on serving,' said Nell, deftly tweaking a sprig of basil into position on a colourful slice of vegetable terrine and pouring a lake of red pepper purée around it. She put down the jug. 'I'll go.'

When she found no one in the Burkes' room, and no sign of them having been in there since it had been cleaned and tidied that morning, she began to panic. Where was Tally? When he hadn't turned up for staff tea she had assumed he'd gone straight down to the Macphersons' house, because he often did. She rang Flora, who was instantly as worried as she was.

'He rang me from Lismore,' Flora told her, 'just for a wee crack – a bit of a chat, you know. He said he was about to start back. That was around four-thirty.'

'Four hours ago!' exclaimed Nell. 'Where *are* they?'

'Well, is the boat there?' asked Flora, practically.

'I don't know. I'll check.'

'I'll ring if Tally turns up here. Let me know what's happening, won't you?' There was no mistaking the deep anxiety in Flora's voice. Her usually gentle tone had become quite sharp.

'Of course,' replied Nell and hung up. She called Rob at the stables and asked him to go to the jetty and check for the boat, and then returned to the kitchen. Dinner would have to be served to the rest of the guests as usual. They couldn't afford to cause any unnecessary upset.

Rob brought a negative report back from the jetty. There was no sign of the boat. Nell wondered out loud what she should do and Calum told her that whatever it was she had better go and do it and leave him to handle the starters. 'You're making a right mess of them,' he muttered, wiping drips of red purée off the edge of a plate where she had carelessly dribbled it in her agitation.

Leaving the kitchen, Nell rang the coastguard's office and told them the situation. There'd been no reports of any boats in trouble, she was told, but a careful lookout would be kept. It was a calm night. The boat was hardly likely to have capsized.

'Unless it's drifted into a ferry lane and been mown down,' said Nell, fearing the worst. 'How else could they just disappear?'

'Are you sure they left Lismore?' asked the coastguard. 'They might have had engine trouble and decided not to set out.'

'But they'd have telephoned,' wailed Nell. 'There are telephones on Lismore, aren't there?'

The man had to agree that there were.

By nine Nell was worried enough to ring Alasdair. 'I'm sorry to disturb you . . .' she began.

'What's wrong?' he interrupted, hearing the note of panic in her voice.

'The Taliska dinghy has disappeared with Tally and two guests on board. I'm so worried they've had an accident or capsized or something. I've rung the coastguard, should I ring the police?'

'No, he will have informed them already. I'll come straight there,' said Alasdair. 'Is Mac back yet?'

'No, I don't think so. Why?'

'He might have some idea where they are. He knows the currents so well. Catch him when he gets in and I'll be with you in a quarter of an hour.'

Dusk was falling when the *Flora* nosed her way into the jetty, a still, soft dusk which gave no hint of danger. Reflecting the dying light in the sky, the loch looked like a shining swathe of pink satin, innocent and calm, disturbed only by the rippling wake off the *Flora*'s snub-nosed bow and the low rumble of her idling engine. But when Mac heard Nell's news his expression gave her no comfort.

'Tide's been on the ebb since five,' he mused aloud, staring across the water. 'If they got caught in the Lorn current they could be off Seil Island by now.'

'Where's that?' asked Nell, hardly wanting to hear.

'Mouth of the Firth. Next stop Newfoundland.'

'Oh, for God's sake, Mac, they can't have got as far as that!'

'That current moves helluva fast on the ebb. Tell the coastguards to alert their man on Easdale. That's the wee island off the south-west of Seil,' he added for her benefit. He then turned to his crew, a lad of no more than sixteen. 'Do you want to get on home, lad, or will you help me search?'

The boy nodded. 'I'll bide wi' you,' he said tersely. 'Man the searchlight.'

Mac touched him briefly on the arm by way of thanks and said to Nell, 'Tell Flora to let this lad's folks know he's still with me and tell her I've gone out again. We'll search the stretch between Lismore and Oban.' He shook his head and added gloomily, 'I warned Tally about the current. Has he got flares?'

She nodded miserably. 'I think so.'

'Good, they'll show up better in the dark, as long as he hasna used them all up before nightfall.' Mac's tone was more sympathetic, as if he recognised her terrible fear and was doing his best to ease it. 'You go and ring the coastguard again. Tell them what I said and wait by the phone. You can do no more.' He vaulted back onto the *Flora*'s deck and dived into the wheelhouse to restart the engine. The lad cast off and leapt nimbly after him. Nell watched for a moment as the *Flora*'s propeller churned the pink satin into white lace and then she turned back to the hotel, hand over mouth, blinking back tears. It seemed impossible that the dinghy and its occupants could have just disappeared without a word or a ripple! What would she do without Tally? How could she cope on her own? She was stupid and helpless and so bloody lonely . . .

'Damn!' she cried out in fear, blundering blindly into someone who had suddenly materialised out of the darkness. That someone caught her tightly to prevent her falling. Alasdair! She would know that scratchy tweed jacket anywhere. Even in an emergency on a summer night he wore it and the fact was strangely comforting. 'Oh God, Alasdair.' For a moment she clung to him, a strangled sob escaping before she could control it.

Hugging her, Alasdair experienced a surge of tenderness such as he had not felt for what seemed like a lifetime, and then he gently backed off, still holding her shoulders and looking down into her white face with its enormous, fearful eyes. 'What did Mac say?' he asked.

She told him and they turned and began walking rapidly towards the hotel. 'Mac was really worried, Alasdair, I know he was,' she panted. 'Do you think they've drowned?'

Alasdair did not voice his knowledge of so many similar disasters, some of which he had subsequently handled as compensation cases. 'No, I think they've had engine trouble and are just drifting on the current. There's very little shipping to spot them in midweek, until the fishing boats come in at dusk. I'm sure we'll hear from the coastguard very soon that one of them has taken them in tow.' He did not add that the fishing boats would come in through the narrow Sound of Kerrera, the island which protected Oban's harbour, whereas a boat in the current would drift past the outer shore, out of their sight, nor that such a small dinghy could be invisible to larger boats in the kind of swell that swept the mouth of the Firth even in the calmest weather.

'What must they be thinking, if they're drifting helplessly like that?' she groaned. 'Poor things, they must be cold.'

'It's a warm night,' he pointed out. 'And a calm one. That's all in their favour. And they'll probably be rowing to try and break out of the current.'

'Might they be able to do that?' asked Nell hopefully.

'It's possible,' replied Alasdair encouragingly, although secretly he knew that it was not. Even an outboard motor could have trouble battling the relentless pull of the tide towards the open sea. It took a powerful diesel engine such as the fishing boats were equipped with to fight the ebb from the Firth.

Flora was in the office when they reached the hotel. 'I couldna wait alone,' she explained. 'I hope you dinna mind?'

'Of course not,' Nell assured her and watched her anxiety deepen when she was told about Mac going to search. For the first time Nell realised that two more lives were now at risk. Navigating at night was always more dangerous. The coastguard agreed to alert their man on Easdale and told her that the Oban lifeboat was standing by. More people prepared to risk their lives, Nell thought, comprehending for the first time how the sea created such tight-knit communities along its shores.

Half an hour later the three of them were drinking coffee in tense silence when the telephone rang. The coastguard at Easdale had seen a distress flare. The lifeboat had been launched and was investigating. The atmosphere of tension lifted a few millibars, Flora and Nell permitted themselves a fleeting, shared smile of hope and Alasdair pulled out his battered book of Norman MacCaig's poetry, opened it and began to leaf through.

'I read poetry sometimes when things get difficult,' he said diffidently. 'There's a poem here that you might like. It's not about the sea, but it's quite appropriate. It's called *In A Mist*. Do you want to hear it?' When Flora and Nell both nodded he read quietly:

'The mountains fold and move.
I'm not quite lost. The thing that troubles me
Is that the easiest way out
Is not the one that's easiest to see.

I know just where you are.
But how to get there when lochs change their place
And the familiar track
Squirms like an adder into the heather bushes?

I curse my senses: and speak
Into the mist: Stay where you are, please stay –
I've got my compass yet.
It'll get me to you, if not by the easiest way.'

Alasdair looked up at the two solemn faces of the women who unmistakably both loved Tally, whether he deserved it or not and whether he knew it or not.

'They've got a bearing now,' he said. 'They'll find him.'

It was nearly midnight when the coastguard rang again to say that the lifeboat had located the dinghy and taken the occupants on board, two men, a woman and a dog. All were tired but well.

'Where were they?' asked Nell with almost hysterical elation.

'Two miles off Easdale,' the coastguard told her. 'Right where your fisherman friend said they'd be, in mid-current.'

'Next stop Newfoundland,' murmured Nell, shivering.

'What?'

'Nothing, it's all right,' she told him. 'In fact it's wonderful! Thank you very much. When will the lifeboat be back at Oban?'

'About one o'clock. The tide's turned now so they'll get a fast trip in.'

'We'll meet them. Thanks again!'

His near-fatal brush with the sea left Tally rather subdued. When he and the Burkes had slept off their exhaustion he invited them to have lunch with him so that he could apologise for the umpteenth time and offer them their holiday on the house, but Mr Burke would not hear of it.

'It was an accident,' he said. 'Any propeller could foul a line and your precautions were excellent. If we had not had those flares aboard we would never have been sighted. I think we'll just send a large donation to the Royal National Lifeboat Institution and thank God the coastguard had sharp eyes!'

'I just hope it hasn't ruined your holiday completely. It's certainly given me a jolt,' Tally confessed ruefully. In the six hours he had spent in the open boat with the Burkes he had come to like and respect them. There had been no panic, no recriminations and no grumbles. Even Lancet had simply lain doggo throughout the entire incident.

'Far from ruining my holiday it has made me see sense,' remarked Burke. 'I must admit that I was desperate at the prospect of my career coming to an end, but now I realise that there is much more I need to do in life before I quit this mortal coil. So I've decided to retire anyway, shakes or no shakes. And the funny thing is,' he held up his right hand, 'it's steadier now than it's been for months!'

Hair smiled happily. Her wig had remained firmly *in situ* throughout the crisis, and only the dark rings under her eyes revealed the ordeal she had suffered. 'There are more than five thousand flowering plants in the British Isles,' she confided to Tally. 'And so far, I've only identified four hundred of them.' She laid a hand on her husband's newly steady right arm. 'And at least the photographs might be in sharper focus now,' she added fondly. The look that passed between them then spoke volumes for Taliska's magic restorative powers. The Burkes might be well over sixty and staring retirement in the face, but they weren't beyond the scope of a little L and R!

Under the table Lancet snuffled up a morsel of cold guinea fowl slipped to him by Ginny. Dogs were not usually allowed in the dining room but this was an exception. The other guests turned a blind eye and raised their glasses to the four rescued mariners.

'When I thought you might have gone for good,' Nell told Tally bluntly, 'I realised that I've been lazy about learning the business side of things. I'm going to start putting in some time on the computer.'

'Oh God,' groaned Tally. 'We'll have gremlins and glitches all over the place.' But he looked quite pleased.

'Too bad,' she retorted. 'It's not good for you to be indispensable.'

'I'd better start learning to cook then,' he grinned. 'The computer and the microwave can suffer together.'

'Shows how much you know about the kitchen,' scoffed his sister. 'We don't even have a microwave and you'll go in there over Calum's dead body.'

'We can't have that. He may be trim but he's not fat-free,' exclaimed Tally. 'But I'm certainly not learning to clean the loos. We've been through that one before.'

'Have you seen Flora yet?' asked Nell suddenly.

He frowned. 'Only briefly when she came down for lunch. She looked tired.'

'She was up half the night worrying about you, you thankless fool.' Nell flushed in sudden confusion. 'She's very fond of you, you know.'

Tally shot her a quick glance. 'I'll go and see her this evening,' he said. 'I want to thank Mac properly anyway.'

'He must be knackered,' Nell said. 'He came in at two o'clock and was back out again before breakfast this morning. It was only because he told us where to look that the coastguard saw your flare.'

'I know,' said Tally solemnly. 'I definitely owe him a drink.'

Flora was pale and listless when she answered the door to Tally late that afternoon. He followed her into the kitchen silently, for once uncertain what to say. The kettle was not simmering on the hob as it usually did. Instead a bottle of whisky stood open on the table with a glass half-full beside it.

He picked up the bottle. 'You shouldn't drink alone,' he said softly. She did not respond but opened a cupboard and got out another glass, handing it to him. He poured himself a measure. '*Slainthe!*' he said, raising his glass in the Gaelic toast.

She picked hers up and touched it to his. '*Slainthe mhor!*' she murmured. They both drank, eyes locked together.

Tally put his glass down and raised his hand to her face, thumb tracing a suspiciously damp cheekbone. 'You've been crying,' he said, wonderingly. 'Not for me?'

She nodded, said nothing for a moment and then sat down suddenly on one of the kitchen chairs. 'Oh God, Tally, I thought you were gone!' She took another gulp of whisky, making a face at its fiery strength. 'I was so feart!'

He was amazed, moved, perplexed. He was used to their relationship progressing along well-established lines. He teased and propositioned, she laughed and demurred. Fear and anxiety had never entered their orbit until now. 'I'm OK, everything's fine,' he told her.

'Everything is *not* fine,' she cried in sudden anger. 'You nearly drowned. I told you – you canna play games with the sea!'

He tried to make light of it, smacked his own wrist and nodded contritely. 'I know you did. I'm a naughty boy.'

She slammed her glass down onto the table, spilling some of the contents. 'Dinna make a joke of it! You make a joke of everything.' Her blue eyes were blurred with tears. 'I couldna hae stood it if you'd died. I canna stand it that you're alive, either.

I love you, Tally McLean, and I'll be damned for it.'

He was on his feet, the other side of the table, and kneeling beside her, his arms around her. 'No, no, you won't,' he said, gathering her up close. 'Because I love you, too. I've always loved you, from the moment you walked into Taliska all shy and beautiful in your blue blouse and skirt.' He stroked the soft fair curls off her forehead and bent to kiss her wet cheeks. Her tears were salty, like the splash of the waves which had so nearly carried him into forever. Distasted with the salt of broken tears, he thought in Troilus's words to Cressida, finding Shakespeare popping up as he so often did in times of stress. 'How can anyone be damned for that?'

'Very easily,' she said, trying to smile. 'You're not a churchgoer or you wouldna ask.' She studied him, her eyes travelling over his face. He could almost feel their passage, like the wings of an insect. 'Do you really?' she asked.

'Do I really what?'

'Love me, like you said?'

He nodded. 'Yes. But you knew that!'

'No. I thought it was always a joke with you. You're English. Everything's a joke with the English.'

'I am not,' he insisted. 'I was born in Glasgow.'

She laughed gently, shrugged her shoulders. 'So you say. But you're English nevertheless.'

'Only on the surface. Deep down where it really matters I'm a Scot, just like you, full of passion and stubbornness and pride.'

'Oh aye?' She raised a sceptical eyebrow. 'Fed on oatmeal and herring?'

He disdained to answer that with words. Instead he pulled her bodily off the chair and into his arms, laying her gently on the rag rug before the kitchen range. 'I forgot to add the one thing that you definitely are, you wee besom,' he whispered, bending over her.

'What's that?' she asked, wriggling slightly to fit her body to his.

She was soft and fragrant and full of contradictions. 'Sonsie,' he murmured, and kissed her curving lips.

For several minutes she was lost to all reason. She wanted him to kiss her. Wanted him to make love to her, open her blouse, ruck up her skirt and simply take her, there and then on the rug, with no thought for anyone or anything other than the whirlpool of their own emotions and the bliss of having at last confessed their feelings for each other. But Flora was a churchgoer, an island girl who had been taught right from wrong at the end of a strap. She came from a community where the minister told newly married couples that sex was all right on Sunday as long as they didn't enjoy it. Inside Flora's head the Hollywood message of instant gratification was all tangled up with the uncompromising teachings of the Presbyterian Church. There was another thing also that troubled her, that hindered her ability to surrender – a secret that she could not speak.

She tore her lips away from his and pulled his hand from between her legs. 'No! No, I can't!' she panted breathlessly, trying to stand up without treading on Tally. 'Please, we must stop. Mac might come home.'

'Oh God,' groaned Tally, rolling over and resting his arms on his knees, his head bowed over his hands. There was a furnace burning in his groin. 'It's all very well to say it just like that but hell, Flora, I want you. I need you! What are we to do?' He looked up at her.

She was fastening her bra, hands curled up behind her. Her skirt was still wrinkled over her hips, her blouse around her elbows. She looked like a modern version of *La dame à sa toilette*, hair tousled, lips parted, luscious, ripe and inviting. No Gemma this with depilated skin and concave belly. Flora had curves and contours and her legs were frosted with a soft, fair bloom of fine hairs. Tally groaned again. He couldn't look at her. He wouldn't be responsible . . .!

When she was decent again she picked up his glass and handed it to him. He was still on the floor, recovering. She had made her decision. 'I will come to you,' she said softly. 'We canna do it here. This is Mac's house, Mac's and mine. It wouldna be right.' She sat down again at the table, taking a sip of her whisky. 'It's no' right anyway but I canna help it. I'll come to you.'

He took a gulp, heaved himself to his feet, put his glass on the table and fastened the waistband of his trousers which seemed to have come adrift! His breathing had steadied. 'When will you come?' He was not sure if she meant it. She *had* to mean it.

She picked up the bottle and screwed the top back on. 'Soon, I promise.'

'Tomorrow?' The next day was Friday. It had to be then! He couldn't wait until Monday – he would burn to death.

'Aye,' she said slowly, smiling at him with her soft, bee-stung lips and her fathomless blue eyes. 'I'll come tomorrow.'

On the tiled terrace of their villa-home on the Costa della Luz, south of Jerez, Isabella Garvey-Byass passed her hand over her tired eyes and ran her fingers back through her thick gold hair. It was three in the morning and their dinner-guests, two British wine importers and their wives, had just left. The débris of the huge paella which Gabriel had cooked over the barbecue lay rather disgustingly scattered among the shadows cast by floodlights slung from the pine trees in the garden; discarded shrimp shells curled in the dust beside chicken legs which even their two golden retrievers were too tired to forage for. Several copitas still half-full of sherry stood on the low terrace table beside an ice-bucket in which the ice had melted to water. A dozen empty half-bottles stood under the table, and sprawled on the nearby sofa were the dogs in question, all tangled up with their snoring master, panda-eyes closed, full red mouth slightly open.

'*Madre mio!*' sighed Isabella wearily. 'Thank goodness we are going to Taliska in two days, otherwise I don't think Gabriel would survive until Christmas.'

Chapter Twelve

Out on the *machair*, the skeleton of a bonfire gradually grew higher and higher. Tally and Nell had decided to throw a Midsummer Eve party to celebrate their thirtieth birthday, and Rob Fraser and Mick Lenahan daily brought fresh loads of driftwood, brushwood and broken fish-boxes to add to the inflammable heap.

'It must be a real beacon,' Nell said with determination. 'I've always wanted to do what they did in the old days and leap the flames at Johnsmas.'

'Why not go the whole hog and have fireworks?' suggested Tally. 'If we're jumping a bonfire we might as well jump the gun on Guy Fawkes as well.'

'Fireworks make such a mess, and we don't want burnt-out old rocket sticks littering the place,' Nell said. 'Let's pop champagne corks instead. Just champagne, a bonfire and birthday cake and Tina playing her clarsach. Craig says she'll be back from college by then.'

'Very minimalist! Shall I get Flora to make shortbread?' inquired Tally.

Nell glanced at him sharply. She had noticed a subtle change in her brother's relationship with Flora, although she could not put her finger on exactly what it was. 'If you like,' she said. 'Should I ask David up from London, do you think?'

'If you want to.' He returned her glance with an equally quizzical look. 'I thought I detected a certain coolness in that direction.'

'I like him fine when he's here,' she shrugged. 'It's when he's not here that I go off the boil.'

Tally gave a hoot of mirth. 'It's the Taliska syndrome,' he declared. 'Presence makes the heart grow fonder – or should that be some other organ?'

She flared angrily at him. 'Don't be foul! He wouldn't be able to come in midweek anyway.'

'Well, you certainly don't want him if he can't come,' leered Tally, with gleeful *double entendre*. 'Not when you have that sexy new shape to flash about.'

Nell made no response to this but flounced out of the office where she had been putting in an hour on the computer. The machine was becoming less of a mystery to her but her own body grew more mysterious by the day. She now went in, in places where she had never gone in before, and could hardly recognise her own backside, which suddenly looked good in Sinead's bondage leggings. 'I am a bit like Mummy after all,' she said to herself in surprise when she screwed round to look at her rearview in the mirror. 'Without my bum and bouncy bits!'

It was true that she had shrunk considerably since starting her drastic vomiting routine. None of her clothes fitted and she revelled in the fact that she could now belt her baggy blouses and wear tight blue jeans, the only desirable garment she had been able to buy in the local shops. She chose to ignore the fact that her hair was lifeless, her throat chronically sore and her complexion pasty. Her temper was also erratic, flaring immediately if she thought she was being criticised. Frequent conversations with the big white telephone brought rewards but were also taking their toll.

When Niamh arrived to start her summer job she was astounded. 'Holy shit, Nell, where have you gone?' she cried when she stepped off the train and flung her arms around her sister in an enthusiastic hug, only to encounter less of her than expected.

'I haven't gone anywhere,' Nell protested. 'Chance'd be a fine thing. And you'll have to cut down on the swearing if you expect to be let loose on the guests.'

'Sorry – it's just that there's about half as much of you as there was last time I came here. Have you been dieting? What a bloody silly question – of course you have! It's obvious!' Niamh opened the door and threw her suitcase into the back of the Fourtrack.

'No I haven't, not really,' said Nell with some truth. 'It's just exhaustion and old age.'

'God, don't talk about age!' groaned Niamh, who seemed to have swapped talking in italics for exclamation marks since her last visit. 'I feel about a hundred and ten after doing all those bloody A-levels! As for exhaustion, I hope you don't mind if I sleep for a week before I start work!'

In the event, one good night was all she needed before she began, with characteristic zest, to delve into all aspects of Taliska's activities. She proved adept at waiting at table, surprisingly prepared to clean toilets, and particularly talented at teasing Mick and Rob, with whom she quickly formed a remarkable rapport. They treated her like a kid sister and she treated them like a couple of black-sheep brothers. She even helped them stack the bonfire, giggling and laughing as the three of them competed to see who could hurl branches, twigs and broken boxes higher and highest onto the heap. She actually rose early to watch the cows being milked and enjoyed walking them to their pasture through the dappled sunlight under the Scots pines, while Mick gleefully expanded her ability to abuse the English language by teaching her Glasgow slang. Away from her sophisticated London friends she lapsed into a lively, fun-loving teenager. Nevertheless Nell couldn't help feeling they were sitting on a time bomb. She waited to see which of the male staff Niamh would eventually select for vamping. Sinead had warned her that there had been plenty of 'incidents' involving a whole string of boyfriends even while Niamh was working for her A-levels. And considering the girl's porcelain complexion, flashing green eyes and mane of Titian red hair, Nell could well believe it.

Meanwhile, Tally's curious triangular relationship with the Macphersons had intensified. Flora had begun visiting Tally's flat two or three times a week but despite this, his friendship with Mac continued unaltered. Flora was anxious to keep her affair a close secret and would slip into the flat in the afternoon before she went home, when the other staff were off duty. She told Tally that her love for him did not affect her love for Mac and she seemed remarkably able to juggle both her body and her mind, balancing the demands of lover and husband not only to the physical satisfaction of all three of them but also apparently in accord with her own spiritual serenity. She kept up her regular attendance at church and told Tally simply that she had come to a personal arrangement with God. He did not feel inclined to probe into the detail of this, since he suspected that he would not comprehend it any more than the minister would if he were told. Alone of the three, Tally was somewhat frustrated by the arrangement because ideally he would have liked to have Flora all to himself. However, he did not want to upset Mac or lose his friendship, nor did he wish to jeopardise his relationship with Flora so, for the time being, he was forced to accept the status quo.

Apart from this small cloud on his horizon Tally was remarkably content, and looked it. He had never imagined during all his tempestuous affairs with London women that the process of love could be so amazingly uncomplicated. There was no elaborate ceremonial with Flora. She did not require wining and dining or taking to fashionable clubs. She did not consider food, drink or any other inducement to be a prerequisite for sex and she had the added attraction of a healthy appetite and a naïve and gratifying enthusiasm for exploring the wilder pastures of love-making. She insisted on staying hidden in Tally's apartment, but would cheerfully adopt any variation of place or position, method or aid to more exciting intercourse. She could be shy maid or whore, temptress or innocent, and she would wear any combination of apparel from suspenders and feather boas to thigh boots and leather waistcoats if that seemed to be what turned him on. She was a chameleon, who could leave her normal everyday persona at the bedroom door, ready to collect it on the way out. Physically she had the whitest skin he had ever encountered and, although he searched industriously, he could find no blemish on her pale, perfect body. It enchanted him to discover that the nipples of her softly moulded breasts were the delicate pink of the inside of a cockle-shell and the gossamer fluff of her pubic hair was the colour of primroses. She was a woman of the north, a true Norse blonde for whom the sun was an implacable enemy.

Far from demanding expensive pre-coital dinners, Flora was always ravenous *after* sex and would come up to Taliska on her 'visiting days', as she rather primly called them, equipped with some of the product of her most recent baking session. Scones and shortbread, bannocks and bridies emerged from her ubiquitous basket and were consumed as she and Tally lay back after sex, blissfully naked and engrossed in the long, rambling conversations which became as much a feature of their affair as their variegated sexual activities. They discussed likes and dislikes, phobias and fetishes, hopes and fears and, as he had never done with any of his previous lovers, Tally listened as much as he talked. After only a few visits, he felt he knew more about Flora than he had known about any woman with whom he had shared any part of his life.

Flora would leave the hotel before the staff came back on duty at six and wend her way home to cook supper in readiness for Mac's late summer-evening return. However, while she would tell Mac she had eaten earlier, Tally would then have to sit down as usual to a Taliska dinner, and light and low-fat as these were, on top of his afternoon feasts they were too much. For the first time in his life, Tally began to put on weight.

'They've started again, have you noticed?' Flora asked him one afternoon, lying across his silk-sheeted bed, a half-eaten piece of gingerbread balanced precariously on her gently rounded belly.

He bent forward and took a bite, kissing her bare flesh as he did so. 'What have?' he asked with his mouth full. Dark crumbs dropped into the pale gold fuzz between her thighs and he nuzzled for them.

She wriggled at his touch. 'That tickles,' she protested mildly, rescuing the rest of the gingerbread which threatened to become squashed in a compromising place, and cramming it into her mouth for want of anywhere else to put it. 'Mac's weird spells,' she mumbled indistinctly. 'He's away with the fairies again, on and off.'

Tally frowned, flicking away some of the crumbs he had dropped and pausing to carefully pick out others from her soft fur. 'When have you noticed that?' he asked.

'Mostly in the evenings, when he gets back. He wanders in quite vaguely, as if he's no' sure it's his home, even. He was like that the other night when you came to fetch him to the Ossian.'

'He was in a mellow mood, certainly. I just thought he'd slipped in a few quick nips after an unequal contest with a lobster.'

She didn't smile at that as she might have done but shook her head solemnly. 'No, it's no' like when he's had a few drinks. He has more gab then, he's no' all quiet and queer. I've seen the same look on Rob's face sometimes, in the afternoon when I meet him on my way home. Do you think he could be getting Mac something?'

Tally pursed his lips. He was still hunting crumbs. 'It's possible. Do you want me to ask him?'

'Well, I'm no' sure that's a good idea,' she replied, squirming a little under his probing fingers. 'I mean, it's illegal isn't it? I wouldna want Mac to get into any trouble.'

'Why don't you ask him, then?'

She looked dubious. 'I dinna think he'd admit anything to me. It'd only make him crabbit.'

'Well, I'll keep a look out for a while. Last time it didn't go on for long. Perhaps it'll be the same this time.' He discarded the last crumb and kissed the place he'd picked it from, raising his head to ask, 'Is Mac coming to the party tonight?'

'Yes, of course. I said I'd meet him at the jetty.'

'Good. Will you jump the fire with me?' He was smiling, teasing her with his eyes and his fingers, which were buried up to the knuckle in gold fuzz.

'No – it sounds a heathen thing to do. Aah, do that some more . . .'

'So it is,' he agreed, obliging her. 'All Nell's idea. It's supposed to bring you protection from evil spirits for the coming year.'

'You should rely on the Almighty for that,' she said righteously, suddenly going pink and breathless because of what his fingers were doing and pulling the duvet over them both as if she suddenly realised they might be naked in His sight. Not for the first time Tally marvelled at her capacity for mingling shamelessness with prudery. 'Anyway, if I do jump, I'll jump with Mac,' she groaned, arching her back to encourage his urgent explorations.

All the staff were going to the party and an invitation had also been issued to the guests, along with an apology in advance in case any noise of revelry reached the bedrooms. In *Comfrey*, the second-floor room into which the circular jacuzzi had been lifted with the help of Leo's 'pulleys in the well', the curtains were drawn all afternoon. Gabriel and Isabella Garvey-Byass were not, however, lustily making use of their luxury facilities but sleeping off the effects of their heavy social calendar and an early flight from Jerez to Madrid and then on to Glasgow. They had arrived at Taliska by helicopter at four and immediately fallen exhausted into the firm embrace of their well-sprung king-size mattress without even bothering to unpack their baggage. When Libby told them at dinner about the party they looked dubious but, being Spanish and used to very late hours, found themselves tempted, especially once they had viewed the stunning clarity of the evening through the dining-room windows.

'All right, Gabriel, if you want to we will go,' agreed Isabella, knowing that his gregarious nature could never resist a party. 'But please promise me that you will not drink any champagne!'

So far Gabriel had managed to refuse all offers of free drink on each of their flights but she knew that the strain was beginning to tell. He looked mutinous but one glance at Libby's lissome physique persuaded him that there might be visual compensations for the lack of alcoholic stimulant. 'All right, no champagne. Just the sparkling Highland air and the odd pretty girl.' He crinkled his panda eyes at his wife who knew his flirtatious ways.

She pursed her soft, pink-lustre mouth into an exaggerated pout. 'Only if she is blonde and beautiful,' she said, making her husky voice even more sexy than usual, 'and married to you . . .'

He rolled his eyes so the whites showed. 'I don't think I am going to be able to stand it here,' he said mournfully. 'No champagne, no *fino*, no Carlos Treseros – and only one beautiful blonde!'

'You'll have to take cold showers and lots of exercise – just like at Ampleforth,' she chided him. 'And at least the food is delicious.'

'Yes, but no cream,' he moaned. 'All this health is not good for me!'

The location for the party had been chosen because it was a reasonable distance from the hotel and near to the boat-shed, which provided somewhere to store the food and drink during the early part of the evening while most of the staff were busy. Niamh had taken over the organisation, telling Nell she shouldn't be working for her own birthday party, and Nell had to acknowledge as she approached the site that, with a little help from nature, Niamh had done a terrific job with the decorations.

The sun had set less than an hour before and a glimmer of luminous twilight still clung to the edge of an ink-dark sky, dusted with diamond stars. Under a white half-moon the *machair* displayed a natural chiaroscuro of light and shade, speckled by a hundred pinpricks of flame which twinkled around the straggly mound of the waiting bonfire. Niamh had put lighted candle-stubs into jam jars and placed them along the jetty, on rocks and ledges, in the grass and at every corner of the tables set out for the occasion. These had been carried from the staff dining room and decorated with flowers and red paper cloths. There were pretty paper plates and paper napkins. People who had already dealt with the débris of a formal dinner wanted nothing to do with any further washing-up, although they made an exception for the champagne glasses. No one wanted to drink Bollinger out of paper cups! Two decorated birthday cakes occupied a central position.

Having decided against asking David, Nell had invited Alasdair McInnes, whom she had not seen since the awful night of the drifting boat. He walked with her down to the bonfire, closely followed by Tally and a small group of guests who had changed from dinner dress into something more suitable for a midsummer picnic in balmy moonlight. Even Alasdair had abandoned his usual tweed suit in favour of a checked, open-necked shirt and blue cotton trousers.

'Quick, let's light the bonfire,' Nell said over the sound of popping champagne corks. 'I know we call the midges friends since they drove away the travellers, but some friends should always be kept at a safe distance. The smoke ought to do it.' She slapped at her bare upper arm, aware that for the midges the party had definitely begun. When she had bought her new jeans in an Oban boutique, she had also found a matching blue denim waistcoat which she now wore with nothing beneath. She was delighted with the rather daring effect of this waistcoat. It fastened reasonably modestly but its cut-away armholes and plunging V neck left plenty of exposed flesh, including an eye-catching cleavage. As well as being her birthday party, she was determined that this night was to be a celebration of the new Nell.

The effect of the new Nell was not lost on the men present. Tally, watching his sister as an alternative to watching Flora, which he could only do surreptitiously, noted the clinging denim outfit and suddenly remembered Nell's words to him twelve months before. '*You are just about everything I want to be. Thin, amusing, clever, sexy* . . .' My God, he said to himself in surprise, she's bloody well done it. She's turned herself into what she wanted to be and I never really noticed it happening. Clever Nell is suddenly quite thin and really quite sexy. He, as her brother, might have realised that the bouncy, amusing side of Nell had lapsed somewhat in the process but he was far too wrapped up in Flora to register such details.

Alasdair, on the other hand, regarded the new Nell with mixed feelings. He had to admit that this denim-clad temptress was quite a stunner and his eye wandered frequently to the tantalising cleavage, but for all the self-confidence displayed by the tight waistcoat and the ironed-on jeans he detected an emotional instability which had not been there before. He marked her rather lank hair and the thick make-up and wondered with some concern just how her new shape had been achieved. Nevertheless as they raised their first glass he said appreciatively, 'Let's drink to the new Nell.'

Her eyes widened in surprise. She had not expected him, of all people somehow, to make reference to her slimline shape. 'New?' she echoed. 'I can hardly be called new when I've reached the venerable age of thirty!'

'I speak figuratively,' Alasdair explained. 'And I do mean *figur*atively! You seem to go in and out in places which I had not perceived you to do before.'

Nell's brows rose even further. 'Perceived? Very legalistic! I didn't know you had an eye for such things, Alasdair. And you a respected Writer to the Signet.'

He cocked an eyebrow back at her over the rim of his glass as he took a long gulp of champagne. He seemed to need Dutch courage tonight. 'Writers to the Signet can be a pretty racy lot, I'll have you know,' he retorted. 'There's something about dusty ledgers which seems to bring out the raffish element.'

'Is that so?' she laughed and twirled slowly, keeping her head turned to watch his reaction. 'In that case I'd better give learned counsel a proper look at the evidence.'

He observed her solemnly, as if considering his judgment, then nodded. '*Definitely* Exhibit A. May I say Many Happy Returns?'

'Not yet, m'lud. Tally was born just after midnight, I came an hour later. Ahh!' Someone had thrown a lighted taper into the paraffin-soaked bonfire and it had gone up with a whoosh, sending sparks high into the dark sky. 'Who needs fireworks?' she exclaimed with exhilaration, following the trajectory of the flickering embers dancing eagerly upwards, clinging to the updraught of heat from the flames until they died, suspended in a void.

From the other side of the conflagration a pair of deep-set, Gallic eyes studied Nell through the blaze. Claude Marchelier had come to Taliska in the company of a lively divorcée called Fenella Drummond-Elliot, a successful knitwear designer from Edinburgh. She had just completed a gruelling sales trip to America, Switzerland and Italy which she had rounded off in Monte Carlo where Claude pursued a lucrative accountancy business. The two had met at an international society party during one of Fenella's previous sales trips and had become lovers. This meeting was a re-match and had developed into a short holiday at Taliska which Fenella had heard about on the fashion grapevine. ' "Low-fat, high luxury, total seclusion",' she quoted to him from the brochure. 'It sounds just what we need.' So far they had spent forty-eight highly satisfactory hours using all the hotel's facilities for exactly the purpose which Tally had intended they should be used. The birthday party was almost the first time they had emerged from their bedroom, apart from making the odd trip to the gym for a sauna or one of Libby's massages. Fenella and Claude were unmistakably on an L and R trip, and all this sex had decidedly whetted his appetite, though not for food.

'What butterfly has caught your roving eye?' Fenella asked curiously, detecting though not resenting her lover's drifting attention. She attracted copious attention herself, being a long-legged, striking blonde in her early thirties with breasts designed for clinging sweaters and a bottom tailor-made for tight trousers. She was also permanently tanned and, in light blue jeans and a sleeveless white cashmere top, looked nothing less than sensational.

Claude nodded in Nell's direction. 'I think not so much a butterfly as a pupa – do you agree?' He blinked his hooded brown eyes lazily. He was much the same age as Fenella, tall and olive-skinned with fine, sculpted lips and a long, straight paper-knife nose. Dark, wavy hair swept his collar and he wore a monogrammed short-sleeved, cream linen shirt and honey-coloured Chinos belted with gold-buckled crocodile-skin. He was stylishly sexy and he knew it, like a debonair French film star.

Fenella regarded the object of his interest through the fountain of sparks. Nell's curly brown hair was dishevelled, her make-up skilfully pale and carefully smudged around the eyes and she was smiling engagingly at Alasdair, standing in a rather provocative way with one hand in the belt of her jeans and the other raising her glass as if in a toast. Yet despite her woman-of-the-world stance there was something vulnerable about the soft line of her jaw and the defiant tilt of her chin. 'Isn't that the birthday girl?' asked the designer, making a swift, professional appraisal. 'Owns the hotel with her brother. He's the yummy one over there, surrounded by chambermaids.'

'I assumed you would have spotted him, *chérie*,' Claude remarked lazily. 'But he is already hatched, wouldn't you say? Whereas his sister looks as if she has not yet quite had the courage to spread her wings.'

Fenella slipped her arm through his in a gesture that was both sensual and proprietorial. 'OK, lover,' she murmured into his ear. 'I get the message. You want to go and chat her up. Well, I confess her companion intrigues me also. He looks wonderfully unassailable, like a craggy mountain, and you know I can't resist a challenge!'

As the bonfire ignited Alasdair had been seriously pondering how best to move his relationship with Nell up a gear and wondering apprehensively whether his advances would be met with indifference or encouragement. He had heard nothing of the London boyfriend lately and hoped that particular liaison had died a natural death. He was aware that his own emotional bruises were still not completely healed but, after nearly two celibate years, was at last beginning to recognise the stirrings of a genuine new attraction. And he thought Nell might be open to his interest, believed he had detected a certain understanding between them on the night of the lost boat but had prudently refrained from seeking to make more of it on that occasion. It was therefore with dismay that he saw the sudden flame of fascination ignite in Nell's eyes because it was clearly not for him but for someone she viewed over his shoulder. He looked round to see who was the cause. A beautiful couple – there was no other way of describing them – were approaching through the glare of the flames.

'I felt I had to wish you a very happy birthday,' crooned Claude exclusively to Nell, while Fenella adroitly engaged Alasdair in a separate conversation. 'I sense that this is a night of great power for you.'

Nell was startled, uncertain whether to take him seriously. He was undeniably gorgeous, with deep, penetrating eyes which seemed to burn with a smouldering intensity, at present flatteringly focused entirely on herself, but she would not have earmarked Claude Marchelier as a psychic or a seer. He was too vibrant, too obviously able to indulge every sense at will without the need of extra-sensory perception. Nevertheless he had certainly touched the nerve of her own secret belief that this feast of St John would launch her into a new phase of her life. In her case the term 'feast' applied only loosely, for in her bathroom before the party she had already dispensed with that night's dinner and the champagne on her empty stomach was making her light-headed.

'Great power?' she echoed, relishing the strange, slightly stilted intonation of his English. 'Well, there is definitely something supernatural happening on a night like this, don't you think? You can almost feel the spirits whizzing about.'

'You are lucky to have been born at such an auspicious time,' he told her, allowing a touch of envy to creep into his brown velvet voice. 'I was born in the depths of winter.'

'Then perhaps you were the spark of new life in a dead world,' she suggested, her eyes dancing. 'Will you leap over the fire later? That's the idea of the party.'

'If you lead, I shall certainly follow,' he told her and touched her bare arm solicitously. 'But you are surely vulnerable. You do not fear the flames?'

His unexpected caress caused Nell to blush hotly. 'No,' she said shakily, feeling goose-bumps speckle her flesh. 'We won't jump till after midnight. The fire will have died down a bit by then but there has to be some element of danger or there's no excitement in it.' She could hear herself gabbling foolishly. In the company of this sophisticated Monegasque she felt gauche and inadequate. Even her years in television had given her no experience of such an intense and vivid male creature. Heavens, she thought, I'm behaving like a moonstruck teenager. I must get a grip.

As far as Claude was concerned everything was progressing satisfactorily. He was looking for amusement and Nell was his party entertainment – someone to practise his technique on. He watched her obvious confusion with intense pleasure. Meanwhile Alasdair found himself disconcertingly subject to Fenella's charm, transmitted at full power. He was startled and intrigued but not enough to divert his attention entirely from Nell. From the corner of his eye he noticed with distaste that the Frenchman's predatory brown hand was on her bare arm and that a heavy gold bracelet adorned his wrist. 'You're a lawyer?' he vaguely heard Fenella cooing with flattering interest. 'I usually find lawyers so unapproachable but you are . . . different.'

Gabriel had instantly latched onto Niamh, breaking all Isabella's strictures about beautiful blondes by gravitating towards the girl's tawny Irish splendour. Principally however, he had spotted that she was smoking what appeared to be an over-sized cigarette, dragging the smoke down into her lungs as if each breath might be her last and letting the exhalation drizzle slowly and sinuously through her nostrils. She reminded him of an old movie, when female stars were not considered sexy unless they smoked – a modern Jane Russell or Lauren Bacall. He was curious to learn more.

'I am surprised that a young girl like you is smoking,' he told her in a tone of avuncular admonition. 'Is it not very bad for your health?'

Niamh favoured him with her most withering green gaze and then softened it by shrugging when she realised he was a guest. She'd get the heave-ho if

Nell caught her being rude to one of them! 'I don't exactly smoke,' she said illogically, on a cloud of something that looked very like it. 'This is different.'

'That's funny. It looks just like a cigarette,' Gabriel observed dryly. 'But perhaps it has another name.' Gently he reached out and took the object in question from between Niamh's fingers and put it to his mouth, drawing on it deeply. Holding the smoke in his lungs he nodded mutely and then said as he exhaled, 'Yes, I think it does.' His panda eyes blinked slowly at her and he smiled. 'And it is just what I need.' Isabella had said no alcohol but she hadn't said no grass . . .

A few paces away Claude was still staring intently into Nell's eyes. 'Tell me,' he inquired, 'do you like clothes?'

Nell's eyebrows made angel's wings. 'What do you mean?' she asked.

He smiled indulgently. 'What I say.' His hand moved purposefully upwards to the cutaway armhole of her waistcoat where he slipped his fingers in, tantalisingly close to her breast, to rub the cloth against his thumb. 'Tonight you wear this denim. Do you like denim?'

'Yes, yes I do,' she said weakly, trying to ignore the effect this apparently innocent exploration was having on the flesh of her nipple, so close to his fingertips. He must surely be aware of it hardening, becoming erect, pushing at the unyielding fabric which covered it.

'But it is stiff and harsh. It scratches your skin, does it not? Why do you not wear something softer, more feminine?'

With a spurt of self-assertion she raised her own hand and slowly removed his from her clothing, holding his gaze as she did so. Their hands remained linked, elbows bent as she said evenly, 'Some people think denim is rather sexy.'

He laughed ruefully, detached his hand and raised it, acknowledging her implication that he himself might be among them. 'It is true,' he admitted. 'It is sexy. But you should wear silk and lawn and cashmere. They would make you *feel* sexy as well.'

'Would Polyester and Botany wool do?' she asked, anxious to nudge the conversation onto more familiar, humorous ground. 'The overdraft might explode otherwise.'

'I know what we should do,' he declared with sudden animation, humour apparently lost on him. 'We should take you to Edinburgh for some shopping.' He swung round to gather Fenella into the conversation, breaking rudely into her charm-assault on Alasdair. 'What do you think, *chérie*? Wouldn't Nell look wonderful in your designs?'

Swallowing an irritable protest at this Gallic lack of manners, Alasdair needed only one glance at Nell's face to understand with a lurch of regret that his moment had passed. He felt sure any approach from him now would appear dull and unexciting in comparison with this conceited but magnetic foreigner. Silently he cursed the circumstances and his frustration showed on his face as petulance.

Nell saw Alasdair's brow wrinkle and his lips purse. Damn him and his obvious disapproval! Who did he think he was?

'What is it you design?' she asked Fenella, although she already knew through staff gossip.

Fenella switched off the quizzical look she'd given Claude and bestowed a friendly smile on Nell. 'Knitwear,' she told the other girl. 'Cashmere, mainly. I have a showroom in Edinburgh. Yes, you must come! I think your hotel would be an ideal place to wear my designs. You'd be a good ambassador for them.'

'Which means you should get them at a good discount,' put in Claude mischievously, slipping his arm round Fenella's shoulders. 'Should she not, 'Ella?'

'Huh!' countered Fenella, pinching his cheek in teasing reprimand. 'I'll make my own arrangements about things like that, if you don't mind, you scheming money-man. But seriously,' she turned to Nell, 'you should come with us when we leave on Thursday. Give yourself a birthday present – a day or two shopping in Edinburgh. And we'll help you. It would be fun.' Over Nell's head she winked at Claude. It was a wink that said, 'You owe me.'

Nell visualised her credit card, sitting in its leather wallet, hardly touched for months. 'Yes, it would,' she agreed thoughtfully. Why shouldn't she go and buy some new clothes for her new figure? 'I just might do that.' An audible snort from Alasdair only served to harden her resolve.

Meanwhile, Mac was the focus of a flurry of activity. Amidst much giggling he was passing round another giant-sized cigarette of the kind Niamh had been smoking. Libby, Rob and Tony had taken deep drags at it one after the other and a sweet, herbal smell drifted on the night air around them. Flora stood at the edge of the circle looking anxious. Tally moved up beside her, asking nonchalantly, 'What gives?'

She shrugged and shook her head. 'They all seem a bit dulally.'

He laughed. 'Good word, dulally. Yes, I bet that's exactly what they are.' He stepped nearer to Mac and took the cigarette firmly from his friend's hand. Nothing was said as he took a deep drag on it and held the smoke for several seconds in his lungs. Exhaling slowly he grinned and passed the reefer to Flora. 'Great stuff, Mac,' he said, nodding at Flora to take a drag. 'Where d'you get it?'

'It's around,' said Mac evasively. 'It's no' hard to find.'

Flora had taken a small, spluttering pull at the joint and handed it on gratefully to Niamh who had now joined the group, having felt obliged to give the rest of hers to Gabriel. She took a deep drag. ''S good shit,' she said with a slur, fragrant smoke drizzling from her mouth. 'Better than you can get in the Time Capsule. Come on, let's go and stare at the moon, Tony. They say it makes you tell anyone anything they want to know.'

Tony looked gratified and glassy-eyed at the same time. The suave, smooth-talking Scottish-Italian barman had been after Niamh ever since she arrived, but this was the first encouragement he had received. Now that Libby's see-saw inclinations seemed to have settled in Rob's favour, the libidinous Tony was restlessly seeking solace. Niamh would more than compensate.

Tally eyed this oddly matched pair curiously. He gave Tony little chance of landing that particular fish. He knew his younger sister was playing the field, testing her considerable man-pulling power without necessarily letting it tug her over any cliffs. He grinned as they wandered off and accepted another drag of the joint from Mac. His senses were beginning to swirl pleasantly. 'Let's enjoy it while we can,' he said. 'But for God's sake, keep quiet about it around the guests. We don't want anyone getting the idea this is a shit-house.' His wits were still sharp enough to file away a mental resolution to investigate the source of the drug tomorrow. He did not want to spoil the party now. 'It's even better mixed with champagne. Come on Flora, your glass is empty!' He took Flora's arm in a brotherly way and marched her towards a table on which rested several loaded ice-buckets. Another cork exploded into the night air.

As Tally left the circle, Gabriel sidled up to Mac and began a softly murmured conversation in which each had to repeat himself frequently owing to the difficulty they had in understanding each other's English. However, by the time Isabella had abandoned a conversation with Tina about her clarsach and wandered over to join her husband it was clear that a deal had been done. Mac looked hazily self-satisfied and Gabriel had a broad smile on his face. Isabella was carrying a glass.

'What is this?' asked Gabriel indignantly, keeping the part-smoked joint he had wheedled from Niamh hidden at his side and indicating the glass with his other hand. 'No champagne, you said.'

Isabella slipped her free hand into the crook of his elbow. Her sun-bleached hair was tied back in a scarf and she wore a bright blue silk shirt tucked into cream linen trousers. There was gold at her ears and throat and she was amiably tipsy. 'That was only for you, darling,' she murmured unashamedly. 'It is you who needs to rest the liver, not me.'

Gabriel gave an indignant laugh but was already too marijuana-mellow to mind. He abandoned caution and took a pull at his joint, staring upwards as he exhaled. 'Well, it is a marvellous place to rest the liver,' he sighed, leading her gently off towards the jetty amidst her protests against him smoking.

Tally sipped champagne as he gazed at the shadowy figures around the fire. 'Everyone's pairing up like kippers,' he observed with amusement.

Flora giggled and gulped from the glass he gave her, wiping the bubbles from her turned-up nose. 'Kippers don't swim in pairs,' she exclaimed. 'They're just smoked that way.'

'Oh well, like gloves then, or turtle doves if you want to be poetic. Look around. It's amazing!'

Sure enough, most of the shadows seemed to have two heads as people stood or sat close together, talking and whispering while the flames danced and died. Gabriel and Isabella were leaning over the rail of the jetty staring into the water, Tony and Niamh were silhouetted against the beaten-pewter sheen of the loch, seated on a log by the shore presumably swapping fascinating truths under the moon's crescent glare, Libby and Rob had broken away from Mac and wandered hand in hand across the *machair*, Calum was leaning against a rock in animated conversation with Ginny whose cheeks were rosy with champagne and firelight, and Fenella and Claude remained intertwined as they pursued their encounter with Nell and Alasdair. Only these last two remained unattached, aloof from each other as if harsh words had been exchanged.

Flora gave Tally's hand a meaningful squeeze, smiled apologetically and left his side to take a drink to Mac. Soon they, too, had their heads together in private conversation. Tally meandered disconsolately off towards Tina who, with Craig's help, had set up her clarsach and was about to begin her incidental music. She, too, looked flushed and distracted as if she had also been at the grass and smiled rather dizzily at him as he approached.

'I'm not sure I'll be able to play very well,' she confided, sitting abruptly on the little folding stool she had brought for the purpose. 'I think I'm a bit squiffy.'

'You're not alone,' Tally told her with an avuncular smile. 'No one's exactly sober.' With a shock he realised that Tina was wearing a low-cut top and jeans which looked even tighter than Nell's. Recalling the girlish white broderie Anglaise she'd worn at the opening party, he thought, Christ, they're all at it! There must be something in the air.

By the time Tally and Nell cut their birthday cakes everyone was either dreamy-eyed or frenziedly animated. Calum had freely admitted that cake-icing was not his speciality and so young Craig had made the cakes, revealing a talent previously unknown to his employers. Nell's was white and decorated with blue scabious and yellow iris, both flowers known to be her island favourites, while Tally's was shaped and coloured like a champagne bottle adorned with the Taliska label. He winced exaggeratedly as he cut into the tip of the 'cork'. 'The first time I've been called on to circumcise anything,' he quipped amidst tipsy cheers. Nell sank the knife into her cake and wished hard but revealed her wish to no one. 'It's bad luck,' she told Alasdair, shaking her head when he inquired.

'Will you really go to Edinburgh with that Frenchman?' he asked tetchily.

'Yes, why not?' Nell demanded, an angry snap in her voice.

'He's nothing but an offshore accountant. I wouldn't trust him further than I could throw him,' he told her unsteadily. The champagne had made him reckless.

'Oh, Alasdair!' Nell exclaimed with exasperation. 'Whatever happened to the "Auld Alliance"? He may be an offshore accountant as you so charmingly put it, but to me that sounds far more interesting than an "old woman", which is what *you* are being.

I'm going to jump the fire.' And she turned on her heel and left him.

'Damn,' muttered Alasdair gloomily, watching with an expression of helpless frustration as she went up to Tally and began to coax him towards the bonfire. It had died down into little more than a heap of glowing embers but it was still quite a substantial obstacle. Tally looked at it dubiously and kicked one of the scattered logs further into the centre, raising a sudden volcano of ash and sparks.

'Pshaw!' He spat in disgust and wiped his eyes free of cinders. 'Pass the sackcloth, I'm covered in ashes. OK, Nell, OK! Let's get this mad business over with.'

Joining hands, they retreated several paces in order to get a run at it. Then, to the accompaniment of a crescendo of sweeping chords from Tina's harp and a swelling handclap from the onlookers, the twins drew a deep breath and raced, laughing wildly, towards the licking tongues of flame and the flickering embers of the expiring bonfire. '*Geronimo!*' they shrieked in unison as they cleared it without mishap. Flushed with success and charged with adrenaline, they both began to dance about like dervishes. 'Come on, everyone. It's easy!' they yelled.

Tina's fingers grew numb with the friction of the harp-strings but she continued to vibrate the night air into climax. Galvanised into action, singly and in pairs, more people began to jump. From the surrounding darkness an onlooker might have feared he had stumbled on a witches' sabbath, a circle of eerily cheering and cavorting figures silhouetted against a hellish inferno. In macabre procession, weird and flailing black shadows detached themselves from the group and flung themselves over the pyre, becoming fleetingly chromatic in the light of its glowing heart.

Even Claude and Fenella abandoned their clinch and leaped like a pair of exotic gazelles. Niamh jumped with Tony, throwing a handful of fire-crackers into the embers as she did so and causing brief consternation followed by hilarity among the crowd. Only Alasdair demurred, firmly shaking his head, even when Nell came to try and persuade him.

'I've confronted everything fate's thrown at me so far without the help of any red-hot embers,' he insisted. 'I'll take whatever's coming in the same way.'

'God, you are stubborn,' she told him irritably. 'Stubborn and unadventurous.'

'Call me what you like,' he retorted crossly. The night was a disaster. He wished he was on a mountain somewhere, miles from anyone. 'I don't need any superstitious nonsense to bolster *my* hopes.' He felt as if all his hopes had been irretrievably dashed anyway, by a greasy, egregious Frenchman wearing a gold bracelet! Angrily he crushed his paper cake-plate in his fist and hurled it into the fire.

'It isn't just superstition, it's symbolic,' protested Nell. For her the jump had been powerfully significant. From now on she vowed that she would assert herself, be less retiring, take a more positive attitude. The fire had consumed her past. 'I will no longer be a shrinking violet,' she told herself determinedly, turning her back on Alasdair and striding up to Claude with what she hoped was a devastating smile. 'I am no longer a fat nobody. I am Jane Fonda, Joan Collins and Shirley Conran all rolled into one. Look out world – here I come!'

'Look Alasdair, there she goes,' muttered the stubborn lawyer to himself dejectedly, filled with self-reproach.

★ ★ ★

When Flora and Mac wove their way down the drive towards home she had to hold him up. His feet kept wandering away from his body as if determined to escape the fierce hangover which could only be a matter of hours away. With a grunt of exasperation Flora grabbed a fold of his trousers to hoist him back to the vertical and her hand closed over something bulky. Mac made a feeble effort to stop her but she deftly dipped her hand into his pocket and removed a wad of notes, crying out in surprise at its thickness and obvious value. Although dawn was already brightening the sky she could not discern the denomination of the notes, but even if they were only tenners there had to be at least two hundred pounds there.

'Mac! Mac!' she shouted, trying to shake him and hold him up at the same time. 'All this money, Mac – where did you get it?'

But Mac was too intoxicated to respond coherently. He simply smiled and nodded as if she had told him the best joke he had heard for days, lifting his arm to wrap it around her neck in a clumsy hug.

Oh well, she thought, tucking the wad safely in the pocket of her jacket. At least whatever that stuff is he smokes, it makes him gassy instead of crabbit! A charming drunk was better than a belligerent one any day. But the money was a worry. She couldn't understand where Mac was getting the drug from, but if he was selling it too that was worse, much worse. Even she knew the penalties for drug-dealing.

She decided not to let him sleep it off. He would be more vulnerable if she kept him awake and pestered him with black coffee and questions. Intuition told her that sooner or later he would crack and tell her the truth, if only to get some sleep.

As is its wont, truth turned out to be every bit as strange as fiction. When she relayed Mac's tale to Tally the next day he gave a shout of laughter and exclaimed, 'It's just like *Whisky Galore*!'

'What's *Whisky Galore*?' asked Flora, not familiar with Compton Mackenzie's comic novel of Hebridean island life.

Tally laughed some more and clutched his throbbing head. 'Why should you have read it when you've probably lived it?' he declared, shrugging. 'It's a book in which a ship loaded with whisky is wrecked off a Scottish island. The story tells of the lengths to which the islanders go to rescue the cargo and hide it from the Customs and Excise. It's very funny. How much grass did Mac find?'

'Grass – is that what you call the stuff? He just said it was a bale, like a wool-bale. He found it on the beach.'

'On Taliska?' asked Tally, perturbed.

'No, on Mull. Just sitting there in a bay where he'd anchored to untangle his nets. He saw it from the boat and put ashore to have a look.'

Tally nodded. 'I've read about it happening. Sometimes smugglers ditch the stuff in the sea if they think they're going to be boarded. Or it just falls overboard when they're transferring cargo in mid-ocean, and it gets washed up. There've been articles in the press about it.'

'He should have told the police,' said Flora, 'but he couldna resist keeping it. He just thought he'd make a wee bit out of it, first from the travellers and now from your staff and mebbe the guests, too. What are you going to do?' Her face was so crumpled with concern that Tally risked a quick, consoling kiss. They were in the office and rather open to interruption but he couldn't bear to see her troubled expression.

'Nothing that you have to worry about. I'll sort it out with Mac. Where is he?'

'At home, in bed. He's no' too good!' She managed a wry smile. 'I dinna think champagne and – grass, is it? Well, they dinna mix too well.'

Tally rubbed his own pounding temples. 'You're right, they don't! I'll drag him out for a hair-of-the-dog at lunch-time.'

'I hope Calum wasn't expecting any fish today.'

'He's got yesterday's prawn catch on tonight's menu. They've been on ice – they'll be fresh enough.' Tally touched her hand in a brief gesture of affection. 'Don't worry, my darling.'

In the Ossian later, Mac was just about *compos mentis*, pale but unrepentant. 'It was only a bit of flotsam,' he grumbled when Tally remonstrated with him for profiting from his windfall. 'There's no harm in making a wee bit out of it.'

'There is when it's my hotel you're flogging it in,' Tally insisted in an undertone. There were few people in the bar at that time but he didn't want them getting wind of the conversation. 'How much more have you got?'

Mac shrugged. 'Most of it, really. I havna got rid of much. It's stashed in a cave near Port Ramsay.'

'On Lismore?' exclaimed Tally. 'Why did you take it there?'

'I knew a good place to keep it. It'll never be found where I've put it.'

'Maybe not, but if the police trace any back to you they'll do you for dealing. You've been helluva lucky so far but whilst it's still there you'll be tempted. You must get rid of it, Mac.'

'How do I do that?' his friend demanded gruffly. 'I

canna just throw it into the sea for somebody else to find!'

'You could weight it with something, for God's sake,' said Tally with exasperation. 'Once it's sunk it'll rot away, although it might give the fish a bit of a trip.'

Mac pondered this idea for a few minutes. 'Well, OK.' He still sounded dubious and reluctant.

'I'll help you,' Tally assured him hastily, wanting to be certain that the fisherman kept his word. 'And don't flog any more in the meanwhile. Too many people know about it already! Look, why don't we go tomorrow? Get it over and done with. Tell your crew to take another day off. He'll think you're still sick.'

'Aye, OK,' said Mac reluctantly. He took a long pull at his pint and winked a wicked, bloodshot eye at Tally. ''S bloody good stuff, though, isn't it, pal? Maybe we could just keep a wee bit for ourselves!'

'Christ Mac, you're incorrigible!' exclaimed Tally, scowling.

Gabriel Garvey-Byass was just thinking the same as Mac. It was bloody good stuff! He and Isabella had taken one of the rowboats out on the loch which was calm and sun-kissed under a sky as clear by day as it had been the night before. They drifted gently in a deserted inlet on the east side of the island watching the sea-birds wheel and dive overhead. On the jetty the night before he'd told Isabella about buying the grass from Mac.

'It is just enough for our stay here,' he assured her. 'I won't be nipping into the bodega for a quick joint when we get home, don't worry. But if I'm not having a drink, this will see me through all this health business. It is just what I need.' He had stuffed the small plastic bag full of dried, brown leaves into his sponge bag. 'You must try it, Isabella.'

So she had. Drifting dreamily in the dinghy, lying on cushions between the thwarts, they shared a joint and let the sun dazzle their closed eyes and gradually they began to fondle and stroke each other as they had when they were teenagers on the beach in Cadiz Bay. The pressures of work and three small children had restricted their love-making to midnight scrambles, frequently interrupted by small, piping voices demanding drinks of water or spoonfuls of cough medicine, until boarding school had removed them for at least eight months of the year. But habits become ingrained, and Gabriel's drinking had escalated by then to the extent that he frequently passed out at night, rather than falling asleep. It had become an exception if he and Isabella went to bed early enough or sober enough to exchange more than a perfunctory kiss.

'We have never done it in a boat, have we?' asked Gabriel, growing more pleasantly aroused by the minute. He had just unfastened Isabella's bra under her cotton T-shirt, a manoeuvre he remembered vividly from his early teenage fumblings with girlfriends who had subsequently invariably pulled his hands away from their gloriously liberated breasts. Isabella, however, did not.

'How do you mean? You can't remember?' Isabella's low, throaty laugh was amused. She opened her eyes to discover his face looming dark and passionate above her. The boat rocked but not threateningly. 'You want to? Here – now?' She wriggled her body as if testing the stability of their position and then smiled, lazily and submissively, the drug blunting all inhibition. 'Well, why not?'

The most perilous moment was removing their trousers but so urgent was their amorous need that they managed somehow, giggling and laughing like the two teenagers they once more imagined they were. Soft, Spanish moans and expletives echoed off the mischievous wavelets, scampering across the surface of the loch and alerting several herring-gulls which swooped and called as if encouraging the giddy progress towards climax they witnessed in the rocking dinghy beneath them. To any human eye it might have been an incongruous sight, two half-naked bodies not in the first flush of youth, writhing and gasping like a pair of netted salmon in the bottom of the bucking boat, but there was no human eye to see and an event which might have inspired mockery or even scorn among their fellow men and women was a wonderful, rejuvenating experience to the two who shared it, who gloriously revelled in each other as they had not done for years, out on the gentle water with the breeze playing on their naked skin and the sea-birds blinking their uncritical yellow eyes.

The next morning, when Tally got up to prepare for his spot of pot-dumping, he peered gloomily out of the window at a wildly changed weather-prospect. Rain lashed the panes, the marram grass was lying horizontal and waving like a streaming banner, and the wind was tearing holes in the canopy of the grove of Scots pines. 'Oh shit,' he groaned, stumbling to the bathroom. 'Give me the Joy Rides. This is going to be a bitch of a trip.'

He took two sea-sick pills and stuffed the rest of the packet into the pocket of his waterproofs. As he did so he noticed a slip of paper lying on the carpet. It was a brief note which Nell had pushed under his door.

Made an early start. Gone to Edinburgh for a few days, it read. *Staying with Fenella. Back Sunday. Keep the hotel fires burning!*

Chapter Thirteen

With amusement and alarm Nell regarded her reflection in the hairdresser's mirror. I look like Sonic the Hedgehog, she thought – a close encounter of the weird kind. Tinfoil-wrapped spikes stuck out all over her head like an heraldic sun in splendour. When they reached Edinburgh, Fenella had driven directly to the salon, a chrome and white mirrored emporium, swept imperiously inside, demanded an immediate comb-up for herself and introduced Nell to the friendly, bearded coiffeur. 'This is Murdo Scott, Nell, the demon barber of Thistle Street. You'll look after Nell, won't you, Murdo? As you can see, she's a complete headcase.'

Murdo eyed Nell's limp brown locks and visibly shuddered, but his eyes twinkled kindly from under bushy brows. Nell had more or less assumed that all male hairdressers were poofs by definition, but this example of the species seemed reassuringly macho, from the tip of his curly red beard to his size twelve loafers. He was six feet tall with the shoulders of a rugby forward. The only delicate thing about Murdo Scott was his touch on the scissors, which he wielded with the skill and speed of a fencing master. Nell's hair had been washed and towelled and subjected to the twinkling twin blades almost before her hackles had time to rise. The only time her opinion was asked on anything was when a girl assistant inquired whether she would like milk in her coffee. Then the same girl had set to with a roll of tin-foil and a pastry brush so that Nell would have felt distinctly like a Beef Wellington or a tray of cheese straws if the viscous liquid into which the brush was dipped had not been a kind of science-fiction blue rather than egg-yolk yellow. 'Give her some style, Murdo, and for God's sake give her some highlights,' Fenella had urged as she raced to rescue her car from the predatory attentions of a traffic warden. 'Hair hasn't been worn mouse brown since peroxide was invented.'

'Fortunately we don't have to use peroxide any more,' the girl with the pastry brush said reassuringly. 'It made your hair fall out.'

Nell made a face. 'Don't tell me that. I have enough trouble with fall-out as it is.'

'Yes, I've noticed that,' commented the girl. 'Have you been ill or something?'

Nell denied that she had but was faintly disturbed that her hair's lack of grip on her scalp should be the subject of comment. Up to now she had chosen to ignore the quantity of fallen strands which recently tended to clog the drain every time she washed her tarnished crowning glory. And she refused to link this fall-out with the chronic soreness of her throat, the ulcers in her mouth or the blotches on her skin. Panadol, Bonjela and moisturiser fought a losing battle with the effects of her ugly new habit while she herself had eyes only for her shrinking body.

At lunch-time Fenella and Claude came to collect Nell from the salon. 'If you had not the same clothes on I would not have known you,' declared Claude fervently in his irregular English. For the first time in her life Nell recognised instant arousal in a man's eyes and it made her feel quite giddy, like the first hectic plunge on a Big Dipper. How could a bit of bleach and a few snips of the scissors achieve such a reaction? It was illogical and absurd – and wonderful.

They ate lunch at the Café Royal, a magnificent Victorian pub which had been transformed into a copy of a boulevard brasserie. Nell could hardly eat because she kept catching glimpses of herself in the elaborately engraved wall-mirrors and experiencing small tremors of shock. She knew that the figure seated between Fenella's vivid flamboyance and Claude's dark sensuality was herself, but when she glimpsed the chic blonde head on the slim angular body, she could not relate to it mentally. It seemed to her that it was someone else whose shining curls reflected the light from the opulent stained-glass windows and drew the eye from the potted palms.

'This afternoon we will buy clothes, yes?' asked Claude, whose eyes seemed to have been flatteringly glued to Nell all through lunch. Her own glance had met his directly once or twice and sent wicked stabs of recognition shooting through her groin. It was as if an invisible cord was tugging her inexorably towards him, like a fish on the end of a fine filament line. She had never experienced such a compelling physical attraction before. It eclipsed reason, morality and common sense.

'I'd love to, darlings, but I can't,' Fenella announced. 'My agent is flying in from Germany and I shall be closeted with him for hours.'

'Then I shall accompany Nell,' persisted Claude, unperturbed. He smiled encouragingly at her. As if it were necessary, thought Nell, feeling the smile like an intimate caress. 'Fenella will tell us where to go and I shall advise what you should buy. I love to watch a woman shopping. She is so intense, like a dancer before a performance. All is in the preparation, no?'

'You have never been shopping with me, then,' sighed Nell. 'I tend to grab anything I think suits me and run. It's never been one of my favourite occupations.'

Claude shook his head disapprovingly. 'We shall not do it hit and miss like that. We shall do it like an audit. We have prepared the spread-sheet,' he indicated her new appearance, 'and now we shall make the entries in separate columns – underclothes, dresses, shoes. Then we shall make a total look.'

Nell laughed nervously. 'You make it sound like Budget Day! I may have a balance of payment problem.'

'This is what she was built for!' yelled Mac, the muscles in his forearms straining to keep the *Flora*'s wheel steady as she tossed and danced over the stormy waters of the loch. The sturdy fishing boat seemed to make little of the violent wind and lashing sea, shrugging it aside as if it were merely a puny jet from a child's water-pistol. Nevertheless Tally wished his feet were planted almost anywhere other than on the heaving, creaking deck of the wheelhouse. Visibility was no more than fifty yards, and water streamed over the gunwales every time the boat wallowed broadside on the swell. The roar of the engine seemed to fill his head with excruciating pain.

'I didn't know the loch could get so rough,' he bellowed at top volume. 'We should have waited for another day.'

Mac gave an incredulous snort. 'If fishermen only went out when it was dead calm there'd be no fish and chips!' He indicated the lighthouse which guarded the strait between Lismore and Port Appin. Its beam was flashing through the grey, sodden gloom of the morning. 'See, we've only to keep that to starboard until we clear the rocks and then we'll round the point and it'll be calmer. Port Ramsay headland'll protect us from the swell.'

Tally shuddered, remembering his previous trip to Lismore, the screeching outboard and the grip of the current. 'This stretch of water is jinxed for me,' he groaned. 'This is the last time, I swear it. Just keep that engine churning!'

Mac laughed rather evilly. 'The Silkie'll no' come for you,' he cried. 'You're too foreign for it.'

'I didn't know your rotten sea-sprites were fussy about their victims' origins,' retorted Tally. 'I just hope you're right, that's all. I got away with it once and I have no wish to be carried off to some watery grave now.'

When they reached Port Ramsay the force of wind and tide had luckily filled the once-silted harbour, for the *Flora* needed the protection it afforded. Even so, when they disembarked after they had tied up in the lee of the sea wall, the north-easterly nearly blew them off their feet before they reached the beach. The horizontal rain seemed to penetrate every seam of their waterproofs as they clambered along the shore to Mac's 'grass-house', as Tally cryptically dubbed their destination.

'How did you get the damned thing up here on your own?' he asked in amazement, flicking the beam of his torch over a battered bale the size of a washing machine. 'You must have had help.' They'd had to scramble several yards up an unstable rockfall to reach the cave, half a mile along the headland and out of sight of the village. Inside it was dry, dark and relatively quiet, only the deep sough of the wind outside disturbing the blessed calm.

In the gloom Mac shrugged and shook his head. 'No. It was the day you first came to see Taliska I moved it. I used the net-winch to drag it off the rocks on Mull. No one saw me. And then I just anchored behind the headland here and floated it ashore. I used ropes to haul it up. It wasna too difficult.'

'And you've been popping back to raid the larder ever since, you sly old rat,' Tally mused, pulling at a ragged hole in the hessian and plastic wrapping which looked as if rodent teeth had, indeed, been gnawing at it. 'Well, we can't use the winch now, not in this weather,' he added dejectedly, moving forward to stare out of the cave-mouth at the greedy waves sucking at the jagged rocks below. They couldn't risk splintering the *Flora*'s planking on those broken teeth.

For the first time Mac looked concerned. He shook his head. 'No, we canna,' he agreed. 'Perhaps we could drag it along to the harbour?'

Tally shook his head vehemently. 'No – can't risk it. I didn't see anyone when we arrived but I reckon a few curtains twitched in those cottage windows. They'll see us load the bale, even if we could get it down there without several slipped discs. Also, it might split open. The last thing we want is a load of wet grass floating about on the tide.'

'Oh, I dunno. It looks a bit like kelp,' observed Mac. 'Maybe we should just spread it round the rocks and coves and leave it at that.'

'I've been told the sheep eat seaweed in these parts,' Tally remarked, pertinently. 'Suppose the crofters' ewes all got as high as kites and fell off the cliffs? No, Mac, burial at sea is the only fitting end for this stuff. We'll have to wait for the wind to drop.'

At Taliska, only Ann was aware of Tally's whereabouts since he had left her a message on the computer. For the rest of the staff the morning passed in the usual pattern of serving breakfasts, cleaning rooms and laying up tables. Of the guests, only the Garvey-Byasses were staying on but they had taken one look at the weather and asked if they could have a picnic lunch in their room. Their rocking-boat episode had started something they were unwilling to stop, and the rain had just brought their activities indoors.

So, as there were no lunches to serve in the dining room, the staff meal was a leisurely affair, consisting of the usual soup and bread. Today the soup was a good thick green cabbage and barley broth which Craig had made and which most of the staff ate hungrily, inspired by the change in the weather. It seemed extraordinary how chilly and damp it had become so suddenly after the velvety warmth of the Midsummer Eve party. Calum did not eat lunch; he was too involved in preparing a complicated shellfish fricassée for that evening's dinner, and Niamh, unusually for her, ate only bread and cheese, declaring that barley broth was her *bête noire*. Had Nell been there she might have detected an impish gleam in her sister's eye but no one else remarked it.

Ginny and Libby were the first to show a strange lack of co-ordination and a distinct inclination to giggle. They had gone to the dining room to put fresh napkins on the tables and it was Libby who began the process of folding the stiff napkins into shapes that looked like falsies. 'Look – Madonna!'

she shrieked hysterically, holding the pointed cones to her chest and doing a wild gyrating dance around the dining room.

'No, Peter Rabbit,' squeaked Ginny, clamping a similarly folded napkin to her head and hopping clumsily among the tables, nudging a display of fruits so that they cascaded to the floor.

'Carmen Miranda,' cried Libby, tripping over rolling pears and plums and squashing them into a juicy pulp on the carpet. She was laughing helplessly, trying to balance a pineapple on her head.

'What the hell's going on?' shouted Calum, alerted from the kitchen by the noise and shockingly sober amongst so much hilarity. 'Pack it in, both of you!' But the Australian girls could not pack it in. Even the usually sedate Ginny was quivering with uncontrollable mirth, staring at Calum with her hands over her mouth and tears streaming down her face. 'What's the matter with you?' Calum demanded incredulously. He and Ginny had been gradually feeling their way towards a more-than-friendly relationship of late, tentatively probing each other's shyness and diffidence and looking forward to the day when they might trust each other enough to take the plunge into commitment. Now, out of the blue, here was a wild, manic creature who giggled and hopped about like a rabbit and bore little resemblance to the calm, sweet girl Calum thought he knew. He became angry, hurt that she could have deceived him and puzzled that she should prove so volatile. 'You been at the gin or something?' he accused her furiously. 'You're both pissed out of your minds!'

'No, they're not pissed, they're high,' said a voice behind him, brimming with suppressed amusement. It was Niamh, who had been passing the dining room and understood immediately what the commotion was.

'What's the difference?' snapped Calum. 'They've both gone bonkers!'

Libby and Ginny were now singing uproariously together, a song learned in their Australian childhood.

'See the Sydney Harbour Bridge,
Standing up so high!
It spans its arch across the sky,
Like a giant rainbow!'

They had linked arms and were lost in a drug-induced memory of sparkling water breaking into a diamond mesh over myriad sail-boats and ferries. 'What did we sing that day we went through the Sydney heads in a gale?' Ginny slurred dreamily. 'It went like this – *Da-a da de-e da da-a de da da de da da da da da de da . . .'*

'Da da da de da,' Libby joined in loudly and rapturously. *'Jesu Joy of Man's Desiring* – that's what it was! 'Member we sang it on the ship crossing the 'Stralian Bight, just so we could say that our Bach was worse than the Bight.' The joke started them giggling wildly again.

'It's not exactly their fault,' Niamh said gleefully. 'They'll be all right later. It's just the grass I put in the soup.'

It was then that they heard a crash in the kitchen and Calum raced through the service doors to find tall, gangling Craig grinning inanely, his huge, gym-shoed feet paddling ludicrously in a sea of curdled cream which he had been trying to pour into a cheese-cloth. The shards of a broken earthenware bowl stood up like macabre islands in a white ocean.

'Christ, dinna tell me they're all the same?' Calum yelled at Niamh, who nodded unrepentantly.

'Yes, all of them,' she gurgled, nodding roguishly. 'All except you and me.'

'Jings, Crivens!' *In extremis* Calum resorted to comic-strip expletives. 'You've really put us up shit creek, you wee besom. There's ten in the house tonight. I hope to God Tally's back soon or you are going to have to be barmaid, waitress and chambermaid – to say nothing of doing the washing-up!'

On Lismore the storm raged more elementally than on Taliska. The wind whipped down the loch straight off the slopes of Ben Nevis and, when the driving rain ceased and the tide turned to flow, the waters backed up into the wind, causing waves of more rather than less power. Mac and Tally both agreed that they were unable to move the bale but Tally was unwilling to make the journey back to Taliska in such a violent sea simply in order to return the next day. 'Now you've got me here,' he told Mac, 'you'd better keep me here until the job's done because, I tell you, I'm *not* crossing that stretch of water again.'

No amount of bullying or cajoling would change Tally's mind and so, when the rain eased, they made their way to the phone box at the road junction above the village and rang Taliska. Ann's airy assurance that all was well and they would see him when they saw him should have rung alarm bells with Tally but it did not. He had no reason to suspect Ann of dereliction of duty. She was the soul of discretion and reliability.

Truth to tell, Tally was too concerned about spending the night with Mac in Flora's father's empty croft on the hill above Port Ramsay. It was not a prospect he relished. On the surface, his relationship with Flora had not changed his friendship with Mac, but deep down it made him feel uncomfortable. He had broken an unspoken male code of honour which, barring incest, made just about all women fair game but did not allow a man to mess about with his friend's wife. It was a measure of his obsession with Flora that he had broken this code, but it would also be a test of his ingenuity to spend a day and a night in her husband's company without revealing any tell-tale signs of his disloyalty.

After Mac had rung Flora to tell her he would not be back they set off for the croft in the wind-tossed, penetrating drizzle. 'Any supplies tucked away anywhere?' Tally asked hopefully, his stomach growling like a starved lion.

'There's plenty of grass to keep us going,' replied Mac with a rare flash of humour.

In the office Ann had just taken the telephone message but it had gone in one ear and out the other as she sat in a contented daze, wondering what had happened to make her feel so calm and untroubled. Nothing could go wrong on such a day. Every guest was a personal friend and would be greeted with a hug and a kiss – they were all such kind and wonderful people. Tally was a kind and wonderful person. No, he was more than that. He was the most marvellous person in the whole world and she would tell him so. She picked up the handset again and Niamh found her several minutes later happily murmuring into it passionate words of endearment which would never reach the ears of the man for whom they were intended.

In the stables Rob and Mick were good-naturedly arguing over who would milk the eggs and collect the cows. A basket full of broad beans, still in their fleshy pods, stood forgotten in a corner beside a bag of shiny green courgettes, freshly picked from the garden – vegetables which might never reach the kitchen. Tony had put on a tape of the kind of music which appealed to his pleasantly fogged senses and the staff quarters echoed to a crescendo of synthesised chords building to a percussion climax which would have shattered the crystal spheres of the ancient astronomers. Tony had experienced the effect of marijuana before and was blissfully aware of it without bothering to wonder how this particular high had come about. He simply lay on his bed and let the music and the mood wash over him before sleep claimed his consciousness.

As predicted, there was nothing hit and miss about Nell's shopping spree with Claude. Fenella had directed them to a particular boutique in one of the narrow streets behind Edinburgh's most famous shopping thoroughfare. 'No one shops in Princes Street unless they want to look like everyone else,' Fenella said firmly. 'And remember, don't buy any cashmere or I'll never speak to you again. We'll raid my showroom tomorrow when I've got rid of Helmut.'

'I didn't know there were places that still did this,' Nell whispered to Claude as they sat, sipping coffee and watching a model parade a series of outfits for their benefit.

Claude gave a dissatisfied frown. 'This girl is much too tall. What looks good on her will not necessarily look good on you. And she does not have good legs. Yours are much better.'

Nell stared at him as if he must be slightly crazed. Never before had anyone suggested that she had good legs. Mainly because it was not true. They were too fat in the thigh and skinny in the ankle. Triangular was how she described them herself, with feet that were far too large, clamped like two great rhomboids on the end. However, when she tried on a Tomasz Starzewski dress with a skirt that ended well short of the knee, she was startled to discover that even without the slimming effect of black tights her legs didn't look half bad. In fact, she was so mesmerised by them that she completely forgot to look at the price tag on the dress, a beautifully tailored shift in pale pink with an intriguing horizontally pleated skirt.

'But I can't have this,' she declared reluctantly. 'Even though it does make my legs look less isosceles.'

'But why not?' asked Claude in astonishment. 'It is absolutely marvellous on you. You look wonderful. You could go to Buckingham Palace in that.'

'In Scotland the Queen invites one to Holyroodhouse,' Nell corrected him primly. 'Should she feel so inclined. Unless, of course, it's for a fishin' and shootin' weekend at Balmoral.' She glared once more at her reflection. God, she looked good! 'I can't have this dress because it's pale pink. I *never* wear pale colours. They make you look big, everyone knows that. I wonder if it comes in black or navy?'

'*Mon Dieu* – look at yourself, Nell. Do you look big?' Claude was exasperated. 'No. That is the dress for you.' He turned to the saleswoman, a pleasant and very chic middle-aged lady who wore black jersey and an abundance of gold chains. 'We will take that one, and perhaps the little cream one with the reveres, the Arabella Pollen . . . here, Nell, try it.'

'Not cream, Claude. Honestly, I told you—'

'No black,' said Claude firmly. 'And no 'orrible navy blue. If you must have blue, let it be French blue, with a bit of *joie de vivre*!' Claude was thoroughly enjoying himself, like Svengali with a Scottish Trilby. Nell's naïve protests had brought out the masterful side of his nature. In Monte Carlo women seemed to be born sophisticated. It was refreshing for him to have an opportunity to take the style initiative.

As she was taking off the pink dress Nell caught sight of the price tag and gave a small scream. 'Oh no – it's nearly five hundred pounds! I can't, Claude, truly I can't.' She was in such a state of shock that she stepped out of the changing room in her bra and pants, causing Claude to utter his own cry of distress.

'*Merde alors!* Look at your underwear, Nell. Did it come from a jumble sale?' He turned to the saleswoman, grimacing in apparent pain. 'If you please, Madame, find her some underthings that do justice to your so beautiful dresses. You have lingerie, do you not?'

The black and gold lady agreed that they did while Nell dived back into the curtained cubicle in confusion. She stared once more into the mirror, trying to see herself as Claude had seen her. Was her underwear a disgrace? Well, it was certainly no longer white. It had not been that since a year earlier when she had washed most of it with a new and poorly dyed black T-shirt. Grey would have been a kind way to describe her bra, although grubby might have been more accurate. Moreover, it was at least a size too large and the cups were wrinkled and baggy over the shrunken swell of her breasts. And her knickers, as she consistently called them, were equally baggy cotton which tended to stay up more by willpower than elastic. She had been too pleased with the disappearance of all the lumps and bumps which used to occupy the midriff space between bra and pants to consider the actual condition of her undergarments.

Now that she did, she saw immediately that Claude was right to be horrified. Nevertheless she felt rather angry with him for making such a song and dance about it. This was why she never shopped with other people. Who needed anyone to make comments on anything, let alone your most personal items of clothing? She was still seething when the gold chains jangled at the curtain and several wisps of satin and lace were handed in for her to try. She had to admit that the feel of silky-smooth oyster satin was delicious on her bare skin and certainly made her look more alluring than the Orphan Annie undies she'd discarded. The trouble is, Nell thought then, viewing the stubbly growth on her calves and shins, satin just doesn't go with stubble. It'll have to be a leg-wax next: I suppose this is what's known as the Domino Effect.

Nell was perilously close to the thousand-pound limit on her credit card when she left Fenella's favourite dress-shop but Claude took the accountant's view. 'They are all clothes you need for your job,' he pointed out. 'Clients who pay much to come to a place like Taliska expect to find people there who dress as they do. These are the tools of your trade. You can claim them as expenses against tax, *chérie*.'

Nell wondered whether the firm of rather tight-collared young money-men Tally had appointed as the Taliska accountants would take the same cavalier attitude as Claude. 'I'll get you to do our accounts next time, then,' she warned him. 'You can attempt to persuade the Inland Revenue that power-dressing is permissible against tax.'

'I do it all the time,' he told her airily. 'My clients all have Many 'Appy Tax Returns.'

Niamh, meanwhile, was not having such a happy time of it. Her prank with the marijuana began to look decidedly less funny around six o'clock when the rest of the staff should have come on evening duty. All she was normally called upon to do while Libby, Tony and Ginny were serving the dinners was slip upstairs to the bedrooms, replace wet towels, tidy dropped garments and check the supplies of soap and bath-salts in the bathrooms, the level of malt whisky and brandy in the decanters and the variety of fruits in the bowls. Then she drew the curtains, turned down the beds and laid out the nightwear (if there was any), leaving a welcoming glow from the bedside lamps for the guests to return to later in the evening. She rather enjoyed these duties, for they gave her an opportunity to learn more about the people who temporarily inhabited the rooms. She liked to play guessing games about what people would wear in bed. Were the women silk or Polyester, or merely two-dabs-of-perfume-behind-the-ears types? Did the men wear pyjamas or just a broad smile? It was fun to see their chosen flavours of toothpaste, to try the fragrances and lotions left by the ladies and to peep into the cupboards and inspect the clothes hung there. Sometimes she even tried some on, just to see what they looked like. There was endless amusement to be had upstairs while the guests were consuming Calum's delicacies downstairs.

On this occasion, however, Ginny, Tony and

Libby were still sleeping off the effects of the grass soup when the guests began wandering into the bar for their pre-prandial cocktails, and the only available person to serve them was Niamh. She was also the only available person to take their dinner orders, fetch and pour their wine, carry each of their five courses to the tables and clear them away afterwards. And, although there was time-and-motionally not a minute left in which to turn down their beds, she had to try and fit that in too. All that, and smile while she did it!

Calum was without sympathy or mercy. 'I don't care if your feet fall off and your head spins like a compact disc,' he said tersely when she moaned that she couldn't cope. 'It's you who has got us into this mess and you who will have to get us out of it.'

'Where the hell is Tally, that's what I want to know,' she said through gritted teeth, slicing bread at such a speed that her fingers were under threat of imminent amputation.

'Tally is the boss. He can take an evening off without asking your permission. It's what he's going to say about your idiocy that should worry you.' And Calum stirred viciously at a saucepan containing rapidly reducing rowanberry sauce. Without Craig he had had to cut back on the number of sweets that were on offer, exchanging complicated apricot and almond parfaits for a simple pineapple and stem-ginger compôte. He did not like having to compromise on his menus.

'The hotel is like an abandoned ship tonight,' remarked Isabella Garvey-Byass after Niamh had to sprint to the bar and back to bring a bottle of Aqua Libra to their table, a task which Tony would normally have performed. After her defection to champagne at the party, Isabella had reverted to teetotalism in order to support Gabriel in his save-the-liver campaign. Their rediscovered delight in each other gave her renewed interest in preserving his newfound zest for life and love-making!

'Well, it's not exactly abandoned,' explained Niamh with a 'butter-wouldn't-melt' expression. 'More like . . . enchanted. They're all sleeping, you see.' And she told Isabella and Gabriel the truth about her soup-pot trick because she knew that they, alone among the guests, would find it amusing. Apart from her encounter with Gabriel at the party when she'd reluctantly surrendered her joint to him, during a subsequent dinner-time foray into their room she had emptied an ashtray and found the telltale stubs of two more spent joints so she knew the Garvey-Byasses to be fellow spaced-out travellers. 'Only I think I overdid the dose a bit,' she confessed, 'and the trick has back-fired on me.'

To the rest of the guests, however, she spun a yarn, explaining that the staff had been struck by 'a sort of virus'. 'There seems to be no cure for it but sleep,' she elaborated, not without some truth. 'Luckily the chef and I seem to have escaped it, but I hope you won't mind if you wait just a little bit longer than usual for each course. They are well worth waiting for, I can assure you.' So bright was her smile and so disarming her youthful enthusiasm that the guests, all new arrivals, seemed to accept the state of play without demur. Fortunately, the couple at Table Two did not see the fate of their fricassée as Niamh slipped on a patch of Craig's spilled cream and went flying in the servery. She did not dare tell Calum she had dropped the shellfish on the floor so she scooped it up, rearranged it on a clean plate and presented it as if nothing had happened. 'What the eyes don't see the stomach won't grieve over,' she told herself, misquoting her mother and blissfully unaware of the bug-count in untreated curdled cream! Fortunately for the occupants of Table Two, their stomachs remained unaffected by it.

It was after nine when the dope-heads, as Niamh wickedly called them, began to wander back to work, rubbing their eyes and wondering where the afternoon had gone. 'To pot,' quipped Niamh, insisting, despite her shrieking feet and over-worked legs, that there was still an amusing side to the incident. Libby and Tony shared her mirth, Ann guiltily remembered Tally's message that he would not be back that evening and Ginny shyly asked Calum if she had been 'very silly'.

Relieved that by some miracle his dinner had not been completely ruined, Calum dragged off his chef's hat and grinned ruefully. 'You were a right case,' he exclaimed with unexpected mirth. 'Never thought I'd see you do the can-can on the sideboard.'

'I didn't!' cried a red-faced Ginny, mortified.

'Oh?' he asked enigmatically. 'How would you know?'

'You'd better go on without me,' said Fenella on the telephone to Claude. 'Helmut and I will have a carry-out in the office or something. We've got to finish our business tonight because he's leaving for Milan at the crack of dawn. I'm sorry, Claude – but you'll enjoy showing Nell off in all her new glamour, won't you?'

Just before six a taxi had delivered Nell and Claude, laden with glossy carrier bags, to Fenella's elegant flat in an exclusive street in Edinburgh's Georgian New Town, only to find that their hostess still had not finished work. Fortunately, she had given Claude a key and by eight o'clock her guests had bathed and changed and begun to grow impatient. The phone call had at least resolved the waiting problem.

'Do you mind very much?' Nell asked Claude, guiltily trying to ignore the leap of excitement she felt at the prospect of dinner alone with this man who made her pulses race. 'After all, it is Fenella you came to Scotland with.'

'And it is you I found when I got here,' he murmured, suavely kissing her hand. Nell had found some Dior *Dune* in Fenella's bathroom and sprayed it lavishly over her arms and neck, and Claude's aquiline nose seemed to twitch with recognition as he followed its trail from her hand to her cheek. She saw his fine lips smile close to hers below his melted-chocolate eyes. His voice was like *crème Anglaise*. 'Fenella is preoccupied,' he purred. 'I understand business. But *we* can enjoy ourselves – OK?'

Prestonfield House had been built shortly after Mary Queen of Scots fled south over her own kingdom's border to throw herself upon the mercy of her merciless cousin, Queen Elizabeth of England. It was now a beautifully restored, beautifully furnished and beautifully run hotel and restaurant set in its own corner of the parkland which surrounded Edinburgh's celebrated city-centre mountain called, for reasons which historians still argued over, Arthur's Seat.

'This is a kind of Taliska in town,' murmured Nell with delight as she stepped from the taxi. An avenue of ancient oaks guarded the drive, lawns and shrubs marched down to wooden posts and rails, and small, shaggy brown cattle grazed the tree-scattered pasture beyond. The house itself stood tranquil and solid as it had for 400 years. It was faced with white stucco, and finished with pale sandstone mullions and parapets. White doves fluttered on the steep, lichen-covered roof-tiles and imperious peacocks strutted among stone urns and statuary in a formal sunken garden. The whole presented a scene of peaceful serenity, in complete contrast to the hectic bustle of traffic and people and the crowded press of bungalows which clustered right up to the gates of the historic mansion. In the few moments it took to pass down the drive, the visitor exchanged the clamour and rush of modern city life for the relative languor of the sixteenth century.

The dining room at Prestonfield was curtained in crimson brocade and hung with portraits of richly clad ladies and gentlemen connected with the mansion's provenance. They were not the product of distinguished artists but their overall effect was to reinforce the sense of history and continuity and there was no electric light to show up their inferior brushwork. Fine silver candelabra provided illumination on each of the tables, glowingly reflected in their polished wood surfaces and in the large, gilt-framed mirror hung above the fireplace. Period silver dishes and implements gleamed in profusion and even the wine was cooled in an old zinc-lined wooden tub at their feet.

Nell's only problem was the richness of the food. Prestonfield was no Taliska with its declared interest in featherlight, low-fat cuisine. Here, old-fashioned standards prevailed and portions were substantial and well laced with butter and cream. It was irresistibly delicious and so, immediately after a starter of creamy mushrooms *en brioche* and her chosen main course of *carré d'agneau Bordelaise*, Nell had to excuse herself and head for the Ladies. Much though she still relished such a feast, she was now an expert at ridding herself of what she had consumed, in the quickest, quietest and least messy way possible. Claude had no reason to suspect that her departure from the table was due to anything more than a sudden call of nature, which Nell told herself it was. Even the pale pink Starzewski dress was none the worse for it.

Unfortunately, much of the delicious Mouton Rothschild '74 which Claude had selected from the wine list went by the board. Nell felt rather guilty about the Mouton as it had been excessively expensive, but no twinge of guilt could spoil her enjoyment of everything else the evening had to offer. The subtle glamour, the admiring glances, these were worth far more to her than a few cutlets and a glass or two of red wine, however rare. The rarer the better, she amused herself by thinking. One might as well be hung for a Mouton as for a lamb Bordelaise!

They had fresh strawberries for dessert, accompanied by some fabulous Château d'Yquem Sauternes. Only a Frenchman, Nell thought, could have introduced her to such a sensational combination. Never again would she disparage the virtues of sweet white wine. They consumed a bottle between them and she never went near the Ladies, with the result that she left the restaurant in a pleasant, dreamlike fog, not unlike that in which, unknown to her, most of her staff had spent the afternoon.

Absolutely shattered! Sorry, gone to bed. Help yourselves. Fenella's note in characteristically flourishing handwriting was propped against a decanter of brandy in her sitting room. This gracious apartment had been the withdrawing room of the Georgian townhouse of which Fenella's first-floor flat was only a part. On the walls were the original gilt candle-brackets backed by mirror-glass. Striped satin curtains adorned three long sash windows which overlooked the large private park across the road.

'That's Treasure Island, you know,' Nell told Claude, accepting the glass he proffered and pointing at a small, shrub-covered islet in the middle of the park's ornamental lake, whose waters gleamed dark in the sodium glare of the street lights.

'Treasure Island?' Claude echoed, puzzled.

'It's a novel written in 1883 by a famous Scottish writer called Robert Louis Stevenson. Fenella told me that he spent his childhood in one of the houses in this terrace. He saw that island every day from his nursery window and later his imagination wove a story around it and peopled it with pirates and buccaneers. Isn't that romantic?'

Nell stared at the lake surrounded by empty lawns, silhouetted trees and shadowy paths, a scene endowed with an air of mystery by the weird ochreous illumination. The wind and rain which had been lashing Taliska when they had left that morning had hardly touched this part of the country. As so often, the weather on Scotland's east coast was proving radically different from that on the west.

'It seems strange to look out and see lights and buildings,' she went on, sipping her drink. The fierce bite of the cognac made her shiver.

'Civilisation,' nodded Claude, standing very close and looking at Nell, rather than the view. 'It is very reassuring to me. I love cities.'

'Really? Well yes, I suppose you must, living in Monte Carlo.'

'You should come and see my city,' he murmured softly. 'Now that *is* romantic. It is very beautiful, clinging to the sides of its bay with all the yachts on the water. Every time you turn a corner there is a glorious vista.'

'More beautiful than Taliska?'

'Just as beautiful, in a different way. Can there only be beauty in nature? Does not man make beautiful things, too – paintings, palaces, piazzas?' He was so close that Nell could feel his breath on her cheek.

'Tower blocks, motorways, power stations,' she continued the list ironically, marshalling her thoughts with difficulty under the full force of Claude's sex appeal. 'I grant that much that is man-made may be lovely, but I think nature is more consistently beautiful.'

'I think you are beautiful. No!' He held up an imperious hand. 'Do not go all Nell-ish and say you are not. The trouble is, not enough people have told you that you are beautiful. How can a woman radiate beauty if she is not fed the compliments that make her glow? You were so lovely in the firelight on the night of your party but you are even lovelier now with your hair bright and soft and your so-elegant dress!' He took her by the hand and led her to a sofa. 'Now, you will sit there quietly while I tell you what else about you is beautiful.'

Nell gave a small, tremulous laugh. Good sense told her she ought to demur, go and sit in one of the more prim, upright armchairs scattered about the room and talk intelligently of Robert Louis Stevenson. But good sense was a still small voice compared with the loud clamour of her less-good senses! Claude was the male equivalent of a Siren and his call was irresistible.

At first his approach was rather like a Barbara Cartland novel, as sweet and intoxicating as the

Château d'Yquem. Claude's itemisation of her attributes began at her toes which he relieved of their black Charles Jourdan court shoes, moved up to her knees, silky in pale, eight-denier Christian Dior stockings, ascended to her thighs where he revelled in studying the finer points of her Janet Reger suspenders, and upwards to her back where he found no difficulty in unzipping the celebrated Starzewski dress. 'And this is too beautiful to crease,' he purred, kissing the hollow of her throat, a place which tended to turn her red light to green. 'It had better come off so that we can enjoy the beauty of that new satin and lace.'

By the time the dress was off Nell had lost all sense of time and place and entered Sybaris. It was bliss to have someone admiring the slim thighs and flat belly she had thrown up so much to achieve. She watched him, mesmerised, as he tenderly rolled each stocking down to the ankle, planting kisses the length of her legs as he did so. In a cogent corner of her mind she thanked heaven that Fenella's razor had achieved a smooth surface, if only for a few hours. God, he was so beautiful himself with his springy dark hair and aristocratic profile. She shivered with anticipation as he removed the stockings and kissed each naked toe. Never again, she felt sure, would she ever be so thoroughly caressed as Claude clearly intended she should be.

Château d'Yquem had a great deal to answer for. She didn't stop to think that what she was doing might be irresponsible, immodest or disloyal. She didn't care, as he obviously did not, that they were abusing Fenella's hospitality, betraying her trust in her own drawing room, on her own sofa without even drawing the curtains . . . Somehow that detail gave added spice to the encounter. Nell had a sudden fantasy that Long John Silver was playing Peeping Tom among the branches of the tall trees in the garden across the road. How the old rogue would have relished such entertainment! By the time Claude began the serious business of praising her breasts, sliding the slippery oyster satin slowly down the length of her newly slim, white body, Barbara Cartland had definitely left the room.

'I don't mind, you know,' Fenella said cheerfully. 'I knew it would happen anyway. Here, this would suit you I think.'

Nell accepted the proffered sapphire-blue cashmere sweater in silence. She felt acutely uncomfortable as she had done ever since greeting Fenella at breakfast. What could she say? There was no denying that she had behaved like a little whore. No, worse! A whore was in control of her actions, performed them with her eyes open and got paid for them. She, Nell, had submitted to Claude's erotic ministrations like a schoolgirl accepting sweets from a stranger and the undeniable truth was that the sweets had been all the more delicious for being stolen. During a subsequently sleepless night, her A-level German Lit. studies had come ironically to mind. She had been Goethe's Margaret to Claude's Faust and, while his technique may not have been diabolically granted, he was undeniably a master of it. How often had she giggled with her fellow pupils over the German word for seduction? *Verführung*. In Fenella's drawing room, on Fenella's sofa, it had been a classic case of *Verführung durch Technik*!

She and Fenella had come straight to the cashmere showroom after a breakfast of black coffee and orange juice. Claude had gone to do some shopping of his own, apparently unperturbed at suddenly finding himself the centre of a *ménâge à trois*. Desperately though she would have liked to talk properly to him, he and Nell had only exchanged the usual morning pleasantries. She felt suddenly as if she did not know him at all, could not discern what made him tick. He was so laid back, so cool! Why did he make no reference to the night before? Not in front of Fenella perhaps, but . . . She was not stupid enough to think that last night's episode meant any kind of commitment on his part, but how did one go about building on a one-night stand? She was so ignorant! Aged thirty, supposedly a businesswoman and yet a complete child in matters of *Verfürhrung*!

'Is it over then, between you and him?' she asked Fenella, trying to disguise the tremor of hope in her voice.

Fenella flashed a wicked smile at the other girl. God, she was so transparent, so naïve! One bonk and she was hooked. 'Maybe. We'll see. He's good, though, isn't he?'

To cover her confusion Nell plunged her head inside the soft sapphire sweater. She did not know how to respond to such a question. He was wonderful! More wonderful than anything she had ever imagined. 'He does nudge the Richter scale, yes,' she managed to murmur when her head emerged. Did she sound casual enough?

'Hardly surprising. He's had plenty of practice. By the way, you don't have to worry about AIDS or anything,' Fenella added nonchalantly. 'He's as straight as they come and has regular blood-tests. He showed me the last one, just to reassure me.'

Nell felt her stomach lurch. She had never thought of that. She was out of her depth, such a fool. She had just done the very thing she was always warning Tally about. No amount of progestogen could protect her from HIV as it could from unwanted pregnancy.

Fenella tweaked at the shoulder-line of the blue sweater, secretly amused at Nell's sudden pallor. Well, a little shock would do her good! She was much too innocent for her own safety. 'There,' she said brightly. 'I told you it would suit you. Try this skirt with it – it's the new, longer length. It went down a bomb in New York.'

Nell eased it over her hips. The skirt was tobacco brown and the colour combination was unusual and stylish, the skirt draping softly from a wide, high waistband into which she tucked the sweater. It would be ideal for Taliska dinners on winter evenings. Oh God, Taliska!

'I must call the hotel,' Nell said suddenly. 'Would you mind?'

'Help yourself,' replied Fenella, indicating the phone. 'I'll look out some casual stuff for you to try.'

By the time her call came to an end Nell was seething. Bloody Niamh and bloody Tally. They were both completely irresponsible! 'I'll have to catch the afternoon train,' she said furiously and then gave a small, resigned shrug. 'Perhaps it's just as well.'

Fenella gave her a quizzical look. 'Trouble?' she inquired.

Nell shook her head and sighed. 'Yes and no,' she said. 'A small case of a mouse playing while the cats are away. Tally seems to have gone AWOL. I'd better go back.'

For the rest of the morning she tried on clothes and thought of Claude. David had disappeared from her mind like a note of music, leaving only a pleasant echo. His amiable strumming at her strings had been a mere ballad compared with the symphony of sensation Claude had summoned from the vibrating instrument of her body. Yet dearly though she would like to think she had also struck a chord on his keyboard, she suspected, stretching her mental musical metaphor, that he was more of an Aeolian harp, singing a different duet with every passing Zephyr.

She saw Claude again only briefly before catching her train. 'You will come to MC, won't you, beautiful Nell?' he asked, his dark brown eyes crinkling at her in a devastating smile.

'MC?' she echoed weakly.

'Monte Carlo.'

She studied him carefully, her heart pounding. Did he mean it – really mean it? 'I'd love to,' she said, forcing her voice into casual lightness. 'When I've solved my balance of payments problem.'

'Good.' He had bought a new hat, a very British panama which he wore strategically tilted over one eye. 'Why not bring your problem with you, and I will solve it?'

You could, she thought. You really could!

'I hope you've enjoyed your stay at Taliska.' Ann handed Gabriel Garvey-Byass his receipt with a bright smile. She had watched the daily improvement in this particular guest's appearance with almost proprietorial pleasure. The Spaniard's twinkling charm had worked on her on his arrival, even exhausted and jaundiced as he had been then, the epitome of a jaded appetite but still projecting an elfin spark. Now she noticed that the panda eyes had lost their puffy bags, the once-sallow skin was a healthier olive colour and there was a spring in his step that had not been present a week before.

'It has been a wonderful stay,' Gabriel assured

her, tucking his receipt into his wallet and pocketing it. His eyes danced merrily as he leaned forward conspiratorially and stage-whispered, 'I have lost two kilos and found a liver, and my wife has shed a few inhibitions.'

'And a few centimetres,' exclaimed Isabella, coming up beside him.

'But not where it matters,' he responded, playfully patting her backside and enjoying Ann's faint blush. 'I think we should book another week in October so that we can come and recover from the vintage. Have you ever been to the vintage in Jerez, my dear?' he asked the receptionist and when she admitted she had not, proceeded to urge a visit on her. 'It is how we celebrate the end of harvest, when all the grapes are gathered and pressed. I am sure you would enjoy it. It is one long procession of parties. Even the mice get drunk.'

'It sounds like you'll need another week here,' laughed Ann, pen poised over the desk-diary. 'What date shall I make the reservation?'

Through July Nell waited for a call from Claude. His silence gnawed at her and yet she made continuous excuses for it, determined that it was temporary and explicable, just as she deluded herself that her vomiting was controllable. The longer she waited, the more she vomited and the thinner she got. And the thinner she got the more clothes she bought. Her appearance became an obsession. She made weekly shopping trips to Glasgow and Perth, but never to Edinburgh in case she bumped into Fenella, or even Claude. She had no wish to discover that he had remained in Fenella's thrall. In spending money and watching herself in mirrors she sought a substitute for what she really wanted. Self-projection replaced self-esteem.

Interest in clothes also displaced interest in food. She ate food, often vastly to excess, but she lost the desire to prepare it. She only filled her stomach in order to have the gratifying sensation of emptying it and to experience the high that hit her afterwards. It was a drug on which she was now firmly hooked. Calum looked surprised but made no complaint when she announced that she no longer wished to act as assistant chef and that he should give some thought to a suitable replacement. She was needed elsewhere, she told him, not admitting the real truth which was that cooking no longer held any appeal for her.

Eager to take a more visible role in the running of the hotel, she demonstrated a desire to assume the day-to-day responsibility for administration and guest-handling and, after only a brief argument, Tally was agreeable. He was totally wrapped up in his love for Flora which, like his weight, waxed greater each day. In six weeks their afternoon sex and shortbread sessions had raised him from eleven to twelve stones and counting! But he was happier than he could ever remember being and even his enforced overnight sojourn with Mac on Lismore had done nothing to rock the boat. The incriminating bale had been disposed of without the police getting wind of it and without Mac getting wind of Tally's relationship with Flora.

As punishment for her pot-prank, Niamh accepted a month on chambermaid duty with reasonably good grace. Tony had become more enamoured of her than ever, admiring her wild streak and pursuing her indefatigably around the tennis court, the gym and the staff quarters. And if she ever succumbed to his ardent wooing he at least had the grace not to boast of his conquest. Mick and Rob now called her 'Souper-Grass' and pestered her for more supplies but, under threat of expulsion from Taliska, she refused. She only had a little left for her own consumption anyway and soon discovered that Mac's source had dried up or, more accurately, drowned.

While Nell appeared more elegant by the day, Tally became a contented soul in jeans and wellies, throwing himself into a scheme to improve the leisure facilities on the island. He designed a mountain-bike track around the summit and bought a range of suitable bikes so that guests could either hire them for scrambling or for making longer cycling excursions onto the mainland. He played tennis with Niamh, Libby and Tony but their leisurely matches did nothing to counteract the shortbread. He missed his sporting tussles with David.

Nell had not heard from David for several weeks and, when he telephoned towards the end of July, she hoped he could not detect her disappointment at hearing his voice rather than Claude's at the other end of the line.

'I've been in Spain,' David told her, 'or I would have rung before.'

'How lovely,' she responded guiltily, trying to make up in warmth of voice tone for what was missing in warmth of feeling. 'Where did you go?'

'To Marbella. A friend has a villa there.' David's voice sounded tinny and false and it was not just the quality of telephone line. 'To tell you the truth, it was Caroline's parents' villa.'

'Oh.' It was all Nell could think of to say.

'We've been seeing rather a lot of each other lately, Caroline and I.'

'I imagine you must have if you've been on holiday together. How is she?'

'She's fine. We're both fine. Look – we're engaged, Nell. We're getting married. I hope this doesn't come as too much of a shock.'

'Oh! No, not really.' She tried to analyse what she did feel. Surprise? Antagonism? Relief? 'I'm delighted for you. When is it to be?'

'In October. Well, you know our parents were always keen that we should get together.'

'Were they? Well, what's the right word – *mazel-tov*! I hope I'm getting an invitation to the wedding.'

'If you'd like one.'

'Of course I would. Definitely. Don't worry that I might mind. It's all right, really. In fact, I think it's terrific!'

And still Claude did not ring or write. Nell knew that any reasonable person would simply cry a bit, call it spilt milk and shrug it off, but she was not in a reasonable state of mind. Undernourishment made her irrational and irritable. The stupid thing was she had no way of contacting Claude herself. When the bill had been settled for their stay at Taliska it had been Fenella's address and not Claude's which had been put into the hotel records, and Nell could not bring herself to ring Fenella and ask for his number.

However, she rang Caroline, wanting to calm any choppy waters onto which their friendship might be thought to have sailed. 'I seem to remember you once told me there were only calories between you and David,' she began teasingly. 'Well, they've certainly raised some heat, that's all I can say. I claim my reward for being the one to make you two see the error of your ways.'

'Oh Nell, you're being so sweet about it. You were right all the time and I'm as dim as a nightlight. I thought you'd hate me for ever.' Caroline sounded relieved and pleased to hear her friend's voice.

'That's because now you've twigged that you love David, you can't imagine anyone being prepared to give him up,' Nell observed pertinently. 'Whereas I was only using him as a port in a storm. He makes a very good harbour, by the way, so just you make sure there aren't any other old wrecks wallowing out there in heavy seas looking for shelter. Though I'm sure you'll repel all boarders quite easily. Are you happy?'

'I am very happy,' Caroline confessed. 'And strangely, the fact that Mummy's thrilled as well makes it even better. You will come to the wedding, won't you? Davy says you want an invitation.'

Davy! 'Naturally I do, idiot. Catch me missing my best friend's hitching! Both my best friends, really, because I hope David won't cut me dead now the old flame's died.'

'Let him try. I'll be keeping an eye on you both, though.'

'Quite right,' laughed Nell. 'Keep you on your toes. We don't want the bride getting complacent.'

One morning at about this time Calum and Ginny came into the office looking rather sheepish. As they stood together in the doorway Nell wondered why she had never noticed before how alike they were, both with red hair and fair skin and the flecked, greenish-brown eyes which so often went with that colouring. Only Ginny's sunny Australian upbringing had endowed her with a plethora of freckles which made Calum look almost insipid beside her. 'Come in, sit down,' Nell said brightly. 'Is this a deputation?'

'No' really.' It was Calum who spoke first. 'It's about the job in the kitchen.'

'Have you decided on someone?' Nell wondered idly why Ginny had come along if Calum wanted to tell her about a new sous-chef.

'Aye, in a way. I'd like to promote Craig. He has real talent and I dinna think I could find anyone better. No' this season anyway. He's got a nice light touch and he already understands the menus as you know.'

Nell was surprised. 'That's true but he's very young. Could he be trusted to cook without supervision? It's your reputation which is at stake, Calum.'

'Well, I thought you wouldna mind keeping an eye on him when I'm no' there. It would only be one day a week and he already does breakfasts on his own.'

'I suppose I could.' Nell knew it was a reasonable request but felt slightly annoyed that it meant she would not entirely escape the kitchen as she had planned. 'And what about an apprentice? We'd need to find someone to replace him in that capacity.'

Calum indicated Ginny and coloured slightly. 'That's why Ginny's here,' he said.

'I was wondering if you'd let me move into the kitchen, Nell.' Ginny's myriad freckles could not disguise the depth of her blush. 'I would very much like to learn to cook.'

Nell was astounded. There must be more to this than met the eye. 'Really?' She stared at the other girl and fiddled with her pen. Then she turned back to Calum. 'And you agree to this? Ginny is hardly a school-leaver. You wouldn't be able to treat her the way you treat Craig. Are you sure she has the aptitude?'

'She's been cooking for me up at the cottage and

I've been very impressed,' replied Calum diffidently.

'I see,' said Nell. 'Cottage pie, eh? Very cosy. Does this mean what I think it does?'

There was silence for a few seconds as Ginny and Calum looked at each other and smiled shyly. Ginny spoke first. 'I would like to move into the cottage if that's all right with you and Tally,' she said. 'Calum and I would like to live together.'

It must be the season for it, Nell thought. First Caroline and David, now Ginny and Calum. She felt rather aged, suddenly faced with such rampant romance. She supposed it must be love that made them look so sheepish and self-satisfied all at the same time. 'Live *and* work together – well, why not? I'm sure it can be arranged. There's enough bed-hopping going on in the staff quarters. It's nice to find someone taking it rather more seriously.'

Calum looked relieved and coughed nervously while Ginny smiled happily. 'You really don't mind?' she asked earnestly. 'We don't want to offend anyone.'

'Heavens – why should anyone be offended? I hope you'll be very happy in your wee butt and ben! Let me know if you want any more furniture or anything.' Nell grinned encouragingly. 'Mind you, Ginny, you're taking an awful risk, putting all your eggs in one bowl. Calum may be a wizard with a whisk but he can be like a tartar over the saucepans, you know. Ask Craig.'

'I already have,' Ginny assured her. 'He seems to think Calum's the best thing since sliced bread.'

'He should know better than to say that,' Calum put in sternly. 'There's no sliced bread in *my* kitchen.'

Chapter Fourteen

Sinead McLean had booked herself a week at Taliska in August, 'To shape me up a bit, Nell darling. Niamh tells me you're pencil-slim yourself these days so Taliska can obviously do the trick.'

Nearer the time she rang again, to ask if Ninian could come with her. 'Not to stay in the hotel, of course. He doesn't need all that luxury. Could you spare a staff bed for him and use him to peel potatoes or something? He's done his cadet corps camp so he could stay until the end of the school holidays if you could find some work for him. He doesn't want paying, he's just very keen to investigate the wildlife on the island.'

'Of course he can come.' It was Tally who took the call. 'He can help me with the leisure side of things. These days there are always muddy bikes to wash and boots to clean. He'd be a godsend through the busy time.'

'I'm glad to hear you're busy. Your father will be pleased. He's been so much in India supervising his second distillery that I've hardly seen him lately.'

'Yes, we had a postcard – a picture of some skeletal, ash-covered guru and a message that said this was what happened to you if you gave up drinking whisky!'

'Huh – there's no chance of him doing that. A

stay with you is what *he* needs really but I can't pin him down.' Sinead paused and her voice became more distinctively Irish as she continued: 'I've got one more favour to ask of you Tally, I'm afraid. God, you'll be cursing me, I expect.'

Really, thought Tally – families! 'No. Ask away,' he said politely.

'You've got a twin-room booked for me, right?'

'Right. That's what you asked for. Why, are you bringing your lover? Do you want to change to a double?'

'No, you wretch – your father would kill me! It's just that a very good friend of mine recently lost her husband and I'd really like her to come with me. She desperately needs a break and I thought Taliska would be just the place to help her recover. The trouble is, she couldn't afford your prices and I thought if she shared with me you could give her mate's rates on the meals and things without telling her, so that she won't be embarrassed. What do you think?'

Tally put his hand over the telephone receiver and sighed. Just at a time when he could have filled the room twice over at twice the price! But what could he say? 'That'll be fine, Sinead. You're not such a wicked stepmother after all, are you? Who is this unmerry widow?'

'Oh, she's not unmerry – quite a lively lady normally, but obviously a bit subdued at the present time. Her name is Grant, Alison Grant. Her husband was Professor of Zoology at Glasgow University and was at school with your father. They called him the badger man because he was always snooping around setts, or whatever badger dens are called. But he had a heart attack in May and never recovered. I'll invite her, then. She wants me to see a Van

Gogh exhibition in Glasgow on the way up and then we'll come on to Oban by train together. Will you meet us? That's great! Thanks, Tally.'

Alison Grant proved to be a tall, slim, rather faded beauty whose once red-gold hair had dulled to pale topaz and whose blue eyes had the washed-out look of someone who has done too much weeping. But she was far from insipid and was plainly captivated by Taliska. Within two days she had explored every nook and cranny of the island and on her third night announced that she was certain there were badgers in the Scots pine grove. 'There are holes in among the roots of the trees and scratch-marks on the trunks where they've sharpened their claws. You hardly ever see the animals themselves because they only come out at night.'

Ninian was jubilant. 'Let's set up a watch,' he cried, thrilled at the prospect of seeing his first badgers. 'I'll go out tonight.'

'I think it would be better if you cased the area by daylight first,' Alison suggested. 'Then you can decide where their paths are and which way the wind's blowing and set yourself up comfortably in a good place. Fraser and I often used to do that.' A wistful look came over her face as she said this and Ninian looked uncomfortable, in the way of the young when confronted with death and its subsequent grief.

'Why don't you come too?' he suggested suddenly. 'We could take a picnic and make a camp. It'd be great!'

Alison looked at the teenager with surprise. Ninian was fifteen – not an age when boys usually wanted to camp out at night with ladies old enough to be their granny. She smiled gratefully at him and shook her head. 'No, no. You won't want me with you. Take your sister or someone a bit younger.'

'Niamh?' Ninian said scornfully. 'She wouldn't know a badger from a bale of hay. She'd probably bring her Walkman and listen to Michael Jackson all the time. No, please, you come with me. I bet you know all about badgers and could tell me what they're doing and why, and where is the best place to watch from.'

'Yes, I could do that.' Alison glanced at Sinead to gauge her opinion and received an encouraging nod. 'Well, all right then. I must admit I'd love to come with you – if you won't be bored with an old lady's company.'

'Oh no,' responded Ninian unselfconsciously. 'I like old ladies. My granny is a great old bird. She used to live here, you know, when she was a kid.'

Sinead had made a sharp protest when her son failed to deny that Alison was an old lady, as a more mature person might have done, but her friend was unperturbed, knowing that to a fifteen-year-old, fifty-five was positively aged.

'My son Ross used to be just like you about animals, Ninian,' she told the boy happily. 'He was mad keen, like his father. He's a vet now.'

'That's what I'd like to be,' Ninian told her enthusiastically. 'But you have to be dead bright. They want higher qualifications for the vet faculties than for the medical schools.'

'Yes, that's right,' nodded Alison. 'Fraser always said animals deserved better doctors than humans anyway.'

'Well he would, wouldn't he, being a zoologist,' exclaimed Sinead.

'He was right,' put in Ninian fervently. 'Animals do deserve the best.'

'I can see that you and I are going to be great

fellow badger-watchers,' said Alison, her smile wider than it had been for months. 'I'm really looking forward to getting started.'

So the next night, while the other guests were tucking into Calum's five-course dinner, Alison and Ninian were bedded down under a rhododendron bush at the edge of the pine grove with thermos flasks of coffee and brown-bread sandwiches. 'I brought these just in case,' whispered Alison, pulling a pair of binoculars out of a leather holder. 'They were Fraser's. He always took them on night watches. They're infra-red lenses so you can see better in the dark.'

'Brilliant,' Ninian hissed. 'Can I have a look?'

He was still scanning the surrounding undergrowth twenty minutes later when Alison nudged him and pointed towards the hole among the roots of the nearest tree. Even in the gloaming the striking black and white stripes of an emerging badger-head were sharply visible.

'That's the boar, the male,' Alison murmured. 'He'll be making a recce to see if the coast's clear.'

Sure enough, after several minutes a second monochrome head, followed by a bristly grey body, emerged to join him, waddling across to the dung pit which the badgers had carefully dug a few yards away from the sett entrance. While she squatted over it two cubs, already half the size of their parents, tumbled into the twilight, snuffling and squeaking at each other. For ten minutes or so the badger family stayed near the sett, going about their toilet, stretching and sniffing cautiously, but Alison had chosen the position of their hide carefully, ensuring that it was downwind and sufficiently far away not to be detected.

'They're much bigger than I thought,' breathed

Ninian excitedly. '*And* much more beautiful.' The adult badgers were about the size of a basset hound but more streamlined and elegantly marked with their famous striped heads, long, sensitive pink-tipped noses, black underparts and strange speckled grey and white backs – like chicken breast or fish with too much freshly milled pepper sprinkled over it, Ninian thought.

'Each of the back hairs is white with a black band just behind the tip. That's what gives them that three-dimensional appearance,' whispered Alison with a catch in her voice. 'You can see why my husband spent so much time watching them, can't you? It's wonderful to think that a family like this is living only a few hundred yards from the hotel and nobody even knew.'

'They're leaving,' said Ninian, following with the night-glasses as the boar led the two cubs and the sow away down a well-defined but narrow path towards the cow-pasture.

When they had moved out of sight Alison sat up and rubbed her cramped calves. 'Ooh, that's better. I'm getting too old for this caper.'

Ninian ignored what he considered an unnecessary interruption to his investigations. 'Where will they be going?' he asked eagerly, using a more normal voice-level now that the badgers had left. 'Can we follow them?'

'Well, I wouldn't. Not tonight,' advised Alison. 'They'll be out hunting and you might stumble over them and frighten them. They grub around for worms and eat fieldmice and voles and also fruit and grass. They're rather like us in their eating habits – omnivores, I think Fraser called them.'

'Would they eat food if we put it out for them?' asked Ninian urgently. 'Could we tame them at all?'

Alison looked dubious. 'I don't know. They're very, very wary of humans, not without reason. They used to be baited for sport, you know. Dogs were bred specially for it. It still happens in some places, I believe, or they're killed for their fur or just because people are frightened of them. They used to be blamed for spreading anthrax and tuberculosis until quite recently. Man is their only enemy – and, of course, dogs frighten them rigid. But if you took it slowly you could probably get them used to you.'

'What would I feed them?'

'Anything, really. Bread, milk, even nuts and apples. Anything fresh and tempting.'

'I'm going to do it,' declared the boy. 'I'm going to try to get them eating out of my hand before I leave Taliska.'

Alison's teeth showed luminous in the dying light from the sky. 'It's a challenge,' she nodded encouragingly, standing up and stretching.

'Maybe I could get them to come up to the hotel after dinner,' Ninian went on dreamily. 'People would love to watch them feeding, wouldn't they?'

'Yes, as long as they're not frightened of them. And you'd have to make sure their sett wasn't disturbed during the day. They'll leave if that happens. And that's just what I'm going to do now.' Alison picked up the groundsheet she'd been lying on. 'You stay and watch for them to come back. Hang on to the glasses and let me know what you see. It's nearly an old lady's bed-time.'

'You're not an old lady,' said Ninian graciously, standing up next to her. 'You're great! Thanks very much for showing me what to do and telling me all about the badgers.'

Alison knew better than to hug him or make him feel stupid by too gushing a reaction but she could feel tears sting her eyes as she said brightly, 'It's been fun. The highlight of my stay.'

She didn't tell him that it was the best thing that had happened to her since her husband died, or that he had restored her faith in goodness and the future. It would have been too much for a fifteen-year-old to take. But she hugged the knowledge to her and felt as if a heavy weight had been lifted from her shoulders. The sturdy silhouette of the old tower loomed reassuringly against the starlit night sky as she traversed the lawn towards its welcoming lights.

It was not Claude but Fenella who made a reappearance at Taliska. Nell did not discover her presence until she entered the bar in order to perform her usual pre-dinner 'hostess with the mostest' role, wearing one of her now numerous little black dresses, relieved by some startling mother-of-pearl jewellery she had found in a boutique in Glasgow. Fenella was sitting at the bar in a clinging red cashmere dress nursing a gin and tonic.

'Nell, darling. How are you? Is that Butler and Wilson?'

The sensual voice and exotic figure took Nell by surprise and she started visibly but recovered quickly and smiled, if a little nervously. 'Fenella! No one told me you were here.' Her hand flew to her throat where the mother-of-pearl gleamed. 'Trust you to know a fake when you see one.'

'Ah, but a fabulous fake. I only got here half an hour ago. They've looked after me beautifully, as usual. I'm in your medieval room – *Ling*, I think it's called. God, it's marvellous! I *love* the ancient loo.'

Nell nodded at Tony to pour her usual white wine. 'Can I get you another?' she asked Fenella. 'Are you on your own?'

'Yes, please. And yes, I am. All alone and cold. Such a shame in that fantastic four-poster. Perhaps you could send me some company.' She indicated Tony who had moved away to the gin optic. 'He looks quite nice.'

Nell raised an eyebrow. She was never quite sure whether Fenella was joking or not. She realised that the designer's fling with Claude had been one of a series of casual affairs she'd enjoyed since her rather messy divorce from an Edinburgh architect, but she suspected Fenella might not be as careless in such matters as she appeared on the surface, might in fact be secretly looking for 'lurve'. 'Tony is our resident Lothario,' she remarked in an undertone. 'He'll answer any female call.'

Fenella pouted. 'He's no good then. I don't like an easy lay – well, who does? Have you heard from Claude, by the way?'

It might have been unintentional that she voiced the two questions in tandem but, knowing Fenella, Nell guessed it was not. The dig should have upset her but there was something strangely likeable about Fenella, however loaded her questions. For all her woman-of-the-world sophistication she was absurdly generous and therefore curiously vulnerable. Nell could not forget the considerable discount which had appeared on the bill for the cashmere she had selected on that uncomfortable morning in Edinburgh.

'No. No, I haven't,' she replied guardedly.

Fenella frowned. 'Really? That's strange, neither have I. Except for a huge bouquet of white roses – sent, I suppose, as a Thank You. White roses, wasn't that sweet? I decided they were intended to be cryptic.'

Nell couldn't help laughing. She felt much better suddenly, now that she knew Claude had not contacted Fenella either. 'You're very philosophical about it,' she said admiringly. 'Don't you feel as if you've been dumped?'

Fenella snorted derisively. 'No way! I think he just got the message. Things were pretty frosty after you left. I didn't fancy playing piggy in the middle.'

'I think I was the piggy,' admitted Nell.

'No, he was a swine. Not to me because I knew what I was doing, but you were like a little pearl, casting yourself before him. Poor Nell – have you been pining?'

Nell shrugged. 'Only slightly. He did cause a bit of an earthquake, I have to admit.'

'And you're still feeling after-shocks? We'll have to do something about that. Let's wave the magic wand!' Fenella gestured accordingly and grinned but in her short, tight dress with gilt chain belt and huge gold hoop earrings she looked more vamp than fairy-godmother. 'Where's that nice craggy mountain you were talking to at the party?'

'Who? Oh, Alasdair.' Nell looked startled. 'I don't know. I think he's away walking in Skye or somewhere. I haven't seen him for weeks.'

'Pity,' Fenella observed quietly. 'He seemed to me the sort of man it might be worth taking up mountaineering for.'

Nell stared at Fenella in amazement. She hadn't taken a fancy to Alasdair, surely? Nell felt a frisson of apprehension and then rather wondered why. Am I my lawyer's keeper? she thought. 'He's still mourning his wife I think,' she remarked casually.

'Didn't look like a man in mourning at your

party,' said Fenella sagely. 'But never mind him. I am not just here for my health, though Taliska is very good for it, no doubt. I have a proposition to put to you.'

'A proposition – clean or dirty?'

Fenella looked affronted. 'Clean as a pair of heels! How could you think otherwise?'

'I can't imagine,' countered Nell with a faint smile. She was beginning to understand this contradictory creature. 'We could talk about it at dinner if you like. Why don't we eat together if you're alone?'

'Chew the fat, as they say. I'd like that.'

'Good, I'll make arrangements in the dining room. Don't say that word too loudly, though. Remember – Taliska is a fat-free zone!'

Fenella's proposition, not unexpectedly, concerned her business. She proposed a link between Taliska and Drummond-Elliot Cashmere which she considered might work to their mutual benefit. The island and the hotel would be used in all her advertising and promoted among her international list of clients, and in return she asked that Taliska should host a pre-Christmas cashmere weekend when the richest of her clients would be invited to inspect her collection over three gala nights and three fashion shows.

'We could import some models and put them up in the village or somewhere, and fill the hotel rooms with different clients each night. There are ten rooms, aren't there? The three nights would add up to thirty clients and there are probably about twenty who live within striking distance. From fifty clients we could clear fifty thousand and split the profits. What do you think?'

'Fifty thousand? That sounds an awful lot,' reacted Nell. 'Are you sure?'

'I'll let you have a breakdown of prices so that you can see what I mean,' Fenella assured her. 'But in principle, what do you think?'

'I'll have to discuss it with Tally, of course, but it sounds interesting. When you say Taliska would host this weekend, what exactly do you mean?'

'Rich people like deals. Put them up two for the price of one and throw in a gala dinner and the fashion show, and they'll think they've had a bargain night – even though they've spent a fortune on cashmere! Meanwhile, you've filled the hotel for three nights at a dead time of year and you'll also get a share of the sales profits. We'll sling in some sexy underwear for the girls to model as well, just to give the husbands and lovers something to dull the pain of parting with their money, and everyone will be happy. It can't go wrong.'

'Unless they don't overdose on cashmere,' Nell pointed out practically.

'They're bound to,' declared Fenella indignantly. 'My collection is irresistible. I'll even model some of it for you and Tally after dinner to show you. Where is he, by the way?'

Nell glanced across at their usual table in the far corner of the dining room. It was empty. 'He's probably having a pie and a pint in the pub down the road. He's gone quite native lately. But he'll be up later to do some after-dinner mingling. I'm sure he'd love you to strut your stuff for him.'

Fenella leaned forward confidentially. 'He's rather gorgeous himself,' she murmured. 'Definitely above five on the Richter scale, I'd say. Is he available?'

Nell pursed her lips and waggled her hand like a balance. 'Sort of. Why don't you try it and see?'

Fenella gave Nell a sideways look. 'In my family

the expression was "suck it and see". I think the allusion was to sweets but my little brother always got his Ss muddled up with his Fs.'

Nell laughed and thought how well matched her own brother might be with this soft-hearted siren. At present Tally seemed totally wrapped up in Flora, a fact Nell could not reveal to Fenella. But you never knew with Tally . . .

Later that evening a private fashion show took place in Nell's flat. At first Tally was polite but unenthusiastic. He had experienced enough of the catwalk mentality with Gemma and was not keen to encourage any more. However, Fenella modelling was another matter entirely. No bored stare and laid-back slouch for her. She prowled like a tiger in her sinuous, clinging designs, vamping Tally at every turn in such a blatant way that he was vastly entertained. And furthermore he understood that Fenella was completely in on the joke, enjoying her act as much as anyone. Colour was the key to her collection, with apricot, grey and pink featuring in one group of garments while in another charcoal and cream made a dramatic stride away from the ubiquitous black and white so beloved of high-street fashion. Her lines were clinging and flowing at the same time. Beautifully contoured little jumpers displayed Fenella's spectacular bust to perfection, revealing just a hint of midriff above flowing loose-legged trousers and sexily slit calf-length skirts. Dresses were sleek and uncluttered, with touches of interest in ribbing and swathing, and a generous quantity of the fifty-pounds-a-pound yarn went into fabulous sweeping scarves, flute-edged stoles and unstructured jackets. Her clothes linked the luxurious softness of cashmere with the sinuous grace of subtle knit and cut and they were, as Fenella claimed, completely irresistible. Her final *pièce de résistance* was a black, scoop-necked evening gown with long sleeves, a tight waist and a deeply slit pencil-skirt, edged at wrist, hem and neck with a narrow band of jet beading. Under it, to sensational effect, Fenella wore nothing at all and the fine black stocking-knit clung to every curve and ridge on her body. It was pure Hollywood and Tally was moved to applaud.

'Give the girl an Oscar!' he declared excitedly. 'I absolutely agree that we should have a Drummond-Elliot Cashmere weekend, but only if Ms Drummond-Elliot herself models that dress *and* what she's wearing under it!'

This sally was greeted by Fenella's lusty laugh. 'As my competitors know, I'll do anything for a deal. So, I'll model the dress, and any others you may nominate, but I leave the underneaths to the under-thirties. There's nothing worse than mutton dressed as lamb, especially when the dress is little more than a cutlet frill.'

'If *you* are mutton, then give me ewe every time,' quipped Tally gallantly.

'That's why I love cashmere,' added Fenella, becoming temporarily earnest. 'I know what wonderful things the right style and colour can do for a body when they're made in cashmere. In my clothes, the average thirty-something can knock the tits off the pertest nymphette in hot pants. So, you see, rich bitches love my clothes because they give them power. And rich men like to buy them for their wives because they make them look as good as their mistresses. You can't lose!'

'Here endeth the lesson,' murmured Nell, 'taken from the gospel according to St Cashmere, chapter five, verse one.' She went up to Fenella and kissed her warmly. 'Your collection is wonderful. I wish I could have it all. Do you think I could wear that dress?'

Fenella cast an appraising glance over Nell's figure. 'To be honest, darling, no. I think we'd have to fatten you up a bit first. You've gone a bit scrawny.'

Nell flushed indignantly. 'Scrawny? You're joking! I'm fat – always have been and always will be.'

Fenella's fine dark eyebrows climbed new heights. 'Get yourself some spectacles, darling. You're wasting away, isn't she, Tally?'

Tally turned to look at his sister. Why hadn't he noticed before? There was almost nothing of her. 'Fenella's right, Nell. You're disappearing fast. If you don't stop soon you'll be a spot of grease on the kitchen floor – and you know what Calum does with spots of grease.'

'God, that's bloody typical,' shouted Nell in sudden rage. 'All your life you're told you're too fat and then, when you start to lose a bit of weight, everyone starts telling you you're too thin. I wish you'd all mind your own bloody business and get off my back!' Agitatedly she began to pick up discarded garments and fold them back into Fenella's large suitcase.

Fenella and Tally exchanged glances and shrugged. 'We're only thinking about your health, Nell,' said her brother gently. 'There's no need to go off the deep end.'

Nell impatiently dashed a tear from her cheek. Why did she have to cry the minute anything untoward happened? It was pathetic. 'I'm sorry, I didn't mean to shout. Sorry, Fenella. You must think I'm awful.'

'Not at all,' said Fenella kindly. 'It's late. We're all

tired, I expect. We can discuss the cashmere weekend again tomorrow.' She, too, was packing her collection away as she spoke. When it was full, she snapped the suitcase shut and smiled appealingly at Tally. 'Would you be an angel and carry it downstairs for me?' she asked. 'I'm only in the room below but those medieval stairs are a bit difficult in these heels.' She was wearing stilettos so high and thin that they might have been classed as offensive weapons.

'Always prepared to help a lady in distress,' replied Tally with a grin. ''Speshally in dis dress, man,' he added, Caribbean-style, patting her skin-tight rump. It wiggled unashamedly at him in response. Fenella had baited her hook.

She was rather put out, therefore, when Tally refused her invitation to a nightcap in her room. 'I might be tempted to help you out of that dress,' he demurred, 'and then I wouldn't be answerable.'

Fenella knew better than to persist. She bestowed her most devastating smile on him, murmured, 'Good night, then,' and shut the door. 'You deserve a medal,' she told herself, feeling every erogenous zone droop with disappointment. 'Or at least a year off for good behaviour . . .'

Tally was both flattered and alarmed. He had been tempted – God, he had been tempted! There was something instantly beddable about Fenella. She made no secret of her need for sex, set out determinedly to get it where she wanted it and yet seemed unsullied by her promiscuity. So why hadn't he accepted the apple and munched it joyfully? The answer of course was Flora. What he loved most about Flora was her uncomplicated simplicity, but it was that very simplicity which meant she would be mortified if he slept with anyone else. Of course, just as she deceived Mac almost daily she, too, could be deceived and might never find out. But Tally would not risk it. He loved Flora and could not bear to hurt her. It was a new experience for him to deny himself but regrettably, Fenella's luscious, juicy flesh would have to go untasted.

Meanwhile Nell was berating herself for being such a fool. 'What is the matter with me these days?' she muttered, dabbing angrily at her wet cheeks with a handkerchief. 'I'm always crying.' Anything set her off. A sad story in the newspaper, a minor disagreement with one of the staff, an imagined slight or a small criticism, like tonight. There had been really nothing to get upset about. Impulsively she stripped off her clothes and stood in front of the mirror naked. Her breasts looked OK, rounded and firm and her bottom was now gratifyingly minimal and undimpled. But there was still room for improvement! She pinched her diaphragm between thumb and forefinger. There was at least an inch of spare flesh. She *was* fat! Nervously she ran her hands over herself, feeling for lumps and bumps. Oh, God – look at her stomach. It was huge! It must be the dinner she had eaten. She had stuffed herself!

She ran into the bathroom, knelt before the toilet and stuck her fingers down her poor overworked throat. Her body convulsed and the sour vomit stung sharply as it erupted through her inflamed gullet but she welcomed the pain, just as she welcomed the smell which had once been so vile to her and the glorious giddy sensation of the void in her guts. There was nothing more satisfying than the wonderful, euphoric emptiness that came after she had retched all nourishment from her stomach.

'Well, that's an edifying sight I must say,' said Fenella's deep voice, pitched to a perfect level of sarcasm. 'There she is, naked and unashamed, worshipping at the throne of crepitation!' She was leaning languidly against the bathroom door-frame, still wearing her seductive dress. Wordlessly Nell grabbed a towel and wrapped it around herself. Her eyes were red and she could feel bile dripping down her nose, burning the sensitive lining. She ripped some tissue from the toilet roll and blew loudly, staring balefully at the intruder.

Fenella was dangling a small black leather purse from its gold chain. 'I forgot my bag,' she said evenly. 'You didn't answer my knock and the door was open so I came in.'

'I think I must have caught a bug,' muttered Nell defensively. 'Suddenly I can't seem to keep anything down.'

Fenella reached for a towelling gown that hung on the back of the bathroom door and held it out to Nell. 'Want to tell me about it?' she asked kindly. 'Only don't bother with the bug story. I know exactly what's bugging you, and it's not viral or bacterial. The proper name for this bug is bulimia – bulimia nervosa, to give it its Sunday name. Only it isn't a bug, it's more like a drug.' She followed a subdued Nell out of the bathroom and sat down with her on the bed. 'You look just about dead,' she told her bluntly. 'Can't you see what this is doing to you? I suppose you puke every day, do you? Eat first, puke later – that's the pattern, is it?'

'No, of course not,' cried Nell hotly. 'I just felt sick suddenly, that's all. It's nothing to do with nerves or bulls or anything you said. If you spy on people you see dirty things, I'm afraid.' She looked coldly at Fenella and then suddenly stood up and rushed back into the bathroom. There was the sound of flushing followed by the trickle of the cistern filling. When she re-entered Nell walked pointedly to the bedroom door and opened it. 'I'll be all right in the morning. I'm just tired. Thanks for your concern but there's really no need.'

'OK, if that's how you want to play it.' Fenella stood up regretfully and crossed the room. 'But just remember, when you decide you need help I know where you can get it. It's nothing to be ashamed of. You're far from being the only one, you know.'

'Good night, Fenella,' said Nell firmly, holding the door-handle.

'Good night, Nell. Don't forget what I said.'

The next day's post brought a letter from *Hot Gryll*.

Dear Nell,

Hot Gryll *has been asked this year to prepare a Christmas Special and with that in mind I have a proposition to put to you and your brother. Caroline Cohen has suggested to me that your hotel might make an ideal location in which to record a festive version of the programme, and of course your knowledge of the finer points of production would be an additional advantage!*

What do you think? Perhaps I and my director might come up for a recce and some discussion on the subject. Could you book us in for, say, the 29th–30th August?

I look forward to hearing your reaction. We miss your wicked ways with the Pelmanism! How about devising a fiendish version for the special?

Yours aye,

Patrick.

Underneath the scrawled signature the producer's full name was typed and underlined, *Patrick M.*

Coyninghame. The affected spelling sent a shiver of recognition down Nell's spine. The M. had always caused speculation among the programme minions. Patrick liked people to think it indicated a distinguished middle name such as Maynard or Manderston, but his secretary once revealed at the office party that it stood for nothing more pretentious than Michael. *Hot Gryll* seemed like another world to Nell now, a forgotten world of precious egos and ferocious temperaments where any drop of human kindness quickly drowned in an ocean of ambition. The thought of Gordon Gryll punning his way around the island, sneering at its remoteness and disparaging its beauty made her consider an extra trip to the – what had Fenella called it – the throne of crepitation! Nell had looked up the word in the dictionary and discovered it meant 'a discharge of noxious fluid, mainly applying to beetles'. Did Fenella then think of Nell as some kind of low, crawling creature? More immediately, what on earth was she, Nell, going to do about Patrick 'Machiavelli' Coyninghame?

Predictably, when Tally read the letter he did not dismiss the idea out of hand. 'We've got to at least see them about it, talk it over,' he said. 'It could be brilliant publicity.'

'Ask Calum what he thinks about *Hot Gryll*,' objected Nell, 'and Gordon Gryll in particular. He'll probably resign if he thinks that egregious toad is coming anywhere near his kitchen.'

But, surprisingly, Calum was not immediately averse to the idea either. He had nothing but scorn for the smarmy presenter, but agreed with Tally that the publicity would be superb and, 'If you run a restaurant you can't afford to be too choosy about who eats in it,' he added.

'The customer is always right?' jeered Nell, realising she was on the verge of being outnumbered. 'But Gordon Gryll is not a customer, he's a parasite! He'll take the mickey out of everything and upset the staff. It's just not worth it, in my opinion.'

But she was out-voted and it was decided that the producer and director should at least be booked in for their weekend. 'If they think to get it free,' muttered Nell darkly, 'they've got another think coming.'

Before Fenella left it was arranged that she would return in three weeks with models and a photographer to take shots for her catalogue, and the cashmere promotion was fixed for the first weekend of December. 'Rich people don't like thinking about Christmas before that,' Fenella maintained. 'Big spenders don't have to shop early.' Neither she or Nell made any reference to what had passed between them the night before but, without Nell's knowledge, Fenella asked Tally for Alasdair McInnes's number. Tally saw no harm in giving it. It was in the phone book, after all.

'Who is this Gordon Gryll you're all so rude about?' Ginny asked Calum that afternoon, sitting in the cool kitchen of their 'wee butt 'n' ben'. They were poring over recipes and cookbooks, planning the menus for September.

'Och, he's no' very important. Just a television jock who has more poisonality than personality. His programme's good though, and lots of folk watch it so we canna afford to give it two fingers.' Calum scribbled something in his notebook and glanced up. 'These menus are more important. Do you no' have any good Aussie ideas that might vary things a wee bit?'

Ginny pondered for a few moments, her eyes squinting into the sun. 'Well, there's always pavlova, I suppose. I haven't noticed you doing anything along those lines.'

Calum made a face. 'Pavlova! The Antipodes' great contribution to *haute cuisine*. I've always thought it tasted like an imitation bath sponge.'

'Not if you make it like my Mum used to. Hers was always like swansdown, just as it should be. It was called after the ballerina Anna Pavlova, you know, because her speciality was *The Dying Swan*.'

'So why's it come from the Antipodes, then?'

'Because she came on tour and someone invented it in her honour. It was like Nellie Melba in reverse. You know – Nellie left Australia to sing in Europe and someone invented Peach Melba for her because they said she sang like peaches and cream with a hint of fire and ice. That's the ice cream and the strawberry purée.'

'I know what Peach Melba is, gum-drop.' Calum looked slightly pained. 'So, how did your good old Sheila of a Mum make such featherlight pavlova, then?'

Ginny jumped up. 'I'll show you, if you like.'

'What, now? Give us a break. We've been cookin' all day,' Calum protested.

'I thought you'd do anything for a new recipe! Come on, you lazy Scotch pancake. There's plenty of eggs, it won't take long.'

'Well, OK. I'll watch – you work,' grumbled Calum, swinging his feet up onto the kitchen table and swaying idly on the back legs of his chair. But the light of interest was unmistakable in his speckled eye.

'It's a matter of getting the egg-whites whipped just right before adding a touch of vinegar,' said

Ginny a few minutes later, shouting over the whine of the electric whisk.

'Vinegar! I thought you added sugar, only less than for meringues,' Calum shouted back.

'Sugar *and* vinegar,' Ginny said, doing both and beginning to enjoy herself. It wasn't very often she had a chance to teach the great *chef de cuisine* anything!

'Huh,' said Calum disparagingly, watching her dribble vinegar into the fluffy mixture. 'It'll taste like salad dressing.'

'No it won't, you disbeliever,' cried Ginny, switching off the whisk and teasingly finger-flicking the top off one of the whipped peaks so that a blob of egg-white landed squarely on Calum's nose. 'Oh, great shot, Ginny!' the Australian girl crowed delightedly, taking aim again. 'But can you do it twice?'

As it happened she could and another blob settled on Calum's fiery thatch of hair like a large, wet snowflake. 'You wee rat,' he muttered, leaping to his feet. 'I'll get you for that.'

He and Ginny had lovingly restored the old Edwardian range in the cottage kitchen and spent leisure hours scouring antique shops for period cook-pots and implements to complement it. Now he delved into a stone jar of wooden spoons and other articles and grabbed one in particular, holding it threateningly before him as Ginny squealed and put down the whisk. A gleeful grin spread over Calum's face as she retreated and he advanced, backing her through the door into the inner room of the cottage which they had turned into their bedroom. Calum's chosen implement of punishment was a turned stick of pine-wood about the length of a ladle with an integral handle carved into a thistle shape. The Scots name for it was a 'spirtle' and such a tool had been used in every ancient butt 'n' ben to stir the porridge over the fire.

Ginny was giggling with triumph and apprehension as Calum waved the spirtle at her and pushed her onto the bed. Then he rolled her over, pulled her across his knee and began to paddle her bottom gently with it. 'There – your just desserts,' the *chef de cuisine* exclaimed with satisfaction, eagerly pushing the skirt of her sleeveless T-shirt dress up to get a better target. The round globes of her buttocks, sheathed rather inadequately in lacy white nylon, glowed at him tantalisingly in the dim light cast through the small casement windows. Ginny kicked and struggled, but only feebly. This game was one she and Calum had enjoyed before.

'Are you sorry?' he demanded, still paddling, while his other hand had almost pulled her dress over her head and was now poised on the elastic of her panties.

'No,' she squeaked, squirming excitedly. 'No, I'm not!'

'Right then.' He pulled at the elastic and her buttocks popped over the white nylon like two white moons, turning slightly pink from the attentions of the spirtle. He renewed his efforts, though actual contact with her skin was only enough to sting slightly and her cries were cries of pleasure, not pain. Under her naked belly he could feel his jeans becoming uncomfortably tight.

'Sorry now?' he asked breathlessly, leaning down to nuzzle the back of her neck. 'Shall we make porridge?'

She turned her head and a glinting, greeny-brown eye widened questioningly up at him. 'You're the expert. Isn't that what a spirtle is for?'

With an exclamation he turned her over and more or less threw her back onto the bed, pulling the panties swiftly off her legs. Languorously she eased the skimpy dress over her head and threw it carelessly away, watching him undo his belt and step out of his jeans. Lying there in the dim golden light she looked small and creamy and softly rounded, like a tasty fairy-cake, he decided, with a frosting of red-gold curls and a dusting of chocolate freckles.

He discarded the spirtle and his underpants in almost the same sinuous movement. 'We don't need *that* spirtle,' he said thickly, leaning over her, his hands braced either side of her shoulders.

Ginny cast her eyes down to his belly and his own, rampant instrument of pleasure. 'So I see,' she murmured, writhing her hips slightly in invitation. 'Yours looks as if it would stir things up much better.'

'Just show me the pot, darlin', and I'll start stirring!' he said, lowering himself gently into position while she willingly obliged.

Later, when the pot had boiled and come to rest, Calum felt in his hair for the blob of whisked egg-white which had caused all the excitement. It was limp and sticky now but he drew it out with his thumb and forefinger and put them to his tongue, tasting and smacking his lips together teasingly. 'Tell you what, my wee Aussie cookie,' he said, grinning and waggling a finger at her, curled like a kitten in the curve of his other arm. 'There's too much vinegar in that pavlova!'

Sinead and Alison left at the end of their week's stay, and his stepmother was so thrilled with the new tautness of her tummy and lightness of her step that Tally felt unable to regret the few hundred pounds he'd been obliged to knock off the bill. Alison, too, looked much brighter and more relaxed than when she had arrived. 'I've loved it here,' she told Ann as she wrote her cheque. 'You are all so lucky to work in such wonderful surroundings. I'll spread the word around the University.'

I hope she doesn't tell them how much she paid, thought Tally, overhearing. The dons will be very disappointed when they find out the real tariff.

'Tell Ninian to let me know how he gets on with the badgers, won't you,' added the slightly merrier widow. 'I hope he's got them coming to the door by the time he leaves.'

As a reward for all the nights he'd spent with the badgers, Ninian was beginning to gain their trust. He'd started leaving bowls of milk and trails of nuts further and further up the path they'd beaten through the rhododendrons until he'd gradually extended their range right up to the edge of the lawn. The big break would come when he managed to get them to venture out into the open ground within sight of the hotel windows.

Alasdair was astonished to receive Fenella's telephone call. He had just returned from three weeks' solitary wandering in the Cuillins and other parts of Skye, and his mind was still full of spectacular ridge walks and empty brown wildernesses. It took him several seconds to recall the beautiful couple at the party. 'Ah yes, now I remember,' he said at length. 'Carly Simon's song.'

'Come again?' asked Fenella, puzzled. The man was cryptic as well as craggy!

'Never mind,' said Alasdair hastily, wishing he had left his obscure reference unvoiced. 'What can I do for you?'

'I'm not sure, really.' Fenella was hesitant, beginning to regret making the call. It was strictly none of her business and probably none of his either but he had seemed so protective of Nell at the party . . . She decided to wade in regardless. 'It's Nell McLean. I think she's in trouble.'

There was no mistaking the instant concern in Alasdair's voice. 'What kind of trouble?'

'Have you seen her since the bonfire?' asked Fenella.

'No. We don't meet regularly and I've been away most of this month. Why?'

'How did you think she looked then?'

'Thin but all right. Why are you asking these questions?' Impatience lent an edge to his neutral lawyer's tone.

'She's even thinner, now – scrawny, in fact. And she's throwing up deliberately. I think she's got bulimia. Do you know what that is?'

'Of course I know,' he snapped. 'Everyone does since all the fuss about the Princess of Wales. But what makes you think Nell has it?'

'I caught her throwing up after dinner. She tried to make out it was just a bit of a bug but I recognise the signs. I've used the "eat now, throw up later" method of weight-control myself, and so have lots of my friends, but Nell has got it bad. It's like a drug with her. I could see the high in her eyes just after she'd vomited. I'm sorry to give you all the gory details but I think you might be able to help her – if you want to, that is.'

Alasdair was intrigued and, for all that he prided himself on his social awareness, slightly shocked. 'Well, I'd like to of course, but surely it's hardly a lawyer's brief. Wouldn't the advice of a doctor be more appropriate?'

Fenella made an exasperated noise. 'It's not as Nell's lawyer that I'm approaching you, Mr McInnes. I thought you were her friend.'

'Well, I am her friend, of course, but hardly an intimate one.'

'Well, she won't let me help her on this, and Tally strikes me as being about as sensitive as a pair of rubber gloves. You at least show signs of human compassion, and she obviously respects you. Couldn't you talk to her?'

There was a hint of the sergeant-major about Fenella when she was in full flow, which possibly accounted for her ability to run a successful business, Alasdair thought to himself. But what she said about Nell respecting him came as a surprise. He had always rather assumed there was more regard on his side than hers. 'She does have a mother,' he pointed out, but it was a feeble attempt at a disclaimer.

'Yes, but I strongly suspect that she is part of the problem,' Fenella explained. 'Nell doesn't talk about her mother much but when she does it's always in relation to some remark about her appearance. No, in my experience a man is always better at handling a woman with this sort of problem because only a man can make a woman feel she's worth a million dollars – and that's the only cure.'

Alasdair found himself laughing at Fenella's blatant sexism. 'Well, you won't win the Germaine Greer award for female emancipation, will you?' he said. 'I've a feeling my wife would have had something to say about that.'

'Forget female emancipation!' snapped Fenella, throwing caution to the winds. 'Forget your wife and go and see Nell. She doesn't need a lover or a lawyer, she just needs a friend – and if she won't accept me as the friend she needs I'm going to find someone she will accept. You're nominated, Mr McInnes. What do you say?'

'Please call me Alasdair,' he replied. 'And I say that you are a very shrewd and kind lady. Nell is lucky to have met you. Of course I'll go and see her.'

'Good. Incidentally, my lawyer will be sending you a draft contract covering a cashmere promotion I'm initiating with Taliska. It should be with you next week. Goodbye, Alasdair.'

'Right. Thanks. Goodbye . . . Fenella.' Alasdair replaced the receiver thoughtfully. How did that Carly Simon song go? He crooned it softly: '*You're so vain, You probably think this song is about you* . . . Well, it might apply to the man you brought to the party, Fenella Drummond-Elliot,' he mused pensively. 'But after what I've just heard I realise that it certainly doesn't apply to you. Beautiful you may be, wild you may be, but vain and selfish you are not.'

It was a mutual admiration party. When Fenella replaced the receiver at her end she smiled regretfully. 'Now there's one worth a dozen Claudes,' she told her office wall. 'I should have made more effort with him when I had the chance. I just hope Nell doesn't blow hers.'

August was drawing to a close. It had been the busiest period of the hotel's season so far, with Americans and Europeans swelling the ranks of British visitors who were attracted by Tally's regular advertising campaigns. He'd bought a page in the Wimbledon programme which had paid dividends despite the cost, bringing people from every walk of wealthy living who shared a common interest in tennis. The hotel court was buzzing even when the weather was not perfect and the twins were glad they'd installed the astro-turf surface which permitted play even in light rain. The squash court, too, proved its worth, as did the Jacques croquet set they had bought at what Nell considered a ridiculous cost.

'How on earth can a few iron hoops and wooden balls and mallets cost five hundred pounds,' she complained when she saw the invoice. 'It's daylight robbery!'

'It'll be worth it, you'll see,' Tally told her with maddening confidence. She had to admit that his instincts had not been far out over other selling-points so she'd swallowed her protests. There had been general jubilation among the staff when the Scottish Tourist Board had awarded Taliska five crowns and a *de luxe* recommendation in their hotel guide. They'd all guessed who the inspector was when he booked in for his dinner, bed and breakfast, but they'd kept up the charade of pretending they hadn't until he eventually revealed his identity just before leaving and congratulated Tally and Nell on their achievement. 'The only quibble I have is the lack of televisions in the bedrooms,' he told them.

'We're always prepared to put one in if people insist,' Tally told him hastily. 'It's just that we don't think television and Taliska go together. Nothing against the box, of course. Watch it myself often but we like to think people come to Taliska to find peace and relaxation and better things to do with their idle moments.'

The significance of his broad wink when he said this seemed to be lost on the inspector. 'Our practice is to recommend that our top-class entries provide television and video facilities in each bedroom and remove them if people make a specific request to do so. It's just a slight change of emphasis we require,' he said solemnly.

'We'll think about it,' Tally responded, and shelved the dilemma until a less busy time.

He was extremely grateful to have Ninian's help with the outside leisure activities. He began to consider an expansion of these for the next season and the possibility of employing a full-time leisure officer to handle them. They were eating into his afternoon sessions with Flora!

Ninian demanded to be allowed to set up the croquet hoops on the lawn so that he could make sure they didn't interfere with his intended badger playground. 'I don't want Bertie catching his leg in a hoop and injuring himself just as he's beginning to trust me,' he said, carrying the set to a corner of the lawn well away from the rhododendron bushes.

'Bertie,' echoed Tally with amusement. 'Don't tell me you've given them names now.'

'Of course I have,' declared Ninian hotly. 'Bertie is the boar – the dad. And then there's Bessie the sow and the cubs are Berry and Bramble because I can't tell what sex they are.'

'So you're not on intimate terms yet?'

'Well, I've got pretty close to Bertie. He's a bit of an old buffer really, always snuffling and blowing like an elderly colonel. He'll let me sit in full view of the sett without diving back down again now but I haven't tried moving about. Mick's been coming with me so that he can take over their training when I've gone home.'

'What are we starting here?' asked Tally suspiciously. 'Some sort of badger circus?'

'No – far from it. We're trying to get people on the badgers' side,' Ninian told him earnestly. 'But they'll never be that until they know and love them.'

'I must say I'm looking forward to seeing them myself,' said Tally encouragingly, not wanting his young brother to think he was being too critical. 'When do you think they'll emerge onto the lawn?'

'I'm going to try tonight,' Ninian confided. 'It's quite clear and the moon should be nearly full. I've got some really tasty hazel nuts, all peeled and shelled for them, and I'm going to leave them scattered near the rhodos just after dinner. So keep your fingers crossed!'

It was a sizeable group of guests who gathered around the windows in the drawing room and bar after dinner when Ninian walked softly across the moonlit lawn, throwing handfuls of nuts down onto the grass. He disappeared momentarily into the bushes to lay a short trail, hoping to lead the badgers on, and then retreated behind the trunk of a large ash tree to one side of the lawn. They all waited, quietly and with excited anticipation, murmuring among themselves in the darkened hotel rooms until they became restless, moving away from the windows to fidget and wonder whether to go to bed.

'There's one,' cried Libby softly, for she had not given up her vigil. 'Look! Jeeze, how beaut!'

The moonlight gleamed off Bertie's broad white head with its two black eye-stripes as he nosed for the first scattered nuts while behind him, slowly and carefully, the other three members of his family peered out from among the dark bushes. Perhaps he gave them a signal or perhaps they just became more confident watching him gorge unmolested and decided to share in the feast, for within minutes there were four badgers browsing on the short grass, raising their heads after every mouthful to sniff and test for intruders but then proceeding tenaciously to search until all the nuts were gone. They were rather like night-sheep, Nell thought, glued to the window in the bar. Rather special sheep who were only too aware of their rarity and kept raising their heads to make sure it was not compromised. All the childhood tales she had ever read, of Brock the Badger or Ratty's friend Mr Badger in *The Wind in the Willows*, came rushing back to her as she guessed they must be rushing into the minds of the other onlookers, because they were all exclaiming and murmuring delightedly at the sight before them on the moon-washed lawn.

'Next time I'll get them to come nearer,' vowed Ninian excitedly when he finally came indoors. 'I'm sure we can get them right up to the hotel eventually. Wouldn't that be great?'

'Yes, that would be quite a coup, little brother,' said Tally, clapping the lad on the shoulder and already planning his next brochure with a wildlife as well as a 'wild life' slant! 'There can't be many hotels which can boast built-in badgers for after-dark entertainment. Bertie, Bessie and babies look as if they might be quite a bonus for us. Well done, Ninian.'

'All part of the service,' grinned the boy. 'I'll try taming otters next.'

'I think that's been done before, hasn't it?' Tally laughed.

Chapter Fifteen

'It's not unethical, just a bit cheeky,' said Alasdair, extracting a folded document from the capacious inner pocket of his tweed jacket and opening it out for perusal.

The bar was crowded with guests of assorted nationalities but the weather was warm enough to sit outside so he and the twins had taken pre-dinner drinks out to one of the tables set under the great sycamore tree on the lawn. A game of croquet was proceeding between four members of a German family, who punctuated the air with loud, guttural exclamations as they marshalled their platoon of coloured balls with brisk clunks of their wooden mallets. '*Achtung!*' came a yell, and Tally lifted his feet as a red ball rolled under his chair. He kicked it back, waved sociably and muttered in an aside to Alasdair, 'I hope they don't start challenging any of the other guests or we'll have World War Three on our hands. I've never known a game like croquet for setting people at each other's throats.'

'Oh? I thought it was a pleasant activity for nice young girls in white pinafores and black stockings,' remarked Alasdair in surprise, glancing up from the document.

Tally raised an eyebrow at the lawyer. 'White pinafores and black stockings, eh? So that's your weakness! But you're sadly misinformed. Croquet is a game for vipers and cheaters who will stop at nothing to destroy the opposition. It will really channel your aggression but I advise you never to play it with anyone whom you wish to keep as your friend. Still, we'd better get on with this contract because it looks as if I'm going to have to wield a corkscrew this evening. We've forty for dinner and Tony's up to his eyes.'

'I'm glad you're so busy. I'll come straight to the point. It's quite straightforward really but there are one or two impudent little additions that Mrs Drummond-Elliot has seen fit to include which might raise your eyebrows a millimetre or two. Here, for instance,' he pointed to a clause, 'she demands free accommodation in the hotel during periods when business is being transacted to your mutual benefit.'

'What? That's crazy!' exclaimed Nell. 'If she took up one of the rooms during the cashmere weekend it would reduce the number of buying customers by three – one on each night of the promotion. That represents a very expensive outlay on both our parts.'

'There's no problem,' put in Tally swiftly. 'Keep that clause worded so that it is ambiguous about whether she stays in one of the letting rooms or in staff accommodation. That leaves it to our discretion. If the place is full, she has to slum it. She can always share with me if we get too crowded.'

Alasdair gave him an old-fashioned look. 'I'll leave that last bit out,' he said, scribbling in the margin. 'But the idea's good.' He began to flip through the pages of the contract for further clauses with Fenella's stamp on them. There was one subtly attempting to doctor the fifty-fifty split in profits, another to establish a permanent showcase for her clothes in the reception hall. The first was discreetly altered to restore the status quo, the second readily granted for a limited period to be renewed by agreement. Ten minutes later Tally heaved himself up and said he must start flashing the wine-list about.

'I'll send you out another drink,' he promised, wandering off in the direction of the bar. Nell noticed with interest that his movements were becoming slightly ponderous with the increase in his weight.

Left alone with her, Alasdair found himself regarding Nell critically. She *was* thin. Zeus, she was thin! Was this the same bouncing, energetic Nell who had wailed like a banshee as she leaped over the embers of her birthday bonfire? She appeared substantially changed, almost the epitome of languid self-assurance, wearing a deceptively simple beige linen dress which Alasdair understood enough about ladies' fashion to know must have cost a three-figure sum, her sheer-stockinged legs elegantly crossed at the knees. Her face was carefully made-up, her nails manicured and finished with pale pink polish and her jewellery distinctive. 'I haven't seen you since the bonfire,' he remarked conversationally. 'Has it produced the required results?'

At least her speaking voice still gave evidence of the old Nell, the voice low and sweet with its habitual hint of irony. 'Well, there were no scorch-marks,' she said. 'At least, not anywhere that shows. How was your holiday?'

'Very relaxing, thanks.' He was wondering whether he liked her new hairstyle. What had once been brown and bouncy was now blonde and smooth and flopped over eyes which were watchful and shadowed. She looks like Tally, he thought with surprise.

'Isn't it lonely, walking on your own?' she asked.

'It can be, yes. But you meet plenty of people along the way. Hillwalkers are a chatty lot.'

'What do they talk about?'

'Oh, the state of the footpaths, the weather, the best treatment for blisters.' He laughed. 'You can imagine.'

'It sounds rather nice,' she said a little wistfully. 'And is Skye as romantic as people say?'

He looked dubious. 'That depends on what you call romantic. The Cuillins are dramatic, certainly – great craggy ridges rising high above sea lochs, glens full of tumbling waterfalls, steep rocky corries – but a lot of Skye is rather featureless really, just barren brown moors scattered with crofts. Its history is probably more romantic than its scenery.'

'Bonnie Prince Charlie and all that? I always thought he was rather wet.'

'Like the climate! Yes, well, he was probably a bit bumptious and rather gullible and yet a whole legend has grown around him.'

'It's depressing, isn't it, when great heroes turn out to have feet of clay,' Nell observed sadly. 'A bit like discovering Father Christmas is a paedophile.'

Heavens, thought Alasdair. Something *was* hurting behind those wary eyes. He gave a harsh laugh. 'Or that Madonna is a virgin! I know what you mean. It doesn't have to be like that though, does it? People one thought were unbearable or wicked can turn out to be rather kind and pleasant when you get to know them.'

She shrugged, clearly not convinced.

Where is the old, generous Nell? he pondered. Their fresh drinks had arrived and he leaned forward to pick up his glass, gesturing with it in a wide arc to indicate the populous lawns and terrace. 'The hotel is very lively. Does the season look like being a success?'

'In financial terms, yes. We're keeping on the right side of the bank manager and we're getting all kinds of stars and rosettes in the tourist guides so I suppose it must be called a success.'

'You don't exactly sound ecstatic about it,' he remarked sharply.

A bleak smile greeted this observation. 'Oh, take no notice. It's just me. I can't help feeling deflated. I thought I would be on top of the world if it all worked out as we planned and now it has, well I'm not. Aren't I a spoilsport?'

He shook his head sympathetically. 'No. I think you're tired. You need a break from it. Do you ever take any time off?'

'Oh, yes. I go to Glasgow for shopping and things. The staff only have one day off a week so I can hardly take more.'

'The staff don't have your responsibilities, Nell. Nor have they been working non-stop for more than a year,' he protested. 'Why not give yourself a real break? Go away for a few days, visit your family or just go somewhere else. Taliska will look quite different to you when you return.'

'Will it?' She looked around at the stately, grey stone house, the smooth green lawn and the gracious trees, the sweep of *machair* beyond the fence and, in the distance, the glint of the evening sun reflecting off the loch. 'I wouldn't want it to look different, Alasdair. I love it, you see.' She said it simply, without emphasis, but emotion was not far from the surface, shining in her eyes.

'And you are very good to it,' he said gently. 'But

sometimes I am not sure it is very good to you. If you won't go away, why not at least take time off just to relax? Walk in the hills, sail on the loch, get some fresh air. I'll come with you if you want company.'

She gave him a grateful look. 'Would you, Alasdair? That's really kind of you. But I truly don't think I can spare the time right now,' she said, shaking her head rather sorrowfully. 'There's just too much going on here. May I take a rain check?'

He smiled and nodded. 'Any time you like,' he agreed levelly. Just don't leave it too long, he thought, or you might break down, rather than out . . .

It was Flora who found a replacement for Ginny in the dining room. Tina Armstrong had filled in for several weeks but was due back at college in September so Flora persuaded the teenage daughter of one of her friends to take on the job. Ginny and Calum meanwhile were like two newlyweds in their wee cottage, and the atmosphere in the kitchen was positively hearts and flowers. Ginny seemed to have the ability to make Calum smile while he worked, she was quick, hard-working and adept, and even Craig had to agree that she was a boon. The three made a formidable team and the reputation of the dining room soared.

Meanwhile, Fenella brought her own team from Edinburgh to photograph her collection. 'Quick, you should see what's going on in the orchard,' cried Tally gleefully, bounding into the office one morning. 'Talk about rustic humour. It's pure Titania and Bottom out there!'

Ann looked up from the computer screen and Nell hurriedly put her hand over the telephone to prevent her brother's voice carrying to the other end of the line. 'Sshh,' she hissed crossly.

Tally was unrepentant. He made a face at his sister and bent over to whisper to Ann, 'Just leave that. I'm sure it will wait for five minutes and you may never get another chance like this.'

Ignoring Nell's frowns and agog with curiosity, Ann followed Tally through the staff quarters and out of the rear door. In the orchard a small knot of people were gathered under an old, lichen-covered apple tree which had produced an unusually numerous crop. The ancient branches were propped up with posts and clumps of almost-ripe apples seemed to cling to every twig and stem. Perched in among them on a fork in the branches, wearing his grubby green and white striped Celtic FC bobble hat, was Mick, red-faced and grinning sheepishly.

'I feel a right Wally,' he muttered to the streamlined model in a moss-green cashmere trouser-suit who stood beneath the tree holding a basket. The photographer was hovering a few feet away shouting instructions.

'Head up a bit, darlin'. No, not that high, you silly bitch – you look like you're apple dookin'. Aye, that's better!' There was a series of camera clicks and then an irritated tut-tut of the photographer's tongue. 'For God's sake look as if you're enjoyin' yourself, dearie. Tell her a joke, someone. Let's have some smiles around here!'

'He'll regret having said that,' muttered Tally to Ann on the sidelines. Asking for a joke in Mick's company was like turning on a tap.

'OK, pal.' Mick grinned down at the model from his tree like some wayward garden gnome. 'How much is Paul McStay's jockstrap worth?'

Tally gave an audible groan and the model gave a puzzled frown. 'Who's Paul McStay?' she asked.

'Omigod!' Mick looked anguished and the photographer tut-tutted several times more and shook his head in exasperation. 'He's only the best player in the Celtic football team. You've heard of Glasgow Celtic, surely?'

Amazingly enough, the model had. She smiled encouragingly. 'My Dad's a Celtic supporter,' she announced.

'Good man!' enthused Mick. 'So – how much would you give for Paul McStay's jockstrap?'

The model had gone slightly pink but responded bravely. 'I don't know. Twenty quid?'

Mick rocked around on his branch with delight. 'Nah,' he cried triumphantly. 'It's no' worth a light 'cos it's a load of bollocks!'

It took a few moments for the significance of the joke to sink in but when it did the model began to laugh uproariously and Mick, who tended to laugh as much as anyone else at his own jokes, joined in. The photographer began to shoot furiously, moving speedily around the tree from one angle to another, to the whirring accompaniment of his motor-driven camera. 'That's great – just great! Keep the jokes coming.'

Mick needed no second bidding. 'OK, pal. D'you know the one about the boxer who went to his doctor with insomnia?' Mick's jokes all tended to be connected with sport. 'Well, the doc told him to count sheep. "I've tried that," said the boxer, "but every time I get to nine, I stand up!" Get it? Ha! Ha!' Mick was off again and so was his audience.

'God, this catalogue's going to be nothing but pictures of Mick surrounded by hysterical women,' grinned Tally. 'Once he starts he'll go on all day. His store of jokes is endless.'

'I know,' responded Ann ruefully. 'He cornered

me in the bar once on his day off.'

'Did he tell you the one about the famous snooker player in the Christmas pantomime?'

'Yes, he did,' Ann bleated in mock distress. 'Don't you dare repeat it! I must get back to the office anyway. Nell will be wondering where I am.'

'Your cue to leave,' cried Tally irrepressibly. 'The snooker player missed his!'

Ann groaned, put her hands over her ears and ran. Behind her retreating figure Mick and another model wearing cinnamon trousers and polo-neck under a chunky camel-coloured cardigan had taken up position around a log-filled wheelbarrow, and Mick launched into a stream of blue jokes about Rangers football team. Tally wandered over to Fenella who was helping the first model out of her moss-green outfit, apparently oblivious to the fact that she wore only sheer tights underneath.

'The view here improves every minute,' Tally said appreciatively. 'We should charge the guests extra at such times.'

The model stared stonily at Tally and pulled on some tan-coloured leggings while Fenella selected a straight autumn-gold tunic from a rack and handed it to her. 'Mick's jokes are better,' she told Tally. 'At least they're not sexist.'

'Oh? What about McStay's jockstrap?' he demanded, watching regretfully as the model pulled the tunic over her naked torso. While relishing his brief glimpse of the girl's small, unsupported breasts, a corner of his mind compared them unfavourably with Flora's more ample, snowy hillocks.

'It would be sexist if I told it,' Fenella replied tartly and nodded approval at the model who wandered off to receive the attention of the location hairdresser working from a garden bench. 'You look as if you could do with using your own jockstrap.' She brazenly prodded Tally's protruding belly. 'Either you're pregnant or you haven't been playing enough sport.'

Tally looked penitent but unabashed. 'It's the good life I lead,' he told her, patting his incipient paunch. 'Do you play squash?'

'Yes, as a matter of fact I do,' she grinned. 'I've even got my gear in the car. Want to take me on?'

'With pleasure! When?'

'When we've finished here. I warn you, though, I'm good.'

'I bet you are,' he observed, appraising her firm, athletic figure.

True to her word, she gave him a better game than Tony and, as Tally remarked appreciatively, she looked a damn sight more attractive in shorts. Their games became a regular feature of Fenella's visits to Taliska, and some close-fought contests had Tally sweating profusely and vowing to lay off the scones. He even occasionally cut short his afternoon session with Flora in favour of one with Fenella, but he carefully did not confuse the games he played with each. His hands-off attitude continued to puzzle and frustrate Fenella. She remained unaware of his relationship with Flora and uncomprehending about his apparent lack of amorous interest in herself. Thanks to Mick, however, the catalogue was a great success, displaying her casual clothes with a spontaneous freshness which made them seem a joy to wear.

At the end of August, the *Hot Gryll* team arrived for their recce and, as Nell had predicted, both Patrick M. Coyninghame and his director brought their wives, in blatant hopes of a free weekend. Which hope Nell quickly dashed while Patrick M.

was still reeling at the change in her appearance. 'I'd never have recognised you, Nell,' he gushed. 'My God – you look com*pletely* different!'

He, on the other hand, made Nell feel exactly the same – to wit squeamish and on edge. He prowled about the premises making notes in the lap-top computer which his rather unkempt wife hauled out of her capacious shopping bag every time he halted. By dinner-time on Saturday night he had confidently decided that Taliska was absolutely right for the Christmas programme but it took until Sunday afternoon and employed the combined efforts of himself, Tally and Calum, whose support for the plan proved the deciding factor, to persuade Nell to agree. Her initial reluctance was partly due to what she considered a derisive location fee offered by Patrick 'Miserly' Coyninghame as she called him to his face, and the substantial increase he eventually made in this fee was due in no small measure to her determined stand.

'Nell can be quite ruthless at times,' Tally told Flora the day after the television team left. 'I always thought she was an easygoing girl but she didn't give an inch to those TV boys. I was quite impressed.'

Flora traced her forefinger down Tally's naked arm. Not for the first time she noticed more flab than muscle. 'She understands them, I suppose, having worked with them so long. But things aren't right with Nell, Tally. Are you sure she isna ill? She looks awful thin these days.'

'I've asked her and she says she's fine. I expect she's just overdoing the dieting. Having been a bit plump she's gone too far the other way. She's bound to put some weight on soon – it's inevitable.'

'I'm no' so sure. It can become a disease, this slimming. I've read about it in my magazine, and the article said it could actually be fatal. The heart fails or summat. Shouldn't you talk to her again?'

Tally rolled over and put his arm around Flora. They were still lying in bed although it was nearly six o'clock. 'Why don't you talk to her? These things are often better between women, don't you think? We men tend to put our feet in it.' He kissed her fondly between the breasts and gazed at them admiringly. Under his avid gaze Flora's skin glowed like moonstones and he craved constantly to caress it.

She shook her head resignedly. Tally was notoriously unwilling to get involved in anything upsetting. With a sinuous twist she extricated herself from his arms. 'All right,' she said, 'I'll talk to her. But I'm going to tell her you asked me to. I'm no' carrying all the blame myself.' Spurred on by her success as Taliska's housekeeper, Flora was becoming more assertive. 'I'll need to go,' she declared in panic, looking at the clock on the bedside table. 'Mac said he'd be in earlier this week. It's getting dark by seven-thirty now.' She began to pull on her clothes.

Tally looked alarmed. 'God, yes. Winter is coming. What shall we do when he doesn't go out at all? When the weather is too awful for fishing?'

She looked unconcerned, continuing to dress methodically. 'I dinna suppose we shall do anything.' Then, seeing his horrified expression, she added, laughing, 'It'll no' be for long – two or three weeks at the most. And it's ages till then – months.'

'I'm a wreck if I don't see you for two or three days,' he said simply. 'I can't live without you for weeks at a time, Flora, I can't.'

'Jings, Tally, you're such a wean,' she chastised him. 'Some fishermen are away to sea for weeks at a time and their wives and lovers have to cope. You'll learn, just like them. Now, I must go.'

It was Tally's turn to shake his head with resignation. Why, he wondered, did women become bossy when they felt in control?

The following day, Flora managed to find Nell alone in the linen room. She was checking towels in response to a complaint from a guest that hers had been threadbare.

'They shouldn't be wearing out after so short a time, Flora,' Nell fretted, in the midst of unfolding and re-folding each bath-sheet on the shelves. 'We've only been using them for five months.'

'One or two of them seem to be a bit weak at the edges,' observed Flora. 'Perhaps they were a bad batch.'

'We did get some seconds at a sale price,' admitted Nell, reaching up to place a pile on a high shelf. 'Oh!' She suddenly seemed to stagger, and clutched at a strut to save herself from falling.

'What is it? Are you OK?' Flora rushed forward anxiously to support her.

Nell shrugged her help away, put a hand over her eyes and stood immobile for a few seconds. Then she raised her head and smiled. 'It's all right. I just felt a bit dizzy, that's all. I didn't have much breakfast.'

'If you ask me, you dinna have enough to eat at any time,' declared Flora sharply, beginning to rearrange the contents of a shelf which Nell had disturbed. 'You canna work as hard as you do and get by on white wine and thin air.'

Nell glared at Flora. 'What are you talking about?' she asked coldly. 'I eat plenty.'

Flora swallowed nervously but she'd started now and felt impelled to continue. She smiled apologetically but resolutely pushed in the knife. 'Oh, come on. You're no' just thin, Nell, you're worn, like some of these towels. You've got to start taking more care of yourself. Tally thinks so, too.'

Nell shook her head wearily. 'Tally – what does he know about it? Or you either, for that matter. No, I'm sorry Flora, I know you mean well but really it's nothing to do with you whether I'm thin or fat. You should both mind your own business.' Her tone was not angry but perplexed, as if she could not understand why Flora should even have raised the matter.

'But it is our business if you're making yourself ill, Nell,' Flora persisted bravely. 'Look, you shouldna be getting dizzy just reaching up to a shelf. You shouldna, honest! Do you no' see that?'

'No, I don't,' snapped Nell. 'I've just got the curse, if you must know, and it sometimes affects me like that. Now, please, can we drop the subject? God knows, you and Tally can hardly accuse me of living dangerously. How you've managed to keep your jolly little afternoon sessions a secret from Mac for so long beats me – but they might not remain a secret for much longer if you start moaning on at me about how to live my life. I think it would be to everyone's advantage if we *all* minded our own business, don't you?'

Flora looked stricken. She had anticipated an emotional reaction, but she had not expected this instant and bitter retaliation, which almost amounted to blackmail. She flushed bright red, muttered an apology and retreated from the room, devoutly wishing she had never agreed to interfere.

'God dammit!' Nell cried out miserably and, for want of anything handy to sit on, slid weakly down against the shelving until her bottom hit the floor. Dragged down by her descent, thick white towels began to fall in heaps around her, dropping like thawing snow off an Alpine roof. She buried her face in one and began to cry hot, remorseful tears. She had not meant to threaten Flora in that appalling way. It was a hideous thing to do. How could she have said those things? She was such a cow! But being called too thin was so hard to take. She had had to put up with 'poor-little-fat-girl' glances all her life and now she was damned if she was going to let anyone start pitying her for being too thin. She *liked* being thin, even though she was beginning to realise that her extreme weight loss was taking a drastic toll. The excuse about the curse had been a lie. She hadn't had it for two months now and she definitely wasn't pregnant. So her body was trying to tell her something. But when for most of your days you'd looked fit to take on Mohammed Ali over fifteen rounds, it was bliss to feel that someone might consider flinging you over their shoulder or lifting you up on a white charger and riding off into the sunset . . . The really bloody part about the whole thing was, though (and now the tears came faster and hotter), that the only person she'd met whom she actually yearned to carry her off was miles away in Monaco and didn't give a shit. Oh God, oh hell! It was true – life got you down and then kicked you in the teeth. Or, as she'd heard Fenella say once: *'Life's a bitch, and then you die.'*

'You can take one Sunday off, surely,' insisted Alasdair on the phone later that day. His secretary was hovering in an agitated way, mouthing that there was another call on the line, but he was determined to make Nell commit herself. 'You'd be doing me a favour if you'd come. I'm sick of walking on my own all the time.'

Nell bit her lip. She wanted to say yes but she was terrified that she might make a fool of herself. Suppose she couldn't climb the kind of hill Alasdair took for granted? Suppose he had to keep stopping to wait for her? She would feel such a drag and then she would get angry with herself and probably with him as well. 'You won't take me up a Munro, will you?' she asked hesitantly.

'No. I promise it will be a gentle Sunday stroll – nothing strenuous and lots of stops to admire the view. You must come this month, Nell, because September is the best time of year. The heather is flowering, the bracken is turning and the temperature is just right – not too hot and not too cold. I'll pick you up first thing on Sunday morning.'

Just before he replaced the receiver he heard her faint, 'OK. Thanks.' He immediately pressed the second key on his line system and addressed himself to a divorce case he was handling, but half his mind was still with Nell. In many ways he shared her misgivings. She was hardly fit and would probably find a day in the hills tough going, but he hoped that the enormous pleasure and sense of achievement to be gained from it would more than compensate for what it might take out of her physically. He knew just how and where to initiate a flabby novice into the joys of hillwalking, the very route that would delight her eye enough to take her mind off her creaking muscles, and then, with any luck, she would be hooked!

On Sunday they made an early start and drove in gathering light and awkward silence through a bleak glen scarred with forestry trenches. It was developing into a dull grey morning, the sky uncertain and pale and the air neither warm nor chill, a wait-and-see kind of day when climatically almost anything could happen, from scorching sun to sudden downpour. 'It's so sad,' Nell observed, peering out from side to side up the newly planted slopes. 'This must have been a rather beautiful glen before the trees came.'

When the Forestry Commission started a new plantation, they first brought in trench-diggers to gouge great drainage ditches, throwing up black piles of peaty soil like dark scabs on the hillside. Then they planted saplings in rows, protected against marauding animals by unnatural-looking grey plastic sheaths. Individually no doubt they were beautiful plants, would grow into beautiful trees, but in their hundreds and thousands, hidden inside their obscene grey condoms, they resembled an army of infant telegraph poles marching across the glen. Collectively they were an eyesore.

'They're only putting back what was there before the sheep destroyed the forests. It will look better when the trees are grown,' Alasdair assured her.

'Better perhaps, but utterly different,' she responded. 'The face of this glen will never be the same again, will it? For years it will look scarred, then it will be totally obscured by sitka spruce and then, when they are felled, it will look like a blasted heath until they decide to plant it again. It has lost its identity; forcibly erased in the interests of newsprint.'

'That's one way of looking at it,' he agreed. 'Another is to say that the land is being put to some use.'

'Yes, but is the land simply there for us to use?' she persisted. 'Or does it have rights, too?'

'Be careful,' Alasdair told her, 'or I will read you another of my favourite poet's poems.'

She glanced at him sideways. His profile was solemn, almost stern, staring ahead at the road gathering under the wheels of the car. 'Well, I hope you will,' she said. 'But please choose a moment when I'm dying for a breather.'

After a time they turned off the scarred glen along the side of a loch. High peaks towered in a grand range ahead of them, dark and rocky and pitted with ravines. They drew up in the car park of a squat, white lodge, already busy with posses of walkers and climbers, for a score of different routes began and ended there. 'I'll just go in and tell them where we plan to go,' said Alasdair. 'It's always wise to leave word in case of accidents.'

Nell gestured towards the mountains. 'Those look suspiciously like Munros to me. You did promise.' Her face was a study in uncertainty.

'I did,' he said. 'And I meant it. We'll just look up at them today. You never know, they might beckon to you.'

She shook her head. 'Don't count on it.'

He laughed. 'We're going up the high dark glen – Glen Dochard, to give it its Gaelic name. It's a slow steady climb but worth it for the views and its mysterious dark loch. Get your gear on, I won't be long.'

Nell's 'gear' consisted of the jeans she was wearing, an old waxed cotton jacket and some trainers. She suspected that Alasdair would consider these fearfully unsuitable, dressed as he was himself in dull-green Gortex jacket, britches and long fawn woollen socks. When he returned he opened the car boot and took out two pairs of strong leather walking boots with rough, corrugated soles.

'I brought along a pair of my wife's,' he said in an expressionless tone. 'I thought you and she might be much the same size.'

Nell stared at him, wondering what it had cost him to unearth the boots and when he had last seen his wife wearing them. She said nothing but removed one trainer and slipped her foot into the right boot. It felt strange but not uncomfortable. 'You're right,' she said. 'They fit me. Thank you.'

'Good. We'll take your trainers in the pack, though, just in case those start to pinch,' he suggested.

They both tied their laces silently, unspoken thoughts hovering in the air between them. 'What was her name?' Nell asked at length. 'If I'm in her shoes, so to speak, I think I ought to know her name.'

'Muriel. Her name was Muriel.' She could detect no quiver in the voice and yet she felt certain the emotion must be there, churning and seething just beneath the surface of his impassivity. He shrugged his shoulders into the straps of a rucksack and handed her a small, sealed plastic bag. Bright-coloured chocolate wrappers showed through, and a round tube of mints. 'Some iron rations,' he explained briefly. 'Just in case we get separated. Put them in your pocket. There's no drink, but burn water is quite safe and very plentiful as you'll discover.'

'You think of everything,' she remarked admiringly, stowing the packet away.

'It's best to be careful in the hills. People get lost and injured every week. There's no harm in taking precautions.'

'No, of course not.' There was still an ocean of unease between them. Taking a deep breath, Nell plunged into its treacherous shoals, hoping she would not flounder hopelessly. 'Was she pretty, your wife?'

They were walking out of the car park now, through a gap in the surrounding wall, heading straight across an expanse of long, tufted grass towards the bank of a river. He had his head down, looking for footholds among the tussocks, so that his reply was slightly muffled by the collar of his jacket. 'Yes, I think she was. Beautiful actually. She was what they call *bhan dubh* – fair dark. Dark hair, dark eyes, pale Highland skin.'

'It must be hard, walking without her when it was a pleasure you shared together. I wonder you still do it.' She could not see how he reacted because she was following close behind him. But close as she was, it seemed uncomfortably as if Muriel was walking between them.

'For a year I didn't. But I started again this season. I couldn't seem to keep away. It's the call of the hills.' He turned, smiling slightly, teasing, banishing the ghost of Muriel. 'The hills *are* alive, you know!'

Nell stopped in her tracks and giggled. 'With the sound of music? Don't tell me!' The awkwardness between them vanished and simultaneously the sun broke dramatically through the high, grey haze above them, pouring golden light onto the bracken-covered slopes with their scattered clumps of gorse and rowan. In a movie, orchestral music would have swelled on the soundtrack but when Nell tucked a hand behind her ear, cocking it up the slope to catch any descending serenade, she shook her head sorrowfully. 'Nope, can't hear a thing.'

He peered down at her from his nine-inch superiority of height. 'You will, little Nell, you will,' he promised and glanced up at the clearing sky, his face bathed in sunlight. There was no sign of the underlying sorrow she had imagined must be there. His kind, open face was calm, his expression eager. He was apparently thinking only of the weather and the walk ahead. 'By the way,' he continued, rummaging in a jacket pocket. 'I brought some sun-cream. I think you're going to need it. It's going to be a lovely day – here.'

She accepted the tube he offered with a smile and a wry nod. 'There you go again, thinking of everything. Thanks.'

They walked in companionable silence after that, saving their breath, for the terrain became more taxing as they followed the river upstream. It grew narrower and narrower until it was little more than a burn, leaping and foaming over fallen boulders, its banks steeper and steeper where it had gouged its way down the hillside. Graceful birches and rowans grew tall in the shelter of the ravine, and as the sun grew stronger the walkers plunged gratefully into the green-gold shade they offered. There was a path of sorts, probably formed by deer and thus occasionally disappearing hectically over some rocky outcrop which the animals might leap with ease but which gave its human followers a little more difficulty. However, with Alasdair hauling her up the more inaccessible bits and steadying her down the sheer drops, Nell managed to negotiate the path with creditable skill. The difficulties of the route made her dismiss all other thought from her mind save the exacting business of putting her hands and feet in the right place and hauling her body after them, although it did occur to her at one time that Alasdair had said that this would be no more than a Sunday stroll. What was a real walk like if this was a Sunday stroll, she wondered.

Just when she began to think that torture would be a fairer prospect, when her lungs were gasping and her arms and legs aching with the effort of the climb, they came face to face with a waterfall where the burn tumbled and splashed musically over an almost sheer rockface and, after one final heave, they emerged from the ravine onto the clear, sunlit slopes of the high glen. Nell scrambled up the last few yards and threw herself, panting, onto a thick clump of purple heather. 'That's it,' she puffed jerkily. 'I've got to stop for a while.'

Alasdair, who seemed to be breathing maddeningly evenly, lowered his rucksack onto a nearby rock. 'That's the worst bit over,' he told her. 'You've done brilliantly. I never thought you'd get up here in one go.' He pulled a plastic bottle from the pack and unscrewed the top. 'Back in a minute,' he said, plunging through the heather to a small, clear pool which had formed at the top of the waterfall. Water dripped invitingly as he offered the filled bottle to Nell.

She sat up. 'Thanks,' she exclaimed and took several gulps. It was sharp, astringent, thirst-quenching, tasting slightly of peat. 'Marvellous!' she exclaimed, handing it back, still puffing. She was bright red from exertion and her hair was damp with perspiration, clinging to her forehead. She pushed it back with both hands, raising her face to the cooling effects of the wind. Now that they were higher up and out of the shelter of the ravine the breeze was quite strong. For the first time she took stock of her surroundings and stared down the slope in amazement. 'God, what a fantastic view!'

The range of mountains at their backs effectively formed the western wall which retained Rannoch Moor, one of Scotland's great wildernesses. Its north-eastern barrier was the Grampian range stretching away in the distance, peak after peak standing clear and sharp against a blue sky edged with pink-tinged clouds, heaped like home-made meringues. Between the two ranges the moor itself appeared to Nell like the surface of the moon, mile upon mile of flat, bracken-covered terrain, pock-marked with hundreds of crater-like pools of every shape and size, from small puddles to meandering, indented lochs dotted with flat, featureless islands. At first sight she could not discern a single tree and yet, on closer inspection, lonely, stunted rowans and alders could be seen here and there, gnarled and slanted by the force of the incessant wind. Apart from the white buildings at the head of the loch where they had parked there were no other houses, no sign of human habitation. The moor almost seemed to shout, proudly and defiantly: 'Here is a place where no human foot has trod!' and although for the most part that was probably untrue, Nell intuitively knew that there must be small stretches of marshy ground between those blank sheets of water where the foot of man had, indeed, never ventured and she felt elated and intimidated by the prospect.

'It's incredible,' she breathed, turning to Alasdair with shining eyes. 'If Emily Brontë had seen this she would never have written *Wuthering Heights*!'

'You think she'd have written a novel called *Rannoch Moor* instead?' he asked, amused.

'Without question.' Nell repeated the name, lingering on the syllables. 'Rannoch Moor. It sounds as bleak as it looks.'

'*Raineach* is the Gaelic word for bracken,' Alasdair explained. 'That's one interpretation of the name. The other is that it's derived from a phrase meaning "watery place".'

'Well, either would be appropriate enough, that's certain. Just look at it.' She swept her arm before her, indicating the vast empty grandeur of the moor. She had forgotten her burning lungs, her aching legs and her broken fingernails.

'Perhaps this is a landscape that will never lose its rights or its identity,' suggested Alasdair, pulling his battered volume of Norman MacCaig's poetry from a pocket of his rucksack. 'I'll read you that poem now, if you like.' When she nodded he continued: 'It's called "A Man in Assynt", and MacCaig is writing about another wilderness, further north, but the same ideas apply here too, I think. He poses the question you more or less asked earlier.

Who possesses this landscape? –
The man who bought it or
I who am possessed by it?

False questions, for
this landscape is
masterless
and intractable in any terms
that are human.
It is docile only to the weather
and its indefatigable lieutenants –
wind, water and frost.'

He shut the book and stared down the mountainside at the wild, untamed tract of moor. 'He is right, isn't he?'

'It makes me feel guilty for owning Taliska,' murmured Nell.

'Ah, but do you own it or does it own you?' he asked enigmatically.

'You sound just like Granny Kirsty.' Nell suddenly put her hands to her stomach as a loud rumble seemed to break the sound barrier. 'God, I'm starving. Is there any food in that bottomless rucksack of yours?'

'Plenty,' he laughed. 'But you can only have some

if you promise to hang on to it. I haven't carried it all the way up here for you to deposit it behind a rock.'

There was a sudden eruption of silence between them like an invisible wall swirling up out of the wind. Nell flushed a deep, furious red but it was not from anger. It was from shame. She did not know how Alasdair had found out about her horrible habit, nor how long he had known, but the fact that he had and he did was cathartic. She felt as if he had caught her in mid-puke, vomiting all over some object of great beauty, defiling it and spoiling it forever. As if the product of her wretched retchings had obliterated the Venus de Milo or the Taj Mahal or was spreading out like some putrid flood over the magnificent, intractable landscape below them.

She shut her eyes, drew in a deep breath and opened them again to meet his candid, demanding gaze. 'I promise,' she whispered, reaching out for the sandwich he offered. There was no point in denial. He had made it plain that he knew her secret and did not condone it, but added no words of reproach or criticism. Curiously, in contrast to her reactions when confronted by Fenella and Flora, she did not feel angry. In fact she recognised distinct symptoms of relief. Perhaps the old adage was true after all, that a problem shared is a problem halved. 'How did you know?' she asked him at length, taking a bite of the sandwich.

He shook his head. 'That's not important,' he said. 'What is important is that you stop. Stop confusing your appetites! I liked the Nell best who had an appetite for life.'

'I still do,' she protested indistinctly, her mouth full.

'No, you don't. You have an appetite for food but now you also have this insatiable appetite for image that makes you throw it up again. You have turned self-discipline upside down and it is making you ill.'

She made no response for several minutes, munching mechanically on her sandwich, forcing it down her throat. Her hunger had evaporated with her self-respect. She felt stripped, vulnerable, perilously close to tears and part of her self-pity she recognised as self-loathing. Was she in so deep that she couldn't stop, or could the sympathetic support of someone like Alasdair help her to kick her habit?

It was Alasdair who broke the silence. 'I only speak of this because I care for *you*, Nell. I don't care about the body that you seem so anxious to reduce to a skeleton, I don't care about the snappy little garments you dress it in or the blonde tresses you achieve on your nut-brown head. I care for the real Nell, the one who exists inside all of that and whom I fear may change or even disappear because of it.'

He smiled at her in such an affectionate way that she was left in no doubt of his sincerity. The tears which seemed constantly to lurk just beneath the surface broke through then and began to slide down her cheeks. The view, the half-eaten sandwich, Alasdair, all converged into a moist blur. She felt something touch her hand and saw that it was a handkerchief, proffered in a strong, freckled brown fist. Thankfully she closed her own fingers around it and buried her face in it.

Alasdair sat quietly beside her as she mopped and sniffed. The reference to her habit had taken all his courage. He was, on the whole, a let-sleeping-dogs-lie man, a lover of the even keel, even if it meant sailing on a sea of repressed emotion. With dismay he felt the boat rocking beneath him, threatening to tip him overboard into frightening undercurrents. He hastened to steady it.

'Believe it or not, this glen is even more beautiful further up,' he said, and Nell noticed gratefully that his tone was kind but not pitying. He rose and held out his hand to her. 'Would the real Nell McLean please stand up?'

Chapter Sixteen

'You look wonderful, Nell darling! For the first time in my life I'm really proud to be seen with you.' Donalda's expertly painted mouth seemed to fill the frame of Nell's vision. That mouth, which always clamped firmly shut in the presence of cream or chocolate but opened volubly on the subjects of calories and cholesterol, was a wide red gash, gushing enthusiasm for Nell's stark new shape. 'You must be down to size ten by now. You won't stop will you, darling? Size eight is the truly *chic* size for a woman. It's nothing to do with bones, you know. Even the largest bones will fit size eight if there isn't too much flesh on them.'

'I feel so weak though, Mummy. Sometimes I don't know if I can put one foot in front of the other, and my throat is sore all the time.'

'It's worth it though, isn't it – to be slim and elegant. A lady must suffer to be elegant, I've always told you that.'

'I get dizzy just walking across the room. Perhaps I should ease up a bit, try to stop vomiting every day.'

'Oh no, darling, don't stop! You don't want to be fat again, do you – not now that you're a civilised shape at last. Please don't stop.'

'But I want to stop, Mummy. It's hurting me, can't

you see that? It's making me ill!'

'It's better to be ill than fat. Much better. Don't stop, darling, don't stop, don't stop, don't . . .' The bright red slash of a mouth kept shaping the words over and over like a computerised graphic until there was no face behind the red lips, no mind behind the words, no heart behind the mother image.

In silver morning light Nell woke with an enormous sense of relief that she had been dreaming. This particular dream theme had started after the walk in the high glen, inspired she was sure by the self-revulsion she had felt when she realised that Alasdair knew about her vomiting. He had made no further mention of it but just the fact that he knew and the few words he had said were enough. For the first time she admitted to herself that she had a problem and in some strange way he managed to share it, treating it as he had treated his own grief for his wife, as something which must be faced and dealt with, not as something to be denied or ignored.

Lying staring at the brightening squares of her bedroom windows, Nell's heartbeat steadied gradually as the image of her mother's red mouth faded back into her subconscious. These dreams always starred Donalda as a wicked, weight-watching witch and yet in her waking life Nell found herself thinking more fondly of her mother. 'I must go and visit her in London now that things have quietened down here. I know – we'll go and stay with her for David's wedding.'

Things had quietened down a great deal at Taliska; frighteningly so. Through September the number of guests held up but as October advanced they fell off drastically. Tally blamed the fact that most of the other country-house hotels in Scotland closed at about that time, financially unable to justify remaining open through the winter months. But he and Nell had decided to stay open at least until New Year, hoping that special promotions like the cashmere weekend and the *Hot Gryll* recording would sustain them. They'd had a successful enough summer to sustain a few weeks' slack period.

Staff numbers shrank naturally. 'Souper-Grass' Niamh left to take up a place at Edinburgh University and 'Lothario' Tony to start a new job as steward at a Glasgow golf club. They made tentative plans to visit each other but Nell guessed that their relationship was unlikely to go any further. In a moment of sisterly intimacy, Niamh had admitted to Nell that she found Tony rather shallow, for all his persistent ardour and dark good looks. Student life was likely to provide friends and lovers of more intellect if not less concupiscence. Encouraged by Calum, Craig, too, went to Perth to pursue the first six months of a culinary course which would release him to return to the hotel kitchen during the next high season. 'Go and learn the basics and get shouted at by someone else,' Calum told him with unconscious avuncularity, 'and come back here in the spring if you canna stay away!' He and Ginny nested comfortably in their little cottage, wielding the spirtle energetically and talking about getting married.

Tally talked to Flora about getting *un*married but she just laughed. 'Divorce Mac? No, no, Tally, I wouldna do that. Divorce is wicked and anyway, I love him. We belong together.'

'You say you love me,' Tally reminded her, unaware that he was becoming the kind of sulky, complaining lover he had always deplored.

'And so I do,' Flora assured him, kneeling over him on the bed and bending down to kiss him, the white, white flesh of her thighs so pale against his. 'In the afternoon.'

'You should not confuse love with sex,' he declared petulantly. 'I love you all the time – morning, noon and night.'

She slid down to lie along the length of his body, moving her hips erotically against him in a way she knew stirred him to ecstasy. 'Well, you'll have to make do with three till six,' she murmured, her lips against his.

'And never on a Sunday,' Tally retorted, pressing her to him and rolling her over. The act of intercourse was becoming one of the few ways he felt he could dominate her.

'Sunday is my day of rest,' she told him, raising her knees and his heart-rate. The subject of divorce was dropped in favour of extra-marital affairs.

The walk in the high glen became the first of several that Nell took with Alasdair. She kept to her promise never to throw up any of the food which he carried on their expeditions and, as a result, she began to find it possible to eat more often without vomiting. She still couldn't bear the sensation of a full stomach and was consistently driven to empty it when her appetite had raged too fiercely but, slowly and gradually, she began to throw up less.

She enjoyed their excursions more as she grew fitter. Walking in Alasdair's footsteps over burn and brae, she sometimes pondered what it was about him that she liked so much. Certainly he was no movie-star heart-throb like Claude! He was kind, but that was not nearly enough. He was not really handsome, his face was too irregular for that, the nose too bent, the mouth too straight, the eyebrows too bushy and the hair too crinkly. Besides, it was going grey. Twelve years her senior, he was considerably older than any of her previous men friends. He was a sugar daddy! And yet he certainly wasn't. Sugar daddies are supposed to shower you with gifts, she thought, gifts in return for favours. But Alasdair did not look for favours nor did he supply gifts. He was neither paternal nor avuncular.

Yet he made no moves romantically, seeming content with the occasional handclasp as he hauled her up a steep path or steadied her over a drop, and the brotherly kisses of greeting and farewell which marked the beginning and end of their outings. He spouted poetry but never the slushy kind, and his conversation was all of the countryside and its beauties, its cruelty and its bounty. He knew about the birds that flew above their heads and the snakes that slithered beneath their feet, he knew about winds and tides, mountains and glens, rivers and lochs and he knew when they were safe or dangerous, welcoming or hostile. He was good company but he showed no signs of becoming or even wishing to become anything more.

Is it he who cannot forget his wife, she wondered, or I who cannot make him?

Her mistake in encouraging David and her conspicuous lack of success in pinning Claude down to anything more than a one-night stand inhibited her. The Claude episode especially had made her feel dirty and promiscuous – sensations which lowered her self-esteem as much as her growing knowledge of her own stupidity in allowing herself to become addicted to vomiting. She saw herself as unworthy of being anything more than a friend to someone like Alasdair and, perhaps because of this, she wanted to be more, much more. Alasdair was a rock to which she longed to cling, a mountain which she yearned to climb, but he was also a cave in which she felt there were hidden obstacles to these ambitions. She hid her muddled longings under a veneer of casual companionship.

For his part, Alasdair was too emotionally diffident to detect any hint of Nell's musings or misgivings. To him she seemed a dispassionate walking-partner – friendly, relaxed and interested in her surroundings but not particularly in him. After her initial inquiries about his wife she had shown no further curiosity about his past, his work or his way of life. She evinced no interest in seeing where he lived and, because his house in Oban seemed to him a cold place without Muriel's presence, he never took her there. Although he knew that she never threw up after any of their picnics, he had no other evidence that her obsession had eased. Walking the hills in jeans and boots she seemed almost like the old, carefree Nell, but once back at Taliska, he saw her retreat again behind her screen of make-up, manicure and model dresses. Her hair grew longer and blonder and her hotel personality grew more brittle and businesslike. The only glimpses he got of the bouncy, artless Nell of old came when, puffing with effort, they reached the summit of a hill or mountain and she stood in rapt delight, gazing round at the wild landscape spread below before turning to grin breathlessly at him and share the thrill of achievement. 'Oh God, Alasdair, it's wonderful!' she would invariably sigh, face flushed and eyes shining and his only regret was that he could not bottle the joy she displayed on the high peaks and pour it like syrup over the other parts of their lives. But his feelings were too earnest to reveal. Fifteen years of happy marriage and two of grievous mourning had left him sadly out of practice in the old-fashioned art of flirtation.

* * *

'Have you noticed?' Tally asked one day over lunch, when the depleted staff were gathered in relaxed mood, 'that although there are fewer guests, those that do come are much randier?'

Mick and Rob pricked up their ears. A conversation on this tack could provide much fodder for gossip and fantasy to warm up their cold outdoor duties. Mick was still basking in the glory of having lured the brochure models down to the Ossian for a joke session with the boys. The two girls had been introduced to whisky with lemonade and snooker, bending tipsily over the green baize table in their mini-skirts in a way that had sent many a local sea-dog back home with his tail wagging.

'It's the short days,' remarked Calum, who had become demonstrably less Calvinist in his attitudes since setting up house with Ginny. 'Short days, long nights and large beds! I sometimes think we should give them their dinner at dusk and let them get on with it.'

'Oh no,' said Nell, entering into the spirit of it. 'Dinner is the interval entertainment. Time for refreshment and then back for the second act.'

'That Lord Whatsisname didn't look on it like that,' contradicted Libby. 'He was at it all through dinner as well. I don't know how he managed to eat anything, with his right hand up his so-called secretary's skirt and his left hand groping me every time I came near him. He was a right octopus.'

'You should have offered him one of your famous specials,' Tally suggested. 'I thought they always damped down the fiery ones.'

Libby blushed. Her talents as a masseuse were always much in demand, but sometimes male guests asked for more than she was prepared to give. When they did she had a secret and extremely effective 'special' which she employed with great success, silencing their demands and forestalling any grievances they might feel. Libby's 'special' had got her out of many an awkward situation but she never revealed what it was, nor had Tally been able to persuade her to give him one. 'It's supposed to deter rather than encourage,' she had told him, in the days when she was giving him all the encouragement he could want.

'Don't tease, Tally,' Nell admonished him. 'Libby's massages have revived many a flagging libido.'

'Speaking of which, why has Guedalla not booked in here for his honeymoon?' observed her brother. 'You haven't put him off, have you Nell?'

It was Nell's turn to blush. 'No, I have not,' she said defensively. 'They're probably going somewhere foreign. Anyway, they'd know that if they came here they'd only get bagpipe serenades at midnight and apple-pie beds.'

Tally grinned and nodded. 'Aye, but they'd have a honeymoon they would never forget!'

David and Caroline's wedding took place in London at the end of October. The twins were both invited and decided that as trade was quiet enough to leave the hotel in the hands of Ann, Flora, Calum and Ginny, they would spend a long weekend with Donalda and Hal. Apart from rather stilted weekly phone calls there had been no real contact between them since Donalda's early departure from the pre-opening house-party.

'God, I'm dreading this,' Nell confided to Tally as they taxied between Heathrow airport and the Marylebone penthouse. 'You don't think she'll bang on about Scotland and Daddy all over again, do you?'

'I doubt it,' replied Tally. 'She'll be too busy rhapsodising about the new Nell.'

'There *is* no new Nell. It's just the same old me, wrapped up a bit differently.' After Alasdair's remarks on their first walk Nell was self-conscious on this point. At the same time she had taken ages to decide on the tailored Cambridge-blue outfit she was wearing for this significant meeting with her mother. Part of her was aching to hear Donalda's ecstatic exclamations of approval, and part of her was longing to hear her mother express concern for her daughter's health now that she was fifty pounds lighter than she had been.

Having spent the best part of Nell's life telling her she was 'a bit too plump', when she answered their ring at the penthouse door Donalda stared in astonishment at her slimline daughter, clearly lost for words. Kissing Tally first, more or less out of habit, she still kept her eyes on Nell and, when she turned to her, said faintly, 'Darling Nell, you look wonderful. Is that a Catharine Walker suit?'

Mother and daughter exchanged kisses on cheeks whose bone structure was now seen to be remarkably similar – high and slanted under skin stretched in one case by youth and the other by surgery. Donalda's hand lingered on Nell's upper arm, ostensibly fingering the fine fabric of the sleeve but actually feeling the lack of flesh layered over the bone beneath. 'You've lost weight, Nell,' she remarked rather obviously. 'Come in and let me look at you.'

While Hal was greeting Tally, Donalda looked her daughter up and down critically and Nell held her breath. It was only by a strong act of will that she refrained from running straight to the nearby cloakroom and throwing up out of sheer nervousness.

That and the fact that she had nothing to throw up, having been hardly able to eat all day. 'I'd never have guessed you could look so glamorous, darling. You must have lost *stones*. And the clothes!' declared Donalda, her eyes still riveted on Nell. 'Isn't she glamorous, Hal?'

'Gosh yes, absolutely great,' responded Hal in a rather toneless voice. He looked distracted, rather than entranced. 'Bit too thin, though, maybe.'

Reluctantly Donalda had to nod agreement. 'Do you know, Nell darling, I never thought I'd say it but he's right. You are actually a bit *too* thin. Congratulations on taking off so much weight, but you mustn't overdo it, darling. You don't want to get ill.'

Mingled relief and exasperation flooded Nell's mind and she began to laugh with mild hysteria. 'Oh, Mummy,' she exclaimed dizzily, flinging her bag and coat over a hall chair in order to hug her mother properly and kiss her again. 'You are amazing!'

With Donalda frowning in puzzlement at Nell's exuberance, the four proceeded into the drawing room, the familiar panoramic view from the penthouse windows now darkened into a black evening vista pin-pricked with thousands of lights. 'Never mind me anyway, Mummy, how are you?' Nell asked as they all sat down, except for Hal who began to busy himself with drinks. 'You look a little tired.'

'We're fine, really, except Hal's had some rather bad news.' Donalda glanced doubtfully at her husband who nodded curtly back, uncharacteristically taciturn. Donalda then proceeded to reveal an anguished stream of misfortune. The recession had hit the computer business and Hal was being retired early in a company restructuring programme. Not only that, but his pension would be larger and go further if they went to live in the States. For an hour over drinks and all the way through a restaurant dinner, Donalda rehearsed the pros and cons of living on one side of the Atlantic or the other while Hal sat morose and silent, concentrating on his food. All his normal ebullience and energy gone, he drank whisky steadily. His eyes were dull and there was a roll of fat above his belt.

'Couldn't you stay here if you really wanted to, Hal?' Nell asked with concern, trying to stir him into conversation. She had never greatly liked her stepfather, but deplored this drastic change in him. 'You've always loved living in England.'

'It doesn't really matter where you live if you don't have a life,' Hal told her bleakly. 'If you're not in a job, as far as I'm concerned you're not in the business of living.'

'Now don't say that, Hal. It's not the end of the world,' soothed Donalda. 'We'll just have to make the best of it.'

Nell felt sorry for both of them, facing this change and the loss of status it entailed. Image and position had always been of great importance to the couple, and from that point of view their future did look bleak and unpredictable. In the circumstances, it was surprising that Donalda had expressed any concern for her daughter's health, being obviously considerably worried about her husband's. It was unreasonable to expect any help with her bulimia from her mother. More than ever it was brought home to Nell that her habit was her own problem and one which she must face up to, just as her mother and stepfather had to face theirs.

Happy though the twins were to have repaired bridges with Donalda, it was a relief to escape to Golders Green on the Sunday to join in the boisterous celebrations which invariably accompany a Jewish wedding. Caroline made a vivid, exotic bride in a dramatic white feathered wedding dress which must have cost a small fortune and which made her look rather like a tiny, restless humming-bird, darting and hovering among her guests with a vibrant happiness which Tally found rather exhausting. He even felt faintly sorry for his old school chum, a trimmer and more solemn David, clearly feeling his responsibilities among this staunchly family-oriented gathering.

'We're going abroad actually,' David confessed rather apologetically when asked about the honey-moon. 'To the Bahamas. Caroline's found this wonderful island hideaway which has little palm-thatched bungalows set in their own private gardens beside a blue lagoon. She fancies going native, I think.'

'Sounds really wild,' drawled Tally, patting the grey waistcoat beneath David's morning coat. 'Is that why you've lost a bit here, old man? Want to look good in the altogether?'

David grinned. 'Something like that. I'm nothing, though, compared with Nell. She's practically disappeared. Caroline couldn't believe it – asked me if she looked fat in comparison. Honestly, with some women you can never win. Can't say you look as trim as you did, though. What's happened to the old "never put on a pound" Tally?'

'Found true love and shortbread. I'm trying to give it up, though.'

'What – true love?'

'No. Shortbread.'

'I suspect you're missing my pulverising squash challenges. Have you found another squash partner?'

'Yes, I have, as a matter of fact. Doesn't play quite so well, but she's much better looking than you.'

'A female? Is she the shortbread lady?'

'No. She's cashmere.'

David raised an eyebrow. 'Aha. One sweet, one soft. Playing one against the other, eh? Still the same old Tally!'

'Not quite,' responded Tally flatly.

As November advanced the days became too short and inclement for excursions into the hills so Alasdair began to be a regular guest at Taliska Sunday lunch – a meal which invariably consisted of a traditional roast and a low-fat 'Calum' trifle. With fewer guests, less work and therefore less stress, Nell began to gain some control over her vomiting and her hip-bones ceased to protrude quite as much as they had. Furthermore this did not plunge her into despair as it might have done a month or so before. She was not deliriously, spell-bindingly, overwhelmingly happy but at least she had not thought of Claude for weeks.

On the Monday before the cashmere weekend Fenella rang. 'Everything is OK,' she told Nell enthusiastically. 'It looks as if we'll have a full house and there are even people threatening to stay elsewhere and come over for the dinners and shows. At the risk of giving custom to other hotels, I don't see how we can stop them.'

'We can't, of course. We'll just have to make them wish they were staying at Taliska.' Nell wondered if any of them might be staying with the Ramsay-Millers, and then she remembered that Lorn Castle was already closed for the winter. She'd heard on the grapevine that they'd had another difficult season despite moving down-market, but she hadn't been there to investigate further.

'You'll do that all right, I'm sure. What about staff?' Fenella asked. She was bringing several of her own girls to organise the fashion shows and had offered more to help out domestically if necessary.

'We're fine. We have enough local part-timers who are only too happy to earn extra cash before Christmas. Everything looks set fair.'

'There is one slight cloud on the horizon,' Fenella told her in a different tone of voice. 'You'll see it anyway when you get the final guest-list. Claude's coming.'

Nell felt her stomach flop and lurch like a water-filled balloon. 'Claude! Why?'

'He's laying a Contessa at the moment and she's one of my biggest spenders. She's named him as her partner for the weekend.'

'Oh shit! Which day are they coming?' The telephone felt like a red-hot poker. No, come to think of it, that's what Claude was!

'That's just it – she's bought two nights, a double booking in more ways than one. They'll be here on the Friday and Saturday. Business-wise I don't mind because she'll probably buy twice as much cashmere as anyone else.'

'Perhaps I'll send for some bromide,' suggested Nell with uncharacteristic malice. 'Why should the Contessa have her cake *and* eat it?'

'Good idea,' cried Fenella. 'Keep her mind on cashmere rather than Claude.'

'I was thinking more of giving it to him,' countered Nell. 'Does bromide work on ladies?'

'God knows – let's give 'em both a dose!' It was wishful thinking, but it vented both women's sense of indignation at the Frenchman's unwelcome return to Taliska. Both considered that if he'd any sense of decency he'd have turned the Contessa's invitation down.

While she was on the telephone, Nell was vaguely aware of the fax machine whirring into life. The noise sounded like an emanation of the Claude-inspired churning of her innards. After she said goodbye to Fenella it was several minutes before she felt calm enough to tear off the message and look at it.

Great idea for Hot Gryll. *Wild boar arrives Taliska Friday for use in festive menu contest. Couldst house until slaughter next week? See you Dec. 15th. Regards, Patrick.*

'Wild boar?' Nell was flabbergasted. 'What the hell are we going to do with a wild boar?'

'Who's a bore?' asked Tally, entering the office from the cellar with a revised winter wine-list. 'Is the computer free?'

'Yes, help yourself.' Nell waved the shiny fax paper at him furiously. 'Look at this. Bloody Patrick "Meddling" Coyninghame wants us to look after a wild boar for him until next week. Honestly, he's got a bare-faced cheek.'

Tally took the fax and read it through. He laughed. 'More like boar-faced cheek! But it shouldn't be a problem. We can keep it at the far end of the byre – the stall there is pretty well fortified. I'll see Mick about it. It isn't just the bore of the boar though, is it? What's really got your goat?'

'Oh ha ha!' snapped Nell. She ignored the question and left him to his wine-list.

If it had not been for the imminent arrival of Claude and his Contessa, Nell and Fenella would have thoroughly enjoyed preparing for their first joint promotion. Over the last few weeks they had become firm friends, the 'crepitation' contretemps buried if not forgotten as Nell began to fill out again slightly and Fenella assumed she was tackling her bulimia problem. They shared similar tastes and were in easy accord over how the hotel should be used and presented during the weekend sales campaign. The conference room was set aside as a showroom-cum-shop where Fenella's two salesgirls would be based and from which they would take selected garments to be tried on by customers in their own rooms. The large folding doors between the drawing room and dining room were to be opened out for the gala dinners and a catwalk built down the middle.

'It's a perfect location,' enthused Fenella when the joiners had finished their work. 'And that ash-blonde panelling just sets off this season's colours to perfection.'

'I hope you haven't forgotten your promise to model,' Nell reminded her. 'Tally will sue you for breach of contract if you don't.'

'Oh, I'm going to,' Fenella assured her. 'And despite his perfidy I'm going to ask Claude to escort me down the catwalk. I've got some fabulous men's sweaters and scarves and even a great chunky knitted jacket which might tempt the husbands and lovers. Claude would model them perfectly. If nothing else it might make the Contessa jealous and he might feel a twinge of regret that he's got hooked up to an old wrinkly rather than something a little more . . . succulent.'

'Supposing he won't strut his stuff?' Nell asked.

'He will,' Fenella assured her. 'He's vain. You'll see.'

The boar arrived as promised on the Friday morning in a van from the Argyll Wildlife Park. He was a massive black-bristled animal about the size of a large Alsatian dog but weighing four times more. His sharp, yellow tusks stuck out from his jaw like the business ends of a pair of old-fashioned can-openers, giving him a rather comical expression. He appeared fairly docile but the warden who delivered him warned that he could move faster than a man over rough ground and was surprisingly agile for his size.

'His name is Basil,' he added, and Nell immediately wanted to save the boar's bristly skin. He reminded her of Bertie the badger who had become quite a pet by now, arriving promptly every evening at the foot of the steps to the bar-terrace to slurp his bowl of milk and snuffle up his brown bread and hazel nuts. Ninian had trained him well but the sow and the cubs were more wary, only taking tidbits that were thrown to them across the lawn. Most guests, however, were only too thrilled to feed them and admire their markings in the floodlight Mick had installed especially for these nightly feeding sessions.

'Poor Basil,' Nell said, watching Mick and the warden use large wooden boards to manoeuvre the wild boar out of the van and into his temporary home in the byre. Mick had reinforced the stall's partitioning with steel brackets and, after a cursory inspection, the warden predicted that it should be secure enough. 'Why have you sold him?' Nell asked.

'We've just got too many,' the man told her. 'Normally they're quiet, unaggressive creatures unless they're cornered but they can get into some pretty dramatic fights when they're disputing territory or sows. We have to cull them.'

'So poor old Basil gets his face on telly with an apple in his mouth,' said Nell sorrowfully, gazing over the partition at the boar who returned her stare with his tiny black-button eyes.

'Well, if it's any consolation, the wildlife park can do with the money he'll fetch,' the warden said.

Actually Nell was finding consolation in the fact that Basil's small, close-set eyes bore an uncanny resemblance to Gordon Gryll's. Perhaps the television audience would see it, too. 'What will he taste like?' she asked bleakly.

'I haven't a clue,' said the warden. 'I'm a vegetarian. So is he, incidentally. His favourite food is potatoes.'

'I'll remember that,' said Nell, making a mental note to ask Calum to reserve the potato peelings for Basil. The condemned boar might as well eat some hearty last meals.

Claude's Contessa turned out to be a dark, animated, jewel-decked Italian in her forties whom Fenella introduced to Nell as the Contessa Valentina de Busto Arsizio. 'All bust and arse, as you can see,' she murmured as the rather buxom lady disappeared up the main staircase talking non-stop to an attentive Claude.

'I bet she busts his arse,' put in Tally crudely.

Nell said nothing. She was trying to recover from the awful realisation that if Claude had crooked his little finger at her, she would probably have followed him up the stairs like a silly, tail-waggling lamb. The lazy smile in his dark eyes and his warm, slow handclasp had turned her lower body to semolina pudding. Red-hot poker? Rubbish! He was a walking stick of Semtex, damn him.

There had never before been such a glittering guest-list at Taliska. Apart from the Contessa, for this first gala night there was a Rothschild, a Guinness and a Vestey, the mistress of an oil billionaire and several international business tycoons mostly accompanied by their various partners and mountains of Vuitton luggage. Helicopters seemed to be landing in swift succession most of the afternoon, depositing the great and glamorous, and the hotel was soon loaded with a cast-list of glossy gossip-column characters. It's like *Hello!* magazine come to life, Nell thought. Fenella's right – if this lot get into a spending mood, our respective overdrafts could disappear overnight.

Aware that his reputation, like a soufflé, could rise or fall on this weekend's showing, Calum had gone into overdrive. His first banquet consisted of wild mushroom feuillettes, a delicate chicken and tarragon consommé, quenelles of salmon with crisp, fried seaweed, saddle of venison with a bramble coulis and baby cabbages spiked with juniper, a Drambuie parfait, and to finish, the unique Taliska oatmeal-rolled cheese with orchard apples and a savoury of devilled lobster blinis. With the mushrooms Fenella showed her coffee and cream collection, with the soup came the cinnamon and tobacco browns, the peach and apricot with the salmon and the deep reds and murreys with the bramble venison. Samples of winter white evening wear accompanied the sweet and cheese, and the savouries, which were served with peaty malt whisky, came with the beaded black evening dress. After careful rehearsing from Fenella and Calum, Nell delivered the catwalk commentary, mingling information about the clothes with brief menu notes, and she found it surprising how the same words could be appropriately applied to both; clothes and dishes alike were 'smooth, piquant, mysterious, subtle, voluptuous and chic' and were 'blended, mixed, teamed, tailored, trimmed and wrapped'. She began to see how easy it was to fall into the Gordon Gryll pun-trap.

As Fenella had predicted, Claude had been unable to resist her invitation to model some men's fashions and, when she made her final prowl down the catwalk wearing the clinging, black beaded dress, he escorted her with such smouldering sensuality that, far from being jealous, the Contessa immediately ordered it in three different colours, blissfully unaware that, with her rather too generous hips, she would fill the dress somewhat less sensationally than Fenella did.

While liqueurs were being served, the men were entertained by a sucession of models in flimsy underwear, specifically instructed to do their best to draw male attention from the number of orders being made by the ladies. During this time the Contessa's red-nailed, generously beringed fingers caressed Claude's thigh so openly and with such demanding possessiveness that Nell found herself cattily wondering how Claude could bring himself to return the embraces of such an ageing nympho. She subsequently noticed, however, that several gentlemen's sweaters and an extremely expensive cardigan-jacket were added to the Contessa's cashmere order, so no doubt the accountant kept the books meticulously balanced in terms of favours granted and gifts bestowed! But by the end of the evening Fenella's sales book was also looking healthily full of entries, and both his ex-lovers could afford to feel some pity for Claude who was clearly suffering from the prolonged grip of the Contessa's claw on his thigh!

The next morning was so bright and crisp that after a lazy breakfast most of the guests chose to clear their heads for their return journeys by taking a restorative stroll in the grounds of the hotel. The lawns were crunchy with frost and the air sparkled like chilled Perrier. It was 'a gin-clear day!' as Tally so accurately observed and, ever alert for additional sales opportunities, Fenella marshalled her four models into the thick, cosy tunics, hooded cardigans and leggings included in her collection and sent them out to wander among the guests. The Contessa and Claude, who was looking rather under the weather, were among those who strolled on the lawn admiring the clothes and discussing further possible orders over mugs of steaming glühwein, hastily concocted and served by Tally and Nell.

Meanwhile, down in the byre Mick had approached Basil's pen with a bucket of potato peelings. The cold freshness of the day combined with the tantalising smell of his favourite delicacy provoked instant energy in the confined boar, who hurled himself bodily at the partition, reducing it almost instantly to matchwood. Mick was literally bowled over by the huge, bristly creature who immediately busied himself among the potato peelings, swinishly unaware that he had knocked the bearer of the delicacy both over and out on the hard, stone-flagged floor. Having consumed what he considered little more than a tidbit, Basil ventured to seek further spud supplies, emerging from the byre like a black thundercloud, snout down, tusks up, intentions apparently totally evil. He quested unsuccessfully through the orchard and blundered on, making nothing of the chicken-wire and paling fence which had been erected to deter Taliska's rabbit population and was no proof against the determined push of a full-grown wild boar.

At this point his loud snorts and snufflings drew the attention of the guests gathered on the lawn, among whom Nell was moving with fresh mugs of glühwein on a tray. 'Oh my God – Basil's loose!' she exclaimed in agitation, slopping glühwein over a sumptuous silver fox fur jacket worn by a tycoon's lady. Nell was torn between stopping to mop up and make amends, and rushing to head off disaster.

By this time Mick had regained consciousness and was staggering groggily across the orchard, uncertain either where he was or what he should do. However, his wild gesticulations startled the boar into further flight, sending him careering straight towards the group of glamorous celebrities. The daunting prospect of five hundred pounds of bristling black malevolence hurtling in their direction had them all momentarily rooted to the spot, except Claude who instantly saw this as an opportunity for glory. 'Here, let me have your stole, Valentina,' he said urgently, removing the Contessa's recently acquired length of cashmere from around her shoulders and advancing rather gingerly towards the boar, waving it aloft like a medieval battle-standard.

The stole was red and Claude, on tiptoe, resembled a Spanish toreador trying to engage the attention of a fighting bull. His intentions were no doubt good but he was not aware that, far from being attracted towards the maddening flap of red cloth as a bull would be, the boar was deterred. Inadvertently, therefore, Claude appeared to chase Basil towards the rest of the guests rather than lure him from their path. The effect was just as if a rogue Catherine Wheel had slipped its fixing and was careering at random among a Guy Fawkes party crowd, except that in this case the 'firework' was a big black hog with yellow tusks and devilish, red-rimmed eyes. The Contessa screamed and began to run and the other guests and the models followed suit, all dashing in different directions. One of the more cowardly male guests shamelessly shinned up a tree, leaving his young trophy-wife at the foot unable to follow because of her tight skirt and high heels. Two of the models ran in panic to the garbage pen and shut themselves in among the rubbish and verdigris, irretrievably staining two outfits of fabulous winter white cable-stitch cashmere. Fenella and Nell stared helplessly at each other and then both shouted at Tally to do something. Tally began to shout at Mick who staggered up holding his head and yelling that he couldn't help it and that the bloody pig had scrambled his brains!

Meanwhile Basil continued zigzagging across the lawn from one side to the other trying to escape the threat which he perceived coming from all directions at once. In the process he caught the end of the Contessa's stole on one of his tusks and tore it from Claude's grip. The red banner flapping around his head frightened him even more and he plunged and snorted and proceeded to prove the warden's observation that a boar could run faster than a human being. Fixing his sights on the dense bank of rhododendron bushes which flanked the drive he put his head down and charged, heedless of who or what stood between him and safety. It happened to be Claude who, having lost the Contessa's stole, was standing irresolutely, trying to work out how best to retrieve it from the boar's tusk without endangering his own skin.

Hesitation was his undoing. Basil saw an opportunity and took it, blasting past and hurling Claude to the ground, trampling the cashmere stole as he stampeded for the bushes, disappearing into the dark security of their deep green foliage. Freed from the boar's tusk, the stole undulated into the air behind him and settled gently over Claude's prostrate body like a tattered red shroud. Winded and humiliated, Claude lay motionless for several seconds.

There was no sympathy from his lady. From the centre of the lawn the Contessa shrieked loudly and shrilly at her ignominiously felled lover. '*Basta!* Get up! You make a fool of yourself and of me! I will not be made to look stupid. My family honour is at stake – and my stole, *mama mia*! Get up! Get up!' She stamped her leather-booted foot angrily.

Leaving Claude to his own devices, Fenella and Nell moved to placate the irate lady. 'Bravo, Basil,' they murmured, nudging each other in secret jubilation.

Claude lifted the tattered stole from his torso and stood up. He had clearly had enough. His eyes were blazing as he brushed the frost off his trousers and approached the Contessa, holding the strip of cashmere away from his body as if it was contaminated. Standing before her he made a minuscule bow, dropped the stole at her feet and said, 'Yours, I believe, Madame.' Then he turned on his heel and stalked angrily off towards the hotel.

'Exit Claude, pursued by a boar,' Tally said to himself in habitual Shakespearean mode, following the retreating Frenchman. 'I suppose I'd better offer him a lift to the station.'

The sound of the boar still crashing about in the undergrowth sent everyone hurrying inside, exchanging excited accounts of their close brush with bristles. The tycoon came down from his tree to be harangued by his angry wife, the models emerged, shame-faced and filthy, from the rubbish pen and Mick shuffled off towards the stables still rubbing his head. It looked like game set and match to Basil.

When Mick had recovered from his 'scrambled brains', he and Rob instigated a boar-hunt but could find no sign of Basil other than damage evidence that he had smashed his way out of the rhododendrons, through the Scots pine plantation and into the island hinterland. 'He could live there forever,' said the wildlife warden when Nell rang him and described the terrain of bracken, grass and whin. 'And he won't harm anyone unless they corner him. Or he might swim for it. They can swim really well, you know. It's a myth that they cut their own throats with their front trotters.'

'We'll leave him to it then,' she said gleefully. 'I hated the thought of him going to the abattoir. Bravo, Basil!'

They did not cheer Basil with such enthusiasm, however, when they realised just how much he might have cost them in lost sales. After the incident in the garden, most of the guests took the first available helicopter flight, failing to pursue further purchases which might otherwise have been inspired by the brisk, bright weather and the glühwein. But there was no time to mourn what might have been, with another batch of guests due that afternoon and another banquet and fashion show to stage. Claude announced his intention of leaving immediately but the Contessa stuck to her plan to stay another night and Fenella allocated to one of her sales girls the unenviable task of keeping her amused and fostering her interest in further purchases.

'Will you come and see me off, Nell?' asked Claude throatily when she went to tell him that the car was ready to take him to the station. The Frenchman appropriated her hand before she had a chance to deny him and she felt an unexpected surge of annoyance. Even when he seductively turned her arm to kiss the inside of her wrist she detected no sign of semolina pudding. Heavens, she thought. Am I becoming Claudeproof? She firmly withdrew her hand before he could kiss any higher up and shook her head. 'I'm afraid I can't,' she said flatly. 'Tally will drive you.'

Claude's pout resembled that of a spoiled little boy denied an ice cream. 'But I had much rather *you* did,' he said, unable to believe she was resisting his blandishments.

She smiled sweetly, the victorious smile of a reformed addict. 'Don't you think we've done our station farewell scene?' she asked pertinently.

His eyes acquired a hurt look. 'I never wanted it to be *adieu*,' he assured her. 'Only *au revoir*. You are always welcome to visit me in Monte Carlo.'

'Oh?' She cocked a disbelieving eyebrow, remembering the deafening silence which had persisted since July between 'MC' and Taliska. 'I think the field's a little crowded, don't you? So many heifers and only one bull.'

Claude pursed his lips, gave an eloquent Gallic shrug and picked up his briefcase. '*Tant pis*,' he said coldly, waving imperiously at his luggage. 'Have that brought to the car, would you?'

'Certainly, sir.'

Nell watched his retreating back and remembered that, naked, his buttocks were tight and muscular and as tanned as the rest of him. He might be a shit, but at least he was a gorgeous shit. 'Goodbye,' she said with a hint of genuine regret.

Chapter Seventeen

'No, I will *not* give permission for a boar-hunt. The only kind of shooting party you can send is a camera crew,' Nell shouted angrily down the phone. 'Basil broke out and as far as I'm concerned he's going to stay out. Get the props department to make you a fake boar's head if you must have one. You're *not* putting an apple in Basil's mouth.'

'The whole script is geared around the chefs creating recipes for wild boar,' complained Patrick M. Coyninghame bitterly. 'It'll mean a complete re-write.'

'It won't be the first time,' retorted Nell unrepentantly. 'I seem to remember that we had to arrange a new programme in two days when Gordon made that poor Yorkshireman walk out by banging on about him being "the man who put the chef in Sheffield"!' Her flesh crawled at the possibility of Tally being introduced as 'the man who is the Tal in Taliska'. She could hear the fatuous Gryll giggle even now as he coined the phrase. To Patrick she added, 'At least you've got nearly a week this time.'

Not a bristle of Basil had been sighted since the boar had flattened Claude and plunged into the rhododendrons, and Nell for one was delighted. She was therefore unimpressed by the explosion of wrath from the producer when she had broken the news that his culinary star-turn had done a bunk from the byre. 'I've already recorded the choir of King's College Cambridge singing the *Boar's Head Carol*,' wailed Patrick, beside himself with frustration.

'Well, go back and get them to do *Good King Wenceslas*,' she said tersely. 'The verse about "bring me flesh and bring me wine" should do admirably. Or what about the *Wassail Song*? That bit about "figgy pudding". I'm sure the chefs could invent some super figgy puddings.'

Patrick M. blustered on some more about the expense of importing a boar carcass from Italy and then rang off in a fury. Nell had not enjoyed a phone call so much in years!

Despite Patrick's threats, four days later the electricians and set-builders arrived on schedule to install three competition kitchens in the drawing room which became a temporary studio, complete with black-out curtains and a complicated lighting rig. The *Hot Gryll* logo of a radiant iron grill surrounded by flames was evident everywhere, bringing back vivid and none-too-pleasant memories for Nell. She had not watched a single edition of the programme since she had left. It had been a blessed relief not to suffer the weekly duty of ensuring that what had been put in the can was exactly what was transmitted. She was dreading the moment when she must re-encounter Gordon Gryll and make him welcome at Taliska. The production team and competitors would be staying in the hotel for three days and she wondered how she would manage to stomach seventy-two hours of the egregious GeeGee.

He arrived two days before the recording with his wife, Norma, a former dancer who had once twirled weekly in chiffon and sequins while escorting hopeful competitors to meet Gordon before the camera in his previous incarnation as the compère of a programme called *I Will*. It had been a quiz-show pitting husbands against wives and although the critics panned it for causing marriage breakdowns it had actually been the making of the Gryll partnership. GRYLL SAYS 'I WILL' the headlines had screamed on the showbusiness pages and the match had proved enduring, though infertile. Ten years together had produced no children and, in the tradition of caring celebrities who publicly air their problems in the hope that 'others might realise they do not suffer alone', Gordon and Norma had given interviews and made celebrity appearances on behalf of CHILD – the Committee to Help Infertile Lives Develop. Being suspicious of their motives, it was yet another aspect of the Gryll phenomenon that made Nell cringe.

The Grylls arrived soon after lunch, when Nell was in the office signing Christmas cards. Seeing Gordon's all-too-familiar visage with its close-set brown eyes, squashed nose and carefully combed pepper and salt hair peering over the reception desk, she shrank back to allow Ann Soutar to handle the formalities. 'This place is a gem,' the presenter told the receptionist enthusiastically in his faintly Americanised drawl. 'We can't wait to explore the island.'

'I love islands,' added his wife excitedly. 'There is something magical about being surrounded by water, isn't there? I do hope the programme will convey that, Gordon.' An anxious expression crossed her pretty, oval face in its frame of short, dark curls delicately frosted with grey. She wore a deep pink fleecy wool jacket and matching pants with short boots and looked as if she might have just stepped off a ski-slope.

Her husband smiled at her in the midst of signing

the register, an intimate, cosy smile conveying an unspoken understanding. 'I'll make sure it does, sweetheart. I can't have my greatest fan disappointed, can I? We'll have to get Nell to give us a guided tour so that we can get the feel of the place.' He looked at Ann inquiringly, apparently unaware of the figure hovering in the shadows behind her. 'Is Miss McLean anywhere about?'

Nell forced herself to step forward and smile. 'I'm right here, Gordon,' she said briskly, offering her hand. 'Welcome to Taliska.'

Gordon was visibly surprised by the emergence of a thin blonde when he had been expecting a plump brownie, but rapidly controlled his astonishment and exposed his famous teeth. 'I am so sorry, Nell. I didn't recognise you. You've changed a great deal since I last saw you.' He took her hand and shook it vigorously before drawing his companion forward. 'I don't think you ever met my wife, Norma, did you? Norma, this is Nell McLean, the owner of this fabulous place.'

'Well, joint-owner,' Nell demurred, shaking Norma's hand. 'No, we haven't met, which seems amazing considering how long I worked with Gordon.'

'I never usually hang around the studio,' Norma told Nell earnestly. 'I know how hard it is to concentrate when there are so many points of possible conflict. A wife would only add to the distractions. But I wouldn't have missed this Christmas broadcast. Gordon is looking forward to it so much.'

Nell found herself warming to this unaffected, eager woman who was so clearly fond of her husband and proud of his achievements. She was appropriately named, it seemed – a genuinely normal Norma whose pretty, level head had apparently not been turned by association with television's infamous 'punmaster'. And in her company Gordon seemed a different character, calmer, less self-conscious and more – well, the term applied again, Nell thought – more *normal*.

'I heard you saying you'd like a guided tour and I'd be delighted of course,' Nell told them. 'I'll be waiting in the office here. Just come on down when you've made yourselves at home.'

All the time she was showing them around the hotel and grounds Nell was on tenterhooks, waiting grimly for Gordon to apply some horrendous pun to each aspect of the island's attractions, but his comments were confined to unembellished expressions of pleasure and appreciation. The only moment of drama came when the wind suddenly gusted cold and biting around their ears and he clamped his hands to the thick greying thatch on his head. 'Keep your hair on, Gordon!' he exclaimed.

Norma gave an infectious giggle and Nell cried out in genuine surprise, 'I didn't know you had to!' before she fully realised what she had said. She blushed furiously, angry at herself for appearing so rude. 'I'm sorry,' she murmured. 'I didn't mean to say that.'

Gordon was grinning, still hanging on firmly to his hair. 'Wind is the toupée wearer's worst enemy,' he said ruefully. 'Fortunately, it doesn't blow in studios, but television lights do glare off a bald head. I like to think that my toupée is an object of practicality as well as conceit.'

'It's a very good one,' Nell observed in confusion. Had she really never encountered the real Gordon Gryll? Was he bald as well as pleasant?

'He doesn't have to worry really,' Norma said loyally. 'I've always told him people don't care what he looks like, it's his personality they relate to.'

'Toupée or not toupée, that is the question,' chanted Gordon with a flash of his on-screen persona. 'I'm afraid it's the image they really relate to, my love.' He put his arm around his wife and turned to Nell. 'And this is the one who makes sure they get it. She puts the wretched thing on for me every morning and, thanks to her, it's never moved yet.'

Nell was not certain whether he was referring to his character or his hair-piece but they were distracted at that moment by Norma's cry of pleasure. 'Oh look – a cow! Isn't she beautiful!' They were standing at the back of the stables and over one of the stalls a dark horned head peered curiously, long-lashed brown eyes blinking. A loud moo greeted them as they drew nearer.

'This is Marsali,' Nell informed her guests. 'We have two Jersey cows to supply our milk. Usually they're turned out during the day, even in winter, unless there's snow on the ground of course. But Marsali is soon to calve and so we're keeping her in.'

'She's pregnant? Oh, how wonderful!' Norma balanced like the dancer she once was on the lowest rail of the stall and hung over the highest, reaching out to pat Marsali's smooth honey-coloured shoulder. Behind her caressing hand stretched the tight, fecund swell of the cow's belly. 'When is the calf due?'

Nell shrugged. 'I'm not absolutely sure. Around New Year, I think. Our cowman Mick is the great expert.'

'How perfect,' crowed Norma joyously, turning shining eyes towards her husband. 'I wish we could be here to see it born.'

Gordon patted her shoulder consolingly. 'Well, you never know,' he said, 'it may be early.' He looked solemnly at Nell and said confidingly, 'We aren't able to have children ourselves. It makes the idea of birth so much more poignant. We've had to come to terms with Christmas for that reason but we love it now.'

'I see,' said Nell, once more nonplussed by this unexpected side of Gordon's real personality. She had known of the Grylls' childlessness because of the publicity it had received, but had never appreciated the personal heartbreak of it. 'We're hoping for a heifer,' she added, for want of anything else to say. 'Then we can keep her and add her to the milk-herd.'

'And if it's a boy – a bull-calf?' Norma asked with foreboding.

'Well, we can't keep him really,' Nell said apologetically. 'Not for very long anyway.'

Before Norma could inquire further about the fate of a bull-calf, Gordon asked: 'What happened here?' He had moved to the other end of the byre where the broken wooden partition still displayed evidence of Basil's breakout.

'That was where we were keeping the wild boar,' Nell confessed. 'He escaped, as you probably know.'

'Yes, I do,' responded Gordon. 'It was excellent news. We didn't like the idea of killing a boar for the programme, did we, Norma?'

His wife shivered and jumped down from her perch. 'Absolutely not,' she declared. 'And I don't think the audience would have liked it either. Where is the boar now?'

Nell laughed. 'We don't know. There's been a camera crew out on the island trying to find him but he hasn't been seen since he broke out. He might have swum to the mainland.'

'Will he be all right?' asked Norma anxiously.

'Apparently – unless he starts digging up someone's potato crop or moving in on their pigs! I think our farming neighbour Duncan McCandlish might resort to the shotgun if his sows start giving birth to bristly little throwbacks!'

'Let's hope he takes care, then,' said Gordon. 'I wouldn't like to think he'd escaped a *Hot Gryll* just to end up a peppered pork steak.'

'What are the chefs cooking instead?' Nell asked inquisitively.

Gordon gave her a mocking smile. 'The script is littered with references to my "goose being cooked" and the chefs taking a "gander" at the ingredients tray, so you may assume that the audience will be "cackling" and the choir will be singing "Christmas is coming . . ." '

' ". . . The *goose* is getting fat"!' Nell and Norma carolled merrily in unison, and burst out laughing.

'Correct,' nodded Gordon. 'In fact, everything you wanted to know about goosing and were afraid to ask!'

'Do you write them yourself?' Nell could not resist asking.

'What – the puns?' Gordon's eyebrows rose steeply. 'Did you never attend a script conference, Nell? I write the best ones and the others arrive by committee.' He made a comical face. 'And if you believe that, you'll believe anything.'

That afternoon spent with the Grylls radically changed Nell's attitude towards *Hot Gryll* and its compère. She was puzzled and astonished that she should have worked so long with someone and have misunderstood him so completely. Now she realised that the Gordon Gryll she had known had been merely the projected image. The grin and the toupée formed a mask behind which the real man hid, and the script full of puns was a disguise for Gordon's true-life diffidence and his unremarkable ordinariness. The man was a chameleon. His programme persona was a false identity, an image created purely and simply for the camera, a larger-than-life character which could penetrate the layers of technical equipment and electronic wizardry and emerge through the screen as a lively, witty personality, whereas the real Gordon Gryll would have been submerged and nullified.

Among the minibus-load of programme staff who arrived the evening before the recording was Caroline, still tanned from her three-week honeymoon in the Bahamas. 'It was wonderful, Nell,' she confided. 'We just lay around all day with no clothes on and swam and . . . well, you know. Davy looks fantastic with an all-over tan, and I really mean *all-over*! No white bits.'

'Well, you look pretty fantastic yourself,' Nell assured her friend. 'And you're really happy?'

'Ecstatic! I can recommend married life – you should try it. Any new men sniffing around your new sexy shape?'

'Not really. Do you think it's sexy? I'm beginning to think I'm too skinny.' As she said it Nell could hardly believe that it was her own voice. She never thought she would ever admit that she might have gone a bit too far and too fast in the starvation stakes.

'Well, I was wondering whether to say so,' responded Caroline guiltily. 'But I thought you'd snap my head off and accuse me of being jealous or something.'

Nell gave a hollow laugh. 'What a two-faced bitch you must think me,' she said. 'But do you know – you're right. A week or so ago I might have, but I seem to have seen the light a bit since then. Perhaps there has to be a happy medium in this shape business. I just hope I can find it.'

'I'm sure you will. Especially if you're happy,' crowed Caroline. 'Happiness is a great figure improver. Look at me – I put on three pounds on honeymoon and Davy says I'm all the better for it. So I suppose I must believe him.'

Nell cocked her head to regard her effervescent friend. 'Yes Caro, I think you must. You've never looked better.'

Standing before her mirror whilst changing for dinner Nell took another fiercely analytical look at herself. In the glass she saw a willowy blonde wearing a svelte, blue cashmere dress but was that really Nell McLean, any more than the cuddly, size sixteen teddy bear had been? Since she did not have the excuse of needing an on-camera persona she had to ask herself which of her own self-images was the real one. Was she a plump, jolly extrovert who liked food and drink, or a thin, languid bulimic who liked clothes and make-up? Every time she threw up, and she shamefully had to admit that she still did so at least three or four times a week, did she metaphorically discard more of her real self? Was her vomiting one of the less savoury characteristics of the person she was turning herself into? Or was the real Nell McLean someone who had yet to be revealed . . . Who would emerge when she had managed to conquer the bulimia? Would she be an elf or an elephant?

She shook herself crossly, reminding herself that meanwhile the hotel was full of television people waiting for dinner. She went down to the kitchen.

'What do you think of Eye-Level now you've met him again?' she asked Calum, watching him unmould the delicate scallop mousses which would start the night's menu.

'Outrageous, ignorant, the same as ever,' muttered the chef, reaching for his whisk to finish the accompanying egg and lemon sauce.

'I think he's changed,' observed Nell. 'He seems quite agreeable.'

'Perhaps it's you who has changed.' The chef was concentrating on his pan and did not appear to notice her sharp glance. 'Now please let me alone! This sauce is a notorious curdler.'

'Just like Patrick M.!' exclaimed Nell. 'He could curdle milk at twenty paces.' She beat a hasty retreat and bumped straight into the object of her opprobrium about to enter the kitchen.

'Major hitch,' cried Patrick, his complexion ruddier than ever, his hands plucking at his hair in agitation. 'I must speak to Calum. One of the competitors has flu!'

The three chefs who were due to compete in the Christmas special had been expected that evening. The news of indisposition in this culinary cohort had reached Patrick only five minutes before.

Nell determinedly blocked his progress. 'Sorry Patrick,' she said firmly. 'Calum won't let anyone in right now. You'll have to wait until after dinner.'

'I only want to ask him if he'll stand in. Do you think he will? He was pretty caustic with Gordon last time he was on.'

No wonder Patrick's hair was thinning, thought Nell. He literally tore it out! 'I thought he was excellent last time,' she remarked, 'but you can't ask him now or you'll get curdled sauce. Come and have a drink.'

She tucked her arm companionably in that of the rather astonished producer and marched him back through the dining room to the bar which, predictably, was crowded with programme personnel. Tally was doing a roaring trade in drinks with help from an uncharacteristically jovial Mac, whose mellow bonhomie made Nell immediately suspect him of being back on the dope. He would do great trade among the media folk if he was flogging the stuff again, she thought. But supposing the police got wind of it? That was all they needed! A drugs raid while they were on television!

'Mac's not on the wacky baccy again, is he?' she asked Tally in an undertone when the fisherman was out of earshot. 'He looks as happy as Larry.'

'Yes, he's been like a dog with two tails ever since he arrived,' Tally replied agitatedly. 'But I'm pretty sure it's not dope. Something's happened. Flora's in the dining room – why don't you ask her?'

Nell gave her brother a quizzical look. Tally looked tense and anxious, a complete contrast to Mac. 'Calm down, will you,' she advised. 'I'll go in a minute. Patrick wants Calum to compete on *Hot Gryll*. One of the other chefs has flu.'

'So fine,' Tally said, tipping tonics into two glasses at once and flicking his head to keep his forelock out of his eyes. 'It'll do him good. Now do go and talk to Flora, Nell, please. I can't leave the bar.'

Nell found Flora polishing glasses, her sapphire eyes shining as brightly as they were. During the winter months she had agreed to wait at table when necessary, in addition to fulfilling her role as housekeeper. 'It's extra money when there's not many fish,' she had told Tally. 'Mac worries about making ends meet in the winter.'

'Mac seems very happy tonight,' Nell observed, watching Flora select another glass and begin to rub at it with a white linen cloth. 'In fact, you're both neon-lit. Have you been at the grass again?' Apart from her ocular sparkle, Flora looked particularly well in the scabious-blue uniform dress worn by Taliska waitresses for serving dinner. It set off her honeysuckle hair and pale, luminous complexion and her full breasts strained the slightly-too-small bodice. She even puts Libby in the shade, thought Nell. No wonder Tally's potty about her.

'Grass?' asked Flora, puzzled. 'Oh, you mean marijuana? No, no!' she laughed delightedly. 'That's all over and done with.' Her lilting island voice made it seem a ridiculous concept. 'We're just happy, that's all. We've had some good news.'

'Well, that's excellent,' Nell said warmly. 'Anything we can all enjoy?'

Flora shook her head. 'Not just now. Later, maybe.' A Mona Lisa smile remained on her lips as if glued in place and she would say no more.

In true media tradition the programme staff got plastered that evening. Patrick went all effusive when, without much persuasion, Calum agreed to stand in for the sick chef-competitor. The Grylls insisted on buying everyone drinks and sat contentedly together in the midst of a noisy gaggle of electricians, floor managers, cameramen and sound men all reminiscing about past broadcasting triumphs and disasters. Then, tiring of a groove which was too well worn, Caroline brought out a cassette player and put on a tape of Christmas carols and soon everyone was singing along, changing the words to fit the occasion.

On the first Hot Gryll *programme*
The network sent to me
Patrick Coyninghame, spelt with an E!
On the second Hot Gryll *programme*

The network sent to me
Two Gordon Grylls
And a Coyninghame, spelt with an E!
On the third Hot Gryll *programme*
The network sent to me
Three Competing Chefs
Two Gordon Grylls
And a Coyninghame, spelt with an E!

So it seemed Nell was not the only one to realise that there were two Gordon Grylls!

The next day the crew filmed an opening sequence from the helicopter and finally got a shot of Basil rooting for acorns at the edge of the ancient oak-woods at the island's north end. So the boar would be appearing in the programme after all, only 'live' rather than dead! In his introduction, while mentioning Taliska cheese, Gordon insisted that shots of Marsali the pregnant cow should be shown and he carefully erased any references to veal from the rest of the script, although he was unable to resist borrowing a seasonal phrase or two to accompany the cow's appearance, such as 'away in a manger' and 'the cattle are lowing'! It had been agreed at the time of drawing up the contract that Tally and Nell should be the guest judges, giving Gordon ample opportunity for twin references throughout – like how they had gone to 'double trouble' to welcome the programme and how their judgment would be 'didy-dandymous' and 'twice as fair' as any other. It was an appropriate irony, Nell thought, that she who had inflicted so many indigestible ingredients on judges in the past should now be placed in the gustatory firing line herself, and even more ironic that she, who had castigated 'Sick Transit Gloria' for throwing up all over her car, would undoubtedly be doing exactly the same as her inglorious predecessor, though hopefully not in transit and not over anybody's dashboard. One complication arose because of Calum's last-minute inclusion among the competitors. The McLeans could hardly select their own chef as the winner without being accused of bias. Eventually, Patrick devised a way of making it impossible for them to know which dish had been prepared by which chef so that their decision would be impartial. With stand-in and compromise all arranged, everything seemed set for a successful telecast.

However, on the morning of the recording Flora waylaid Tally after staff breakfast and asked if she could talk to him. Puzzled, he went with her to his flat and was about to give her the good morning kiss they could not exchange in public when she blurted out her news.

Avoiding his lips she said huskily, 'I'm pregnant.'

His immediate reaction was ecstatic. He grabbed her hands. 'Pregnant? Flora, that's wonderful. God, it's marvellous. A baby – fantastic! When did you find out?'

'A week ago. I went to the doctor.'

'A week! Why didn't you tell me before? Did you think I'd be angry? I'm not, I'm thrilled. Honestly – absolutely delighted. Flora, what's wrong?' She looked uncomfortable, withdrew her hands from his and began fidgeting with the button of her housekeeper's overall. 'Is everything all right? Is the baby all right?' he asked anxiously.

'Aye, everything's fine. The doctor said I was very healthy and there shouldna be any problems.'

He looked relieved. 'That's great,' he said. 'When is it due?'

'In June,' she said, still fiddling. 'The middle of June.'

'It might be born on my birthday. Wouldn't that be a coincidence!' He did some swift calculations and then frowned. 'But you're nearly three months gone.' He reached out to take her by the shoulders, gazing down into her wide, dark-blue eyes. 'Why didn't you tell me before? Are you worried about Mac?'

She shrugged his hands off but kept her eyes steadily on his. 'No, Tally, I'm not. He's delighted. Canna wait to be a father.'

Tally looked stunned. He shook his head violently, rejecting what he had heard. 'But he isn't the father. This is our baby – we have to get married,' he stuttered, groping for the right words.

She shook her head back at him. 'No, Tally. I *am* married. Mac and I have prayed for this for ten years. This is our bairn, Mac's and mine. Nothing to do with you.'

He grabbed her arm. 'What do you mean, nothing to do with me? You know that's not true. You never got pregnant in ten years with Mac and now you are. This is my baby, Flora – you know it is. It must be!'

She shook her head, remaining stoically calm in the face of his growing agitation. 'No. I am married to Mac. He is my husband and he is the father of my child.'

'That's rubbish. Crap! It must be mine,' Tally cried almost hysterically. 'There are tests – we can have blood-tests! I love you, Flora, and I love our baby. It is mine – I have a right!'

'You have no right, Tally,' she said stubbornly. 'God has answered our prayers. Mac is the wean's father, just as I am its mother.'

'God? What has He got to do with it? This is no

immaculate conception. This baby was made here, in my bed, under my roof. It is not God's or Mac's, it is *mine*. You can't do this to me, Flora. You can't!' He sank down into a chair, his face white, his eyes staring at her, pleading. 'I love you.'

A look of great pity crossed her face. She sat down opposite him, one hand on her belly. 'What am I doing?' she asked mildly. 'A woman knows who is the father of her child, and Mac is the father of this one. Dinna make things difficult, Tally. We have sinned for too long, you and I, and we have to stop now. It's over, you understand. Over.'

'How can it be over?' he asked, his voice breaking on a sob. 'I love you. Just think, Flora – think about it. You've been married ten years. Ten years without becoming pregnant and now you expect me to believe that this child is Mac's – that some miracle has occurred. Well, there's no miracle, Flora. I am the father of your child and you know that to be so. I'll talk to Mac – he'll understand. He won't want to be the father of another man's child.'

The stubborn expression on Flora's face became mutinous. She stood up in agitation. 'You willna tell him, Tally,' she said, leaning over him, spitting out the words. 'Because if you do, you'll kill him! You've seen what this baby means to him. He's over the moon – so proud and happy. It would kill him to think that you and I had . . . that there might be some doubt about it being his. You wouldna do that to him, I know you wouldna!' She was pleading but she was blazing. Her whole body was shaking with the effort of persuasion. 'And if you do I'll deny it. He'll believe me because he wants to believe me and nothing will change. Even if he threw me out I'd no' marry you. This is Mac's baby. He married me when I begged him to take me away from my father. He knew what that man was doing to me and he rescued me. I owe him, Tally. I owe him a child in return.'

At first Tally did not comprehend her meaning. 'He *rescued* you, from your father? What do you mean? Are you saying your father abused you? Incest – is that what you're saying?'

She nodded, her face flaming with shame and anger. 'It happens. I'm no' the only island girl who's suffered. I didna want to tell you, I didna want anyone to know! But Mac knew and he took me away and married me and loved me and gave me respect. You see now, don't you? The bairn is his. I owe it to him!'

A terrible realisation came to Tally in that moment. He sat stock-still, cheeks ashen, tears welling in his eyes. His handsome face crumpled in despair. He knew now that the whole affair had been a farce. Flora had never loved him at all.

'You did this on purpose,' he whispered, still hardly able to credit in his mind what his intuition had discerned. 'You never loved me. It was all for this!' He gestured towards her belly, to the place where the baby, his baby, was still only a few centimetres long. But what plans and machinations had she employed to achieve that momentous bundle of cells? 'How could you do it? You used me. Christ! I see it now.' He sank his head in his hands and let the tears flow. His voice continued, thick and gasping. 'You only came to me to get pregnant. That's all it ever was. What an almighty fool I am!' His voice trailed off and he began to shake as if boneless, like a rag doll.

Flora stretched her hand out towards him in a gesture of contrition but she did not touch him. Tears were slipping slowly down her cheeks. 'You're wrong, Tally. I didna just do it for that. You're no' a fool. I told you after you nearly drowned that I loved you and I did – I do. But I promised God I'd stop if I ever got pregnant. I'm sorry, Tally,' she said softly and turned and left the room, closing the door gently behind her.

A small excited 'studio' audience came from Salach for the programme recording. The BBC designers and set-dressers had been hard at work and the hotel was decorated as it might have been in its Victorian heyday, with garlands of evergreens and pine cones tied with ribbons and looped down the banisters of the great staircase and along the dados in the hall, where a huge Christmas tree was hung with ropes of silver beads and painted trinkets and tiny, pinprick lights. Against this background the competing chefs were introduced on camera before they trooped into the drawing room 'studio' where the quiz itself was to take place. Apart from Calum there was a gay, middle-aged chef-proprietor from a hotel in the Lake District and a buxom lady cook who had won awards for her farmhouse high teas in Devon. True to his 'on camera' persona, Gordon Gryll annoyed them all by immediately giving them nicknames. They were 'the Windermere Wonder', 'Devon Dora' and 'Calum-netics' and he grouped them together with enormous personal amusement as 'Lakes, Teas and Bumpsidaisy'.

Watching the first half of the recording from the audience, Nell had to admit that it was outrageous, but she still couldn't help laughing. The laughter took her mind off Tally, who was sitting beside her looking like a candidate for intensive care. When he had not appeared for lunch she had gone to look for him and found him still slumped in his sitting room, his eyes swollen from weeping, a well-nudged bottle of whisky between his knees.

'What the hell is wrong?' she asked with concern. 'You look as if the world has come to an end.'

''S about right,' he muttered, nodding stiffly at the floor. 'My world . . . come to an end.' His voice was slurred from the whisky and husky from the paroxysm of despair which had overcome him after Flora left. Men don't cry, he'd always believed, and he had certainly never really felt the urge to do so since the age of five. But now he knew that men did cry, wretchedly, and with great physical distress. Misery had erupted from him like lava from a volcano and the great love which had grown in him over six months had withered and shrunk in six minutes leaving him emotionally crumpled like a tin used to demonstrate a vacuum. And into that vacuum he had poured whisky, the only thing he could think of to fill it and deaden the pain.

'What's happened?' asked Nell, wondering in a panic whether she would be able to sort him out and sober him up in time for the recording. 'What's wrong?' She sat on the edge of his chair and put a tentative arm around his shoulders. To her amazement he turned to her like a child and burst into fresh howls of grief, burying his face in her armpit. It was an uncomfortable position, not to mention a somewhat embarrassing one, but she did not pull away. She sat and awkwardly patted him, murmuring reassurances, her mind racing to try and guess the reason for this sudden and total collapse.

Like thousands of male graduates of the English public school system Tally had gone through life concealing his feelings, sheltering behind a façade of cynicism and witticisms, denying himself emotional peaks and troughs in order to prevent any face-losing lapses of control. It was a technique learned in the early days of boarding-school life when the trembling misery of banishment from the parental home was quickly disguised by the acquisition of a stiff upper lip, hastened by the heartless teasing of boys only slightly more senior who had been forced through the same torture themselves in the previous pupil intake. It paid to appear cynical and carefree because there was no joy in teasing a boy who did not react, or who responded only with a quip or a joke.

The men who were the product of this system worked admirably in most of the offices of British government and in the boardrooms of the City of London, but such sangfroid had one great drawback. It tended to crumble under really severe stress. And a frozen upper lip which has not been allowed to quiver for many years tends to shatter if tapped by the mallet of misfortune. Tally's cool façade had collapsed like a house of cards.

'It's Flora, isn't it?' Nell probed gently, raising her voice above the tearing sound of her brother's sobs. 'It must be Flora. Who else could put you in this awful state?' She was more or less talking to herself, hardly expecting Tally to hear, let alone respond.

'She's a witch,' breathed Tally on a gasp of air. 'A scheming, calculating witch!' He withdrew his head from Nell's oxter as if he had suddenly realised where it was and buried his face in his hands, jolting the whisky bottle so that it fell from between his knees. Nell grabbed it and lifted it to the light to see how much was left. A quarter. How full had it been when he started?

'What has Flora done?' asked Nell, putting the bottle on the nearby table. When there was no response from Tally she tried again. 'She looked all right at lunch. I've just seen her.'

Tally raised his face to regard his sister with bloodshot eyes. The pull of his fingers on his cheeks gave him the mournful look of a bloodhound. 'She's a bitch,' he slurred angrily. 'A fucking bitch!'

Irritated by such uninformative slagging off of Flora, Nell stood up and went next door into Tally's kitchen. It was pristine. There was no evidence of any recent tea parties, no tins of shortbread or used cups. She wrung a tea-towel out under the cold tap and took it through to him, placing it against his flushed cheek. The chill of it seemed to perk him up a little. 'Well, if you won't tell me what's wrong at least tell me how pissed you are,' said Nell. 'Are you going to be able to do the programme this afternoon or aren't you? I think we should tell Patrick.'

'No!' Tally held up a hand and took the cloth, wiping it around his ravaged face. 'Don't tell anyone anything. I'll be all right in a few minutes.' His breathing was beginning to steady.

'Well, you don't look all right. Maybe a cold shower would do the trick.' Nell did not want to appear unsympathetic but was aware that tens of thousands of pounds' worth of programme staff and equipment were waiting on their presence downstairs. 'Come on, stand up.' She grasped Tally's hands and heaved and he came up from his chair far more readily than she had hoped. She pushed him gently in the direction of the bathroom. 'Go on. Have a shower and a shave. I'll wait.'

At the door Tally turned towards her. 'Get Flora out of the place,' he said thickly. 'I don't want to see her when I come down.'

He let the water sluice down over his face and chest, closing his inflamed eyes to the shower's stinging jet. I feel like one of those Gulf War pilots who were questioned by Saddam Hussein's bullies, he thought, almost expecting to find the evidence of torture all over his body. It was bruised and aching, as if wracked by a sudden and virulent virus. 'Flora *is* a virus,' he protested aloud to the echoing tiles. 'She took me over and now she's knackered me! A stud bull – that's what she's made me. She might as well have taken my semen like the AI man. That would have been fairer, instead of pretending to love me. Making me love her – it was cruel and evil! I hope the child is a cuckoo in the nest. I hope it grows up to hate them. I hope it murders them in their beds.'

Misery flowed out of him and was washed away in the flood of water. There was no instant return of the old, perky, cynical Tally but at least he no longer felt as if he would implode and disappear into some spatial black hole inside his head. As he towelled himself down, he reflected that he had handed out some pretty shitty treatment to women in his time, but he'd never actually pinched their identity as Flora had done. She had stolen his genes. It hadn't been love in the afternoon, it had been daylight robbery!

So it was not a hundred per cent Tally who sat beside Nell at the recording of *Hot Gryll* but at least he was there in body. He had peered over the precipice and he had not jumped, but it had been a close shave.

When it came to the judging, however, faced with a choice between a rich *confit d'oie*, a supreme of goose with gooseberries and a spicy, mango-flavoured rice dish called Coronation Goose, Tally was utterly at a loss, unable either to make up his mind or to offer any worthwhile comment. It was all he could do to force down a morsel of each, thinking even under the arc-lights of Flora and the baby that was his but not his.

It was the reverse of the twins' previous television appearance together, during the New Age travellers incident. After one glimpse of herself on a monitor, Nell knew she was now of a size and shape beloved by the camera and appeared cool and smiling, making pleasant remarks about each of the dishes, declaring them all to be delicious and unique in their own way. Carrying Tally and Gordon along with her, she opted for the gooseberry goose, mainly on the grounds that it was unlikely to be Calum's. Sure enough, it turned out to be Devon Dora's and the beaming farmhouse cook gratefully received the accolade of *Christmas Chef of the Year* and the prize of a tour of the famous goose-liver paté country around Strasbourg, which had been swiftly swapped for the original prize of a week's boar-hunting in the Apennines. Bless Basil for escaping, Nell thought. How much happier the buxom Dora will be among *paté de foie gras* than she would have been among guns and tuskers! For his part, Calum was reasonably content to win the quiz section outright and to have resisted murdering Gordon Gryll for his overworked Calum-netics joke.

When the recording was over, as soon as she politely could, Nell retired to the Ladies and stuck her fingers down her throat, justifying her action with the thought that almost anyone, faced with the richness of the dishes she'd been forced to consume, would have done the same. She very much doubted if she would ever be able to eat goose again.

Chapter Eighteen

'Granny Kirsty's got a toyboy,' Nell announced to Tally, replacing the telephone receiver with a smirk.

'What!'

'She says she can't come for Christmas because someone called Jim Menzies is taking her to Rothesay.' Nell began to giggle. ' "I'm going doon the watter, Nell," she says. "Doon the watter wi' Jim!" '

'Who the hell is Jim Mingy?' spluttered Tally.

'I suppose it's spelt Menzies but she pronounces it Mingies. He's a member of her bridge circle. She's mentioned him before. They're an unbeatable partnership, apparently – and he's only seventy.'

Tally caught his sister's eye and burst out laughing. 'Good old Granny Kirsty,' he cried between gusts. 'A dirty festive weekend.'

'They won't be on their own,' Nell informed him primly. 'The whole bridge circle is going. I expect they'll have a rubber between the turkey and the trifle. No, Tally – not that kind of rubber.'

He stared at her innocently. 'Did I say anything? Still, I hope even geriatrics practise safe sex. It would be a shame to die of AIDS before the telegram comes from the Queen.'

'God, you don't get any nicer, do you?' Nell made a face. 'Still, it's good to hear a touch of the old Tally back again. I was beginning to think you'd signed the solemnity pledge.'

He sobered down suddenly. 'It feels like it sometimes.' He didn't mention Flora but they both knew he was thinking of her, as he still did a hundred times a day. 'What are we going to do for Christmas? Sit and stare at each other?'

'Well, I don't know about you, but I'm going to enjoy a lovely relaxing weekend without any guests in the hotel, before the rush starts again at Hogmanay.'

'It's all right for you. Alasdair's coming, isn't he?'

'Well yes, but he's your guest as much as mine.'

'Huh – I'm not the one he stares at like a mooncalf when he thinks no one's looking.' Tally stood up and went to the office window. 'God, it's raining again. It's been raining ever since the TV boys left.' He glared at the drops which joined forces to trail little rivers down the panes. 'It's going to seem really weird having Christmas without any of our family.' And without Flora, he thought grimly. He hadn't spoken to her since she'd told him about the baby.

'I thought you'd be quite glad,' said Nell. 'Our last family get-together wasn't exactly a roaring success.'

The McLean clan would be scattered around the world over Christmas. Donalda and Hal had finally decided to set up home in New York and had bought themselves an apartment in mid-town Manhattan. There was a parcel each for Nell and Tally already lying under the Taliska tree, gift-wrapped from Bloomingdales. Ian had spent most of December in Bombay following a disastrous explosion at his much-vaunted distillery which had injured several workers. Sinead and Ninian were flying out to join him over Christmas and Niamh was going on an Alpine skiing holiday with some student friends.

'I know, but it's a mess, isn't it?' Tally said

dejectedly. 'We've cut ourselves off here good and proper, haven't we, and what have we to show for it? An overdraft, an island and turkey for two!'

'Five actually,' Nell reminded him. Mick and Ann were spending Christmas with their respective families and Rob and Libby were taking off to a Highland ski-resort where the snow had come blessedly early to boost the flagging Scottish winter-sports industry. It would be a farewell trip for them because 'Women's Lib' had finally declared herself homesick and announced her intention of returning to Australia in the New Year. Of the staff, only Calum and Ginny would remain at Taliska and the hotel would be closed until 30 December when a satisfactory number of guests was booked in to celebrate the New Year in what was hoped would be a healthy manner. 'Although health and Hogmanay simply don't go together,' Tally had been heard to observe.

The telephone rang and Nell picked it up. 'Wondered if you'd take in a stray at Christmas, darling?' Fenella's familiar voice asked. 'Nobody loves me.'

'I don't believe that,' her friend retorted, sensing a Fenella scheme afoot. 'But you'd be very welcome. You might be the answer to a bit of a problem, actually. I was beginning to think a terminal depression had settled over the island!'

'Why? Hasn't the man-mountain pounced yet?'

'There's been no sign of the mountain moving, since you mention it. But it's not me that's low, it's Tally.' All the same, as she said this Nell reflected ruefully that it was a week since Alasdair had been to Taliska and then he had only come to swell the audience for the *Hot Gryll* recording.

'Is Tally looking for a shoulder to cry on, by any happy chance?' asked Fenella.

'Yes. Yes, I rather think he might be,' said Nell, eying her brother, who was still gloomily staring out at the soggy view.

'Good. I'll bring some Kleenex,' said Fenella and rang off.

There was an indignant miaow as Nell thrust back her chair and stood up. 'Oh, God. Sorry, Thatcher,' she said as a tortoiseshell streak scatted from under her desk towards the door. 'I didn't know you were there.'

Prior to the general family exodus from Hollywood Gardens, Nell's cat had been ignominiously doped and put in a crate to be air-freighted to Glasgow. She had arrived three days ago and been collected just as the drugs were beginning to wear off. Nell had been gratified when, oblivious to the change in her mistress's appearance, the little cat had instantly recognised her. But the said mistress had subsequently been less impressed at having to spend two agonising hours driving through the glens of Scotland listening to the Thatcher *Miaow-moirs* delivered at a deafening decibel level. Later Nell could not be sure whether it was her own personal magnetism, the constant rain or some well-buttered paws which kept the little cat at home but she appeared to be adjusting well and had already brought several gifts of dead mice, gleaned from the hotel policies.

'Yuk!' said Nell, bending down to retrieve another small furry offering from under her desk. 'That I can do without.'

'What's wrong with Fenella?' asked Tally sharply, not turning around. 'I thought you liked her.'

'I do,' replied Nell, strolling across to him and dangling the mouse in front of his face. '*This* is the yuk factor.'

'Bloody cat,' he said moodily. 'What have the mice ever done to her?'

'Oh cheer up, Tally,' said Nell crossly, moving towards the door. 'If you won't tell me what the row is all about, for God's sake go and see Flora and Mac and clear the air. You're as miserable as sin.'

She was brought up short by his bald statement, hurled loudly over his shoulder. 'Flora's having a baby!'

Startled, Nell dropped the mouse in the waste-basket and stared at her brother's back. She did not know what to say. 'Oh!' was the sum total of her primary inspiration.

'She says it's not mine.' When he turned to face her Nell could see that there were tears in her brother's eyes.

'And you don't believe her?'

'How can it be Mac's? After ten years? It's improbable, if not impossible.' Tally sank into the chair behind his desk, his head in his hand. 'But what can I do?'

'God, Tally, I don't know. How awful.'

'It's pretty ironic isn't it, coming at Christmas? Child in the manger and all that. Goodwill to all men. Flora hasn't shown me much goodwill.'

Nell perched on the desk beside him. 'I don't suppose she knows what to do either. It's a pretty awkward situation. I mean, maybe it is Mac's. They've been dying for children, haven't they?'

'Yes, and isn't she clever? She's got just what she wanted for Christmas.' Tally's voice was hard and cold, brittle with anger.

'You don't think she did it on purpose?' asked Nell, aghast. 'Oh no! I'm sure she wouldn't.'

'Why not?' Tally asked dully. 'We never talked about taking precautions. I adored her so much I just never thought about anything like that. I suppose in the back of my mind I just assumed that she couldn't have children. I keep telling myself what a complete fool I've been. I wouldn't have told you but I've got to talk to someone. I even thought of telling Mac. I mean, he has a right to know that the baby might not be his, hasn't he? But somehow I just can't.'

Nell's reaction to this idea was instant and instinctive. 'I'm sure that would be the wrong thing to do.'

'Poor old Mac. She's made just as much of a fool of him as she has of me, only he doesn't know it.'

'What the ear doesn't hear the heart won't grieve over,' said Nell flatly, reflecting that this role reversal was becoming a habit. She could not remember ever feeling sorry for Tally before last week when she had found him poleaxed by Flora's withdrawal, but now here she was full of pity once more. 'It's not poor Mac but poor Tally. I'm so sorry. What a miserable situation – and a miserable end to the affair. You loved Flora very much, didn't you?' At his wordless nod, Nell paused reflectively, then added, 'You were like chalk and cheese though, you know. It would never have worked.'

'I don't see that,' he said truculently. 'But that's by the bye now, isn't it? I look like being an unmarried, unacknowledged father. I wonder how many men look at their children and wonder if they're really theirs? Well, I can look at mine and know it's mine but he or she won't know me.'

'What's the alternative? If you tell Mac you could condemn the child to no father at all. Flora would never forgive you and Mac would probably throw her out. After he's killed you, of course! He wouldn't be gentlemanly about it.'

'You're on her side,' declared Tally angrily. 'You women always stick together.'

'No, I'm not,' Nell responded indignantly. 'I just think she's making the best of a difficult situation. Anyway, if she loves Mac she won't want to leave him, especially if he is the father.'

'But she said she loved *me*,' moaned Tally.

'And she probably did. Perhaps she still does. But a baby can only have one father, can't it? You've got to face that, Tally. And Mac is the one who belongs here – who belongs with Flora, if you like.'

'Are you saying I don't belong? We don't belong, you and I?'

She nodded regretfully. 'Not in the way they mean, the people who were born and bred here. We're incomers, strangers, always will be. It's natural for them to stick together.'

Tally shook his head in bewilderment. 'You've changed, Nell. You were the one who thought we could make our lives here. I only wanted the place as a business proposition.'

'You changed too, though,' she told him gently. 'You tried to become part of the place as much as I did. And in a way you've succeeded.'

'No, we've both failed.'

'Well, we've hardly started. You can't fail before you start.'

'At least we've done one thing,' he observed with a lopsided half smile. 'We're not the same people we were on our twenty-ninth birthday. Do you remember saying how you didn't like who you were and I agreed? Well, I'll tell you something for nothing, Nell McLean. Whether you like yourself now or not, I do. *Not* because you're thinner or blonder or more stylish, but because you've become a force to be reckoned with. You're tougher and smarter than you were and you don't let people walk all over you.'

She shrugged, not certain whether to be pleased or displeased. 'I may look like that to you, Tally, but inside I'm a disaster. I used to be complacent and comfortable and now I'm a mass of insecurities. It's you who have changed – you're more compassionate, more sensitive. You're not the person who came here from London.' She paused and smiled to lessen the emotion of the moment. 'There's more of you, for a start.'

'I'm fat, let's face it,' agreed Tally, patting his paunch and lapsing once more into gloom. 'It's because I was happy. I'll soon be thin again now, I suppose – as if it mattered.'

'Well, while we're indulging in a spot of navel-contemplation I'll just give you the full confession.' Nell put her hand to her throat. Her much-abused gullet was never entirely free from inflammation. 'I'm not nice at all. I puke up my food.'

'I know,' said Tally.

'*You know?*' She was startled, incredulous. 'How do you know?'

He looked at her pityingly. 'We're twins, remember. I may be a fool but I'm not blind,' he said. 'I've watched you regularly shoving five courses down your throat at dinner. No one could do that and lose as much weight as you have unless they're ill or throwing it all up. I'm afraid you're addicted, Nell. You couldn't go on doing it if you weren't.'

'I know.' She frowned distractedly. 'I'm trying to stop but it's so hard. Believe it or not, I like the bingeing and I like the puking. They both satisfy me somehow. Isn't that disgusting? God, we're a messed-up pair, aren't we? You're love-sick and I'm sick-sick.'

'You make us sound like a couple of giant pandas. WILL LOVE-SICK AND SICK-SICK FIND TRUE LOVE AND PERPETUATE THE SPECIES? Watch this space!' Tally forced a faint, lopsided grin, leapt to his feet and strode to the door. 'I feel better,' he said as if convincing himself. 'Thanks for listening. I think I'll go Christmas shopping.'

'Well, don't buy any cashmere,' Nell called after him slyly. 'Fenella's got plenty of that.'

She herself decided to go and visit Flora. She couldn't help thinking what a shame it was that there should be a shadow of unhappiness over the conception of a baby for which Flora had waited so long. She, for one, would go and congratulate her.

Flora was in the throes of her weekly bake. She had flour on her chin and wore a rather old-fashioned frilly apron over her jumper and skirt. She looked pale and wan. Leading Nell through to the kitchen she said apologetically, 'I'll need to get these in the oven or they'll no' be ready for Mac's tea. Sit down, please.' Gesturing to a chair she picked up a fluted round cutter and began to press it into a thick square of rolled-out dough in which several circular holes already showed.

'You can't have had much time for baking lately,' Nell said, occupying the chair indicated. 'We've been so busy at the hotel.'

'Aye, Mac's been missing his scones. I promised him some today.' Flora was concentrating on her task, avoiding Nell's eye.

'You look a bit peelie-wallie. You must be feeling tired,' Nell said sympathetically. 'Tally told me about the baby,' she added and Flora shot her a startled glance. 'Congratulations! You must be very excited.'

'I think Mac's the most excited,' said Flora, blushing furiously. 'He's always wanted weans.' She hardly spoke above a whisper, her words scarcely audible.

'I expect he wants a boy, to take over the boat.' Nell hoped her voice sounded casual, merely interested.

'Aye, maybe.' Flora completed cutting the scone-rounds and began to paint them with milk, using a wooden-handled pastry brush. Once this was done, she picked up the full baking tray, opened the Aga door and deposited it inside, glancing at the kitchen clock. It was three-thirty. 'Would you like a cup of tea now, or shall we wait for the scones?' she asked more confidently.

'Tea would be lovely,' said Nell. 'I've only just had lunch so I'm not really hungry.' Oh God, she thought, the same old excuses! She'd had no lunch but did not want to eat.

Flora put the kettle on and began to clear away the evidence of her baking. Board, cutter, rolling pin and pastry brush all went into the sink with a clatter. Nell waited for Flora to speak, Flora waited for Nell. The silence between them might appropriately have been called pregnant.

'How is Tally?' Flora asked eventually.

'Confused, depressed,' Nell began tentatively. 'He misses you, I think. He says you're a witch but he doesn't mean it. He hurts.'

'Yes, I expect he does. I'm really sorry.' Flora spooned tea-leaves into the pot and set it to warm. She sat down opposite Nell and gazed at her with troubled blue eyes. 'I didna mean to hurt him, but what could I do? It has to be over between us.'

'Is it his baby, Flora?' Nell asked boldly.

There was another tense silence while Flora looked as if she was trying to decide whether to confide in Nell or not, and then she simply shrugged inconclusively and said, 'I'll no' be able to work at the hotel next season. Mac wants me to stay at home with the baby.'

'We'll miss you greatly, but of course I understand. Perhaps you might be able to do some part-time work later on? I'd hate us to lose touch.'

'I dinna know.' Flora stood up and poured water into the teapot. 'It might be better if I stayed away from Tally.'

'Oh, I don't think so,' put in Nell hurriedly. 'He's not one to harbour grudges and whatever he feels now I know he'll want to see the baby. It's only fair, isn't it?'

'As long as he disna make trouble. I dinna want Mac upset. He's so happy about the bairn.' Flora sounded genuinely distressed.

Nell shook her head. 'He won't, Flora, I'm sure he won't. He understands, you know. Deep down he understands. As long as it wasn't deliberate.'

'Oh no, it wasna that,' she said hastily. 'I loved him. I love them both.'

'*Torn between two lovers*,' crooned Nell softly, invoking the words of a pop song she recalled from her teens. 'Poor Flora!'

'Let's put Taliska to the test,' suggested Tally with sudden animation. It was Christmas Eve and the Taliska house party was gathered a little morosely by the tree in the hall. A log fire blazed in the great perspex-ed fireplace from which not a whiff of smoke dared escape to sully the festive atmosphere.

'How do you mean?' asked Nell. They were drinking pink champagne and nibbling roasted almonds. Ginny and Calum shared an armchair in a rosy glow, Tally perched rather awkwardly alongside Fenella on the bottom step of the carved staircase, and Nell and Alasdair lounged with studied casualness at opposite ends of the sofa. The only illumination came from the tree lights and the flickering flames in the hearth. There was a sharp smell of resin and pine cones.

'Well, the brochure says Taliska will put a pep in your step and a gleam in your eye,' Tally went on, his glance roving from one dimly lit face to the next. 'Let's see if it can do it for us. We can pretend we're guests who have just arrived. We're tired and jaded, we've unpacked our bags and it's . . .' he glanced at his watch '. . . six o'clock. What do we do next?'

'The jacuzzi!' said Nell and Fenella together, catching each other's eye.

'Right. It's full and it's hot!' cried Tally, leaping to his feet. 'Cast off all our cares and woes, here we go, swimming low!' He offered his hand to Fenella.

'I take it by "cares and woes" you mean clothes,' she drawled, accepting his hand and rising sinuously. 'Well, I'm game. My mother always told me that my underwear should be suitable for being run over by a bus, though I personally prefer the idea of death by Lamborghini.' She had already begun to unbutton the brilliant embroidered silk waistcoat she wore over a floppy white silk shirt and black cashmere trousers.

Nell glanced uncertainly at Alasdair. His face remained sombre and impassive in the dancing firelight but she fervently hoped she could detect a twinkle igniting somewhere in the speckled grey depths of his eyes. 'Hang on, Fenella,' she warned hurriedly, switching her attention to her friend. 'I shouldn't strip here if I were you. It's a cold walk through the tunnel to the gym.'

'Last one in's a Wally,' announced Tally and he pulled Fenella unceremoniously towards the main entrance. 'Come on, 'Ella!' The sound of their scampering footsteps echoed through the tunnel and a cold draught of air banished the cosy glow which had cocooned them all hitherto. The gym was in the old billiard room, reached through the ancient guardhouse on the ground floor of the tower.

Ginny began to smirk nervously, wishing she had put on more substantial underwear than the flimsy cream lace bra and bikini pants she wore beneath her short turquoise dress and thick black tights. Calum frowned and opened his mouth to protest that he did not want to take part in any heathen bathing ritual and then his Calvinist streak seemed suddenly to evaporate in a surge of Yuletide goodwill. 'What the hell!' he declared robustly, shoving Ginny off his knee. 'Why not? C'mon, cookie!'

As they disappeared into the cold air Nell raised an eyebrow at Alasdair. They were still emotionally jousting with each other, neither risking the first move, though both were aware that this Christmas must be make or break. Nell was increasingly and depressingly of the opinion that it might be break. In these circumstances, surely Alasdair was the last person to throw caution and his tweed suit to the winds? 'Last one in's a Wally?' she repeated, testing.

Alasdair frowned. There was a tense pause when Nell stopped breathing for what seemed like minutes. She was telling herself that it didn't matter, that a romp in the jacuzzi was a stupid idea anyway, that a responsible lawyer like Alasdair couldn't be expected to play silly games like the rest of them. Then his brow cleared and he grinned boyishly. Even in the dim light it utterly transformed his habitually serious expression. She realised that she had never seen him smile quite like that before.

'Don't tell the Law Society,' he exclaimed,

extending his long legs and rising, holding out his hand to pull her up. 'They might all want to join in!'

Hurrying through the cold gloom of the tunnel Nell felt her stomach churn nervously. When the trousers were down supposing he did not like what he saw? Supposing she disliked what she saw? In more ways than one it looked as if they were about to take the plunge.

The communal jacuzzi in the gym was a large, round pool which could hold six reclining bodies in relative comfort. Its suction pumps and air pipes produced a fair impression of a maelstrom at the touch of a button. Tally already had it swirling joyously.

Fenella's bus-defying underwear consisted of what the lingerie shops called a 'body' but it barely concealed any of hers, being fashioned out of clinging black lace, stretched to a revealing transparency. 'What you see is what you get,' declared the refreshingly shameless Fenella, posing like a centrefold on the side of the big circular bath, before slipping into the churning water.

'And I'm coming to get it. As soon as I've fetched some more champagne,' Tally told her, down to his distinctive red-and-white houndstooth boxer-shorts and risking pneumonia to rush for fresh supplies. The cellar was conveniently situated down a short stone staircase reached by a trapdoor in the gym floor. He was gone only moments.

Calum's red hair was only one shade darker than his face by the time he had stripped down to tight blue briefs which exposed all but the crucial bits of a surprisingly muscular white body. 'Contrary to what they say about too many cooks spoiling the broth, the ingredients of this soup are improving by the minute,' said Fenella, winking at him mischievously as he stepped into the seething cauldron beside her. Ginny leaped in hurriedly after him, anxious not to air her scanties any longer than necessary. There was a flash of freckled ivory flesh and cream lace followed swiftly by a splash as they disappeared beneath the bubbles.

Tally re-emerged from the trapdoor bearing two green bottles as Nell and Alasdair entered the gym, still fully clothed. He waved the bottles at them and stepped into the pool shouting, 'Looks like we have us a pair of Wallies!'

Alasdair removed his clothes quickly and methodically, hanging his jacket, shirt, tie and trousers on a hook and tucking his socks carefully into his brown brogues before placing them neatly on the floor beneath. Nell cast surreptitious glances at him as she slowly removed her ankle boots and socks and draped her black leggings and bulky Arran sweater over the handlebars of an exercise bike. With gentlemanly *sang froid* Alasdair stood in his shorts and waited for her, frankly enjoying the gradual emergence of her limbs and body from their outer shell.

'What do you call this?' he asked with genuine interest, indicating her white cotton crop-top, deeply edged with stretch lace. 'It seems to be neither vest nor bra.'

'Well, it's either neither or both,' said Nell blushing, her voice sharp with shyness. 'Either way it's not coming off!'

She herself was slyly remarking, though not mentioning, his neat, white boxer shorts, just tight enough to contain a pleasantly muscular stern and a pleasantly bulging prow. But there was no bulge above the waistband. Regular hillwalking had kept middle-age spread at bay. With relief she thought,

Trust Alasdair to be shipshape, even in his nether regions!

'I've been warmer on Ben Nevis in a white-out!' he exclaimed, shivering. 'I hope that water's hot!'

It was. He and Nell sank gratefully into its embracing warmth, arranging themselves among the already-present legs and bodies, and Alasdair was the last person who was going to tell Nell that her pristine little white crop-top became as transparent as clingfilm the moment it hit the water. He was a breast man. It was her cleavage that had first aroused his physical interest and nothing had changed in the intervening year and a half. She was thin now, far too thin in his opinion, but the perky twin mounds wrapped closely in the fine cotton cloth were still sufficiently ample to be highly desirable to him, putting Ginny's swollen bee-stings and Fenella's luscious melons gloriously in the shade. In the heat and steam of the moment the mammary perfection of Muriel was erased from his memory.

'Fizz 'n' bubbles,' announced Tally as a cork popped in his hands. 'No glasses, I'm afraid. They are too dangerous. I don't want Fenella's gorgeous fanny pierced by broken glass.'

'We won't ask what you do want it pierced by,' murmured Fenella irrepressibly, accepting first gulp at the bottle. Pink champagne foamed out over her chin and throat as she inexpertly tilted it towards her mouth.

'It's easy to see that you are not sufficiently adept with the tongue,' Tally said, regarding her critically as his thumbs pushed suggestively at the second cork.

'These things come quicker for some than for others,' giggled Fenella, passing the bottle on. 'Sadly, you won't be able to lick up what I've spilled because it's already been washed off.'

The second cork popped and disappeared into the gloom of the gym. Tally took an expert swig and passed the bottle to Nell. 'There's an art to it, you know,' he observed slyly. 'You have to tilt it just enough and play it just right or you end up spraying it about like those wasteful racing drivers after a Grand Prix.'

'I can't bear the way they do that,' said Fenella with feeling. 'I always want to hover below the platform with my mouth open.'

'You'd better be careful where you do that, my girl, or you might end up swallowing something else entirely,' Tally told her solemnly.

'Who said swallow?' demanded Nell, adding prosaically, 'What's for dinner, Calum? I'm starving!'

'You always are!' Tally said rudely. 'You should try keeping it down a bit longer.'

'Keep it down yourself,' Fenella told him indignantly, seeing Nell's embarrassed flush and rushing to her friend's defence. 'It's Christmas-time, not criticism time.'

'Dinner's in the oven,' declared Calum happily, having shown great skill at lowering the level of liquid in the champagne bottle. 'Boiled beef and carrots.'

'It is not,' Ginny reassured them, unable to allow such a culinary blasphemy. 'It's *boeuf bourguignon* and it's delicious!'

'Pity,' remarked Alasdair, scissoring his legs in the current so that one thigh brushed against Nell's. 'I rather like boiled beef and carrots.'

'I bet,' Nell grinned, unable to decide whether the thigh-brushing was deliberate or accidental. 'Out of a tin and preferably eaten in some mountain bothy, no doubt.'

'I'd share them with you though,' he responded generously. 'I'd even share my bivvy bag if you'd let me.'

Nell glanced at him in surprise. He now held one of the bottles and his lean, weathered face was flushed from the effects of steam and pink champagne. 'Does it have to be up a mountain?' she asked cautiously, and Ginny giggled. Nell was not certain whether the giggle was in response to overhearing her exchange with Alasdair, or to something Calum was doing under the water.

Then she realised that Alasdair was doing something to her under cover of the surface disturbance. His hand was gently feeling the inside of her knee, his forearm resting on her thigh. It was a pleasant, tickling sensation and for several minutes she lay back dreamily and enjoyed it, turning her head once to look at him with mild inquiry. There was a slight smile on his lips and his eyes were closed. A sudden chill ran through her, despite the warmth of the water. Oh no! she thought in panic. Please don't let him be thinking of Muriel! Resolutely she tried to drown this ulcerous thought in the erotic whirlpool building around her. The jacuzzi seemed to have become one big erogenous zone as the level of breathing in the pool began to be audible above the noise of the pumps.

'Enough, children, enough,' declared Tally, standing up in his magnificent houndstooth boxer shorts which were stretched just a bit too tightly over his newly developed paunch and over something suspiciously swollen below it. He reached awkwardly over to press the switch that controlled the swirl of the bath, causing it to subside gradually. 'As master of ceremonies I declare a recess. We will reconvene in fifteen minutes in the kitchen for serve-it-yourself dinner.'

'Fifteen minutes isn't very long,' murmured Fenella, eying the suspicious swelling with interest. 'Not to test out the increase in our pep and gleam.'

'That's just it,' said Tally with magisterial solemnity. 'I detect altogether too high a level of pep and gleam and I think it should be cold showers all round and twice as cold for Fenella Drummond-Elliot. Ouch!' He dodged Fenella's attempted grab at his thigh, encountering only her long, sharp nails, and leaped with surprising agility out of the pool.

'You bastard, Tally McLean,' yelled Fenella excitedly, rearing from the water like a black-lace Botticelli Venus and pursuing him out of the jacuzzi and across the gym in a shower of droplets. 'I'll get you!'

'Yes, I rather think she will,' observed Alasdair with amusement, pulling himself upright and shaking the excess water from his arms and shoulders. 'Brr! It's freezing out. I'd forgotten!' He offered Nell a steadying hand from the pool which, mysteriously, she seemed to need, finding her legs disconcertingly wobbly. Calum and Ginny seemed content to remain floating sensuously for the time being, their eyes closed and their hands delicately exploring each other's limbs and torsos.

Alasdair eyed them speculatively and then, letting actions speak louder than words, he pulled Nell gently towards him and raised his hand inquiringly to cup her cotton-clung breast. With an explosion of relief and arousal she saw love and lust in the grey speckled eyes and no hint of Muriel. 'Four's getting to be a bit of a crowd in here isn't it, Crop Top?' he whispered, brushing her ear with his lips. 'Could you remind me where I stowed my bivvy bag?'

It was never really clear where everyone slept that

night. Certainly Calum and Ginny never made it up to the cottage but Nell couldn't be sure which of the first-floor rooms they occupied. Fenella had been allocated the comfrey but again, Nell couldn't be sure that she slept in it because soon after they had all greedily tucked into fragrant *boeuf bourguignon* with bowls and spoons and hunks of bread and liberal quantities of Beaujolais, she herself settled contentedly into the *Wild Iris* suite with Alasdair.

It was like coming home. She supposed it had been inevitable, but all the same she had not been sure until that moment in the jacuzzi whether the current of feeling between them was flowing in the same direction. Perhaps it had taken the swirling water to conduct their emotions and switch them on to each other, or perhaps it had simply been the right mood and the right moment, but now that they had exchanged caution for passion, it was extraordinary how natural and wonderful it was, as if it were nothing new to either of them but a love which they had shared for a long time. For her this was something altogether richer and more rewarding than anything she had experienced with David or Claude, even though it was markedly less sexually adventurous. Alasdair was a conventional and satisfactory lover and one with whom she felt it might be comfortable and desirable to share a bed for ever.

'The awful thing is,' she murmured into his warm, smooth shoulder, when they were lying curled together in the centre of the suite's imperial-sized bed, 'that Santa won't know where to go to fill our stockings.'

'Let him corridor creep like the rest of us,' replied Alasdair, his lips in her hair. He was still amazed at the lightness of her. She was like a child in his arms, so thin and fragile. Physically he could do with a bit of the cuddly old Nell back and he intended to get it. 'He probably enjoys a good game of Hunt the Stocking. I know I do. There are too few of them around in these tight-infested days.'

'Well, maybe they'll come back now skirts are being worn longer, you shocking old-fashioned male chauvinist,' she said, pushing herself up on one elbow as a sudden thought occurred. 'Supposing Santa thinks we've all been too naughty to deserve any presents?'

'He'd be right. This place is a den of iniquity. How many of these rooms have you slept in?'

The question was asked in fun but Nell detected a note of vested interest beneath the flippant tone. 'My own, of course, and *Scabious*, but then you knew that. That's all. I'm not quite the scarlet woman you suspect me of being.'

'Pity,' he grunted, gathering her back into his arms. 'I was hoping for some lessons in wild outrageous love-making.'

She stroked his back, letting her fingers trail from his shoulders to the soft curve of his buttocks. What was it about his back? It was smooth and muscular and incredibly sexy. 'We could take a correspondence course,' she whispered, feeling a renewed stirring in those nether regions she had admired earlier, so tidily encased in his white shorts. Eat your heart out, Claude, she thought wickedly, encouraging the stirring with a wriggle of her hips. You may be well placed in the beauty stakes but compared with Alasdair you're seriously lacking in the endowment chase!

'I think we correspond rather well already,' Alasdair said, demonstrating what he meant. 'This bit of mine corresponds with that bit of yours. And they definitely seem to move each other to giddy heights.'

'Yes, I see what you mean,' Nell agreed, her breathing increasing in speed and tempo as the wild yellow irises Leo had painted on the walls began to bob and writhe as if in the grip of some violent storm. Lucky Muriel, she thought, just before thought became random. She had him for fifteen years of this. But I mean to have him for longer!

The six exchanged presents late the next morning, gathering around the tree after assorted self-service breakfasts, wearing slightly sheepish smiles and displaying a happy, relaxed camaraderie. It was as if Cupid had spilled his quiver and scattered his arrows among them so that not only had they each discovered an irresistible attraction for their own chosen partner but at the same time had developed an unquestioning affection for the other four members of the party. They were united in a secret sect, marooned together on an island of adventure where every personal joy seemed one of many invisible threads which wove them in a communal web of delight. It's pure Mills & Boon, thought Nell, enjoying it enormously while remaining acutely aware that reality lurked the other side of Boxing Day.

With a contented smile Alasdair presented her with a pair of walking boots for Christmas. 'If I'd known you were going to seduce me I'd have given you something more romantic,' he said, watching her struggle with the laces as she tried them on.

She frowned up at him briefly. The boots were masterpieces of the cobbler's craft, stitched and moulded out of many pieces of leather and canvas, every seam waterproofed, every eyelet waxed. 'I think these are very romantic,' she told him softly, standing up to kiss him gratefully. She hoped he didn't notice that she found it hard to keep her hands off him. He was so warm, so kind, so real, so exactly what her battered body and ego needed. 'They've already walked all over my moral fibre, shattered my resistance and turned me into a shameless hussy.' She glanced shyly up at him, flirting.

Alasdair's square, lived-in face crinkled with laughter as he wrapped his arms around her, wishing there was a little more of her to wrap. She hadn't been out of his sight for twenty-four hours so he knew for a fact that she had not thrown up in that time. If he could keep her eating normally for a week he reckoned she would be on the way to a cure. 'They work fast,' he said, smiling down at her. 'But you haven't broken them in yet. You might get a few blisters but steady, gentle progress will make them the perfect fit.'

'You know I'm not very good at steady, gentle progress,' she protested. 'I want to rush headlong and hurl myself up the mountain!'

'You'll just run out of puff,' he warned, stroking her hair and kissing her sparkling eyes. 'The view from the top is always worth a steady climb.'

'Just who is seducing who here, that's what I want to know.'

'I'll show you,' he said, stepping back a pace. 'This is how you seemed to me the last time I saw you, at the *Hot Gryll* recording.' He took an envelope from his pocket and put it in her hands. It contained a Christmas card. 'I wrote that before I came for Christmas. I was going to give it to you with your present.'

She opened the card. As well as the usual printed message it bore a short poem in his handwriting.

'Party'

Watching your face
That makes an emptiness of this crowded place,
I stand, not speaking, terrified to see
You grown more lovely, and still lost to me.

She read it through twice, frowning. 'Is this more Norman MacCaig?' she asked, and when he nodded she closed the card and slipped it back into his pocket. 'He got it wrong that time, didn't he?'

He smiled and sighed. 'Today it's wrong but yesterday it was exactly how I felt. You *were* "still lost to me".'

She shook her head. 'Well, it's wrong today and it'll be wrong tomorrow and for a long time after that, I hope.' She led him to the Christmas tree and took a small parcel from among the pungent branches, stirring some tiny, decorative silver bells into their own intimate festive peal. In other parts of the hall the other two couples were making similar private exchanges of gifts and embraces.

'I remembered the poem you read us when Tally went missing,' Nell said, placing the gaily wrapped little gift in Alasdair's hand. 'I know you already have one of these but I hope this one will be special.'

It was a compass. Not a heavy, brass-bound instrument but a light, practical, miniaturised dial in a small black leather pouch. A black silk cord was attached to a ring in its side and Alasdair slipped it over his head. 'A Silver,' he said admiringly, tracing the maker's name with his finger. 'They are the best. How did you know?'

'I didn't,' she admitted. 'I asked in the shop in Glasgow. I bought it because N is for North and N is for Nell and the needle always points to the North, doesn't it? Wherever you are, I thought it would remind you of me. So, you can't be lost to me now, can you?'

He stared down at the compass, moving a little so that the needle pointed directly at her. He raised his head and looked hard at her with an expression that made her heart miss a beat.

In a gentle whisper she quoted:

'Stay where you are, please stay –
I've got my compass yet.
It'll get me to you, if not by the easiest way.'

'I never imagined you would remember,' he said, wonder breaking in his eyes.

'Oh yes,' she told him. 'I remember.'

Fenella, predictably and generously, had chosen cashmere garments for each of them. Tally opened his parcel and found a luxurious double-yarn cable-stitch sweater in a deep shade of indigo. When he tried it on Fenella stroked him like a favourite cat and whispered something in his ear. Nell was astonished to see her brother blush. He looked pleased and happy in a way she had not expected to see so soon after Flora, and Fenella, clinging to his arm, looked like a purring lioness. She picked up Tally's wrist, turning back the cuff of the sleeve. Embroidered secretly under the welt was a tiny red heart. 'There you are,' laughed Fenella. 'You wear my heart on your sleeve!'

At that moment Mac burst in through the staff door. His face was flushed and his breath uneven from running. 'It's Marsali,' he panted, staring anxiously around the group. 'She's calving!'

Mick had asked the fisherman to see to the cows while he was away for Christmas because Mac, with his crofting experience, was the only person Mick trusted to milk them and make sure they were warm and comfortable.

'How fabulous,' cried Nell excitedly. 'Oh, poor Mick – he'll be heartbroken to miss it. Does she look all right? Is she in pain?'

Mac looked dubious. 'I think she's doing OK. Perhaps we should ask Duncan McCandlish for a hand. He's the expert. I think she's a wee bit early, before her time you know, so the calf may be weakly.'

Nell glanced at Tally who looked distinctly uncomfortable and tongue-tied at confronting Mac so unexpectedly, with the drama over Flora's baby still unresolved. 'Oh Mac, would you ask Duncan?' Nell pleaded, hastily covering her brother's awkward silence. 'He'll come if you ask him, I'm sure, even if it is Christmas Day.'

'He'll no' be having much of a Christmas anyway,' said Mac, agreeing readily enough. 'Being all on his own, that is. Probably be glad of summat to do.'

Nell felt unaccountably guilty. She had never asked herself if the irascible farmer might be lonely at Christmas.

Mac went out again, bent on his errand.

'Could we all go and watch?' Fenella asked Tally timidly. 'I've never seen a calf being born.'

'I don't know,' said Tally doubtfully. 'We mustn't upset her. But I'm sure we could watch over the partition. She's in a pretty big stable so we wouldn't crowd her.'

'We'll be as quiet as mice,' Fenella promised. 'She won't know we're there.'

As it turned out, Marsali appeared unperturbed

by the arrival of six human observers. She was a mature cow having her fifth calf. It was not a situation she seemed to regard with any surprise. On the other hand, her human audience all agreed afterwards that they found it a magical experience.

It was cold in the byre. Breath rose in misty clouds, swirling around the single electric bulb which dangled on a cable high above Marsali's head. She stood in deep straw, head down, jaw moving rhythmically as if she was chewing the cud. Her eyes were huge and slightly bewildered but she did not look distressed. The waves of muscular contraction flowed across the stretched hide of her swollen belly like wind flurries across a calm loch, temporarily halting the methodical motion of her jaw and widening the long lashes which fringed her eyes. She looked calm and patient, waiting for the powerful spasms and the inevitable process of birth to take their course.

Mac arrived with Duncan about forty minutes later when the cow's tail was up and there were already birth stains on the straw behind her. She was bellowing loudly from time to time but was otherwise calm.

'Thanks for coming, Duncan,' said Tally who had been at the cow's head for some time, keeping her steady. 'I'm no expert but she seems OK.'

'Aye. Nature'll do her work fine in most cases,' the farmer muttered gruffly, putting down the steaming pail of water and other equipment he had brought into the stall with him. 'Let's hope we won't be needing any of these ropes.'

'Ropes?' Fenella whispered to Nell in alarm. 'What do they use ropes for?'

'Well, sometimes I think they have to haul the calf out bodily,' said Nell, who'd watched a television series about vets at one time. 'If it's a breech birth or something. I suppose the same sort of things can go wrong with cows as go wrong with humans.'

'Don't show me a rope if ever I'm about to give birth,' said Fenella faintly. 'I think they ought to hide them from that poor cow.'

'How is she doing?' asked a soft voice from the dim stable passage. It was Flora, hands thrust into the pockets of a padded jacket, a white knitted hat on her head. 'Mac rang me,' she added, almost apologetically.

'Gee,' said Ginny in surprise. 'I'm not sure I'd like to be here, if I were in your condition.'

'I hope you don't mind?' Flora asked Nell, approaching the knot of people hanging over the partition. 'I've helped at calvings before. My father always had a cow on the croft.'

'Of course not,' said Nell, moving along to give her a view of proceedings.

As if irresistibly drawn, Flora ducked under the rail and went straight to the cow's head, stroking her neck on the opposite side from Tally. His eyes met hers over the lowered horns. They said nothing to each other but there was communication in the way they both murmured encouragement to the cow. 'Good girl, brave girl, canny beast.'

The birth was easy and uneventful. Soon after the head presented, the rest of the long body slipped quietly and smoothly into the cold world in a cloud of steam, to be received by Duncan and laid gently in the straw. An accompaniment of muted exclamations of wonder was heard from the enraptured onlookers. Duncan and Flora both worked with handfuls of straw, helping Marsali to remove the sac mucus and stimulate the little calf into movement. 'It's a heifer,' crowed Flora in delight. 'A heifer,' repeated Tally to the others behind the barrier.

'Thank goodness,' breathed Nell, squeezing Alasdair's hand in relief. 'We can keep her!'

As the soft baby pelt began to fluff up it soon became evident that instead of being the colour of ripe corn, denoting the pure breeding of the pedigree Jersey, the calf was rufous. Ten minutes after emerging from the birth canal the little heifer was staggering on unsteady legs, her moist pink mouth nuzzling at Marsali's udder, but the face was not dark Jersey brown, shading to honey, it was a white mask, contrasting with the russet curls of the neck and back.

'Well, I'm going to have a word with that AI man,' Tally said in bewilderment, scratching his head. 'He must have got the semen muddled up. It's a right little mongrel we've got here.'

'Not a mongrel, Tally,' murmured Flora hurriedly. 'Don't call her a mongrel.'

He looked at her quizzically. 'What would you call her then?' he asked pointedly.

'A mixture,' said Flora. 'A sturdy, healthy, precious little mixture!'

They stared at each other accusingly but, after several tense moments, suddenly began to laugh helplessly.

Their laughter was infectious, spreading through the entire company, until all those gathered under the dim, single bulb were chortling merrily, although the rest did not fully understand the joke. They were laughing from a sense of relief, a sense of wonder and a sense of peaceful joy at the sight of cow and calf, mother and daughter, placidly getting on with the business of suckling and giving suck, unaware of the network of human emotions weaving invisibly around them.

It was Mac for whom a penny dropped. 'It wasna the wrong semen,' he exclaimed with sudden enlightenment. 'The AI man came too late! Marsali, you wicked coo.' He struck the beast playfully on the rump and Marsali turned her limpid gaze towards him in mild reproach. Mac then swung round to point an accusing finger at Duncan McCandlish who had retreated to a corner, busily organising his ropes and pail. 'McCandlish – I think your Shorthorn bull's been playing away!'

McCandlish smirked noisily. This was clearly a conclusion he had come to some time before. 'Aye well,' he said impishly, 'he can swim fine, that Ruairidh!'

Tally did a doubletake between Mac and Duncan. 'What?' he expostulated. 'Are you telling me Ruairidh swam across to Taliska and got to Marsali before the AI man was even called?'

'It's possible,' nodded Duncan sagely. 'I had to put him in the far field while they travellers were here. The fencing's no' so good there. Come to think of it, I found him real damp one morning afore I moved him back. Still, dinna fash! He's good stock, my Ruairidh. The wee heifer could do worse for a sire.'

Nell was staring at Flora who had gone bright pink and appeared to be studying in some detail the properties of the straw at her feet. 'Well,' said Nell thoughtfully, 'what's done is done. Nature makes damn sure that life goes on, it seems. The calf's here now and I'm sure she'll be a great member of the herd.' There was a loud moo from the other end of the byre which seemed to endorse her statement. In the excitement they had all forgotten Bride, the other Jersey cow, who was bellowing a welcome to the newcomer.

'Well done Marsali, I say,' declared Fenella. 'She's struck a blow for females everywhere.'

'How d'you make that out, Fenella?' asked Ginny in her flat Australian twang.

'If it was a choice between a real bull and a man in a white coat with a bloody great syringe,' Fenella said with feeling, 'I know which I'd rather have!'

Leaving the stable in the dying light of the winter-solstice afternoon, Nell tugged Alasdair off in the direction of the loch, rather than returning immediately to the house. 'Let's watch the sun set over Morvern,' she suggested. 'It's my favourite view from the island.'

The sun had almost sunk below the horizon and the jagged range of Kingairloch stood outlined starkly against a deep terracotta sky, with the crouching hump of Lismore still showing faintly green like a sleeping dragon in the foreground. A cold breeze had whipped the loch into waves like the icing on a frosted Christmas cake, and sponge-like heaps of spume were lying beached and luminous on the stony shore. Seal-grey rocks gleamed silvery pink where the waves broke and retreated, leaving their smooth, wet surfaces reflecting the light of the sky. There was no sign of life, and apart from the soughing of the wind the only sound was the creak and snap of the *Flora*'s rigging as she bumped and swayed against the dark silhouette of the jetty.

'You still haven't seen the summit of Ben Nevis,' Alasdair remarked, placing a hand on each of Nell's shoulders and rubbing his cheek against her wind-blown hair.

'No, but I know it's there, and I'm sure I will see it,' said Nell contentedly. 'I have the feeling those new walking boots are a statement of intent.'

'We'll stand at the top together,' Alasdair promised, dropping his hands to hug her to him from behind. 'It shall be your first Munro! The first of many.'

'Oh God! How many are there?' exclaimed Nell.

'Well, Mr H. T. Munro, who listed them first, said there were two hundred and seventy-seven. Enough to keep you going for a few years!' Alasdair told her. 'People who climb them are called Munro-baggers. Once you get hooked you won't be able to leave Scotland until you've climbed the lot.'

'No, I won't be one of them. Anyway, I don't need an excuse to stay here. Nothing would tear me away, now.' Nell turned within his arms and sought his lips with her own. Their kiss was cold and deeply tingling like vintage champagne and it had the same overall effect, sending rivulets of pure melted pleasure rippling down their limbs. They were oblivious to the icy clutch of the wind.

'Break it up, you two,' came a familiar voice to their rear. 'It's too cold for a beach party.'

'Don't be a spoilsport,' Fenella protested as she and Tally strolled up, arms entwined. 'It's good to see these two having a party at all. They've taken long enough to accept each other's invitation.'

'And do we gather that you've both got a party going too?' asked Nell teasingly. 'Or is this one of Tally's notorious flings?'

'Just a fling,' agreed Fenella, snuggling into Tally's shoulder. In the dim light her face looked mischievous and almost childlike. 'I've flung myself at him and he's flung himself at me.'

'She's cradle-snatching, actually,' murmured Tally, stroking the top of Fenella's head. 'She's going to swaddle me in cashmere and sing me to sleep every night.'

'Sounds wonderful,' breathed Nell. 'I'm only going to get brisk walks and a bivvy bag.'

'What on earth is a bivvy bag?' inquired Fenella.

'It's an instrument of torture. Alastair sleeps in it when he goes walking and he swears he can climb in soaking wet and be dry in half an hour.'

'That's right. Water only goes out, never in.'

'Sounds like the flow of money in the Taliska bank account,' quipped Tally.

'Rubbish,' exclaimed Nell. 'We've done very good business this season, considering it's our first. Even the bank thinks so.'

'Yes, I have to admit that's true,' Tally observed, picking up a stone and throwing it into the water. Ripples spread rapidly and were broken up by wavelets. 'I think I'll give it another year.' His teeth gleamed in the twilight.

'Good of you,' Nell retaliated dryly, but she knew that for all his mocking tone, in his own way Tally was expressing commitment. 'Be careful it doesn't give you a kick in the arse.'

'That's funny, I thought it already had,' he said cryptically and reached out for Fenella again. 'But it's also given me a shot in the arm.'

'That's the most romantic thing anyone's ever called me,' she responded, kissing him lightly on the lips and shivering at the same time. 'Can we go in now?'

However carried away Calum and Ginny might have been by the later events of Christmas, they had not let it interfere with the important business of preparing the feast. Having decided on a medieval theme to complement Taliska's ancient history, they had asked if they could use the vaulted tower room for a setting, and most of Christmas Eve, up to the time of the jacuzzi party, the two had spent behind locked doors, either in the tower or in the kitchen. Anxious to give herself some practice in the art of boning poultry, Ginny had started with a quail, stuffing its boneless flesh inside a boned partridge which, in its turn, fitted nicely into the soft tissue of a plump boneless pheasant. All these were then wrapped in the flesh of a guinea fowl, which was finally sewn inside a turkey from which the body carcass but not the legs and wings had been removed. Each layer of poultry had been lubricated with duxelles of mushrooms and then the whole parcel had been pummelled and persuaded back into the shape of a plucked bird, skewered and tied. Ginny called it a *Christmas Cockatrice*.

The *Cockatrice* had been roasting slowly all day, through the birth of the calf and the interrupted present-giving by the tree. When darkness fell the company, now including Duncan, Flora and Mac who had been hastily invited to share the feast, gathered in the vaulted tower chamber which was hung with boughs of holly and balls of mistletoe, collected by Tally and Nell and transported in the Fourtrack from the wooded end of the island. Ivy twined up the posts of the antique tester-bed which had been pulled into the centre of the room, its mattress covered with boards and a dark green cloth decorated with garlands of pine and laurel, and laid for the meal. Chairs had been brought from the dining room. Bowls of nuts and fruit compôte, or ‘compost’ as Calum disconcertingly called it, stood at each corner of the board and the massive pewter candlesticks, which normally rested on the ancient oak chest between the windows, had been placed in the centre, adorned with foliage and berries and supporting two thick red wax candles. It might not have been a Hollywood film-set ideal of medieval splendour, but it was probably nearer the true picture. On the east wall the beautiful tapestry of native flora and fauna with its deep border of heather and bluebells added to the impression that there was about to be a bucolic Christmas broadcast on behalf of the Green Party.

'Fantastic! Incredible!' declared everyone in a babble of admiration as Ginny and Calum, grinning broadly, paraded their fabulous culinary creation like a pair of varlets setting a dish before the king. They had garnished the golden-roasted *Cockatrice* with a neck and head of driftwood and pine-cones, and a tail fashioned from the feathers of each bird represented therein. The head was painted and gilded and the tail spread like a huge, plumed fan, glinting with the iridescent green of the cock pheasant's proud plumage. Around the edge of the great Scottish platter, or ashet, upon which it sat, were scattered piles of roasted apples and onions, heaps of fried croûtons, mounds of crisp bacon curls and little cairns of peeled chestnuts and baby turnips. It was indeed a dish fit for the laird of Taliska and his clan.

'I feel as if I should slice it with a claymore,' grinned Tally, bending over the ashet with carving knife and fork.

Ginny deftly removed the head and tail which she placed decoratively alongside the candlesticks in the centre of the table. 'When the legs and wings are off you should be able to cut it like a loaf of bread,' she said helpfully. 'I hope it's cooked.'

'Marsali should have seen to that,' said Nell.

'Her timing was perfect,' Calum declared. 'Had she taken any longer, the *Cockatrice* might have been cinders.'

'Here's a "mixture", if ever I saw one,' remarked Tally, glancing at Flora after he'd made the first slice. 'I wonder what cocktail of different species makes up this fabulous creature?'

'It's a bit like one of those painted Russian dolls, Mamoushka Dolls I think they're called,' said Ginny eagerly, describing the sequence of poultry packed inside the turkey while plates were being laden with meat and vegetables. As he carved, Tally studied the exposed centre of the *Cockatrice* with more than passing interest. The various colours of white and brown meat lay moistly marbled with the mushroom filling. 'Were it human flesh,' he said with macabre delight, 'we would have here the famous melting pot!' To himself he wondered which flesh would identify itself most strongly among the mingled meats and which would have lost all individual flavour. When it came to dominance would the white flesh have it or the brown? It was an interesting metaphor for life. Would they ever know who was the father of Flora's child – and did it really matter? Would not the child itself find its own identity, regardless of whose flesh and blood were mingled in its make-up?

Alasdair noticed Nell staring balefully at her plate. 'It is dead already, you know,' he murmured to her. 'You look as if you want to murder it!'

She turned her head with a start. 'I'm sorry,' she said hurriedly. She had been wondering whether she could possibly enjoy this feast without the heinous pleasure of throwing up afterwards, knowing Alasdair would be angry if she did and knowing that to upset him was the last thing she wanted. She also knew, in her heart of hearts, that she must take responsibility for ridding herself of her habit, not rely on Alasdair to keep her on the straight and narrow. But it wasn't going to be easy!

'I was thinking of the calf,' she lied, diverting attention elsewhere. 'We haven't chosen a name for her yet. Does anyone have any ideas?'

'You could call her Christmas,' suggested Mac.

'Ye-es,' acknowledged Tally doubtfully, slicing the final portion. 'It might sound a bit funny calling her in for milking in the middle of summer, though.'

'There used to be a type of sweetie when I was young,' put in Flora in her low, soft voice. 'They called it Dolly Mixture.'

'Dolly – that's it!' Tally roared with delight and blew a kiss to Flora. It was a kiss of forgiveness as much as thanks. 'We'll call her Dolly because she's a mixture.'

'Brilliant, darling. That's a great idea!' exclaimed Mac, patting his wife on the back, animated by red wine and the prospect of his heaped plate.

'And now,' said Nell, lifting her knife and fork, smiling at Alasdair and making a firm resolution that what went down would not come up, 'if everyone's served, let's start.'

'A Merry Christmas to all our eaters,' cried Tally happily, nodding encouragement all round and winking at Fenella. 'And after the feast we can all enjoy more of Taliska's celebrated island games!'